Alec dismounted and stood before her, tall, broad, immovable....

"You're leaving," he stated flatly.

Elizabeth's eyes flickered over the expanse of his chest, snugly encased in a heavy cloak, the same cloak that she had pressed her cheek against just two days ago. The same arms that had wrapped protectively about her hung loosely at his sides. The same lips that had claimed hers beneath the mistletoe were fixed into a hard line that hollowed his cheeks.

"I told you I had to."

"Without saying goodbye." Silence hung between them for several moments. Alex shifted his weight. "I'd like it if you'd come again sometime."

"I . . . thank you, but I don't believe I shall."

"When will I see you again?"

"Oh . . . In passing, of course."

"Of course." The mocking tone drew Elizabeth's gaze upward, and she was rewarded with a smile that set her blood churning in her veins. "I *will* see you again, Elizabeth. You can count on it."

Dear Reader,

Welcome to Harlequin Historicals and to a world of adventure and romance where almost anything can happen.

This month we bring you Barbara Bretton's debut novel for Harlequin Historicals. *The Reluctant Bride* is the delightful tale of the battle over a dilapidated hotel between a stubborn American woman and a cynical Englishman.

Rose Among Thorns is Catherine Archer's first published work. This talented newcomer is sure to delight with her story of a conquering knight and the proud Saxon woman who meets his every challenge.

In *The Naked Huntress* by Shirley Parenteau, a society columnist finds herself at the mercy of a notorious saloon keeper when she unwittingly poses for a scandalous portrait.

Kit Gardner's *Arabesque* was one of our 1991 March Madness promotions. In her second novel, *The Dream,* straitlaced schoolteacher Elizabeth Burbridge must match wits with the dashing Lord Alec Sinclair. Those of you who recall the author's fast-paced, lighthearted writing will not be disappointed.

Next month look for new titles by June Lund Shiplett, Isabel Whitfield, Suzanne Barclay and Mary Daheim.

Sincerely,

Tracy Farrell
Senior Editor

Harlequin Books

TORONTO • NEW YORK • LONDON
AMSTERDAM • PARIS • SYDNEY • HAMBURG
STOCKHOLM • ATHENS • TOKYO • MILAN
MADRID • WARSAW • BUDAPEST • AUCKLAND

Harlequin Historicals first edition August 1992

ISBN 0-373-28738-0

THE DREAM

Books by Kit Gardner

Harlequin Historicals

Arabesque #117
The Dream #138

KIT GARDNER

A former C.P.A., Kit Gardner lives in Southwestern Pennsylvania with her husband and two young sons. When her busy schedule allows, she enjoys skiing, golf, travel and reading anything from romance to the latest in sensational thrillers.

To Lee and Jo, for laughing in all the right places.
And to my sister, Victoria,
for always being there in those wee hours
to read one more just-finished chapter.

Chapter One

London, 1872

She trembled with anticipation. Then, as before, as he always would, he emerged from the depths of that fathomless milky haze. He loomed silent and mighty before her, enveloping her within a warmth that was his alone, a heat that branded her to her core. He caressed her cheek, brushing aside her ebony tresses as the mists parted to unveil a face so ruggedly handsome her breath caught. His eyes, dusky gray and clouded with some potent emotion, captured hers in their smoky depths as he pressed her fingers to his lips. His breath upon her trembling hand soothed but a moment then brought a sudden parchedness to her throat. He bent his head and the unruly russet locks, curling in a deceptively innocent manner over his collar, beckoned for her touch. Then her fingers, trembling with uncertainty, poised hesitantly upon that chiseled jaw before venturing deep into his hair to draw him closer, and her lips parted in sweet anticipation of the gentle caress of his mouth upon hers ... again....

A soft thump and what proved an unsuccessful attempt to muffle a giggle snatched Elizabeth from her dream. For a moment she stared into the darkness, her hand fluttering over the soft muslin covering her heart as if to banish forever the last vestiges of that wicked creation from her subconscious mind. A despondent groan escaped her lips and her arm fell heavily across her lids. Of late, every innocent pursuit of slumber resulted in some vision of seduction by a man of whom she knew nothing, but whose face and manner were so hauntingly familiar she was certain he was not solely her creation.

A scrape accompanied by a hushed whisper brought Elizabeth bolt upright in bed. Instinctively, her hand shot out in the darkness to fumble for the bedside lantern and her wire-rimmed spectacles left purposely within reach. Vainly, her eyes searched the darkness for movement and her heart hammered a staccato within her breast as the window nearby slid closed with a dull thud. She swept her legs from beneath starched sheets as shaking fingers struck a match to the lantern.

"Oh! Miss Burbridge!" the intruder gasped, swinging about to clasp a hand to the gaping bodice of her nightdress in a gesture Elizabeth deemed more from outright shock than any attempt at modesty. Color suffused the girl's plump cheeks and a hand rose to pluck self-consciously at the mass of unbound golden ringlets tumbling about her shoulders.

Blinking the sleep from her eyes, Elizabeth adjusted the spectacles upon her nose and heaved a sigh of relief, though she managed to purse her lips with disapproval. "It would serve you well to find your tongue, Miss Sinclair. Perhaps Headmistress Percy would aid you in your plight."

Phoebe Sinclair flung herself in a desperate heap at Elizabeth's feet. "Oh, dear Lord, no! You mustn't summon Mistress Percy! It was an awful mistake! You see, I thought yours was the window to *my* room! In the darkness I must have erred!"

Erred, indeed. Elizabeth could not help but muse that Phoebe's humble and contrite expression must have been practiced countless times before a mirror. Surely one so young, barely fifteen, and so prone to mischief and nonsense, would not find humility a state to which she instinctively aspired. With every batch of young ladies, at least one darling girl—and Phoebe was surely that, poised just this side of beautiful due to a decided plumpness and a pert little nose—would choose to squander her educational opportunities in favor of girlish pranks and ne'er-do-well ventures in the dead of night.

Elizabeth smoothed her own thick braid, lying against the heavy muslin of her nightgown. The child was merely an innocent product of questionable upbringing. Her parents were the cause, of this Elizabeth harbored little doubt. She silently cursed those responsible for fostering such a wild nature. Her eyes darted over the girl's hands, which were clutching at her torn nightdress, then settled upon the brown wool cloak slung over her shoulders. The garment was far too large and coarse to belong to Phoebe.

Elizabeth couldn't suppress a gasp. "Miss Sinclair! You cover yourself with a gentleman's cloak! I demand some explanation."

"Miss Burbridge, you must promise not to tell Mistress Percy. I fear my father would not find favor with me."

Elizabeth nearly snorted with disgust. "Perhaps it would enlighten him to the error of his ways." She contemplated her dewy-eyed pupil, so obviously in fear of Edwina Percy, headmistress and founder of the Dunlevy Public School for young women, Elizabeth's teacher, mentor and inspiration for the past fifteen years. A woman most revered, yet whose wrath was obviously feared by even the most rebellious of pupils. And rightly so, for Mistress Percy ruled Dunlevy with an iron fist.

Indeed, it was fervently discussed in hushed whispers that even the slightest transgression could find a young woman thrown from the great hall in a heap of shame, forever to bear the burden of her folly. Edwina Percy, peering over her thick bifocals, could dismiss a pupil with but a blink of an eye. Elizabeth had witnessed it countless times. The headmistress, pursing her lips and slapping her hands together as if to rid them of some unwanted dust. Then, turning on the heavy heel of her ever-so-sensible brown shoes and striding purposefully, as was her wont for any occasion, to settle herself behind her desk and matter-of-factly purge the unfortunate young woman from her "active" files.

Phoebe Sinclair's folly this evening would undoubtedly prove her final act of rebellion beneath Miss Percy's rule. Yet for some reason Elizabeth found Phoebe's innocence, perhaps the promise of what she could possibly achieve if properly channeled, plucking at her resolve to do what the other teachers, and certainly Miss Percy, would in such a situation.

"Miss Sinclair, if you could confide in me the nature of your business this evening, with the promise that you shan't again pursue activity that could possibly threaten your situation, perhaps I shall not feel compelled to report to Miss Percy that anything remarkable occurred this evening."

"Oh, Miss Burbridge, would you? Could you? Why, one would never have thought you capable..." Phoebe raised a hand self-consciously to her mouth and rushed on. "I mean, rather, well...you see, you're viewed as somewhat of a priss and a prude, both of which, mind you, I find truly... er...enchanting, though this has proven a trifle baffling for us, for you're not really that old—perhaps only a score and five or so...."

Elizabeth stared openmouthed at the girl.

"And Charlotte Lambert says you could possibly be pretty if you didn't wear your hair so...severely, and if you perhaps chose something besides that god-awful brown muslin for your dresses. And if you took your spectacles off and smiled every now and again. Though, if you ask me, 'tis a gentleman friend that you lack."

"Miss Sinclair! It is not *my* future at stake here!" Elizabeth exclaimed, an uncharacteristic heat climbing in her cheeks. She drew her heavy muslin nightgown closer about her neck. "The reasons for your adventure this evening interest me far more than any thoughts either you or Miss Lambert harbor regarding my appearance or state of well-being."

Phoebe drew a deep breath. "I...I met my beau, Miles. He attends Hastings, the nearby boys' school." The smile flirting with her Cupid's bow mouth suddenly widened and her amber eyes sparkled. "Oh, Miss Burbridge, he's so handsome, I fear I can't help myself when I'm near him!"

"You must!"

"But he has such a persuasive air!"

"All the more reason to avoid him. You've far too much at stake. If you must see this young man, then do so in the proper manner. But for heaven' sake, do not tempt the fates and your future by wandering about in that...that thin nightdress."

"I fear I misplaced my robe beneath an elm."

Elizabeth stared at Phoebe. "You removed your robe?"

Phoebe shrugged and grinned guiltily. "Miles wished to see my gown and I could not deny him."

"Dear God!"

"Oh, but, Miss Burbridge! 'Twas all that happened, honestly! He asked for but one kiss, and to see my gown, but other than that..." The young girl's amber eyes flew wide beneath Elizabeth's suspicious gaze. "Oh! I didn't allow him to touch my bosoms, of course, though he said he wanted to."

"Enough!" Elizabeth fairly shrieked, pressing her hands to her pounding head. "Phoebe, we shall discuss this at great length, I'm afraid, at a proper hour. Until such time, you must promise me that you shan't meet this Miles fellow again, or I shall be forced to speak with Miss Percy."

Phoebe pouted and chewed her lip dejectedly. "But I fear I shall miss him dreadfully. 'Twill undoubtedly be the death of me!"

"A small sacrifice, I can assure you, and one you will not regret."

With a happy sigh of the painfully innocent, Phoebe leapt to her feet and flung her arms about Elizabeth in a hearty embrace. "I won't forget this. Thank you!" And with that, she skittered from the room, leaving a befuddled and shaken Elizabeth with far more than a hauntingly seductive dream to keep her from slumber for what remained of the night.

Elizabeth's sigh seemed to echo through the empty classroom, obliterating, for the moment, the jingling of sleigh bells and the voices of those readying themselves for the Christmas holidays. She stared from the tall windows, contemplating the gently falling snow, the bustling scene below, all through a blur of unshed tears. She'd watched it now...how many times? Horses stomping impatiently, polished black coaches filling with trunks and eager young women bound for home and hearth and a joyous holiday season.

Melancholy welled in her throat, lodging there with her tears; the lengthening shadows had stirred memories of other holidays when her mother had failed to arrive altogether, leaving

Elizabeth to fabricate some believable lie before taking to her room to spend the holiday alone. Thank heavens her mother's letter had arrived before Elizabeth had set about packing her trunk, allowing her sufficient time to drum up some excuse, some dreadful lie, some further perpetuation of this sham.

She had to struggle to suppress a painful wince, a wince born of shame and humiliation, and, yes, resentment, at perpetuating such deceit with Miss Percy. All because of her mother's true identity, an identity that, if exposed, would condemn Elizabeth to a life far removed from the one she cherished at Dunlevy. Had she not been so supremely certain of her fate were this secret ever to come to the fore, perhaps she would have confronted Miss Percy with the truth long ago. As it was, she'd managed to look the headmistress square in the eye and lie through her teeth...something about her mother's dear sister and a sudden raging fever that required Leonora Burbridge's prompt attention, regardless of the holiday. Elizabeth could only imagine Edwina Percy's reaction had she known Leonora had no sister, that the only soul requiring her prompt attention was her latest inamorato, Lord Reginald Davenport. He was yet another in that endless stream of beaux, each and every one of whom, at one time or another, Leonora had breathlessly proclaimed "the one."

Elizabeth could not help but muse that the only qualities she shared with her mother were those most visible—vibrant violet eyes and a bountiful bosom Leonora no doubt cherished but one which Elizabeth deemed a nuisance and therefore bound tightly within her clothes. Her anger flared, bristling to life within her, not because of her mother's laying ruin to a holiday yet again, not even because of the blasted lies, but because after all these years, all the disappointments and those to come, the tears still slipped from her eyes.

"Oh, Miss Burbridge! I'm so dreadfully sorry!"

Elizabeth spun about to confront a wide-eyed Phoebe Sinclair lingering half in, half out of the classroom doorway. Phoebe grinned guiltily as she bent to retrieve the traveling bag she'd dropped and adjusted the emerald velvet hat atop her blond ringlets, her expression reminding Elizabeth of the nocturnal incident a few weeks prior. "My coach has just arrived and I'm awfully anxious to go now. I've waited *all day* to leave!''

Elizabeth smoothed her hair and averted her cheeks lest the child spy a stray tear. "For heaven' sake, don't let me keep you," she replied.

Phoebe gathered her cloak about her and looked as if to leave, when she paused, as if struck by a thought. "And where are you spending the holidays, Miss Burbridge?"

"I…uh…I've an enormous amount of work to occupy me." Elizabeth felt atrociously silly lying to this young girl, yet was incapable of anything but. "My mother was called away to see to her sister, who suddenly developed a raging fever." She almost winced, so inept was she at lying.

Phoebe's brow knitted with genuine concern. "I'm so dreadfully sorry for your aunt, especially at this time of year. Dear God, how terribly lonely you shall be, remaining here."

Elizabeth shook her head dismissively. "Actually, in years past I've found the peace and quiet rather conducive to accomplishing a fair amount of work."

Phoebe wrinkled her nose in distaste. "Oh, heavens, *I* could never spend this holiday away from home. 'Tis such a gay time, what with Cook's divine Christmas dinner…a goose roasted to absolute perfection and plum pudding!"

Elizabeth swallowed heavily at the thought. Goose…plum pudding… She'd never tasted plum pudding.

Phoebe fairly smacked her lips in anticipation, then her amber eyes widened. "Why, of course! You shall join us as our Christmas guest! Father always has an unexpected guest or two over the holidays."

Elizabeth blanched and shook her head. "Oh no, I couldn't. That would be unseemly…."

"Nonsense, Miss Burbridge!" Rushing forward, Phoebe linked her arm through Elizabeth's and dragged her toward the door. "Now fetch your bags and be speedy about it. Hiram, our coachman, cannot abide tardiness."

In spite of herself, Elizabeth allowed the willful young girl to pull her along toward the stairs that led to the third floor. Gathering her senses, she planted her feet firmly and twisted her arm from Phoebe's grasp. "Miss Sinclair, I simply cannot."

Her hands upon her hips, Phoebe clucked impatiently. "Really, you must call me Phoebe if we're to spend the holiday together. Now hurry! Hiram won't wait forever, and Cook no doubt has some delicious dinner piping hot and awaiting us."

Sighing with exasperation, Elizabeth opened her mouth to plead some aversion to roast goose and plum pudding, when she was struck by a sudden thought. Was this not the opportunity for which she'd been hoping? The chance to confront Phoebe's parents about the child's wild and irrepressible nature, a nature, albeit charming, that harbored little but grief for her future? Perhaps if she presented her case in the proper manner and paid great heed to the source of Phoebe's wayward upbringing, she would be better prepared to take the child firmly beneath her wing and ensure a suitable future for her.

"Miss Burbridge?" Phoebe's questioning tone drew Elizabeth from her thoughts. "We must hurry now if we're to arrive before dark. Shall we?"

Without hesitation, Elizabeth laid a hand upon Phoebe's velvet-clad arm. "I shall be just a moment."

Phoebe clapped with glee then hugged Elizabeth fiercely, gushing, "Oh, Miss Burbridge!" before Elizabeth pulled herself from the girl's embrace and dashed up the stairs at a pace heretofore unknown to her.

Elizabeth's eyes swept for what seemed the hundredth time from the coach window over the plush red velvet interior to settle upon Phoebe's plump form nestled within the folds of her voluminous cloak upon the seat opposite. Drawing her own brown wool cloak more closely about her shoulders, Elizabeth wondered how a child could chatter unceasingly. She talked of her home, or rather the family's "home in the country." It was far more prestigious, she informed Elizabeth, to own a house in the country than a "country home." Elizabeth simply smiled, wondering what gaudy facade awaited her. She'd gleaned that current fashion dictated decorating one's home as ostentatiously as possible, and the more class-conscious one was, the more garish the home. From Phoebe's offhanded remarks and the cut and cloth of the girl's stylish clothing, Elizabeth harbored little doubt that her family was upper-class.

Of her father Phoebe spoke briefly, of her mother not a word, confining herself to comments regarding the family's unusual circle of friends, who joined them every Christmas for dinner. Elizabeth gathered her father was somewhat of an eccentric, no doubt aging and, as a result, terribly removed from his daughter's life while he pursued his own idle amusements.

Her lips twisted contemptuously at the thought, when Phoebe leaned forward eagerly upon her seat and gestured frantically from the window. "We're home! And there's Father!"

Craning her neck to achieve a better view, Elizabeth gasped as the coach slowed along a snow-covered curved drive and stopped before an enormous brick-and-stone mansion. Phoebe's impatience allowed Elizabeth only a moment to catch her breath at the enormity of the home and to seek some glimpse of this father. She followed Phoebe from the coach, though at a somewhat restrained pace. Her gaze was immediately drawn to two men and a horse. Of the latter, she was immediately terrified.

She kept her distance from the animal, a huge black steed, which was pawing the earth and prancing delicately about as the younger of the two men attempted to keep his seat aboard the mutinous mount. Elizabeth's eyes flickered briefly over the rider to settle upon the gray-haired gentleman standing before the horse and struggling to retain some control over the beast with a rope secured to the halter. He was older than Elizabeth had expected, somewhat stooped, with thin hair and a crooked, rather hooked nose, which gave him an air of superiority that Elizabeth immediately relished as a challenge.

Suddenly, the horse reared up on his hind legs, pawing the air before him and letting loose a piercing whinny. With a terrified howl, the older man abandoned his task and, in his haste to flee, lost his footing in the snow and fell to his rump.

"Casper! My goodness, are you hurt?" With a gasp, Phoebe rushed forward to assist the older man to his feet. "Why in heaven's name do you allow Father to talk you into helping with this wild beast! Father—" Phoebe lifted her gaze to the young man aboard the mighty stallion and Elizabeth's eyes followed . . . and her mouth fell open.

"Welcome home, Phoebe," the man drawled with a lazy half smile, running a hand through thick russet hair. He swung the stallion about and his smoky gaze settled upon Elizabeth.

With a face drained of color and the blood thumping fiercely through her veins, Elizabeth stared blankly upon the handsome visage of the very man she'd thought but a haunting figment of her imagination. The man in her dreams.

Chapter Two

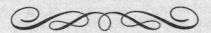

Basil Christy's disposition had known better times. He should have kept to his chamber all day after being awakened well before dawn by that infernal excuse for a dog his stepfather insisted upon keeping in the house. Not only was the damned animal deaf, he was nearly blind, which may have caused his confusion over the room he had sought in the darkness. The swift kick Basil had seen fit to deal the mangy creature had sent him farther down the hall with a whimper and a few soft whines to scratch and mewl before his stepfather's door. The idea! Allowing so ghastly a creature free roam in so stately a manse! Simply another peculiar whim of his aging stepfather, Lord Nigel Cosgrove.

To make matters worse, Lady Luck seemed to have deserted Basil of late at the faro table, though he supposed he'd tempted fate overlong. Then again, his penchant for brandy had not only warmed his belly but loosened his purse when he should have snapped it tightly closed. His luck had proven equally as distressing with his usual gaggle of female friends. Perhaps his appeal had waned of late as word of his sagging luck had spread, though surely no soul was foolish enough to doubt that his purse would ever see bottom.

With a snort of disgust, he splashed a liberal draft of brandy into a snifter and drained the glass in one gulp. With a smack of his lips and a guttural belch, he scratched his belly through the fine silk of his scarlet dressing gown and poured himself yet another liberal libation.

Lifting his glass, Basil made a mock toast to Lord Cosgrove, ensconced within his upstairs chambers. He supposed he owed a token of thanks to his enormously wealthy stepfather, for his access to funds was limitless. He was, however, more than certain the old man would raise one of those infernal bushy white brows and glare upon him as if he knew damned well why Basil requested a hefty advance on an already hefty weekly allowance. Yet Nigel still doled it out, perhaps out of some perverse loyalty to the memory of his wife, Eugenie, Basil's mother, who had died nearly ten years ago of cholera.

Strange old man, for Basil knew his stepfather had never taken a liking to him, even after these twenty-seven years beneath the same roof. As if Basil cared. Something about Basil's penchant for idleness, the old man had growled time and time again. He couldn't abide Basil's decided lack of interest in business affairs, which Basil viewed as nothing short of drudgery. Were Nigel to die, which appeared more imminent of late due to a lingering hacking cough, Basil was certain that the estate, along with that bothersome shipping conglomerate, would all be his. And he intended to sell the business, posthaste.

With a self-satisfied smirk twisting his ruddy face, he ran a hand over his sleek black hair and strolled before the cozy fire, sipping from his drink. Keen black eyes darted about the richly appointed parlor with its wall hangings of deep blue velvet, the matching armchairs and an overstuffed sofa flanked by finely carved Sheraton tables. All very elegant but a bit too plain for his tastes. It mattered little, for Eugenie had been unable to produce a child for Nigel, making Basil the sole heir. One day, as sure as the sun's rising, this would all be his. Perhaps things weren't so bad after all.

Settling himself upon the sofa, he pulled a pillow beneath his head and stretched out, mindful that his satin slippers marred the velvet but uncaring at the moment. A bit of unwanted dust would give all those twittering maids something with which to occupy themselves besides mindless chitchat. He attempted to balance his glass upon his belly, but due to his paunch, caused predominantly by his swayed back, the glass refused to remain steady. Drawing a deep breath, he rubbed his soft middle and contemplated his lost youth, though he found that train of thought more than a trifle disconcerting as he was but two and thirty, hardly an old man. That he hadn't managed to accomplish much in his lifetime caused him a certain disquiet from time to time, though what better position could he be in? Heir to a bloody fortune, a lifetime of excesses of liquor and women . . .

His musings were brought to an abrupt end when the parlor doors swept open and the high-pitched voices of two of the maids announced their arrival. Just as he was about to spring from his comfortable position and launch into a tirade on maintaining a man's privacy, a comment by Felicity, the younger of the two maids, stilled his movements. They were unaware of his presence, concealed as he was behind the tall back of the sofa.

"Now why on earth would Lord Cosgrove summon that solicitor, Mr. Boyd, at such an hour?" Felicity mused in the same breathy voice Basil knew all too well. It had taken him less than a week after her arrival at the Cosgrove household to coerce the frightfully young but ever-so-nubile maid into his bed. For a fleeting moment he allowed his thoughts to linger upon the vision of her gasping beneath him, but the hollow laugh of the other maid, Brunhilde, brought him crashing to earth.

"Seems like Lord Cosgrove's finally come to his senses, saints be praised," Brunhilde snorted in a tone Basil deemed not unlike that of the brood mares stabled behind the grand house. "Now, careful, child. Ye don' want to fuss with the flowers too much. Just a touch of disarray, like ye threw 'em in the vase and they fell just so." Brunhilde heaved a heavy sigh. "Aye, lass, I couldn't be more pleased Lord Cosgrove finally saw a spade fer a spade."

"Ma'am?"

"That *Basil*, child! He's no good, I'm tellin' ye, like I been tellin' Lord Cosgrove fer years now, ever since poor Eugenie died an' he had no one but us servants to confide in. Seems he's finally opened his ears. Cut Basil entirely out of the will, he did." Brunhilde paused and Basil stared unseeing at the ceiling overhead, listening to his heart racing. "That Mr. Boyd took care of it, he did. Signed and freshly sealed. I saw it with me

own eyes. 'Course, Lord Cosgrove an' me, we discussed the
matter many a time. Why, if he didn't feel such an obligation
to poor Eugenie, I'd wager he'd have thrown that good-fer-
nothin' Basil out on his floppy ear long ago."

"He must have loved her very much."

"Oh, 'course he did, child. But 'tis more'n love that eats at
him, I tell ye." Brunhilde lowered her voice to just above a
whisper, barely audible above Basil's frantically thumping
pulse. "'Tis the matter of that other woman."

"There is another woman?"

"*Was* another woman. Now, child, I don't want ye flappin'
yer tongue te all the help, ye hear what I'm tellin' ye? More'n
likely Eugenie herself didn't even know 'bout this woman. Or
the child."

"Child?"

Basil nearly bit his fist to keep from crying out.

"Aye, there was a child. A daughter."

"Why didn't Lord Cosgrove marry the woman?"

"Child, use that thing between yer ears once in a while, will
ye? He was married to Eugenie at the time! Had been for jest
about a year or two, maybe a little longer. But poor Eugenie
couldn't get with child, and perhaps Lord Cosgrove, bein' a
man an' all, found himself taken with this young woman. Oh,
she was 'bout yer age, maybe a few years older. A real beauty
with fine copper-colored hair and sweet as sugar. Oh, he was
taken with her and she with him, I suppose. She bore him a
daughter."

"How sad."

"Sad? Ha! Full of pride, she was, even refusin' Lord Cosgrove's monthly stipends. Probably thought he was goin' te
marry her, she did. Foolish lass. Hopelessly in love with him,
I'd wager. He could never have left Eugenie, for he did love her,
ye know, an' she had young Basil, at the time but five years old
and fatherless since a wee babe. I'm tellin' ye, Lord Nigel Cosgrove's always been a fine man, an' smart. Done the proper
thing. Jes' wait 'til that Basil hears of this! Ha!"

"He . . . he doesn't yet know?"

"Oh, for heaven' sake, child! 'Course he doesn't know! And
ye shan't go squawkin' te him, neither! Nay, 'twill be a sweet

revenge to let him go on thinkin' 'twill all be his. That good-fer-nothin'... Why, 'twill make Lord Cosgrove's passing on jest a tad bit bearable when Mr. Boyd announces that nearly everythin' will go te Lord Cosgrove's blood heir, this daughter.''

"He knows who she is?"

"'Course he does, child! Why, he's kept a watch on her since the very day she was born, and the woman, as well. All very discreetly, mind ye. But, like I says, he's a fine man an' all, and not one te go shirkin' his responsibilities.'' Silence filled the room once more, then the muffled sound of feet scraping against the polished floors. "There. See how beautiful they are arranged just so. Takes practice, child, but ye'll learn in no time. Now we must see te Lord Cosgrove. He'll be wantin' his afternoon tea quite soon.''

"Aye, ma'am. Though if you don't mind my asking, this daughter and the woman...''

The sound of their feet shuffling to the door caused Basil nearly to leap from the sofa with a panicked cry.

"Do *you* know who they are?" Felicity asked.

The parlor door opened and Brunhilde replied, "'Course I do, but, like I said, I'll tell ye what I know, but ye must promise that ye shan't breathe a word.''

"Oh, I promise I shan't...''

What remained of Felicity's breathy reply was lost behind the soft closing of the door. Basil rose like a man possessed and almost hurled his glass at the solid wood. Thinking the better of it, he gulped down what remained and rose on unsteady legs to stumble to the brandy decanter. His hands shook uncontrollably. His vision blurred. Acrid bile rose in his throat despite the soothing burn of the liquor. He gripped the sides of the table as his legs threatened to collapse beneath him, then he turned and stared disbelievingly upon the flames that not moments before had soothed him with their gentle warmth. Sweat beaded his brow and ran in unheeded rivulets down his face and along his neck.

A plan. He needed a plan. And the sooner the better.

Opportunity presented itself later that evening. His nerves were stretched like taut string, his step purposeful yet wary, as if every shadowed doorway concealed yet another servant who wished ill will upon him. As he ventured past the open dining room door, the soft sounds of a woman humming to herself stilled his slippered feet and caused his heart to leap. Daring a peek inside the room, he spied Felicity and another young maid whom he'd never seen before busily polishing silver.

His gaze settled for a moment upon the newcomer, a rather plump young thing with milky white skin and a mass of curling jet black ringlets tumbling from her cap. His eyes fell immediately to the bodice of her crisply starched gray poplin dress. Too young, or far too underdeveloped for his tastes. His eyes strayed immediately to Felicity's well-filled bodice, and the tightening in his loins, despite his distress, reassured him that he was indeed functioning up to snuff.

Drawing himself up with a pat to his belly, he sauntered rather casually into the room, pausing at Felicity's elbow as if to inspect the maids' work. True to form, and no small nudge to Basil's ego, Felicity's tiny hand upon the silver began to tremble slightly and Basil was quite certain he detected a sudden irregularity in her breathing. For a moment, he peered upon the blond head a good six inches below his, aware that she had ceased her work and no doubt stared with her luminous blue eyes at some spot directly before her. Her lips were softly parted and her bosom heaved enough to draw Basil's roving eye once more. That her disconcerted state could well be the result of her newly gleaned knowledge caused him but a moment's pause. He cared naught for the reason for her distress, only that *he* was the underlying cause.

The swiftly bobbing head of the other maid and her blubbery attempt at conversation drew Basil's attention reluctantly from Felicity.

"Yer...yer...lordship..." The young girl stammered, sweeping a hand to the polished silver before her. "Are ye pleased, sir?"

Basil raised a lofty brow and narrowed his gaze upon the trembling young maid, purposefully ignoring her query. Intimidation had always suited his purposes far more than an amiable air. "You're rather new, aren't you? State your name."

"Ab-Ab-Abigail, sir."

He fingered a silver bowl that to his eye was polished nearly to perfection, purposefully marring the shine with a smudge of his thumb. Fixing a hooded black gaze upon the young maid, he remarked caustically, "I shall overlook, for the moment, your rather obvious shortcomings, Abigail, because you are new to this household."

"Th-thank ye, sir, I..."

"Now, Abigail, I believe Brunhilde wishes you to attend to some matter in the kitchen."

With a nervous bob of her head, Abigail turned and fled.

Silence filled the room, broken only by the distant scurrying of Abigail's feet as she hurried to oblige. Felicity still poised like a stone statue at Basil's side. Slowly and with definite purpose, he laid his hand close to hers upon the table and watched with a growing amusement as her eyelids fluttered and her lips parted with a breathless gasp. He was quite certain that if he were to bend his lips to nibble upon the smooth skin of her throat, she would undoubtedly swoon dead away. This power he wielded over her brought him an inordinate amount of pleasure.

In one bold movement, his hand covered hers and he bent his head until he was certain his breath tickled her ear. In his most seductive tone he murmured, "Darling, Felicity, I must have you tonight or I shall be a man possessed."

Felicity swayed upon her feet and dropped her rag to the floor. "I...perhaps I could get away...but only for a few hours, and 'twill be very late. Brunhilde sleeps so lightly...I...oh!"

With a wicked chuckle, Basil nipped at her tiny ear. "I shall count the hours." Giving her hand a final squeeze, he resisted the urge to pat her rump, turned on his heel and sauntered as casually from the room as he'd entered. The smirk twisting his lips was one of grim self-satisfaction.

A soft tapping at the bedroom door snapped Basil's head up and he fumbled with his scarlet silk dressing gown one last time to achieve the desired effect. Adjusting himself into a half-reclining position upon the huge mahogany four-poster, he leaned casually upon one elbow, lifting a knee to allow the silk gown to drape provocatively between his bare legs, then bade his shy visitor entrance. Any doubts he harbored regarding his ability to perform this evening, brought on by the distinct feeling that a noose was tightening with painstaking slowness about his neck, were tossed to the four winds as Felicity entered his chamber.

The small lamp she carried cast a pale glow into the shadowed room and illuminated her lovely young face, wan, wide-eyed and framed by a sleek fall of honey blond hair. She was no classic beauty, to be sure, for her forehead was a tad too wide and her jaw a bit too square for Basil's tastes, but the lovely body concealed beneath her thin nightgown brought an insistent pulsing to his loins. Indeed, the vivid memory of their last "lesson" loomed quite suddenly, reminding him that this shy maid harbored a boundless capacity for learning and improvisation that had nearly proved the death of him. Perhaps these recently acquired talents would ease whatever misgivings her future bridegroom might harbor regarding her lack of virtue. Of course, were *he* ever to take a bride, which he thought atrociously unlikely, he would demand that her virtue be intact, and the more inexperienced the wench, the better.

Felicity's hesitation upon entering the room fueled Basil's gnawing suspicion that she struggled with the knowledge of his fate. He knew well that some part of her attraction to him stemmed from his title and wealth. Without that, he would have to play upon her weaknesses. Within the boudoir, he knew these well, but he also had every intention of pursuing his hunch that Felicity all but overflowed with sympathetic, motherly instincts.

Rising from the bed, he moved slowly to take the lantern from her and lay it upon the bedside table. Ignoring her breathy reply, Basil pressed his ever present glass into her shaking fingers and tipped the brew to her lips. After she'd taken several sips and raised a thankful gaze to him, he drained the glass and set it aside. He lifted his hands to her shoulders, rubbing her warm skin and drawing her to him until he felt her breasts pressing against his chest.

Brushing his lips over her brow, he murmured, "Darling, what troubles you so? You know you can tell me. For God's sake, after all that we've shared, and what you've come to mean to me, it would tear at me to know that you keep something from me.''

Felicity's hands fluttered over his back and she sighed as his mouth moved to nibble along her throat. '''Tis nothing, really...I...I...oh, I don't know.''

Light as a feather, and with a gentleness Basil had never before found necessary to use, he moved his fingers over her collarbone to hook in the high neck of her gown. His fingers tugged lightly at the thin cotton, as if he wished to rip it from her, which, in all truth, he did, though his intent was to obtain far more from her this evening than a satisfied libido.

"Dear God, but you drive me to distraction," he rasped against her neck. His efforts were immediately rewarded as her hands moved to part his dressing gown, slipping within the folds to caress his back, which, like the rest of his body, was densely covered with thick black hair. She had long since overcome her aversion to his rather beastly appearance, as he'd convinced her that excessive body hair bespoke tremendous virility.

Easing from her, he imitated a shudder before turning from her as if in pain.

"Wh-what is it?" Felicity asked, surprise evident in her voice. "Do I not please you?"

Basil shook his head with what he hoped appeared to be intense frustration. "You please me too much, for I fear I become an animal at the very sight of you. That is what pains me so greatly, for I know something troubles you, darling. Would you have me no better than a rutting stag, to take you so...so callously, without heeding what plagues you?"

Felicity slipped her arms about his waist, rubbing her full breasts against him. "But 'tis a matter involving *you.*"

Basil swung a disbelieving look upon her. "Me? Oh, my darling." He pulled her against him, running his hands over her back and for a moment venturing lower, to her derriere. "If you wish to protect me in some way...oh, but you are sweet..." His pursuit became bold and he moved his hands to cup her breasts through her gown in a manner he knew she loved. "Tell me, darling, you must, or I shall die of wanting you." He nearly had to suppress a delightful chuckle as Felicity's will crumbled and her hands clutched at his shoulders. He bent to nibble at the peaks of her breasts pressing against the cotton gown, reminding himself to move slowly, unhurried. "Tell me . . . you must . . ."

"Oh, Basil. 'Tis Lord Cosgrove's will." Felicity gasped at his boldness. "He . . . he has cut you out, and . . . oh!"

With a soft growl, Basil tore her gown from neckline to waist, dropping to his knees before her. "Go on, darling, tell me."

"I—I cannot . . . oh . . ."

"You must, darling, or we must cease this foolishness and I shall die of this torture."

"Oh . . . I . . . there is a daughter. A schoolteacher . . . Oh, Basil!" Felicity gasped breathlessly. "This daughter, she is Lord Cosgrove's daughter by this woman . . . this Philippa V-Valen . . ."

Basil lifted his head so suddenly he glimpsed a fleeting shock spread across Felicity's sweat-dampened features. "Not the courtesan, Philippa Valentine?"

With a somewhat befuddled expression, Felicity replied, "I know not who the woman is, Basil."

"Of course you don't, darling," he soothed, rising to his feet to sweep her into his arms. "Enough of this, for I fear I cannot wait another moment to have you."

"But you aren't even troubled . . ." Felicity murmured in awe as she was deposited rather unceremoniously upon the bed.

Sweeping his dressing gown from his back, Basil raised a wicked brow as he paused on the edge of the bed, allowing Felicity ample opportunity to view his appropriately swollen manhood. Her look of amazement always brought a smirk to his lips. "Perhaps later I shall realize the enormity of the situation. But for the moment, my darling, I need only to feel you beneath me."

And with that, he lunged forward, pinning her beneath him and driving himself deep within her.

"Basil . . . darling, what is it?"

At the sound of Felicity's sleepy voice from the tumbled bed behind him, Basil took yet another sip of his brandy before turning from the tall bedroom windows. He adjusted the silk sash at his waist, allowing his hooded gaze to settle upon the pleasing form displayed unabashedly in all her naked splendor upon the rumpled sheets. She swept aside the curtain of golden hair and rubbed the sleep from her eyes, which was all well and good, for the time had long since passed for the wench to find her way back to her quarters. For quite some time now, Basil had listened to her soft snoring as she'd slept sprawled across the entire bed while he carefully schemed the evening away. Dawn was but a few hours hence and he could not risk their liaison being discovered. Especially now, with so much at stake.

Drawing upon his most humble of expressions, he approached the bed to gaze upon her with what he hoped appeared to be uncertainty. "Dearest Felicity, it would be a dreadful lie to say that this...change in my stepfather's will caused me no great concern. Truly it does, though it is not so much for the lost inheritance that I grieve but the obvious lack of...of affection my very own stepfather feels for me."

"Oh, Basil, darling!" Felicity flung herself into his arms, cradling his head to her bosom. "I shall always be here for you. Why, to think the man could be so callous!"

Lifting his head, Basil cupped her face in his hands and shook his head as if in disbelief. "Whatever would I do without my lovely Felicity? Perhaps together we could...oh, but no...you couldn't possibly..." He lifted a gaze fairly brimming with unabashed hope. "It would be for *us,* darling, for *our* future, the future I have planned for us."

Felicity's mouth sagged and a tiny hand fluttered to her breast. "Y-you mean marriage?"

Basil chuckled softly and drew her into his arms. "Of course, darling! Whatever else could I possibly mean? But we must work together on this, if only to— Dear God, I loathe the very word, but perhaps it is necessary—to *avenge* my lost inheritance and the pain of a father's love denied."

"Whatever it takes, Basil," Felicity murmured softly.

"Very well, then." Basil had to suppress the matter-of-fact tone looming in his voice. "It will call for all sorts of wheedling on your part, which shouldn't be too difficult, as Brunhilde appears comfortable taking you into her confidence. You must simply learn all that you can of this daughter and her mother, this courtesan. The daughter, is she perhaps unwed?''

Felicity gave him a rather startled look. ''I wouldn't know, though 'tis an odd question.''

''Perhaps...'' Basil rubbed his beard-stubbled jaw in thought. Sensing the slightest withdrawal in Felicity, he clasped her hands in his and drew them to his lips, reveling in her immediate softening of manner. ''Darling, if we play our cards properly, I'm quite certain that my stepfather's fortune will one day be ours.''

Lifting doe eyes, Felicity murmured, ''I only wish to please you, Basil. Surely you know that.''

''Of course, my darling.'' With a final brush of his lips against her hands, he released them to pat her soundly upon the rump. ''Now, off you go, back to your bed. The hour is so dreadfully late and I fear I'm rather...'' Allowing himself a huge yawn, he gave her a sheepish smile as he shooed her from the bed and flopped among the sheets. ''I'm rather tired. Oh, darling, be sure to close the door softly behind you.''

With a look of motherly concern, coupled with what Basil hoped with all his might was not a lovesick tender regard, Felicity gently brushed his hair from his eyes before turning to gather what remained of her nightgown and the lantern and tread silently from his room.

Chapter Three

With a thump and a smack, Elizabeth closed her empty trunk, slid it to the foot of her bed and rose to her feet, wiping her hands against her muslin skirts. She glanced about the charming pale yellow and cream bedchamber as if at a loss for something to occupy her mind. Unpacking what few items she'd brought had taken but a moment to accomplish. Biting nervously at her lip, she heaved a shaky sigh and allowed her thoughts to wander, then reached for the nearby dressing table to brace herself as she felt an uncharacteristic weakening in her knees. Easing herself from a cushioned stool, she clasped her icy hands in her lap and contemplated this cruel twist of fate.

Alec Sinclair. *Lord* Sinclair. Phoebe's father. The very man who'd had the audacity to invade her every dream with an intimacy so seductive and lifelike that she'd been rendered an openmouthed, wide-eyed ninny upon their introduction. Little wonder his gaze had flickered over her so briefly, as if she were but another of his daughter's silly friends, despite her introduction as Phoebe's teacher. If only she could render him a fleeting apparition, one she could keep safely tucked within her subconscious mind.

This, of course, was not to be, for here she sat, ensconced within *his* home, a home that, from what little she'd noticed, seemed to lend itself to unaffected comfort while still maintaining an air of understated elegance.

The crackling of a healthy fire burning within the hearth drew her attention for a moment. A vision of russet hair and smoky dark eyes loomed so suddenly she had to snatch her gaze

away from those flames. The reflection she then beheld in the
oval mirror before her proved equally disturbing, yet somehow captivated her, for at the school, duties did not allow time
for ogling oneself before a mirror. Although she admitted that
this was slim excuse for such a vanity.

Twin pools of deep violet, fringed by sooty black lashes,
stared from an oval face devoid of any color save for the pale
pink splashes high upon her prominent cheekbones. Some
would call her skin luminous; her mother often quipped in a
rather chastising tone that such a fine translucence was the result of not enough fresh air and sunshine.

Elizabeth sighed and lifted a hand to smooth her hair into the
tight chignon at the back of her neck, mindful of the wayward
ebony tendrils curling against her forehead and cheeks. Pursing her lips, she cursed Mother Nature for the thousandth time
for bestowing upon her this thick mass of unruly blue black
hair, which adamantly refused her every attempt at an impeccably sleek, very Miss Percy-like coiffure. Were it not for a
dreaded fear of resembling a well-groomed poodle, she would
have cut her hair very short long ago.

Pursing her lips yet again, she brushed impatient fingers over
her dark brows, silently cursing the arch that lent her that look
of wide-eyed innocence, certainly not the commanding air given
by Miss Percy's very dark, rather heavy upward slashes. Indeed, with her blastedly full lips and small upturned nose,
Elizabeth's entire face beheld a look of such unabashed naiveté, it was a wonder she commanded any respect from her
pupils. No doubt this was also the very reason Alec Sinclair's
hooded gaze had swept with such finality over her.

To be sure, her face had struck no chord of recognition in
him. But, apparently, in the few times she must have chanced
seeing him about the school, *his* had embedded itself so firmly
within her psyche that she could not rid herself of that rugged
visage even as she slept. That she would, in a short time, be
expected to dine with the man, knowing full well that his hair
was springy yet surprisingly soft, that he smelled woodsy and
clean and his lips were firm and... Why, it was absolute lunacy!

"Oh! You *are* here!"

Phoebe's animated voice snatched Elizabeth from her ru-
minations with a start. She self-consciously leapt to her feet as
if the bright-eyed child peering around the bedroom door had
been privy to her thoughts not moments before.

"Yes, of course," Elizabeth managed as she smoothed her
hair yet again and did the same with her gown. Not that she had
ever been given to primping. Indeed, she found this sudden
transformation into a fussy, tongue-tied simpleton most disturbing and not in keeping with the role model she was determined to be for Phoebe. If she did not gain control of her wits,
all her high-necked brown muslin gowns and severe coiffures
would be seen as mere facades, concealing a character far
weaker than that of the effervescent young girl standing before her.

"Perhaps you were preoccupied?" Phoebe toyed with a
golden ringlet lying innocently over the poufed sleeve of her
gown, then giggled and spun around before Elizabeth, spreading wide her full emerald satin skirts. "So? Don't you just love
it? Father is such a dear, realizing, of course, how *dreadfully*
boring I find those hideous brown garments we are forced to
wear at the school. So drab, so tedious, so frightfully ugly!
Don't you think?" With a sudden twist of her mouth and a roll
of amber eyes, Phoebe plucked at the emerald satin bow atop
her head. "This, and the blastedly high neck, were not my idea,
mind you. Undoubtedly Father still thinks me a child." Her
eyes widened and she clasped Elizabeth's hand in hers in what
Elizabeth could only deem a beseeching manner. "Perhaps *you*
will be able to convince him otherwise, hmm?"

Elizabeth bit her lip, willing to her tongue some response
other than that with which she truly wished to fill Lord Sinclair's ear. Phoebe, however, seemed bent upon asking rhetor-
ical questions, for she allowed Elizabeth scant opportunity to
respond.

"So! What gown have you chosen for this evening?" She
cast a wary glance at Elizabeth's frock.

Elizabeth could not resist raising a curious brow. "This *is* the
gown I've chosen."

Phoebe stared dumbly at the gown for a moment. "Oh."

"Is it not appropriate?"

"Do you have any others?"

"Why, yes, but they're all along the same order."

"Brown?"

"Yes."

"Brown muslin?"

"Yes."

"Oh."

"Phoebe, if there is a problem . . ."

"Oh no, of course not!" Phoebe waved her hand and seemed to force a lighthearted giggle. "I just thought . . . perhaps . . . well . . . that you wished to dress up a bit for the holiday. Oh, but Father won't mind. Why, he probably won't even notice. We must hurry now or Cook will be frightfully angry with us."

Without pausing for breath, Phoebe turned and scurried to the door with Elizabeth in tow, a frown creasing her dark brow and a heretofore unknown feeling of self-consciousness about her attire bringing a hesitancy to her step. Her distress was complete when, upon finding herself nearly at the first floor, she realized she had yet to ask Phoebe about her conspicuously absent mother.

Upon entering the massive dining room, Elizabeth found her step faltering once more. The room was bathed in the soft golden light of three enormous crystal candelabras set at equal distances upon the dining table. The table, which looked as if it could comfortably seat twenty, was draped with a rich creamy cloth of the finest damask and set rather cozily at one end with three place settings of sterling and white bone china. Situated between the candelabras were two large crystal vases overflowing with holly and pine, caught up with enormous red velvet bows to match those flouncing the creamy velvet draped across the wall of floor-to-ceiling windows. Against the enchanting reflection of the candlelight in the windows, fluffy flakes of snow fell peacefully in the darkness. The air was filled with the enticing aroma of pine and cinnamon, which seemed to blend perfectly with that of the dinner lying in wait. In all her imaginings, Elizabeth had never anticipated so exquisite a room, one that instantly brought a warmth to her belly and a melancholy over holidays spent alone.

Phoebe cooed and fluttered and smacked her lips as if the mere thought of what Cook had prepared were too wonderful to imagine. Anxiously flopping herself into one of the chairs, she lifted sparkling amber eyes and nodded encouragingly to Elizabeth. "There's little use waiting for Father. He'll be along shortly. He won't mind if we start without him."

Elizabeth settled herself in the cushioned seat opposite. "Really, Phoebe, it's not proper."

"Oh, poohey! Miss Burbridge, Father places very little emphasis on proper decorum."

Elizabeth lifted a reproachful brow, though she found herself idly admiring not only the impeccable place settings but the immaculately attired servants moving noiselessly about. For a man unconcerned with proper decorum, Alec Sinclair's home could not be found lacking. Of course, one could only assume he'd been lucky enough to employ servants who knew better.

"Ah! A veritable feast! Jennings, serve it up, man! I'm famished!" A deep resonant voice echoed off the rafters as Alec Sinclair strode purposefully into the room, shaking his head and running a hand through the unruly russet locks to shed the clinging snowflakes.

For some unexplainable reason, Elizabeth's heart flip-flopped and her eyes skidded about the room as she vainly attempted to rise to her feet and acknowledge his arrival. She had, however, positioned her chair well under the table so that her movements were seen as nothing short of a scrape and a bounce that lightly jostled the table. With cheeks flaming, she raised a hand in silent apology then hastily withdrew it to the safety of her lap, if only to still its noticeable trembling. Venturing a glance at her host, she found her throat suddenly parched as her gaze met his curious one.

He had paused, bent over a serving dish as if to sniff its delightful aroma. In the soft candlelight, his skin glowed a deep bronze, shadowed by the sharp planes of his cheekbones and chiseled jawline. His brow was strong, two dark slashes over a nose that hooked slightly and lent him a decidedly predatory air. He held his mouth in a lopsided version of a smirk, deepening the lines that creased his skin. Had it not been for the tousled fall of richly hued hair, Elizabeth would have deemed his rather harsh countenance in keeping with one far more advanced in years. As it was, his attire, which consisted of snug-fitting black riding breeches and a simple open-necked white shirt, and the undeniably arrogant manner in which he carried his impossibly tall, broad-shouldered frame lent him an air of roguish bravado better suited to a man just a few years her senior. Certainly not befitting the father one would envision for Phoebe Sinclair. Indeed, to Elizabeth's appraising eye, he appeared the embodiment of those swaggering roués who avoided fatherhood like the plague. He was handsome enough, possessing a decidedly captivating air...

"Is there some problem, Miss...?"

The dulcet tones reverberating throughout the room, dangled with some uncertainty, leaving little doubt that the man had forgotten her name. Indeed!

"Burbridge. Elizabeth Burbridge," she managed with a jaunty lift of her chin. Realizing his curious gaze lingered upon her, she averted her eyes to the steaming venison stew served upon her plate and sought to temper the flush mounting in her cheeks. "Lord Sinclair, I...I wish to thank you for receiving me as your guest on such short notice. I fear I—"

"Phoebe's friends are always welcome, Miss Burbridge," he muttered, settling in his chair and nodding to a hovering servant. He eyed the heaping portion of stew Jennings deposited before him in a manner that was, to Elizabeth's eye, not unlike that of a ravenous lion. Reaching for a generous chunk of crusty bread, he swung his gaze to Elizabeth. "Phoebe tells me your mother was called to her ailing sister's bedside." He lifted his fork and proceeded to attack his stew alternately with both fork and bread. Pausing between bites, he remarked, "No doubt that tragedy has cast a pall over your holiday."

"Yes...it has, at that," Elizabeth replied with a decided lack of heart. Fingering her own utensil, she found, however, that she could not take her eyes from the man as he made quick work of the food upon his plate. Not that he was in any way slovenly in his manner. Indeed, though he appeared to have an enormous appetite that he wished to appease, he seemed to savor every bite, pausing frequently to sip from his wine and spilling not a drop of either the food or drink upon himself or the tablecloth.

She found the sight far too interesting to suit her and, realizing she was all but staring at him yet again, decided that her fascination stemmed from her inexperience in dining in the company of a man. She had been taught, like any proper young lady, to pick at her food, though, truth to tell, picking at one's food was remarkably easy at Dunlevy, for Miss Percy appeared to have devoted scant of her exhaustive efforts in finding good teachers to the task of acquiring a competent cook.

As a result, when Elizabeth tasted the stew, she understood Lord Sinclair's gusto. The dish was divine, the venison melting in her mouth, and the bread, dipped into the rich gravy, absolute perfection.

Raising her eyes momentarily to an uncharacteristically silent Phoebe, she noted the young girl's own absorption in the meal, then balked as Phoebe lifted her wineglass to her lips. The girl was but a child! To allow her spirits . . . !

"Father, had I not intervened, poor Miss Burbridge would have spent the holiday alone at Dunlevy. Why, the mere thought! Though she says the peace and quiet aid her in accomplishing her work."

Those smoky eyes found Elizabeth. "This is not the first holiday you've spent alone?"

Elizabeth managed a weak smile. Seeking some diversion, she lifted her own wineglass to her lips. The liquid was surprisingly warm, smooth, with a robust flavor that tickled her throat and encouraged another bite or two of stew. "I . . . my mother . . . she travels rather frequently."

A dark brow rose. "More ailing relatives?"

"No." Elizabeth willed her gaze to remain steady with that of her host, which, for a moment, appeared almost challenging. "It is more a matter of her own boredom, which she has the means to alleviate, traveling as she pleases. Unfortunately, the itineraries of those she visits are less flexible, and she's often confined to holiday travel."

"And you choose to remain at the school?"

"Why, yes, Lord Sinclair. My devotion to my work does not ebb and flow with the comings and goings of holiday seasons."

"I was not questioning your devotion, Miss Burbridge."

Elizabeth detected a slight lift to one corner of his mouth. Mocking or amused, she could not discern. Lowering her eyes to her plate, she ventured quietly, "The meal is delicious."

"Oh my, yes!" Phoebe piped up, reaching for her third slice of bread. "It makes enduring that awful food at Dunlevy a bit easier."

"Still just as bad?" Lord Sinclair shook his head, then pushed his plate away and drained his wineglass in one huge gulp. "Phoebe once remarked on meat pies so tough they could be thrown with the greatest force against the ceiling without breaking."

"The fare is adequate!" Elizabeth blurted in defense, though her response stemmed almost entirely from the decided feeling that Dunlevy's shortcomings had been freely discussed at this table quite often. That in itself was troublesome indeed, but that Phoebe was allowed such freedom to voice what Elizabeth deemed disrespect for so honorable an institution... Why, the food wasn't *that* bad!

"Perhaps the teachers enjoy a more palatable fare than the pupils," Lord Sinclair ventured, leaning back comfortably in his chair and drawing Elizabeth's eye to a waist so trim she could not help but wonder where the man put his food.

"No, it is the same," Elizabeth replied, raising her eyes then quickly averting them. Words seemed to have tremendous difficulty forming on her tongue when her eyes met his. Blast that dream and the myriad feelings thumping through her veins, invading her psyche, rendering her so blastedly weak-kneed. The man was a *father,* married. Where *was* Lady Sinclair?

"At the risk of spreading something besides good cheer during your stay with us, Miss Burbridge..." His deep voice interrupted Elizabeth's thoughts. "I would like to discuss at some length, if I may, my daughter's progress at Dunlevy. You *are* at liberty to do so, are you not?"

Elizabeth nearly snorted and struggled to bite her tongue. No doubt he wished some tedious account of Phoebe's ability to conjugate Latin verbs and perform the required arithmetic skills. A token statement of achievement to satisfy what little interest he harbored in his daughter's education. From what she'd viewed this evening, if his attitude toward Phoebe's schooling mirrored that of his attention to fostering the proper manners in his daughter, what Elizabeth intended to tell him would undoubtedly whiten his skin beneath that confounded bronze glow and open those steely eyes to what disaster ultimately lay in store for his precocious daughter.

"Of course," Elizabeth replied. "Miss Percy encourages such discussions."

"Really, Father, need we bother Miss Burbridge with such matters?" Phoebe's eyes widened as a dish of warm custard was placed before her. "It's such a dreadfully dull subject."

"And one that needs discussion, Phoebe, you know that very well." Lord Sinclair's eyes fell upon Elizabeth once more. "Perhaps tomorrow, fairly early, we could find a moment, Miss Burbridge. After that, you are free to do as you wish. There are the stables with many mounts from which to choose."

"I don't ride." Elizabeth glanced from her host's inquiring look to Phoebe's openmouthed stupefaction and felt compelled to offer some reason. "I never learned."

"Oh, how awful!" Phoebe exclaimed.

"That can be easily remedied," Lord Sinclair said. "You simply have to learn."

Elizabeth's spoon wavered over her custard. "I...uh...you see, I'm not overly fond of horses."

"How awful!" Phoebe exclaimed once again, as if the mere suggestion were unthinkable.

Lord Sinclair raised a dark brow and that infernal lift to one corner of his mouth returned. "I see. Miss Percy, no doubt, has not seen fit to encourage that pursuit, eh? Well, there is the library. You do *read* for pleasure, do you not, Miss Burbridge?"

For some godawful reason, Elizabeth had the distinct impression the man was mocking her. She leveled an unwavering glare at him. "Yes, Lord Sinclair. Reading gives me an inordinate amount of pleasure."

"Good, then perhaps the library will occupy you sufficiently. Phoebe, of course, must have an enormous amount of mischief making to be accomplished and, no doubt, intends to include you. And I believe you may find the dinner guests rather interesting, Miss Burbridge." Begging off the custard Jennings sought to place before him, he turned to his daughter, who was gamely attempting to coerce yet another dish of the dessert from the servant. "What the hell, man, just give it to her." With a grin, he observed his daughter's obvious delight as the servant complied. "Phoebe, I'll be tending to matters in my study for the remainder of the evening. If you need me, you'll know where to find me. Miss Burbridge."

Rising from his chair, he tossed his napkin upon the table, executed an overblown bow before each of the women, which drew an amused giggle from Phoebe and a cursory nod from Elizabeth, then strode from the room, whistling softly to himself.

The bedroom door opened so quickly after the light rapping that Elizabeth had but a moment to whirl about with her mouth open and arms raised to cover her bodice. Her gown and her stiff muslin wrappings lay discarded upon the bed, yet just beyond her reach. She stood helplessly in the center of the room clad only in her chemise and pantaloons.

"Hello! It's me!" Phoebe announced as she slipped into the room and closed the door behind her. Her hair was unbound, her face freshly scrubbed, and, clad in her high-necked pink flannel nightgown, she looked a far cry from the tousled waif who had climbed through Elizabeth's window not so long ago. And certainly incapable of any impure thoughts. "I thought perhaps we could talk and...oh! Miss Burbridge!" Eyes wide, Phoebe simply stared unabashedly at Elizabeth's bodice. "Miss Burbridge! You have bosoms! And so large they are!"

"Phoebe!" Elizabeth gasped in humiliation, turning her back upon the younger girl and casting a mortified look at the high curves and deep cleavage exposed by her chemise.

"Oh, but, Miss Burbridge, I didn't mean to offend you!" Behind her, Elizabeth heard, with sinking heart, Phoebe flop comfortably upon the bed. "Indeed, what I meant to say is that

I would give *anything* to have large bosoms, and yet you are so thin. Oh, to be so doubly blessed!''

"It is no blessing," Elizabeth muttered, reaching within the mahogany wardrobe for her wrapper, which she hastily flung about her before turning toward the young girl once more, arms still crossed over her breasts and eyes darting nervously about the room. Without the muslin wrap binding her breasts and before this child's all-seeing eyes, Elizabeth suddenly felt unusually exposed.

"Oh, indeed it is!" Phoebe replied with eyes wide. "Why, have you any idea, Miss Burbridge, the men! They *love* large bosoms, especially if you also have such a tiny waist."

Elizabeth's jaw fell open, clamped shut, then opened once more. "Wherever did you hear such nonsense?"

"Why, Charlotte Lambert says that of all the maids in her father's house, the one with the largest bosoms gets the best treatment. And, she's neither the youngest nor the prettiest. Indeed, Charlotte's even seen her father—now mind you, her mother is long dead and buried, so please don't judge Charlotte's father harshly—but it seems Charlotte's even seen her father promise all but the queen's jewels to have a go at a pinch and a squeeze. He becomes rather foolish in his pursuit, but as Charlotte says, men just adore big bosoms." Phoebe shook her head in amazement as her eyes flickered over Elizabeth's modest high-necked robe. "Surely you were aware of this?"

"I'm afraid I was not." Elizabeth could not help but wonder what impact the sight of one's father chasing a maid about, begging to fondle a well-rounded breast, would have upon a young child like Charlotte. "I've had very little experience with men."

"Have you no brothers?"

"No, I'm an only child."

"And your father?"

"He died when I was very young, and Mother never remarried." For a moment, Elizabeth stared at Phoebe in sudden shock. "Surely your father did not contribute to this . . . this *theory* you and Charlotte have invented."

Phoebe giggled and waved a plump hand. "Oh, I wouldn't know of Father's preferences, though all of Father's female friends fill their bodices well. You see, Father has always had an eye for beautiful and curvy women. Perhaps I should ask him his preference in bosom size.''

"Oh, for heaven' sake, don't do that!" A searing heat climbed in Elizabeth's cheeks at the mere thought of Lord Alec Sinclair's opinion on the subject. For some reason, the idea brought a strange tightening in her belly.

As if lost in thought and entirely unaware of Elizabeth for a moment, Phoebe cocked her head and her winged brows drew together in a frown. "Now that I think about it, Lady Astrid has large bosoms, though not as large as yours, I wouldn't think.''

Elizabeth gaped at Phoebe. "Who is Lady Astrid?"

"You shall meet her tomorrow. She and her parents, Helmut and Marisa Farnsworth, dine with us every Christmas Eve." Phoebe waved a dismissing hand. "She's just tripping all over herself to become Father's light-o'-love."

Elizabeth could not conceal her shock. "And your mother allows this?"

Phoebe took her turn to stare openmouthed. "Oh, my goodness, no! Why, I simply assumed you knew, though how you would... Why, I never thought to tell you, and of course Father never mentions it. It's a matter even the servants have long since abandoned discussing." She paused, lowering her eyes to contemplate her hands, which plucked almost self-consciously at her nightgown.

For the first time, Elizabeth detected a melancholy air about the child, an endearing wistfulness. Almost without realizing it, she found herself sitting beside the young girl upon the bed, wishing to take the plump hands within her own. "I'm so sorry, Phoebe, if she's passed away."

"Oh, she's not dead. At least, I don't think she is." Phoebe's voice was small, her eyes downcast. "Last we heard she was in Paris, but that was some time ago. You see, I haven't seen her since she ran off...with that...that *man* some nine years ago. After Father obtained the divorce, they married, or so she said in her letters." With a shrug, Phoebe lifted a wistful gaze. "It was an awful scandal."

"Of course," Elizabeth replied, at a sudden loss for words. She understood completely Phoebe's unspoken grief over an absent mother, albeit the type who would desert a husband and five-year-old child. But thoughts of that nature hit too close to home for Elizabeth. How could she advise young Phoebe on rationalizing those feelings when she herself struggled in vain almost daily with the very same task?

Giving in to her instincts, Elizabeth reached for Phoebe's hand and was astonished when the young girl's fingers clasped tightly about hers. Liquid amber eyes seemed to cling to Elizabeth and she had to struggle yet again for the proper response. "Phoebe, perhaps we should see ourselves to bed."

Phoebe nodded, though her hold upon Elizabeth's hands did not lessen in the least.

"Have you no scheduled bedtime?" Elizabeth ventured softly.

Phoebe shook her head and sighed. "Father allows me to sleep when I wish and rise when I wish, simply because at school we're not allowed any freedom."

For a moment, Elizabeth bit her lip in thought. "I once heard, though I believe it was an old wives' tale, that a good night's sleep was essential for growing large bosoms. Of course, that sounds a bit silly."

Phoebe's eyes widened. "Indeed?"

Elizabeth shrugged. "I wouldn't know it to be fact, though I've always seen myself to bed early and risen early, as well. And..." Risking a mocking glance at her bodice, she gave Phoebe a sheepish smile. "One never knows."

"Indeed! Well then, I must be off to bed!" Phoebe sprang from the bed, obviously delighting in the notion that she could perhaps alter her preordained bosom size. "Sleep well, Miss Burbridge!" Squeezing Elizabeth's hands, she scurried to the door. "It's so lovely to have you here, you've no idea. We shall have such fun, I promise!"

After she bade Phoebe good-night, Elizabeth could not help but wonder if her haste to see the child off to bed had anything at all to do with her desire not to upset the young girl unnecessarily. Or if, perhaps, the true reason lay in her own shortcomings.

These very thoughts plagued her early the next morning and she sought solace in the library after some direction from the ever helpful Casper. The room was enormous for a library and smelled of the rich lemony oils used to polish the mahogany walls lined with shelf after shelf of books. For quite some time she stood in the center of the thick green carpet, enjoying the early morning silence filling the house and allowing herself the luxury of scanning the floor-to-ceiling bookcases.

Obviously, his lordship enjoyed reading, though she knew not what particular works inspired the man, for his tastes seemed to run the gamut. One entire column of shelves was devoted to the classics. And another, to textbooks and grammar books, atlases and gardening, wood carving and even furniture making. He had also accumulated an enormous number of the latest periodicals, even *The Ladies,* the women's magazine that had recently devoted an inordinate amount of space to women's education.

Elizabeth moved on, reaching in her pocket for her spectacles. From her vantage, she was nearly blind to the titles lying on the top shelves over the fireplace. From what she could discern, they looked to be books on poetry. Her heart skipped a beat. For months now she had searched high and low for Tennyson's works but to no avail. The man possessed every book imaginable. Why not Tennyson?

On impulse, she hastened to the ladder resting against a nearby shelf and slid it directly before the fireplace. Testing the bottom step, she found it secure, though the entire ladder seemed to sway shakily as she began her ascent, perhaps more out of her own fear of heights than any lack of stability. Her progress was slow but determined, and she had to climb nearly to the top to begin her search through the myriad volumes.

Obviously, his lordship did not indulge regularly in poetry, though the man was organized, a trait she deemed highly commendable, for he kept his works arranged alphabetically by author. As a result, once she'd passed Shakespeare, which was nearly out of reach to her right, she was more than certain that whatever Tennyson the man kept would be just beyond that. If only she could reach a bit farther... And then her eye fell upon a volume of Tennyson's works and her heart leapt once more.

She stretched her arm to its greatest length, rising on tiptoe, then took one last step and leaned precariously over the side of the ladder. At that moment a deep voice echoed throughout the room.

"I would wish you a good morning, Miss Burbridge, if you weren't standing on the one step I'm quite certain is broken."

"Wha . . . !"

Over her shoulder, Elizabeth caught but a glimpse of Alec Sinclair's wicked grin before a splintering crack filled her ears. With arms wheeling helplessly, she felt the sagging board give way beneath her foot, her spectacles slide from her nose, and she was cast into the air, tumbling with a silent cry poised upon her lips.

Chapter Four

Elizabeth would always wonder how a man of Alec Sinclair's size could move so swiftly. At the moment, however, finding herself within his embrace, pressed against a chest that felt far too masculine for so early in the day, she experienced a flare of indignation that had more than a little to do with the rather curious look he leveled upon her spectacles, dangling lopsided from her nose. Indeed, she deemed his version of a barely suppressed smirk entirely not in keeping with her near disaster, which in all likelihood would *not* have occurred had he not startled her so unnecessarily.

"Lord Sinclair! If you please!" She fairly bristled, wondering how her arms had managed to loop themselves about his neck so that her fingers clung in a most desperate manner to the fine linen of his shirt. She groped ineffectually for her glasses, averting her gaze to some spot in a far-off corner and chastising herself for the blush she could feel heating her cheeks. "If you could please put me down. Thank you."

Without ceremony, he lowered her to her feet, though one hand lingered firmly upon her arm as if he were unsure of the steadiness of her legs. "Are you quite certain you're all right?" he asked in that blastedly deep voice.

Shaking his hand from her arm, she turned away from him to smooth a wayward tendril into her chignon while attempting to control the agitation looming in her voice. "Indeed, my legs are far sturdier than that...that..." One hand waved disgustedly in the general direction of the ladder. "To keep such a contraption about! Why, I could have been killed!"

"My humblest apologies, Miss Burbridge," the deep voice intoned behind her, though Elizabeth was quite certain she detected a hint of mockery.

With a huff, she clenched her fists, determined to swing about and voice her disapproval of his quirky sense of humor, when she realized her glasses still sat upon her nose. Hastening to conceal them within her pocket, she stiffened as he spoke again.

"I shall have Casper attend to repairing the ladder immediately."

With a sigh, Elizabeth replied, "Thank you. Until such time, I shall confine my reading to that easily within reach."

Silence filled the room, broken only by the ticking of a clock upon the mantel. Elizabeth fiddled with her fingers until she realized they were nervously clutched at her waist, then nearly jumped from her skin when he spoke again.

"You're about rather early, Miss Burbridge. I trust you slept well."

"Yes, quite well, thank you. The bed was very..." With cheeks flaming, she groped for words, refusing to turn and look at him. Discussing the merits of a bed with this man seemed atrociously lacking in good taste. "It is habit, I suppose, rising with the sun."

"Indeed. I, too, enjoy the early morning. A wonderful time for a ride or a brisk walk through the snow." He paused once again and Elizabeth could not help but feel his eyes upon her back. "Some tea, perhaps, Miss Burbridge? Casper always keeps the brew on hand, though I care little for the stuff."

Willing her skittishness to rest, Elizabeth drew a deep breath and attempted to paste on a smile as she turned to face him. Her breath instantly caught in her throat and the skittishness returned full force as her eyes met his for the first time that morning.

He sat perched against the huge mahogany desk occupying the space before three enormous windows. His arms were crossed casually over his chest. His legs were crossed, as well, encased in dark riding breeches and tall black boots, which emphasized their lean, muscular length. His head was cocked slightly, and the sun caught the tousled russet locks and set them to flame against the bronze of his skin. Even in a half-sitting position, he loomed over her, a feat rarely accomplished by any man due to her own stature. For some reason, that thought alone brought a sudden weakening in her knees. Her utterly baffling and disconcerting awareness of him as a man, and of herself as a woman, made her want to flee to her room in shame. Instead, she stared, transfixed, aware of the rushing in her ears as he rose and strode quickly toward her to grasp her hand in his.

"Miss Burbridge! You're extremely pale. Over here, to the chair. Casper! Fetch some cool water, man, and be quick about it!"

"I'm . . . I'm quite all right," Elizabeth heard herself murmur. She allowed him to lead her to a very deep leather chair, where he lowered himself to one knee close beside her.

Casper appeared with a glass of cool water. Shakily, she drew it to her lips. What in God's name was the matter with her? She'd never been one to boast of a delicate constitution in any way. Surely this man and his piercing gray eyes were not to blame? If only he weren't sitting so close. "Really, I'm quite all right. I'm actually rather sturdy, you see."

He rose to his feet, much to Elizabeth's relief, for she could detect about him the scent of outdoors mixed enticingly with that of horseflesh, a scent she found surprisingly pleasant.

"One would expect nothing less of Miss Percy's finest." For a moment, the gray eyes studied her so closely that Elizabeth was certain he detected her confusion at his dry remark. Whatever did he mean? He offered her little time to ponder. "Perhaps our discussion would be best left to another time."

"Our discussion?" she asked.

"Of Phoebe's progress."

"Oh! Of course! No, by all means, the matter is one of utmost importance and concerns me, as well."

"Indeed?"

The infernally raised brow caused Elizabeth pause for a moment, and she found herself wishing that the chair in which she sat were not so impossibly deep and low to the floor. With him standing before her like some broad-shouldered, slim-hipped fortress of bronzed brawn, she felt pinioned to her seat, small, insignificant and incapable of standing erect, much less possessing the ability to speak her concerns.

Elizabeth shook herself and attempted to rise from the chair. True to form, that ever present hand grasped her elbow, causing her to yank her arm from his touch in a most obvious manner.

"You're rather jumpy, Miss Burbridge," he drawled, his gaze narrowing upon her.

Elizabeth cast him a wary glance as he settled himself once more against the desk and folded his arms over his chest, drawing her eye to the white sleeves stretched taut over his arms. "I would venture to say you've very little contact with men, since you teach at a women's academy."

"Why, yes, but I—"

"Apparently Headmistress Percy does not feel this would contribute significantly to a suitably well-rounded character."

Elizabeth's ire sputtered to life. Why did she feel the man relished challenging her? "That is of little consequence. I have a responsibility to teach—"

"Responsibilities need not become life sentences."

Her chin lifted a notch. "My life's ambition was to be a teacher, Lord Sinclair. To be sure, that which brings me the utmost satisfaction could never be called by even the most cynical a life sentence."

"Highly commendable. But at the expense of a husband and a family?"

"Those were never considerations, though I suppose this vocation does not lend itself to such pursuits. Indeed, I've barely time to attend to my duties."

"Ah, the old work-for-work's-sake ideology."

"The luxury of acquiring knowledge is its own reward, Lord Sinclair. I give little thought to the opportunities I may have forgone in attaining that goal."

"And you expect the same of your pupils?"

Elizabeth shook her head and a stray ebony tendril curled mutinously against her flushed cheek. "Miss Percy expects a certain dedication to pursuing the very best in education from every young woman who passes through Dunlevy's gates. She does *not* expect every young woman to aspire to the vocation of teacher, however."

"And as a role model for these young women she puts forth herself and you, of course, destined as you are to follow precisely in her footsteps."

Elizabeth's chin lifted yet another notch. "It would be blasphemous to assume I could ever adequately fill the woman's shoes."

His eyes fastened upon hers. "Does Miss Percy also insist upon worship from those under her employ, or is your reverence simply a result of sacrificing all other relationships in your life?"

Elizabeth pursed her lips with mounting frustration. "You pass an overly harsh judgment upon Miss Percy and I fail to see the reason behind it. Perhaps you require enlightenment on her accomplishments and what she has set out to achieve."

He waved a hand before him. "By all means, Miss Burbridge. The floor is yours. Perhaps I shall gain some understanding of your fascination with the woman."

Resisting the urge to slap the bemused expression from his face, Elizabeth drew a deep steadying breath and eased her clenched fists against her coarse muslin skirt. "Contrary to what you undoubtedly believe, Dunlevy is an academy devoted to ceasing the proliferation of young women, supposedly educated, who harbor naught but the practical skills to manage a household. These so-called accomplishments leave them with little function but to find a husband and become yet another amusement in his busy life. Indeed, they can execute the proper dance steps, be they Scotch, French, or Italian, and can entertain for hours at the piano and harp and even compose and sing a melody or two. They can sufficiently mend socks and produce multitudes of needlework, and even speak, on those rare occasions when it is deemed appropriate, though they've received but a smattering of education. Indeed, they've been taught never to wish for more, for a 'serious' education would surely be fatal to finding a husband. Men, of course, feel that women should not be presented with intellectually taxing pursuits for fear that acquiring any knowledge whatsoever will drive them entirely mad. Indeed! The idea that simple linear equations brighten women's intellects while quadratic equations drive them into lunatic asylums is atrocious!''

Ignoring the widening of Lord Sinclair's smirk, Elizabeth drew another deep breath and plunged on. ''Miss Percy and I believe women should not be content to be inferior to men. Women should have a choice, Lord Sinclair, besides that 'life sentence' of marriage and the vapidity of tending to a household so full of servants that the wife's very existence seems superfluous. Women are, therefore, forced by lack of activity into a totally wasted life. Ah, but therein lies the very reason for acquiring so many empty accomplishments. After all, she must fill up all those solitary hours of the day. It is indeed a sad state of affairs, and one that *I* intend to alter by my contributions.''

Lord Sinclair's gaze narrowed upon her for a moment. ''Would I be remiss in assuming that your efficient and very sound denouncing of men and the institution of marriage in general has been sufficiently pounded into the heads of each and every one of Dunlevy's eager pupils?''

''Why, no. We simply emphasize our desire, through a challenging curriculum, to provide the *choice* to succeed at something besides being a wife.''

''Ah, that lowly debauched state.''

''I would never presume to call it that.''

''A few moments ago I would swear you did just that.''

Elizabeth clenched her fists with mounting indignation. ''Lord Sinclair, with the proper education, women make fine teachers, headmistresses, nurses—why, the choices are endless! And they may still choose marriage in conjunction with one of these vocations.''

He rose from the desk, a thoughtful expression creasing his dark brow, and began to pace slowly about the room, causing Elizabeth to turn to and fro to follow his progress lest he speak. Which he did. ''You deem your curriculum challenging, Miss Burbridge?''

Elizabeth drew herself up proudly. ''Indeed. It is one of if not *the* finest in all of England.''

''I see.'' The booted feet stilled directly before her. ''Amidst all of Dunlevy's opportunity to enrich oneself through—'' he waved a very large hand "—all that you spoke of, could you tell me why my daughter is bored, Miss Burbridge?"

Elizabeth stared at the man. "Bored?"

"To distraction."

"Why...I...her tendency toward mischief making has always been viewed as a lack of proper guidance."

"Ah, her lax upbringing. Of course."

"Do not mock me, Lord Sinclair."

He gave her what could only be viewed as a mocking half bow. "Forgive me, Miss Burbridge. It is only my frustration, you see, for I sincerely believe Phoebe's wayward tendencies are a direct reflection of the education she is receiving. Were she properly challenged, she would have little time or energy for mischief." His piercing gray eyes locked with hers. "Miss Burbridge, I deem it *your* failure and insist that you do something about it. If not, I will be forced to withdraw Phoebe from Dunlevy in favor of another academy."

"What!"

At the precise moment that Elizabeth decided it would not be improper to fly into a rage and ease her frustrations with a few well-placed kicks and a pounding of fists against that confoundedly broad chest, Phoebe skidded breathlessly into the room.

"Good morning!" she greeted cheerily. "Such a lovely day!"

Lord Sinclair glanced at the clock upon the mantel and raised a curious brow at his daughter. "You're about unusually early, Phoebe. I was certain the sun would see its zenith before you arose."

Lightly kissing her father upon the cheek, Phoebe gave him a huge grin and chirped, "Oh, but, Father, Miss Burbridge told me that if I get myself to bed early and rise early, I will grow large bosoms like hers!"

Elizabeth stood unmoving, wide-eyed and as thoroughly humiliated as she'd ever been in her entire life, when a pair of smoky gray eyes swept appreciatively over her bodice. "Oh, she did, did she?"

"Why yes, Father, you should see..."

With one hand pressed painfully against her flaming cheek and the other clutching at her skirts, Elizabeth fled the room in search of a fluffy pillow in which to bury her face and cry like a baby.

Elizabeth found herself the object of Phoebe's determined pursuit to enjoy the day to its fullest, despite its dreadful beginning, and by late afternoon was begging off learning to ride a blasted horse in favor of a brisk walk. Much to her relief, his lordship had made himself scarce for the better part of the day.

That the man unnerved her was troublesome enough. That he intrigued her and aroused a multitude of unknown feelings of awareness within her brought yet another flush to her cheeks that had little to do with the frosty air. Gathering her cloak about her, she lifted her eyes to the windows above, knowing full well that she could not escape Alec Sinclair even in her sleep. With a frown, she swept her gaze about the softly sloping horizon, bathed in the downy softness of newly fallen snow.

The walk did indeed rejuvenate her sagging spirits and seemed to bring about an inner peace, albeit momentary, a peace that had been sorely lacking from the moment she had set foot upon Lord Sinclair's massive estate. And massive it was, extending as far as the eye could see to the west. To the east, several small dwellings dotted the horizon, the thin trails of smoke extending from their chimneys attesting to some inhabitants. Elizabeth found herself musing that perhaps Lord Sinclair was one of those heartless land barons of whom she'd heard so much.

As she strode briskly along, listening to her hearty breathing and the rhythmic crunch of her boots upon the snow, she found herself ruminating upon the divorce. Contemplating the myriad reasons *why* such a thing happened was none of her business, though she could not imagine a woman tolerating for long such perverse leniency in a man, such indulgence in lax attitudes. Perhaps that was the very reason he had not taken another wife, though God only knew poor dear Phoebe was in dire need of maternal guidance. True, theirs appeared to be a pleasant companionship, an easy camaraderie that paid little heed to the rules of conduct imposed upon most children, but Elizabeth felt compelled to remind Lord Sinclair that he was perpetuating a supreme injustice by raising his daughter in so casual an environment. Yet, at the same time, Elizabeth could not deny that Phoebe seemed happy and content, without a care except for those feelings for her mother she kept hidden beneath her ready smile.

For a moment, Elizabeth allowed herself to consider the preposterous notion that Phoebe's mischief might be due to some fault of hers. Why, at best, the theory was ridiculous. Lord Sinclair no doubt possessed an abominable ego incapable of grasping the idea that perhaps he and his flimsy methods of raising a child were to blame.

A tickling of snow upon her nose accompanied by a sudden bitter gust of wind brought her head up with a snap. Her heart lurched when she realized she'd been frightfully unaware that the clear skies had been obliterated by what appeared to be a low-hanging cloud driven by bitterly cold winds and icy snow. In panic, she whirled about and attempted to retrace her steps, but the snow beating against her cheeks like icy pellets erased the imprints before her eyes. A frigid gust whipped her cloak about her legs and she stumbled as her feet embedded within a deep drift. Uttering a cry into wind that snatched her breath away, she struggled to her feet and bent her head, attempting to move in what she desperately hoped was the direction of the house. Another fierce gust tore the pins from her hair and painfully whipped the ebony curls against her cheeks and across her eyes. She stumbled to her knees with an anguished cry. For the first time in her life, she felt utterly helpless, nearly overcome by the possibility that she could die....

And then a sound rose above the agonizing howling of the wind. As if borne from the depths of her dream, a huge black phantom in the shape of a horse emerged through the murk, eyes blazing fire and smoke rising from his coat and streaming from his flaring nostrils. With a shriek of pure terror, Elizabeth lurched to her feet and stumbled from the advancing animal, plunging into the void of gray, hoping desperately to be swallowed by the wind before being ensnared by that beast. And then powerful arms, human arms, swept about her waist from behind and lifted her with an ease Elizabeth had little time to ponder. Indeed, as she was rather unceremoniously hauled toward the black beast, she kicked and twisted frantically to escape her captor.

Above the wind, a mighty voice roared, "For God's sake, Elizabeth!"

Elizabeth! When had she given Lord Sinclair the liberty of addressing her as Elizabeth?

"I *refuse* to get on that animal!" she cried into the wind, struggling to sweep her hair from her face and his hands from her waist all at once.

His step did not falter. "Damned stubborn woman." His mutter was loud enough for Elizabeth to hear, and she gasped with indignation even as he paused beside the animal to place her none too gently upon her feet. "Now get on!" he barked, grasping the reins.

Elizabeth cringed from the horse at her side and clutched pleadingly at the man before her. "I—I can't. I—please . . ."

With a groan of mounting frustration, Lord Sinclair bellowed, "Get on the damned horse, Elizabeth!"

"No!" With an agonized cry, she flung herself from the animal, plunging into the wind with nothing but irrational terror spurring her onward. From behind, she heard the steady drum of hoofbeats and the animal's grunting as he surged through the snow after her. Her panic intensified. Eyes wide with fear, she screamed her agony into the unrelenting wind before she was lifted clear of her feet and set crosswise in front of Lord Sinclair upon the steed.

Her arms wrapped fiercely about Lord Sinclair's waist and she buried her face in the coarse wool covering his chest, sobbing uncontrollably. The animal moved briskly, undulating smoothly beneath her, then stumbling and uttering a recalcitrant grunt and a whinny before plunging on. Burrowing her face against Lord Sinclair's coat, Elizabeth heard his soft murmurings to the horse and wondered if the animal could possibly hear him above the wind. She grew dimly aware of a throbbing pain in her ankle that seemed to stretch its painful claws through her leg with every jostle and bounce, bringing a wince and a broken sob to her lips.

After a time, she found herself relaxing ever so slightly, perhaps due to the deep voice still reverberating through the chest pressed close to her cheek. Or perhaps the steely arm wrapped tightly about her offered a certain comfort far more than it piqued her ire with its bold familiarity.

When the storm intensified, Lord Sinclair muttered a curse and swung the stallion sharply to the right and directly into the wind. "We'll have to wait it out!" he shouted above the mournful howl.

A short time later their pace slowed to a walk, then the mighty steed stopped altogether. With some surprise, Elizabeth realized she no longer felt the painful bite of the snow and wind upon her neck, and lifted her head to peer curiously about. They had stopped beneath a ramshackle wooden structure consisting of three sides and a sagging roof, boasting no door and only a scattering of hay for a floor. At the moment, to Elizabeth's eye, the place was a godsend.

"May I get off now?" she croaked, keeping her eyes fixed upon the black wool coat before her.

"If you wish," came the muttered reply. "There's little telling how long it will take to subside. Squalls such as these are fairly common in the winter but rarely last even this long." He shifted his weight and attempted to dismount, but a pair of clinging arms flung desperately about his waist and Elizabeth's startled cry stilled his movements.

"Oh! Dear God! Don't leave me here!"

He erupted with a coarse laugh. "Elizabeth, this fear that possesses you is highly out of character, though certainly endearing, for it lends you a decided warmth you otherwise appear to lack." He paused a moment, obviously anticipating some response, which she had no intention of providing, so tightly did her fear hold her within its grasp. "Elizabeth, if I can't dismount first, I shan't be able to assist *you*. Now, hold on to my arm...that's it." With an agility younger men would envy, he slipped to the ground and, without pause, placed both hands about Elizabeth's waist to ease her from the stallion's back.

The moment her left foot touched ground, she uttered a cry of pain and her arms swept about his neck. "My ankle...I believe I may have wrenched it."

He bent to one knee, forcing her to cling to his shoulders as he lowered his head to examine her ankle. Her eyes skidded over the broad planes of his back before coming to rest upon the snow-sprinkled russet hair curling against his collar. Her idle fascination shattered as she felt his hands sliding slowly over her ankle, then venturing several inches up her leg and lowering again. His touch was firm yet infinitely tender, and the vision of those long fingers tracing softly over her cheek loomed so clearly in her mind that her breath caught in her throat.

He seemed oblivious to her response as he straightened, though his hands remained firmly about her waist. "You only twisted it." His tone bore a hint of reproach and he cocked his head to study her through hooded eyes. "Perhaps if you hadn't been so damned foolish. What the hell did you think Sebastian was going to do to you?"

Averting her gaze, Elizabeth loosened her hold upon his shoulders and attempted to hobble away from him until his insistent hands upon her waist stilled her feet.

"Now don't do something equally foolish with that ankle," he muttered, bending slightly so that he was eye level with her. "Surely you know that *I* won't bite you."

Through a tumble of dark hair, Elizabeth shot him a glance that strayed instantly to the animal at his side. "Your horse, he . . . rather, I'm terribly afraid."

With a grin, Lord Sinclair turned to pat the stallion heartily upon his sleek neck, receiving a nicker in response. "Did you hear that, Sebastian? You arouse such fear in the lady that she would rather succumb to nature's fury than associate with the likes of you." His gaze settled once more upon Elizabeth. "Perhaps if she knew the gentleman within the beast, she would find him likable enough to sweep aside any preconceived notions she may harbor."

His disarming smile coupled with an innuendo Elizabeth found difficult to ignore, and one she immediately wished to cast aside as her imagination, brought a warm tingling sensation to the pit of her belly and tied her tongue in a knot. No doubt he was completely unaware that his hands resting upon her waist felt like firebrands against her skin, some four layers of thick muslin beneath. And of course only she realized her bosom brushed softly against his chest with every movement, sending waves of something akin to excitement shooting through her limbs. All the man cared about was his dumb animal, who, at the moment, gave her an appraising glance and snorted.

Grudgingly, Elizabeth realized the beast proved a welcome diversion from Lord Sinclair, and she kept her gaze fixed upon Sebastian. The animal suited his master. Indeed, they even looked alike with their immense statures, black coats and wind-tossed manes, not to mention that barely distinguishable regal bearing that could easily be mistaken for outright arrogance.

"He's beautiful..." Elizabeth murmured, then cringed with fear as Sebastian shoved his black nose directly at her.

Lord Sinclair grasped the steed's nose and patted it affectionately. "I believe he thinks the same of you, Elizabeth."

She stared uncomprehendingly at him for a moment then found her hand soundly encased in his. Struggling for breath and some semblance of a response, she managed only to open and close her mouth several times in succession.

He appeared unaware of her straits, intent upon some purpose. Drawing her closer to his side with one powerful arm, he turned and grasped Sebastian's reins with his free hand. "Now hold your hand still, Elizabeth. For God's sake, you're trembling. Trust me, he won't bite you."

Placing his hand firmly upon hers, he guided it beneath Sebastian's muzzle. His bronzed fingers clasping her slender white hand fascinated her, until a soft tickling accompanied by warm moist breathing upon her palm snatched her attention. With a gasp she stiffened, though the hold upon her hand kept it steady beneath the muzzle.

"I do believe he likes you, Elizabeth." His voice was so close beside her ear that Elizabeth didn't dare meet his gaze. "He can sense your fear. There. Keep your hand steady. He will come to know you by your scent. That's it... place your hand gently upon his nose. Slowly... don't *you* balk, Elizabeth."

For several long moments, Elizabeth found herself caught up in the spell woven by the sudden hush of falling snow and the enigmatic man at her side. Even his beast of a mount contributed to the magic, dipping his head such that Elizabeth's fingers played between his ears. As her eyes studied yet again the hand covering hers, she grew very much aware that her breathing was ragged. She was struck by the sudden thought that, given any other situation, she would have blushed crimson to the very tips of her wool stockings were she to be found in such a familiar position with any man. At the moment, however, his voice close beside her ear, his hands upon her and the intimacy of their contact seemed almost natural. Too natural. And she was powerless to break the spell.

Sebastian, however, was not. With a grunt, he shoved his nose at her then attempted to nuzzle her boldly down the entire length of her bodice, which drew forth an uncharacteristic giggle.

"A man after my own heart." Lord Sinclair firmly shoved the horse aside, then glanced at Elizabeth. "Why, Miss Burbridge." His mocking tone banished the smile from her face in an instant, replacing it with a rosy blush. "With your hair all atumble and a smile upon your face, one would be hard-pressed not to find oneself as enamored of you as Sebastian."

Elizabeth glanced quickly away, though she was certain his eyes had fallen for a fleeting moment to her mouth. Dear God! "Perhaps we should get back."

He grunted in reply, and before Elizabeth could draw a steadying breath, he swooped her into his arms and placed her upon Sebastian's back. Swinging himself up behind her, he slipped one arm about her waist and guided the stallion from the haven.

They found themselves in a dusky cocoon of softly falling snow with nary but the slightest of breezes teasing Elizabeth's tousled locks and stirring the low-hanging, ice-laden branches. The stillness hung about them, broken only by Sebastian's muffled footfalls and Lord Sinclair's occasional murmurings to the steed. The pace was slow due to the sporadic terrain and the deep drifts that threatened to swallow them with the slightest misstep. Elizabeth was supremely conscious of Lord Sinclair's arm wrapped about her waist, as well as his chin brushing against her hair. Neither uttered a word until they stopped before the manor and a female shriek, accompanied by the bang of the front portal and scurrying feet, brought Elizabeth crashing to earth and rendered her motionless aboard the stallion.

"Oh, Father! Miss Burbridge! Thanks heavens!" Phoebe careered from the house in a flurry of red velvet and lace. "We've been so worried!"

Elizabeth watched in mute fascination and mounting embarrassment as Phoebe skidded to a halt directly below them. Her wide amber eyes flickered from her father to Elizabeth and back again, then widened even further, if that were possible, when they fixed upon the arm wrapped about Elizabeth. The child's jaw dropped open momentarily but she said nothing, perhaps due to the bustling of those at her heels.

When Elizabeth's eyes darted to the sea of unfamiliar faces before her, her discomfort knew no bounds. Standing before them, as if dumbfounded, mouths agape and eyes wide, were a balding, rotund older gentleman, his lovely wife and a beautiful auburn-haired young woman, who remained motionless despite the scampering of three young children about her skirts.

Much to his credit, Lord Sinclair was the first to find his voice, though his words, uttered in that infernal drawl, which seemed entirely out of place at the moment, did little to ease Elizabeth's disconcertion.

"Helmut. Marisa. Lady Astrid." He bowed his head and bestowed upon them a dazzling smile. "Merry Christmas."

Chapter Five

"Auntie Astrid!" The youngest of the trio of tots, a bright-eyed little girl sporting a tumble of orange ringlets, tugged at Astrid's skirts. Shoving a plump finger at Elizabeth, the child declared in her most precocious voice, "Saint Nicholas brought Uncle Alec a wife, Auntie Astrid! See! See her!"

Astrid stroked the child's head and attempted a lame smile, though her dark eyes flickered over Elizabeth and settled with some confusion upon "Uncle" Alec.

"Wife?" Marisa Farnsworth shrieked, casting a heated glare upon Alec and fanning herself furiously.

Alec merely shook his head in reply as he dismounted and swept Elizabeth from the saddle and into his arms before she could catch her breath and voice any protest. Despite her distress, Elizabeth was certain she detected a huge sigh of relief pass through the group, though her attention remained upon the hint of amusement flickering in *his* gray eyes as they swept over the guests. "Miss Burbridge is visiting for the holidays. She teaches at Dunlevy, Phoebe's school." Shifting Elizabeth in his arms, he remarked, "We were caught up in the snow-storm and Elizabeth—"

"Elizabeth!" Marisa shrieked once again.

"And Elizabeth twisted her ankle," Alec continued without so much as a pause. "Nothing that a good hot soak won't ease."

"Oh, thank heavens!" Phoebe exclaimed. "Why, the way you were...I mean, Miss Burbridge, your hair and...I thought... Oh, I don't know what I thought."

"I think I do!" Helmut Farnsworth chuckled deep in his belly, giving Alec a conspiratorial nudge and a wicked wink, neither of which was lost upon Elizabeth. "Nothing like a little merrymaking before the holidays, eh, Alec?"

Elizabeth's jaw sagged but the words remained lodged painfully in her throat when Alec swung a knitted brow upon Helmut Farnsworth. "I'm sorry, Helmut, what was that you said? Ah, I hear Mrs. Pettibone and Casper, squabbling once again. What *does* one have to do to acquire good help these days? I'd best break it up before Mrs. Pettibone destroys the remainder of the china."

He strode swiftly into the manse and past a stone-faced Casper, who without hesitation swept the cloak from his lordship's back. To Elizabeth's eye, the servant did not appear at all engaged in any brouhaha with Mrs. Pettibone, nor was he in the least bit shocked at his lordship's "baggage" or the manner in which his lordship proceeded, without pause, to mount the stairs. Despite what had undoubtedly become routine in the household with many a female guest, Elizabeth could not abide these actions a moment longer.

"I demand that you put me down!" she snapped when he'd reached the first landing, then continued on as if she hadn't spoken. "'Tis no doubt simply another heathenish habit you have acquired, this . . . this . . ."

"Some would call it being a gentleman." That twinkle of mischief returned to his eyes.

"Hardly that!" Her eyes widened as his long strides gobbled up the hall leading directly to her room, her tone growing more beseeching with every stride. "This is fine. Right here. Put me down."

"And have you hobble along and injure yourself further?"

"I won't hobble, I promise!"

"And here I thought you'd be thanking me." Alec shook his head and raised those sweeping dark brows as if he were shocked, though his pace remained steady and his eyes fixed directly before him. "Perhaps I should inform Miss Percy of your astounding lack of good manners."

"*My* lack of manners?" Elizabeth screeched.

"After all, had it not been for me, you would still be hopelessly lost in that snowstorm."

"I would have made my way, thank you. And my ankle would have been no worse for wear."

Alec threw back his head with a huge guffaw that nearly proved the end of Elizabeth. "Aha! A crack in the armor! Could it be that I've discovered that thoroughly infuriating, entirely feminine art of convoluted logic that you women choose to employ when it best suits your purpose? I must admit, Elizabeth, and God only knows why, but this trait actually makes you more likable."

"What the devil are you talking about?" Elizabeth glared at him, then nearly died of humiliation when one powerful leg kicked her door open. Before she could even bury her head against his chest in shame, Alec strode unabashedly into her boudoir. Though she wasn't the type to leave all sorts of unmentionables strewn about the room, this offered her little comfort at the moment.

"Put me down!" she demanded hotly as he paced about the room as if unsure of what to do with her. When he paused beside the bed, Elizabeth's eyes flew wide and swept to his.

She was suddenly very much aware that his eyes were nearly a transparent crystal gray, tinged with mirth, she guessed, and something more, something that sent a tremor through her. In spite of herself, she felt her ire sputter and die and her thoughts scattered like leaves to the four winds. She could no more voice a coherent thought than she could stop his eyes from moving slowly over her face to linger on her half-open mouth until she had enough sense to snap it shut. When he spoke, the warmth of his breath fanned her cheeks.

"Some women are incredibly beautiful when they blush, Miss Burbridge," he murmured with a smile that sliced through mountains of reserve.

"If... if you would please... put me down..." she managed in a shaky voice, averting her eyes to the floor.

"As you wish." Lowering her to the bed, he paused a moment, drawing her gaze to the muscled legs planted directly before her. For several long moments, the sinewed length of thigh disappearing into knee-high boots captured her attention until she realized with a start what she was doing. What was *he* doing?

"I'll send up Mrs. Pettibone with a tub of warm water for that ankle. Perhaps a wrap, as well, to help you walk." He paused. "Try to overlook Helmut's asides, however embarrassing they may prove. He's a very old family friend, rather an odd character, but one I believe even you could enjoy. Until dinner, Miss Burbridge."

Even as she cursed her traitorous eyes for following those legs as they stalked so magnificently from the room, Elizabeth decided she much preferred the way he said "Elizabeth" to "Miss Burbridge."

"My dear Miss Burbridge," Helmut Farnsworth murmured close to Elizabeth's ear, so close she could almost taste the wine on his breath. As a result, she found herself leaning away from him in what she deemed a rather obvious manner to all those seated at the dining table, especially, she hoped, to Marisa, who was seated directly opposite her. The older woman dripped with jewels, stretching the limits of good taste, as she did with her conspicuous zeal to see her lovely daughter, Astrid, become the next Lady Alec Sinclair. So intent was Marisa on her quest, she failed to notice her husband's own enthusiasm for Elizabeth. At the moment, Elizabeth cared for nothing more than to flee from Helmut Farnsworth's overly solicitous nature and the brooding man seated at the head of the table.

"Alec, our Astrid looks exceptionally lovely this evening, don't you agree?" Marisa piped up between bites of plum pudding and cream.

"Lovely and charming, as usual." Something in Alec's tone and the look in his eye as it swept over Astrid made Elizabeth fervently wish that she had at least one gown that wasn't brown muslin. Perhaps a beautiful satin frock in just the shade of violet Astrid had chosen.

Her eye lingered for several moments upon that young woman seated to Alec's right, who was now blushing from the tips of her upswept chestnut hair to the toes of her violet satin shoes. Indeed, with her huge brown eyes and milky complexion, coupled with the look of complete adoration she had fixed upon Alec since dinner had commenced, Astrid looked as if she needed little in the way of prodding from anyone, much less her mother. The girl seemed on the verge of leaping out of her chair and into the strongest pair of arms this side of London.

Stupid girl! Elizabeth grumbled to herself. She nearly jumped from her skin when Helmut shoved an elbow into her side.

"Miss Burbridge, perhaps you are aware of Alec's penchant for a good wine. One might even call the man a connoisseur of sorts. Hence the need for both white and red at his table. You did notice, of course?"

"Miss Burbridge does not habitually partake," Alec offered, settling in his chair and observing her through hooded eyes.

"Why, Miss Burbridge, one would think that a woman of your age . . ." Marisa paused as if catching herself in the midst of some outlandish slip of the tongue and mouthed a silent "oh!" "Well, you are a trifle seasoned, hardly a young girl."

Elizabeth stared in mute horror at the woman for a moment until Helmut, well into his cups by this time, hastened to her rescue.

"Marisa, for bloody hell's sake! Who gives a fig how old the girl is? She's far younger than you were when I took you for my wife!" Ignoring his wife's rather undelicate, blustering gasp, he leaned toward Elizabeth and spoke in a voice for all to hear. "Gets her every time! Can't abide the fact that she was once an old maid herself."

Old maid!

"Helmut? Cease your blubbering this instant!" Marisa huffed. "I was simply pointing out that Miss Burbridge need not concern herself with maintaining decorum for our sake, lest we think she too innocent to partake, like our lamb Astrid, here. Why, our precious daughter is on the verge of blooming into womanhood, Alec, right before our very eyes. So tender at barely eighteen. And just the perfect age to become a blushing bride. Why, Alec, I seem to recall you were wed at barely seventeen, if I'm not mistaken."

"Marisa! For bloody hell's sake!" Helmut pounded a meaty fist on the table. "We all know the man's history. Drink your wine, woman. It will take the lash out of your tongue."

Elizabeth's eyes swept to Alec, to a gaze so hooded she could not discern who it held within its unwavering grasp. She had a notion Marisa was a likely choice. When he spoke, Elizabeth detected a barely suppressed emotion held in check.

"Indeed, Astrid would make a beautiful bride at any age." The smoky gaze shifted and Elizabeth suddenly felt ensnared by those steely orbs. "As would Miss Burbridge."

Silence filled the room, though Elizabeth was certain she detected a distinct *plop!* as Marisa's jaw fell open.

"Ah, touché, Alec. Well done!" Helmut lifted his glass to his host, then, thinking the better of it, hoisted both his glasses and leaned close to Elizabeth. "Care to see a wine connoisseur drop his silk socks, Miss Burbridge?" And with that, before Elizabeth could reply and much to his wife's chagrin, Helmut poured a generous portion of his red wine into his white wine, swirled this new concoction, toasted Alec yet again and drained the glass in one gulp.

Elizabeth burst out laughing before she even realized. Her laughter echoed and died within the massive dining room, vanishing in a matter of seconds, though to her ears it seemed like hours. Color suffused her cheeks, her eyes fell to her dessert and she thought she would die of shame, when the thunder of many tiny feet upon the polished mahogany filled the room.

Phoebe bounded into the room, followed closely by the three youngsters and their parents, Willie Farnsworth and his wife, Constance, who had accompanied the children on their inspection of the Christmas tree just before dessert had been served. The children gathered close about Phoebe's skirts as Willie and Constance reseated themselves at the dining table.

"May we open the presents now, Father, please? And roast the chestnuts?" Phoebe bobbed on her toes beside her father's chair, though Elizabeth noticed that one hand absently stroked the hair from one of the cherub's faces and the other almost instinctively grasped another's plump hand. *Such a way she has with the children . . .* "The children are so anxious!"

Alec gave the group a smile that crinkled his eyes and set Elizabeth's heart aflutter within her breast, as did the casual manner in which he ruffled the hair of one of the boys. "The children, eh? I'd wager none of you is as anxious as I to see what lies beneath that tree. Let's not waste another moment at this table!''

Amidst a tumble of squeals of the purest delight, the children scurried from the room, tugging at Phoebe's skirts. Moments later, the adults found them on hands and knees beneath the tree. And such a tree Elizabeth had never seen before. Reaching nearly to the ceiling, it stood in the center of the large living room, directly before a crackling fire that filled the room with the fragrant warmth of freshly cut pine. Candles burned softly on nearly every branch, illuminating the room in a dusky glow that filled Elizabeth with poignant melancholy and a sudden overwhelming gratitude to Phoebe for sharing this holiday with her. Elizabeth would have expressed her thanks had a deep voice, directly behind her, not scattered her thoughts for the hundredth time.

"Miss Burbridge, would you care for some sherry?'' For some reason his voice, so soft and low, reminded Elizabeth of smooth warm honey, soothing yet strangely disquieting all at once, and so god-awfully close above her.

She turned and nearly jumped from her skin when her bosom brushed against the entire breadth of his chest. If Alec were even remotely aware of the contact, which left Elizabeth wishing with all her might to vanish into thin air, his infernally arched brow did not let on. Elizabeth's scarlet cheeks, however, spoke volumes.

His eyes narrowed with his smile as he pressed a glass into her hand. "Some sherry... to warm your blood.''

He brushed past her to attend to his guests, leaving her to ponder his effect on her senses as she searched for a chair in which she would be the least conspicuous. The sherry was surprisingly nutty in flavor and did indeed warm her blood, so much so that when Helmut ventured by sometime later to refill her glass, she accepted with a smile. She found she rather liked the eccentric little man.

The children made quick work of their presents and were soon immersed in their play before the fire. Elizabeth enjoyed her sherry, nibbled on roasted chestnuts and settled quite comfortably within her chair before the fire, snug, warm, a soft smile curving her lips as she listened to the cozy holiday sounds.

The crackle of a last dying ember accompanied by the muffled scrape of boots upon the mahogany brought Elizabeth awake with a start. Her eyes flew open to meet Alec's as he bent close before her.

"Elizabeth," he murmured softly with a lazy half smile she assumed was in response to her look of wide-eyed horror. Or perhaps he had consumed as generous an amount of sherry as she.

"Oh my, I—I—"

"You fell asleep."

"The others?"

"Upstairs asleep, all of them. Some time ago."

"And you left me here?"

"Marisa was nearly apoplectic but I assured her you needed your rest, and, of course, she's well aware that I'm every kind of gentleman."

"She must not know you very well."

Alec chuckled and turned to retrieve something from beneath the tree. Elizabeth seized the opportunity to ease herself to her feet, albeit shakily, due to her unsteady ankle and that blasted sherry.

"I see the sherry has not dulled your wit." He moved between her and the doorway, curtailing, for the moment, any attempts to flee.

She presented her best smirk. "I thought the brew's sole purpose was to warm the blood."

"I think there's little chance of that." His eyes bored intently into hers for several long moments and Elizabeth sensed a faint trembling beginning in her limbs. "I find other... pleasures warm my blood far more than simple food and drink, Miss Burbridge."

Elizabeth stared at him in confusion and her mouth opened and closed ineffectually several times before the words formed on her tongue. "I...you..." Her gaze skidded about the room in a valiant attempt to break the viselike grip his eyes had upon her. Suddenly she found herself cursing the fragrant warmth of this room and the tricks it played upon her senses. "The evening was lovely, but I'm certain it is very late."

The smoky gaze flickered to the mantel clock, then locked upon her. "Midnight."

Gathering skirt in hand, she made as if to brush past him. "Well then, I must see myself to bed."

A steely grip upon her arm stilled her feet. "Merry Christmas, Elizabeth."

For some inexplicable reason, her eyes fell to his mouth and she gulped, then nearly jumped from her skin when he pressed a package into her hand. She stared in confusion at the package, rather crudely wrapped in brown paper but sporting a beautiful red velvet ribbon.

"What's this?" she asked dumbly.

A corner of his mouth lifted. "A present. Surely you don't deem gift giving some heathenish custom."

"For me?"

"Open it."

Her gaze wavered between the package and him. His eyes twinkled with something akin to mirth, which she deemed atrociously out of place at the moment. "I have nothing for you."

"You're dampening my holiday spirit. Open the package."

"I can't, truly..."

He peered intently at her and lifted a brow. "I expect nothing in return. And you needn't fret that accepting my gift implies that you perhaps harbor some fondness for me."

Elizabeth stared blankly at him for a moment then felt the telltale blush sweep her cheeks yet again. Dear God, but her thoughts were transparent. Dropping her gaze, she trailed slender fingers over the velvet bow. "It's not that I don't like you, but..."

"For God's sake, Elizabeth. Open the damned package."

"You needn't resort to profanity." She nearly shrank from the murderous look that suddenly filled his eyes and decided to open the package. With fingers that refused to remain steady, she slipped the ribbon aside and parted the paper.

"Oh..." she breathed, her fingers tracing the scrolled imprint of Tennyson's works. She lifted a radiant smile. "How did you know?"

He flashed a self-satisfied grin. "A lucky guess."

Elizabeth glanced down and sighed wistfully. "I can't accept this."

With a grunt of rekindled irritation, Alec folded his arms over his chest. "I've never been overly fond of poetry. Besides, you nearly killed yourself attempting to reach it. The book will find a better home with you."

Elizabeth lifted a wide smile. "Thank you... for this... for having me. It was a lovely holiday." Growing decidedly uncomfortable beneath his intense regard, she clasped the book and the red velvet ribbon close and brushed past him. "Good night, Lord—"

"Elizabeth."

She found herself rooted to the spot when he moved before her with that same intense look about him.

"I prefer that you call me Alec."

Elizabeth found she couldn't meet his gaze for the life of her, much less argue with the man. Her heart began an erratic thumping that had little to do with sherry or any joy over the gift she'd received. It was his blasted white shirt, so crisp, so elegant and so incredibly masculine. And his scent, mixing with the heady aroma of Christmas...and the downy flakes of snow falling silently outside the huge windows...and the sudden intimacy of a sleeping household.

"We have another custom at this time of year, Elizabeth, one that I would take great pleasure in demonstrating for you." He moved a step nearer and her throat became dry as a bone. "Look at me."

Without forethought, she did as he asked, God only knew why, then instantly wished she hadn't. He stood so close to her she could hear his breathing—short and ragged, like hers—and his eyes were the deepest gray she could imagine without being black. His hands lifted to hers and she clutched her precious items closer. He raised his eyes to the ceiling and Elizabeth's gaze followed. Dangling from the doorjamb directly above her was a sprig of small yellowish flowers surrounding tiny white berries.

"Mistletoe," Alec murmured. "You're familiar with this custom?"

Elizabeth gulped past her parched throat, willing herself to sweep his hands from hers, that look from his eye, but she was powerless. "No..."

"Let me show you." His face moved closer, his eyes fell to her mouth, and she froze, suspended in time for an instant, listening to the roar of her pulse in her ears. Her lips parted but the words remained unspoken, aching in her throat as her world careened out of control. And then his lips were upon hers, warm, firm, just as she'd dreamed, only far more intoxicating than she'd ever imagined, moving with an infinite tenderness that swept aside coherent thought. She felt his breath mingling with hers, his bearded face brushing over her cheek, and she was seized by an uncontrollable trembling that threatened to dissolve her limbs in a heap.

With a groan, she sagged against him and he caught her, perhaps mistaking her sudden weakness for wanton surrender. His arms swept about her, crushing her, her book and the ribbon between them, and his mouth slanted fiercely over hers.

With a terrified wail, she twisted from his grasp and fled the room as quickly as her ankle would allow, still clutching the book to her bosom as tears fell unheeded to her cheeks. She was not to find solace upon her pillow that Christmas Eve, or for many nights to come.

Though Elizabeth found occupying herself a relatively easy task in a houseful of guests, keeping her eyes from Alec Sinclair proved far greater an endeavor for what remained of her visit. The man appeared intent upon thwarting her every attempt to avoid him. He was forever in her sight, or so it seemed, despite her precautions always to be in the company of at least one other adult. For a moment, she had to wonder if perhaps it was her imagination, though she had little intention of allowing him opportunity to explain himself. Indeed, though her eyes strayed to that hulking figure far more than she deemed appropriate under the circumstances, she spoke not a word to him.

He deserved far more, however. A thorough tongue-lashing would have sufficed, had that not required her to find her tongue, which seemed to tie itself into a knot whenever he was about. The man had seduced her with no more than a few glasses of sherry and a Christmas present! The idea! She had more than a mind to give him back his precious book, if only that wouldn't also require speaking to the man. As it was, she decided to keep it, and the velvet ribbon, as well, which she tucked between the pages for safekeeping.

After a vain attempt at a nap late afternoon on Christmas day, she ventured from her room to seek the warmth of the fire in the sitting room below. Upon closing her bedroom door behind her, she spied Phoebe, on her knees, peeking between the slats at the top of the staircase.

"Phoebe, what on earth . . . ?"

"Shh!" With a frantic wave, Phoebe motioned Elizabeth down beside her and shoved a finger in the direction of the sitting room. "How revolting! Just look at Lady Astrid all over Father. And you think *I'm* up to no good, Miss Burbridge!"

Elizabeth's curious gaze followed Phoebe's wagging finger and she found herself on her knees beside the girl. Visible just inside the sitting room were Lady Astrid and the children, gathered alongside Alec, who was on all fours. The children erupted with peals of laughter and begged for a ride. Alec complied with a chuckle and each was given a turn aboard his broad back while Astrid looked on with twinkling eyes that revealed far more than they concealed. Indeed, the young girl looked as if she positively hungered for the man, and made this abundantly clear when the children bounded from the room in search of hot cocoa, leaving her alone with him. With a giggle, she tugged upon his sleeve until he stood directly beneath the mistletoe. Apparently Astrid was more than familiar with the custom, for when Alec bestowed a confused look upon her, she unceremoniously yanked his head to hers.

Spying was a vice heretofore unknown to Elizabeth, but one that she deemed more than necessary in this case. To her eye, it was Alec's place to set the nubile and ever-so-eager Astrid from him with a sound scolding and a pat on the head before sending her off for some cookies and milk. This, apparently, was not Alec's intent. The kiss dragged on interminably, with Astrid, on tiptoe, her head flung back, clinging desperately to those brawny shoulders and uttering moans that sounded like some unfortunate animal caught in a trap. Alec's hands were at the girl's waist, to embrace her or to support her weight lest she swoon dead away, Elizabeth could not discern, though her first instinct was not to give the man the benefit of the doubt. As far as she could tell, he was enjoying the kiss nearly as much as Astrid.

The commotion of the children returning finally put an end to their reverie, causing Elizabeth to wonder at the outcome of such a kiss had they been left undisturbed for some time. She nearly snorted in disgust as a flushed and breathless Astrid patted a trembling hand first to her coiffure then to her stomach, where no doubt a score of butterflies danced away. Alec ran a hand through his hair then placed both upon his hips before muttering something to Astrid that sent her spinning from him with a girlish but decidedly wicked giggle. With a shake of his head, Alec spun on his heel and would undoubtedly have noticed the two spies all but painfully squeezed between the staircase slats had Phoebe not yanked upon Elizabeth's arm and dived for cover around the corner of the hallway.

"For heaven' sake, Phoebe!" Elizabeth exclaimed, seeking to right herself amidst her jumbled muslin skirts.

"Well, Miss Burbridge, the way your mouth was gaping open, I wasn't sure you'd control of your senses!" Phoebe fumbled ungracefully to her feet. "Father most certainly would have seen us!"

"It would serve the man right," Elizabeth grumbled half to herself as she tucked a stray tendril into her chignon and rose to her feet.

"Indeed!" Phoebe retorted in a manner that left Elizabeth wondering at the girl's sudden abundance of moral conscience. "It's almost pitiful, the manner in which Astrid is throwing herself at Father. Why, everyone knows he has no intention of ever marrying again! And who could blame him! Why, he was no more than Astrid's age when he and Mother had to wed." Color flooded Phoebe's plump cheeks and she cast her eyes downward. "It was me, you see. I...I was the reason."

Elizabeth stared in momentary confusion at the girl. "You? How could— Oh, my! Of course... they did... before they were...I see." Blinking several times to rid her cheeks of embarrassment, Elizabeth hastened to appease her. "Surely you don't blame yourself for their indiscretion?"

Phoebe shrugged in a casual way that Elizabeth thought was less than genuine and her amber eyes flickered toward the stairs. "Of course, Father would *never* consider Lady Astrid more than a casual dalliance. He, as I, feels this household is much better off without a woman."

Casual dalliance? God only knew, she'd never in her wildest imaginings thought she'd consider herself labeled as such. Dear God, a fallen woman, bereft of moral fiber...a tarnished soul!

"Miss Burbridge? You needn't look so stricken. It's not so awful, you know. Life without a mother."

"I'm sure you'd feel otherwise if the right woman—"

"The right woman?" Phoebe waved a hand. "Believe me, Miss Burbridge, even if she did exist, neither Father nor I would want her. You are enjoying yourself, are you not, Miss Burbridge?"

Elizabeth summoned a game smile amidst all her distress. "Oh yes, but I must be back at Dunlevy early on the morrow."

"I shall inform Hiram, but, Miss Burbridge, I was hoping you'd stay on for a few days." With a dramatic huff and a pout, Phoebe pleaded, "Are you quite certain I can't change your mind?"

"Quite." With a sudden desire to avoid setting her eyes upon Alec Sinclair for fear of what she could possibly say or, worse yet, *do* to the man, Elizabeth grasped Phoebe's hand in hers. "Would you like to help me pack up my things?"

Phoebe's face lit up. "Oh, of course, but first..." Her eyes twinkled with mischief. "The cocoa really does smell so tempting, and Cook is sure to serve some cakes, as well. Would you care for some?"

Begging off, Elizabeth returned to her room while Phoebe bounded down the stairs in search of her treat. Leaving the door ajar in anticipation of the child's return, Elizabeth slid her trunk from beneath the bed and set about packing her few items. In all truth, this was a mindless excuse for keeping herself closeted in her room.

"Self-indulgent, egotistical man," she muttered half to herself as she plucked a cotton shift from the pile and began carefully folding it. "The poor child is doomed . . . doomed!"

A movement from the doorway drew her attention and she turned, a smile playing upon her lips. "How was your cocoa?"

He stood, one shoulder against the doorjamb, his arms crossed over a chest whose breadth seemed to fill Elizabeth's sight, his gaze sweeping long and leisurely over the flimsy garment clutched in her hands. With an appreciative smile, he raised smoldering eyes and drawled, "Delicious. Absolutely delicious."

Chapter Six

The crystal decanter twinkled brilliantly in the soft glow of the fire, its amber liquid beckoning until a liberal portion was splashed rather impatiently into a glass. The harsh clinking of the two containers grated upon Basil's nerves nearly as much as the sounds of merrymaking from the parlor just across the hall, but this did not in any way temper his abrupt movements.

"Damned holidays," he muttered, gulping from the glass. He closed his eyes as the brandy warmed his belly and eased the painful grip of anxiety that had plagued him of late.

His eyes flickered contemptuously toward the parlor before rolling heavenward as his stepfather's boisterous bellow echoed from the room, audible above the chuckles of his Christmas guests, Lord and Lady Castlethorpe. The old man had one foot in the grave, yet he could still yammer and bark like a man a score younger until that hacking cough rendered him a doubled over mass of white hair and shrunken old bones. A sneer curved Basil's thin lips. It was only a matter of time.

Abandoning the decanter, Basil clutched his glass in hand and began a determined pacing about the deserted sitting room. Elizabeth Burbridge...devoted teacher, old maid, *virgin,* and, from what Felicity had divulged, rather plain if not homely looking. In other words, ripe for the picking.

Basil nearly rubbed his hands together with glee. He knew the type. Wooing her would prove a grossly simple task, if he could find it within himself to mask his repugnance. He could bear a gap-toothed smile and a scrawny frame if she weren't simpleminded. But God help him if the wench were horrendously fat and sporting a hideous wart or two upon her nose. Taking *that* for a wife would indeed test his resolve to see his plan to fruition. Even he would find it physically impossible to bed such a wench, though that might not be necessary. A few intimate caresses coupled with some feverish kisses and hoarsely whispered words of undying devotion and she would be putty in his hands. After all, what had the wench to compare him to?

His slippered feet stilled before the fire and he stared blankly into the flames, pondering the unknowns. Did Elizabeth know her father's true identity and simply wish to deny it? Did her mother, this Philippa Valentine, even know? And what of the courtesan? Basil stroked his stubbled chin thoughtfully. One could only imagine how vital this secret was to both Philippa and her daughter.

The sudden popping of an ember shook Basil from his musings and he moved again about the room. Damn, but he needed a device, some way to ingratiate himself into Elizabeth's life without arousing her suspicions—and Nigel's. Laying his glass upon a polished table with a disgusted grunt, he ventured into the hallway. As he passed a low table just inside the front portal, he paused, as was his wont, before a mound of correspondence left for Nigel's perusal. With a quick glance about and little hesitation, he sifted through the pile with a keen eye. No telling what he could find.

With a disgruntled sigh, he flipped through the last of the papers, finding nothing to arouse his interest. A perfumed note from that dowager of society Mrs. Prudence Proudfit, more notes inquiring about his lordship's health and, of course, endless gibber jabber about that damned benefit for improved education for the poor....

Basil's heart leapt and he grasped the letter with both hands, his eyes scanning the elegant scroll.

... regret that you shall not attend the benefit in your honor... gala event for furthering educational opportunities of those most in need ... appreciate as always your continued unparalleled generosity and support.

The gleaming black eyes swept feverishly over the letter once again, then rose to stare unseeing before Basil clutched the letter to his breast and nearly whooped with joy.

Several hours later, while venturing past the parlor, he spied Nigel alone before the fire. Spinning on his heel, he entered the room, albeit at a measured tread, pausing just inside the doorway. He stared at the back of Nigel's very still, white head and experienced for the briefest of moments a mind-numbing terror that the old man had died.

Then the head turned and Basil was presented with that hawklike profile before Nigel growled, "The stench of your brandy precedes you, Basil. Don't linger in doorways, man. Make up your mind."

Gritting his teeth, Basil moved to stand before the old man. Nigel was seated in a deep leather chair, which seemed to swallow his slight frame within its folds. He wore a dark silk dressing gown and a wool blanket was slung across his narrow legs, causing one less familiar with him to infer that he was a decrepit old man. Basil, however, knew better, and noted yet again the large hand, albeit wizened with age, that gripped the edge of the chair with a strength younger men would envy. The other hand hung loosely over the arm of the chair, absently stroking the mongrel snoring at Nigel's slippered feet. Basil's eyes flickered to his stepfather's face, deeply lined and pale, with its hollowed cheeks and piercing dark eyes beneath thick white brows; eyes that could see right through a man. That, coupled with the snide curl to his lip and the undeniably wild mass of untamed white hair had caused Basil to conjecture on more than one occasion that his stepfather was perched precariously on the brink of lunacy. If only wishing so would make it true.

Basil was graced with a disparaging sweep of those glittering eyes. "What is it, Basil? Do you suddenly find yourself desperately in need of yet another advance on your allowance?" The omnipotent gaze swept over him again. "Lest you harbor any illusions to the contrary, the holiday spirit, as heartwarming as it may be, has not left me eager and willing to keep your purse weighted."

Basil shifted from one foot to the other and bit his tongue. He even managed a half smile, which brought a resounding *humph* from Nigel. Willing his rage aside, Basil bowed perfunctorily before the old man. "No, Stepfather, I only sought to wish you a Merry Christmas. An innocent quest."

"Your first, if it is indeed so," Nigel growled, frowning again into the fire.

Basil's gaze flickered over the stoop-shouldered frame. "I also wished to inquire of your health."

Twin black orbs fastened upon him. "One can't help but wonder at your sudden concern."

"In all truth, the holiday has served as a reminder."

The wizened face broke into a caustic smirk. "Perhaps that brandy you enjoy so freely has somehow managed to render you a conscience. If so, indulge, man, indulge! With my heartfelt blessings!" Raising a hand as if to emphasize his point, Nigel suddenly doubled over as hacking coughs engulfed him.

Basil stared with a perverse curiosity and a snide curl to his lip as wave after wave racked the tortured body. In a gesture he deemed essential to his purpose, he retrieved Nigel's ever present glass of water and pressed it into the shaking hands once the spasms subsided. If he expected a token of thanks from the old man, he was to be disappointed. The eyes that focused on him over the rim of the glass were undaunted in their suspicion. Damned old man!

Lowering the glass from his lips, Nigel drew several deep breaths and muttered disgustedly, "As you can see, I'm ailing. And a bloody nuisance it is! Confined to this house with Brunhilde hovering about like a mother hen. It's almost enough to make a man lose his mind!"

Basil raised his brows and nodded as if he understood entirely. "I'd wager you're sorely missed at all your social functions. Why, just a short while ago I overheard Lady Castlethorpe mention something about that gala benefit two weeks hence . . . the one for education for the poor?"

A tic began in Nigel's jaw and Basil could guess he ground his teeth with frustration. "Aye, if I could summon the strength to make my way about, it would be for that one occasion."

"It's in your honor, I gather?"

"Aye, and another benefactor. An eccentric chap, generous to a fault, nonetheless, and a shrewd businessman. Alec Sinclair's his name."

Basil shook his head absently, for he didn't know the man, nor did he care. He donned his most thoughtful expression for a moment. "I seem to recall that Mother took particular interest in the underprivileged."

Nigel's eyes clouded and probed the depths of the fire with an intensity that made Basil shiver. Swallowing past a suddenly parched throat, Basil ventured into uncharted waters. "I would consider it an honor and a privilege to attend the benefit, if only in Mother's memory. I, er, certainly not in your stead, but perhaps as a member of the family."

The black orbs held Basil within their grasp. "I'd never imagined you possessed a philanthropic bone in your body, man, and in all truth I question your motives. However..."

Basil released his breath in a sudden rush, which caused Nigel to glance sharply at him for a moment before he continued. "If you so wish it, for Eugenie's sake, then I will allow it, though I feel it would be grossly negligent on my part not to warn you to temper your consumption of liquor on that particular evening. And keep your tongue in check." Nigel glared ferociously upon him. "Do not embarrass me, Basil, and if you care naught for the family name, for God's sake, do it for your mother."

For the briefest of moments, Basil considered dropping to his knees and kissing the old man's hands. "I shall look forward to it."

He lingered not a moment longer for fear that Nigel might detect something in his manner that could possibly give him away. Nigel's words of wisdom caused him little pause. Indeed, though his stepfather didn't know it, he had little reason to fret. Basil had every intention of maintaining a very low profile at that event, lest some philanthropic woman with a wagging tongue take it upon herself to bend Nigel's ear with details, especially about the woman upon Basil's arm.

It was a risk Basil was prepared to take, for an event such as this would prove all but irresistible to a spinster teacher brimming with philanthropic notions of her own. A teacher whose identity must be kept secret from Nigel, for he would indeed see Basil's plot for what it was when he learned her name was Elizabeth Burbridge.

Chapter Seven

"Oh, there you are, Alec dear! I've been searching high and low for you!" Marisa Farnsworth's voice rang shrilly from just down the hall, her brisk footfalls upon the hardwood attesting to her haste.

Though Elizabeth all but collapsed in a heap of relief at this untimed but much appreciated interruption, Alec appeared more than a trifle annoyed. His smirk dissolved into a tightly clenched jaw, and the eyes that surveyed Elizabeth were suddenly stormy. They managed to hold her captive for an instant longer than was decent. This alone brought the color high in her cheeks, and she blushed even more fiercely as an astounded Marisa materialized in the doorway. That she still held her flimsy undergarment for all the world to see made Elizabeth want to cry in shame. She didn't pause to consider that flinging the shift into the trunk as if the garment were aflame would be viewed, especially by Marisa, as a guilt-ridden action. Her only thought was to remove the thing from Alec's all-seeing gaze. If only she could remove herself half as easily.

Marisa's wide eyes darted suspiciously between Alec and Elizabeth. "Why, Miss Burbridge, leaving so soon?"

Elizabeth swallowed the lump in her throat and managed to reply airily, "Yes, I must return very early tomorrow."

"And, Alec, lingering in doorways?" Marisa cast a mildly reproachful glance over Alec's brawny figure that to Elizabeth's eye made lingering an indecent act. "Wherever are your manners, hmm? Let the dear girl tidy up her—" Marisa's critical eye swept over the modest pile of coarse brown muslin frocks "—her *things*. My dear Miss Burbridge, in the future, to avoid embarrassment and perhaps a wagging tongue or two, you might keep your door closed when tending to such tasks." Linking her arm through Alec's, Marisa gestured down the hallway. "Alec, shall we? Cocktails await us."

The booted legs remained firmly planted. "I'll be along in a moment."

The woman gaped openly then forced a gay smile. "Oh, come now. You can't stay here and—"

Smoky eyes flickered briefly over Marisa. "A man can do as he damn well pleases in his own house."

With a nervous laugh, Marisa gave a wave of her bejeweled hand. "I never meant to imply otherwise, but, Alec, 'tis the girl's bedroom and she's . . . and you . . ."

"I fear I've suddenly developed a raging headache, of all things!" Elizabeth exclaimed rather boisterously, hurrying to the door. "Please don't hold dinner for me. I may just keep to my bed until the pain subsides. Good night."

With that, she closed the door soundly upon a very self-satisfied smirk and a brooding dark scowl, which lingered with her for what remained of the night.

Early the next morning, well before the house stirred, Elizabeth found herself pacing across the snow-covered porch as Hiram ambled about, preparing the coach for her departure. The man apparently had not been hired for his ability to function this early in the day, for he mumbled to himself as if to clear the cobwebs from his brain and scratched his head in a distracted manner. If Elizabeth didn't know better, she would have thought the man was stalling. She had, however, impressed upon him her urgency.

Drawing her cloak about her against a brisk gust of wind, she cursed her lack of gloves and cast a vexed look at Hiram. Never had she seen a man move so slowly! A claw of anxiety twisted in her and she nearly stomped her foot in exasperation. Blast, but his lordship in all his masculine glory could emerge at any second from that doorway.

A snort and a whinny, accompanied by the crunching of snow beneath four prancing hooves, snapped Elizabeth's head up. Instinctively, she knew it was not the sounds of the horses that Hiram tended to. Indeed, her pulse leapt for a score of reasons as Sebastian, with Alec astride, appeared from nowhere. In an instant, Alec dismounted and stood before her, tall, broad, immovable.

"You're leaving," he stated flatly.

Elizabeth's eyes flickered over the expanse of his chest, snugly encased in a heavy cloak, the same cloak that she had pressed her damp, windburned cheek against only two days ago. The same arms that had wrapped protectively about her hung loosely at his sides. The same lips that had claimed hers beneath the mistletoe were fixed into a hard line that hollowed his cheeks. His hair was windblown; his face looked cold, reddened by a brisk wind and a hard ride and still sporting a day's worth of stubble. He must have risen very early.

"I told you I had to."

"Without saying goodbye."

"I thanked Phoebe."

Silence hung between them for several moments, broken only by Hiram's soft mutterings and a grunt from one of the horses. Alec shifted his weight, drawing Elizabeth's attention to his boots as they crunched upon the snow. She felt his voice as it rumbled through her. "I'd like it if you'd come again sometime."

"I . . . thank you, but I don't believe I shall."

"When will I see you again?"

"Oh, perhaps at the school. In passing, of course."

"Of course." The mocking tone drew Elizabeth's gaze upward and she was rewarded with a smile that set her blood churning in her veins far more than any sherry ever would. "I *will* see you again, Elizabeth. You can count on it."

Hiram appeared at Alec's side with a lame smile and a tip of his hat. "Are ye 'bout ready, Miss Burbridge?"

Elizabeth nearly embraced the little man but thought it better to dash to the waiting coach as quickly as possible with a breathy, "Oh, yes!" She managed to reach the coach step when a large hand encased hers without warning to assist her aboard. Once settled upon the cushioned seat, she sought to withdraw her hand, only to find it soundly grasped within his. Then suddenly Alec's broad shoulders filled the doorway. Feeling her heart palpitating, she raised wide eyes to his and tugged upon her hand again. Instead of releasing it, he brought his other hand to rest upon her trembling fingers.

"'Twas a pleasure, Miss Burbridge. A pleasure." And with that, he lowered his head to brush his lips softly over her fingers before disappearing through the doorway, leaving a pale and trembling Elizabeth to stare in shock at her burning fingertips and attempt to make some sense of her jumbled thoughts.

The hollow halls echoed plaintively as Elizabeth hurried along, toting her trunk. She breezed past the empty classrooms and mounted the back stairs, all three flights, at a spirited gait. She didn't even pause to gaze, as was her wont, from the huge third-story window that overlooked the sun-drenched snow-covered countryside. She only wanted to surround herself with *her* belongings, meager as they were, in the fervent hope that this would restore a sense of normalcy to her world. With a weary sigh that dissolved into a smile of relief, she flung her door wide and stopped short as a blast of cold air assailed her. Her bed and her bureau were gone, and a large portion of the floor, as well, and where a wall and a small window once stood was nothing but open air. Her room was no more.

With stunned disbelief, she dropped her trunk and spun from the demolished room, lurching down the dark hall. What in God's name had happened?

Her frantic pace took her to the headmistress's office, where she paused to draw a few deep breaths before rapping urgently upon the thick wood. If only Miss Percy wouldn't know at first glance that she'd been swept into a man's embrace and soundly kissed beneath the mistletoe....

The oak swung open and the headmistress's solid form filled the doorway. Heavy dark brows shot up and keen eyes fixed upon Elizabeth over thick bifocals. "Elizabeth! Come in."

Stepping aside, Miss Percy waved a sturdy arm before her to indicate a chair in front of her desk, then closed the door and reseated herself behind the massive immaculate desk. "Did you enjoy yourself with Miss Sinclair?"

Elizabeth stared blankly at the headmistress for a long moment. "Oh...yes! Yes, indeed! A lovely girl."

Miss Percy snorted in a manner that accentuated her double chin. "Lovely? Perhaps, but more than a trifle wayward, don't you agree? Hers is a situation I've encountered numerous times. You oversee a majority of her subjects, Elizabeth. Could she perhaps be bored?"

"Bored?" Elizabeth squeaked.

"Yes, Elizabeth. After all, Phoebe Sinclair is not a stupid girl." Miss Percy drew the pencil from behind her ear and tapped it lightly upon her desk. "You, of course, met Phoebe's father. Did you, by chance, happen to discuss the matter with him?"

"I...uh, briefly."

The heavy brows lifted. "And?"

Elizabeth swallowed and managed to respond in an airy voice, "He—we disagreed...in a manner of speaking. I feel her behavior is a result of lax upbringing."

Miss Percy inclined her head as if she were giving the notion some thought. "Perhaps. And what was his opinion?"

"He—he was rather intent on the idea that she is...perhaps, as you said, bored."

"Did he? Well, now that you've met the man, Elizabeth, what do you think?"

"About what?"

"For goodness' sake, Elizabeth! Whatever is the matter with you?"

Elizabeth stared wide-eyed at the woman. "Miss Percy?"

With uncharacteristic impatience, Miss Percy tossed the pencil aside and folded her hands before her upon the desk such that Elizabeth's eyes were drawn to the thick fingers with their sensible short fingernails. "My dear girl, you stare blankly at me with those huge eyes and find composing a complete sentence beyond your realm and you expect me to infer that something is not amiss?"

"I—I—" She knew! Dear God, how could she have expected to keep such a secret from the woman?

"Oh, for heaven' sake, of course!" Miss Percy threw her hands into the air in a helpless gesture that made Elizabeth nearly jump from her seat. "Your room! Whatever was I thinking? My dear, we had a dreadful storm on Christmas Eve. The wind blew that ancient elm outside your window into the building, demolishing your room and a few others. You saw the hole? I had workers here all Christmas Day just to remove the tree and what remained of your belongings. What a mess." The headmistress shook her head disgustedly and pursed her thin lips. "I'm afraid this leaves me in a quandary, my dear, for we've not a room to spare, and everyone expected back tomorrow."

Something in the depths of the headmistress's eyes and the tone in her voice set Elizabeth's stomach churning with trepidation. She all but hung on the woman's every word. "Elizabeth, I'm afraid you will have to find other lodgings for a time. The inevitable withdrawal of one or two pupils this term will make a few rooms available. However, I must tell you that the students who have been displaced by this tragedy will receive those rooms first. I can't very well do otherwise, for they've all paid for room and board and yours is part of your compensation. I will, of course, pay you for that portion of your wages."

Elizabeth searched frantically for a response, which came in a voice poised just this side of hysteria. "Why can't I stay on with one of the students?"

Miss Percy shook her head with finality. "Oh, that would never do. It would not be in your best interests or theirs. No, I'm afraid you'll have to look elsewhere. Perhaps your mother's home. She lives in London, and that's not too great a distance."

Elizabeth burst forth with the first thought that entered her mind. "Oh, of course, yes. Mother's."

Miss Percy clasped her hands together and gave Elizabeth an encouraging smile. "Very good, then. This evening, make yourself comfortable in any of the vacant rooms. Come, I'll show you where your things are. They all fit quite nicely into one small box."

Elizabeth's step held little of its usual springiness the following morning when she ventured past Miss Percy's office bearing her trunk, laden with all her belongings. The door was ajar, perhaps in anticipation of the arrival of the students from their holiday. As yet, none had appeared, which suited Elizabeth's purpose. She had little desire to be found traipsing through the halls, lugging her trunk like some abandoned orphan, while the girls settled in.

Just as she passed the open doorway, Miss Percy's commanding voice resounded through the office and echoed into the hallway. "Oh, Elizabeth! Could I have a moment of your time before you leave? There's someone here I'd like you to meet."

Abandoning her trunk outside the door, Elizabeth loosened her cloak and stepped into the small office, her eyes settling upon the tall dark-haired gentleman standing before her. He had risen from his chair as she entered, holding hat in hand, bestowing a bow upon her as Miss Percy made the introductions.

"Elizabeth Burbridge. Basil Christy, a local philanthropist who is in need of my finest teacher to assist him with his most recent project." Miss Percy gave Elizabeth one of her rare smiles, which, much to Elizabeth's surprise, dimpled the woman's doughy cheek and made her appear a score younger.

Elizabeth swung her eyes back to this Basil fellow. He peered at her closely, almost too closely, down the length of a hooked, slightly crooked nose that looked as if it had been broken a few times. In retrospect, Elizabeth would forever wonder how she had failed to detect the glitter in the depths of those black eyes as they carefully assessed her, but at present she was blissfully unaware of it. Instead, she found herself thinking that with his closely cropped, sleek black hair and ruddy complexion, coupled with the elegant fall of his black cape, he cut an imposing figure. His intense perusal only added to her assessment, though after several moments she found herself growing decidedly uncomfortable and her eyes darted to Miss Percy and back again several times. When he spoke, she almost jumped from her skin.

"Have we met before, Miss Burbridge?"

"I don't believe so." Elizabeth gave him a weak smile. *Basil Christy.* The name struck no chord of recognition. She shook her head for emphasis.

His stony visage dissolved into a soft smile. "My mistake. For a moment I was certain... though I must admit, you've a face a man would find difficult to forget."

Elizabeth stammered a thank-you, well aware of the critical look Miss Percy leveled upon the newcomer. The headmistress, in an attempt to rein in the young man's wandering thoughts, cleared her throat overtly and remarked, "Your business, Mr. Christy? Perhaps you could enlighten Elizabeth." Her chair scraped against the floor as she stood and clasped her hands before her. "Tea, Mr. Christy? Elizabeth? No? Well, I find myself in need of some. If you'll excuse me." The headmistress brushed past Elizabeth with what, to the younger woman's eye, could only be described as a wary look, then strode purposefully from the room.

Basil indicated the chair beside him and reseated himself once Elizabeth was settled. "My project is one that I hope you will find of interest, Miss Burbridge. You will, of course, understand why I came here to look for an assistant. What better place to find a woman... a teacher, rather, who embodies the spirit of education today. And from what Miss Percy has told me, I could hope to find no better a teacher than you."

Elizabeth flushed. "It is an honor indeed to be so highly thought of by Headmistress Percy, and one that I do not take lightly. Tell me of this project."

Flashing a smile, Basil drew a deep breath then glanced toward the closed window. "It is a trifle stuffy, Miss Burbridge. Would you mind if I removed my cloak? Perhaps you wish to do the same."

Elizabeth shrugged, attempting to remove her cloak. Basil, however, hastened to her aid in a flash, all but leaping from his chair with a murmured, "Allow me," and easing the garment from her back with a light touch upon her shoulders. Were she the type to anticipate such things, Elizabeth may have smiled inwardly as his hand lingered just a moment too long upon her arm. As it was, she merely experienced a fleeting disquiet while he stood near, though she knew not why.

With a flick of his wrist, Basil swept his cloak from his shoulders to reveal a handsome topcoat of deep blue, with matching trousers and crisply tied ascot. He cut a rather dashing figure, though to Elizabeth's eye he seemed completely unconcerned with his attire. She did notice that he quickly perused her from head to toe before he settled once more into his chair. They sat in silence for several long moments while he studied her yet again, which caused Elizabeth to wonder at what was keeping Miss Percy.

A smile slid across his face. "Do forgive me, Miss Burbridge. I cannot help but think that we've met before." He flashed a toothy smile. "You see, my stepfather, Nigel Cosgrove..." He peered closely at her again as if anticipating some response.

Elizabeth offered a lame smile. "Perhaps it is my somewhat sheltered existence, Mr. Christy, but I fear that name is new to me, as well. Should it be otherwise?"

"Oh, my goodness, no, Miss Burbridge. Please, lest you infer anything to the contrary, you could never be found lacking for my purpose. It is only that my stepfather and I have, for some time now, donated quite generously to the education of the poor and underprivileged. And I have been actively involved with the cause, as well."

Elizabeth could not help the flush of embarrassment that crept from the high neck of her gown. "I'm sorry to be found so uninformed, particularly of a cause that I hold dear." Her eyes lifted to the twin black orbs fixed intently upon her. "If there is anything that I could do to aid you, please—"

"Oh, Miss Burbridge!" In his enthusiasm, this Basil apparently forgot himself and grasped Elizabeth's hands in his. "Oh, my goodness! Do forgive me, Miss Burbridge!" He gently released her hands with a look of such penitence that Elizabeth nearly reached a hand to his to ease his discomfort. He smiled weakly. "You are more than I could have hoped for. Such enthusiasm! Such devotion I have never encountered in all my philanthropic work, and need I reiterate that I have been heavily involved for quite some time now. Oh, Miss Burbridge, my dearest wish is that you shall agree to work alongside me."

Elizabeth smiled. "It would indeed be an honor for me to work alongside a man who shares my ideals, my dreams, all that I hold dear."

Basil erupted with a hearty chuckle and rubbed his hands together with glee. "Such a team we shall make! Now, the project. I *must* tell you of the project." The black eyes lingered thoughtfully upon her, unsettling Elizabeth yet again, until he murmured, "Miss Burbridge, we may have never met before this day, but I must tell you, I feel I've known you for a very long time." His gaze held hers for several moments until he seemed to force himself to glance away with a deep sigh. "Now, then. I would like to set about establishing a school for young children, not so much in London proper, for much has been done in the last few years to improve their situation."

"There still remains as much to be done."

"Oh, of course, I agree wholeheartedly. Nevertheless, the children in the country are far worse off, not only due to the state of the school buildings alone—"

"Most are mere one-room shacks!"

"Yes, yes, they are at that. But the teachers—"

"A dreadful lot! The majority lacking in formal education of their own! A horrendous crime!"

"Indeed! I agree wholeheartedly."

Elizabeth shook her head in awe. "Yours is indeed a marvelous project, Mr. Christy. When shall we begin?"

Basil looked startled for a moment, then leaned forward eagerly upon his seat. "Well, as a matter of fact, I find my presence is required at a gala benefit a fortnight hence. It is being held in my honor, as well as that of my stepfather, who is ailing, I'm afraid, and won't be able to attend."

"I'm awfully sorry."

Unabashed grief clouded Basil's ruddy features. "Yes, it is indeed a dreadful shame. You see, I have come to feel for the man as I would my own father. His illness tears at me daily, but henceforth I vow to uphold all that he cherishes." The sorrowful dark eyes looked deeply into Elizabeth's. "Miss Burbridge, do me the honor of accompanying me to this event, which benefits the cause we both so desperately wish to pursue."

Elizabeth hesitated not a moment. "Why, of course I will accompany you." She paused at the boisterous sounds filling the lower hallways. The girls were returning, full of Christmas goose and holiday spirit, as yet unrestrained by the thought of the schoolwork that awaited them. Eager to extricate herself from this place as soon as possible, Elizabeth rose from her chair and bid Basil Christy a polite but curt good-day, then watched thoughtfully as he strode jauntily from the room.

Heaving a weary sigh, she donned her cloak, retrieved her precious trunk and hurried below. She still had to summon the one coach Dunlevy employed for the express purpose of conveying visitors to and from the school, visitors who otherwise had no means of transportation. Had she departed earlier as planned, chances were that the coach would not have been detained elsewhere. As it was, upon inquiring of the stable hand as to the whereabouts of the conspicuously absent coach and its driver, she was informed that it had departed for London but a few minutes past and was not expected to return until late afternoon.

With a sinking heart and mounting desperation, Elizabeth returned to the main hall. She unceremoniously dumped her trunk at the foot of the back stairs, well out of range of the hustle and bustle, and plopped herself upon it. Chewing thoughtfully at her lip, she contemplated her next course of action when a tinkling voice sliced through her thoughts and sent her head to hang woefully between her hands.

"Miss Burbridge!" Phoebe Sinclair bounded down the shadowed hallway, skidding to a halt with a rustle of crisp petticoats. She dropped to her knees beside Elizabeth and peered with some concern at her teacher. "Miss Burbridge, are you ill? It's the awful food, isn't it? It has finally done you in!"

"No, Phoebe." Elizabeth looked up, amused in spite of herself and her circumstances, and heaved a weary sigh. "A tree, if you can believe it, fell into my room during a storm, destroying it and a majority of my belongings. As a result, I'm off to find a place to stay for a short time, a room somewhere on this side of London. However, the coach has departed and I fear I shall not—"

"Oh, how dreadful!" Phoebe leapt to her feet and started down the hall, tugging Elizabeth along with her. "But, Miss Burbridge, I've just arrived and Hiram is sure to be outside. Please! You *must* take our coach."

Elizabeth attempted to plant her feet. "No, I couldn't."

Phoebe tugged all the harder and huffed indignantly, "Oh, stop it! I won't hear of it! What an awful thing to happen! Thank heavens you were with us! There's little telling what would have happened had you remained here!"

Before Elizabeth realized, Phoebe hauled her through the front entrance and deposited her before a rather startled Hiram. With an airy command to retrieve Elizabeth's trunk, Phoebe clasped Elizabeth's hands in hers and raised shining eyes. "I hope you find a place, though I would prefer if you'd stay on in my room." Choking on a sob, Phoebe flung her arms about a startled Elizabeth and croaked, "I shall miss you dreadfully! Perhaps I could sneak away and visit you."

Elizabeth could not suppress a hearty laugh. "Phoebe! For heaven' sake! I will be here every day. I fear you will grow rather tired of me."

Phoebe wiped a tear from her rosy cheek. "That will never happen, Miss Burbridge. Oh, there's Charlotte Lambert! I *must* speak with her! Oh, and here's Hiram. Now off you go! Goodbye, Miss Burbridge!"

With a shake of her head, Elizabeth watched the young girl bound eagerly off to share all sorts of sordid tales with her friend. She turned with a resigned sigh and strode to the coach as Hiram secured her trunk atop the vehicle. He turned, giving her a huge smile as he held the door wide, and nodded at her instruction to take her to the city.

Elizabeth had little time to wonder why the man was grinning from ear to ear like a Cheshire cat, but when she ducked inside the shadowed interior of the coach and flopped upon the seat with a weary sigh, her eyes lifted and locked with those opposite her; smoky, smoldering eyes that belonged to none other than Alec Sinclair.

Chapter Eight

If the coach had not leapt forward at that instant, Elizabeth would have flung herself through the door of the vehicle without hesitation. As it was, she would never know if the brawny arm that shot out to steady her as she swayed precariously upon her seat would have done the same to thwart any attempts at escape. Bristling, she sought to sweep his hand from her arm and glowered at him as best she could despite the blood hammering in her ears.

In return, she received a deep chuckle as he released his firm hold upon her. Settling his bulk comfortably upon the seat, he rested one elbow upon a black-clad knee and fingered his cleft chin as if in deep thought, though the amused glitter in the depths of his unwavering gaze hinted otherwise. "A fine mood for so early in the day, Elizabeth. Have you had a bad morning?"

Gritting her teeth against his mocking tone, she clutched the edge of her seat with whitening knuckles. "My mood has little to do with the events of this day, prior to entering this blasted coach."

"Ah, your ankle ails you."

Elizabeth glared at him. "No."

"Then perhaps you're finding Dunlevy's *food*, for lack of a better word, a trifle difficult to digest after several days of Cook's fare."

"No! Your penchant for discrediting this noble institution before your impressionable daughter has weighed far more heavily upon me than any meat pies Dunlevy has to offer!"

"You don't particularly like me, do you, Elizabeth?"

Her mouth snapped shut at his look of amusement. Attempting to regain her composure, she pursed her lips and sniffed, "I find arrogance exceedingly distasteful. Indeed, I don't seem to recall granting you the privilege of addressing me by my first name."

"One would think a kiss shared beneath the mistletoe would grant far more privileges."

Elizabeth managed to find her tongue, though her eyes had somehow focused themselves upon a ray of sunlight slanting across his chest. "If one were arrogant enough to assume that the kiss was indeed shared, then any ghastly assumptions regarding one's privileges would merely be in keeping with one's wretched character."

"And being the arrogant cur that I am, I shall overlook your obvious distress over that kiss and certainly won't allow myself to even consider the ridiculous notion that you perhaps did not enjoy it as much as I."

He shifted in his seat, drawing Elizabeth's attention to the muscled length of leg lying almost innocently beside her. He was casually garbed, as was his wont, in black breeches and riding boots. No doubt he'd spent the morning aboard his beast, though his boots sported a flawless polish and the shirt spanning his wide chest was crisp and immaculate. His cloak draped over shoulders so broad that his bulk seemed to fill the coach and left Elizabeth feeling small and powerless.

She started as his voice rumbled through the velvet interior. "Now that we've determined that your churlish mood is none of my doing..."

She shot him a frigid look, which served only to lift the corner of his mouth another notch. Was the man ever serious?

"Where is it that you're going, Elizabeth, and with your trunk in tow?"

Elizabeth sighed. "I am in need of lodgings for a short time, until my room is repaired. It was damaged in a storm several nights past and my—my mother's home is too great a distance from the school to travel daily."

"Ah, the venerable Miss Percy has tossed you out on your ear."

Elizabeth gasped with indignation. "How dare you question the woman's decisions with such casual disdain? I cannot help but wonder why you allow that very woman, of whom you obviously think so little, to oversee your daughter's education."

"I never once questioned the woman's ability to run the very best of educational institutions, Elizabeth. Only your unfailing devotion."

Winged brows drew together and her voice quivered with emotion. "It would be impossible for me to perform to my abilities with such conviction if I did not feel as I do about the headmistress."

He replied with a hollow laugh. "I've come to expect nothing less of you, Elizabeth. Now, where in all of London do you propose a woman of your sterling character and moral self-righteousness will find suitable lodging?"

Clenching her jaw tightly, she shrugged as casually as possible. "I . . . I know not exactly where. I suppose I could use a bit of guidance."

His dark brows shot up. "You mean to say the remarkably self-sufficient and ever-so-sensible Miss Burbridge finds herself in need of assistance?" His mouth twisted with a wry grin. "Surely you aren't asking the likes of *me?* After all, we arrogant cads associate with only the most debauched and depraved of characters, none of whom inhabits any dwelling you would dare to step foot in."

Elizabeth glared at him. "I am compelled to wonder at whose expense you found humor prior to my landing upon your doorstep."

"I must admit, Elizabeth, I've never found myself responding to anyone as I do to you. Perhaps it's your blasted morality and unblemished virtue that have captured my fascination. Whatever the reason, I can't seem to help myself."

"Perhaps you aren't trying hard enough."

"I'm trying, all right," he muttered. Any hint of a smirk vanished. "That's what makes you so incredibly appealing."

Elizabeth stared dumbly at him for several long moments until a horrendous and thoroughly unsettling thought occurred to her. He was by far the most handsome man she had ever seen.

Beneath his unreadable and unsettling regard, Elizabeth suddenly realized how she'd wound up beneath the mistletoe with him. It was his manner, an undeniable urgency about him that drew her hypnotically, rendering her powerless to stop him.

He was evil.

Shuddering, she pressed a hand to her chest to still the violent quaking just beneath the surface, and then, dear God, he was leaning toward her, his hair as it passed beneath the ray of sunlight flaming into a burnished russet that beckoned for her touch.

"I know of a place that you would find comfortable." His words sliced into her consciousness, serving to remind her that she stared unabashedly at his mouth, which hovered but a hand breadth from hers. She all but jumped from her seat when he raised a brawny fist to pound upon the roof of the coach. As the vehicle slowed to a stop, he remarked, "It is modestly furnished but well located and vacant. Would you care to see it?"

Elizabeth found herself capable only of an airy shrug and a dumb nod, for she had grown all too aware of his enticing scent as he leaned even closer to her and braced himself upon the seat on either side of her. Surely he didn't intend to kiss her?

"Very good," he said. Then, much to Elizabeth's surprise and dismay, he swung the door wide and jumped agilely from the coach.

When he returned, Elizabeth's limbs had ceased their trembling, though her heart leapt and lodged in her throat when he brushed the entire length of her leg as he resettled himself opposite. She kept her attention on the world outside the coach, all too aware that the smoky gaze that had held her within its grasp was now focused as intently upon the blasted newspaper he held just below eye level.

After a time, the coach pulled to a stop on a narrow cobble-stoned street lined with elegant town houses. Alec offered his arm, which she attempted to lean upon as lightly as possible as she disembarked. This drew a smirk from him, little else. He gestured with his hand, indicating a stately white-brick town house sporting tall windows and an imposing black door.

Elizabeth glanced about the street, noting that all the homes were exceedingly well kept. "Is it owned by a friend of yours?"

"Of sorts." He produced a key, much to Elizabeth's surprise, and made quick work of the lock. Swinging the door wide, he bade her enter.

Elizabeth lifted a brow at him as she passed. "Does this friend realize you keep your own key?"

"He wouldn't have it any other way."

"A trusting soul," Elizabeth mused as her eyes appraised the charming foyer, its cream damask walls and highly polished floors, which filled the air with a warm beeswax scent. Suspended from the ceiling two stories above was an enormous crystal chandelier, glittering brilliantly in the sunlight slanting through twin windows above the front portal.

"Discriminating, nonetheless," he murmured close to her ear, which caused Elizabeth to jump like a frightened rabbit and scurry into the front parlor with him close at her heels. This room was as elegant and tastefully decorated as the foyer, as was the remainder of the house. Light, airy, with an irresistible understated elegance, the home welcomed Elizabeth immediately and she ventured up the staircase without hesitation. Upon peeking into one of the three bedchambers, decorated in the palest of violets, she could not help the huge smile she bestowed upon Alec.

"You like it." He had stopped at her elbow and was peering closely at her.

"Oh, yes. It's wonderful."

"Then it's settled. You need look no further."

"But I haven't spoken to the owner... about rent, food...?"

"Yes, you have, and you owe nothing."

Elizabeth stared in momentary confusion. "I...you... You!"

Alec flashed a dazzling grin. "I keep the place for those rare occasions when it serves my purpose to stay in the city for a night or two." At her look of pure horror, he held up a hand and shook his head. "You needn't fret, Elizabeth. Your virtue and your reputation will not be threatened in the least. I have no imminent plans to stay here, nor will I impose my arrogance upon you, unless absolutely necessary, of course. It's up to you. You're more than welcome to use it."

Elizabeth glanced about the place once more. "I will consider it only if you allow me to pay sufficient rent."

"As you wish, though your coin could be put to better use."

A winged brow lifted curiously. "Such as?"

His eyes unabashedly surveyed her from head to toe. "A new dress or two."

He spun on his heel and strode purposefully down the stairs before she could retrieve her voice. She hurried after him, feeling more than a wee bit miffed.

"I shall summon the maid, Winifred, and Holmes, the butler," he called over his shoulder. "Expect them sometime this afternoon."

"That's really not necessary."

"Oh, and you will require a coach."

"Lord Sinclair, really, I don't think . . ."

"I suppose I should also summon the coachman, and of course the cook." He stopped short at the foot of the stairs and cast an apologetic smile at her as she lurched to a halt on the step above him. "I'm afraid she's not quite as good as my cook, but then again, based upon what you've grown accustomed to dining upon at Dunlevy, I suppose anything would be an improvement."

Before Elizabeth could give him anything more than a black look, he grinned, then turned and strode cheerily from the house. Elizabeth stared at the door, listening to the echo of his departure resounding through the foyer. Her eye fell to her trunk, lying innocently upon the floor inside the front portal, and she pursed her lips with vexation. He'd known all along she'd accept his offer.

With a sigh, she retrieved her belongings then remounted the stairs, heading directly for the violet bedchamber, her words obliterating the silence filling the house. "Arrogant man!"

On more than one occasion during the next several days, Elizabeth seriously questioned her decision to stay on at the Sinclair town house. Not that the place or the servants could be found lacking in any way. Indeed, the servants were a friendly lot and, much to Elizabeth's chagrin, full of only the highest regard for "his lordship."

In spite of this, Elizabeth found that, although he remained conspicuously absent, "his lordship's" presence could be felt in nearly every room, as evidenced by the fluttering deep in her belly whenever she happened upon something of his. A book left open upon a table elicited a quick peek to discover what the man enjoyed reading, before being hastily replaced exactly where it had rested lest she be found out. A pair of gloves, his illegible scrawl across a notepad, even the servants' idle talk proved equally upsetting and served as a constant reminder of her inability to function when he was about. He was nowhere to be seen, yet her limbs seemed forever to be on the verge of trembling as the vision of his ruggedly handsome visage filled her thoughts, sweeping aside every attempt to concentrate upon schoolwork. And God only knew she nearly swooned dead away each and every time the front portal banged and the floor echoed with heavy footsteps. It took her several days' worth of clutching a hand to her thumping heart before she discerned it was only Holmes retrieving the mail or the daily paper. Never once did she venture near the large bedchamber directly across the hall from hers, the one sporting an enormous mahogany bed draped with rich burgundy velvet.

Telling Phoebe the news proved far easier than Elizabeth anticipated, though she knew not why she felt a trifle guilty and uncomfortable doing so. The child's eyes flew wide with glee and she flung her arms about a startled, though much relieved, Elizabeth while hoarsely whispering that she would indeed sneak away for visits from time to time.

In response to Miss Percy's inquiry, she felt it unnecessary to burden the woman with details and told her only that she had indeed found suitable lodgings, temporary though they were. That she neglected to mention the Sinclair name caused her a moment's pause, as if she were harboring some tremendous dark secret.

To her mother, she penned a missive that included her new address but little else, lest Leonora deem a visit appropriate. Elizabeth did not anticipate any such calls and, as a result, found herself gaping with surprise when her mother appeared upon her doorstep early one evening.

"Mother?" Elizabeth flew into the front parlor to embrace Leonora, resplendent in a burgundy silk gown and matching velvet cape. Perched at an angle upon her fashionably up-swept auburn coiffure was a matching silk hat sporting an enormous taffeta bow. Elizabeth cast the hat a wary glance as she kissed her mother's powdered cheek, then nearly dissolved in a shameful heap at her mother's response.

"Elizabeth! Darling! Who is he? Do I know him?"

"Mother!"

Leonora gave her daughter a wink and a dimpled smile. "Well, what's a mother to think?" Her eyes assessed the room, taking in every last detail. Arching a delicate brow, she drawled wickedly, "I think I like him already."

Elizabeth let out an exasperated sigh. "Mother, this is not what you think."

"Oh, really?" Leonora spoke in a low conspiratorial voice. "That's what they all say, darling."

Elizabeth rolled her eyes and crossed her arms over her chest as her toe tapped rhythmically upon the thick carpet. "Mother, you're far too preoccupied with affairs of the heart."

Leonora gave her daughter a knowing look. "Be that as it may, but you, dear daughter, have no idea of the fun you've been missing. Then again . . ." Her eyes appraised Elizabeth once more. "Perhaps you've had a sudden change of heart. One can only hope. Your note was so vague, I simply had to come. Now I know why." She gave a throaty laugh and her violet eyes twinkled mischievously. "Sooooo?"

Elizabeth stared dumbly at her mother. "Sooooo? What, Mother? I'm afraid you're in for a disappointment."

Leonora's eyes gazed heavenward and she pressed a hand dramatically to her chest. "Oh, dear God, don't tell me he's married?"

"Mother!"

Leonora wagged a stern finger in admonition. "Elizabeth, don't believe a word of it, do you hear me? He'll never leave his wife, mark my words, and you'll be left night after night to stew and fret in this—"

"Mother! For God's sake, he's not married!"

"Oh, thank heavens!"

With dawning realization, Elizabeth shook her head in self-disgust and hastened to explain. "No, I mean . . . *he* is not the reason for my being here. It was Phoebe who—"

"But there is a he, nonetheless."

"Yes, but he's merely her father."

"He's a father? Dear God, Elizabeth, you've taken up with an older man!"

"Mother! He's but eight years my senior and . . . Oh, for heaven' sake! I haven't taken up with anybody, least of all *him*. He had nothing to do with it. Do you understand? I spent the holiday with Phoebe and him and he was generous enough to offer their town house to me for a while."

Leonora studied her daughter thoughtfully for a moment. "How very kind of him. And how was your holiday?"

Elizabeth shrugged. "As good as can be expected under the circumstances. They have an enormous home in the country."

"He's fabulously wealthy, I gather."

"We're back to 'he' again? Mother, Alec Sinclair played little part in this."

"Alec? Why, the name alone conjures up all sorts of delightfully wicked thoughts."

"Mother!"

"Is he handsome?"

"I . . . I didn't notice."

Leonora erupted with a throaty laugh that resounded with innuendo well suited to Philippa Valentine. "Elizabeth, your face betrays you, darling. And here I'd thought you were immune! Tall?"

"Mother, stop it this instant!"

"Ooh, I just love them tall! And dark?"

"Mother!"

Leonora shivered with delight despite the cloak draped about her slender shoulders. "And just oozing virility, hmm?"

"Mother, cease your mindless prattle or I shall insist you leave!"

"Rich *and* handsome. You could do worse, Elizabeth."

"Mother! Lest you forget, I'm not in the market. Besides . . ." Elizabeth wisely chose to ignore her mother's rather unladylike snort in favor of further explanation. "I find I don't particularly like him. Or his blasted arrogance."

"Ooh!" Leonora squealed with delight. "They're the best kind! Elizabeth, go after this one! Do not let him get away!"

Elizabeth gasped. "Mother, are you daft? I can barely tolerate the man, much less his ill-bred behavior."

Leonora clasped Elizabeth's hands in hers and spoke in her most seasoned voice. "Tell me, what other men do you have in your life, hmm?"

"As a matter of fact," Elizabeth piped up with a self-satisfied smirk, "I have been solicited by a well-known philanthropist to assist him in his quest for better education for the poor. A young fellow, perhaps five years my senior. Mother, he shares my ideals, my hopes for improving the wretched state of the educational system."

Leonora nodded and her brows lifted. "Now that sounds promising. What's the fellow's name? Perhaps I've heard of him. Reggie's into that sort of thing, you know."

"Mother, I have little desire to get married, despite what you think."

"Oh, give it a rest, Elizabeth! Don't be such a wretched prude! Have some fun! What's the fellow's name?"

"Basil . . . Basil Christy, and he's merely a friend."

"What did you say?"

Elizabeth hesitated at her mother's sudden pallor. "I said he's merely a friend."

"No . . . no, his name."

Elizabeth repeated the name. "Why, do you know him?"

Leonora waved a hand dismissively and forced a cheery laugh. "Oh, I . . . no, for a moment I thought perhaps . . . But no . . . no, it couldn't possibly be. No, I don't know him."

"Well, perhaps you should familiarize yourself with his circle, for he's rather influential. Indeed, he's being honored at a gala benefit ten days hence and has asked me to accompany him."

"What were you planning to wear? Surely not one of those blasted brown sacks."

"I hadn't given the matter much thought."

"Perhaps you should from now on. How on earth did you become so entirely unconcerned with fashion and..." The violet eyes suddenly flew wide. "Of course! What a wonderful idea! Elizabeth, darling, just leave it to me! I shall send for my personal couturier. Oh, Gigi's simply marvelous with a needle and thread!"

"Mother, really, that is not necessary."

"Of course it is, you silly goose!" Leonora swept a gloved hand before her. "Why, you can't go looking like *that,* for heaven' sake!" Drawing Elizabeth's hand into the crook of her arm, she gave it a reassuring pat and proceeded toward the door. "Now, tell me, does Alec know anything of this Basil Christy?"

Elizabeth eyed her mother warily. "No, but what difference does it make?"

"Oh, Elizabeth, the things you've yet to learn!" Pausing inside the front door, Leonora squeezed her hand affectionately. "Now, I must be off. Reggie's expecting me, you know."

Closing the door behind her with a grim shake of her head, Elizabeth turned and spied her reflection in the mirror. She gave herself a vexed look. So she preferred a simple chignon to some elaborate and pretentious conglomeration of swirls and loops and enormous bows. Severe though it was, it suited her. Yet...

Her eyes traveled over the high-necked "brown sack." True, it did little for her figure, and the color was anything but complimentary, but it was serviceable and as comfortable as could be expected with her breasts so tightly bound. Yet...

A slender finger gingerly plucked at the tendrils escaping her chignon, as was their wont, much to her constant frustration. Without thought, she pulled the pins from the tightly knotted hair until the ebony curls fell unheeded to her waist. She shook her head and ran her fingers through the silky tresses, then stared blankly at her reflection. Now what? She hadn't a notion how to concoct anything but a thick braid or chignon. Perhaps this Gigi could assist her. Her heart beat a tad faster at the thought of a new dress, and she found, as she idly threaded her fingers through her hair, that she couldn't help but wonder at Alec's reaction were he to see her newly attired and sporting the latest in fashionable coiffures.

At that moment, the front door burst open and Phoebe, never one to practice a measured tread, bounded headlong into Elizabeth.

"Phoebe!"

"Miss Burbridge! I'm so awfully sorry I . . . Why, Miss Burbridge, your hair! It's so beautiful!"

Elizabeth stared blankly at the girl for a moment and idly twirled her hair in the very same manner she found so blastedly irritating when done by her students when they were lost in daydreams. "Thank you. I . . . I just washed it. What the devil are you doing here?"

Phoebe dropped her traveling bag with a weary sigh and doffed her cloak. "I came for a few nights' stay, until school resumes. Surely you must be frightfully lonely!"

"How did you make your way?"

Phoebe gave a lighthearted shrug. "I took Dunlevy's coach." She leaned closer and glanced covertly at Holmes, hovering stoically in a nearby doorway. Giving the servant a fake smile, she whispered hoarsely, "But don't tell Father, for he would not approve of my venturing about alone. I wished to summon Hiram, but Father is out and about somewhere so I had little choice. You see, I wished to come very badly!"

Elizabeth gave the girl a huge smile. "And I'm so very glad that you did. I was not relishing the idea of another night alone before the fire, despite my book and Cook's hot cider and macaroons."

Phoebe's eyes flew wide. "Ooh! That sounds divine! I shall come every weekend from now on."

For a moment, Elizabeth bent a knitted brow upon the younger girl. "Heed your father's advice, Phoebe, and come only if Hiram can bring you. Or summon Lewis. But for heaven' sake, don't venture about alone. Agreed?"

Phoebe's eyes twinkled with mischief. "On one condition."

"Condition?"

"I shall abide by your rules if I can brush your hair."

"What?"

"Oh, please, Miss Burbridge! It's so beautiful . . . so long and thick and shiny! Why on earth do you wear it so . . . so . . . well, it would be lovely coiled loosely and draped just so."

A sudden thought wriggled into Elizabeth's mind and she looked at Phoebe with new eyes. "Why, of course! I find I am in need of a new coiffure for an upcoming event I must attend."

Phoebe's brows shot up. "*You're* attending an *event?*"

"Why, yes, Phoebe."

"Alone?"

"No, I'm accompanying someone."

"A gentleman?"

"Why, as a matter of fact, yes. But—"

Phoebe squealed with unabashed glee. "Ooh! Miss Burbridge! You have a beau!"

"Phoebe! I have no such thing! Basil is merely a fr—"

"Basil? Ooh, what a lovely name for a beau! He sounds delightfully mysterious!"

"Phoebe, you've been reading far too many romance novels."

"Oh, poohey! Now, hush up! We must concoct a truly wonderful coiffure." Phoebe paused and made little effort to hide her distaste as her eyes swept Elizabeth from head to toe. "Are you perhaps considering a new dress?"

Elizabeth erupted with an exasperated sigh. "My mother is seeing to it that I am."

"Oh, thank heavens! Get into your nightgown and robe, Miss Burbridge, and we can cozy up to the fire down here."

Elizabeth could do nothing but comply with the young girl's instruction and a quarter of an hour later found herself padding into the front parlor wearing nothing but her nightgown, a wrapper and soft slippers. Phoebe awaited her, as did a crackling fire and a huge steaming mug of spiced cider. Once settled upon the floor and sipping the delicious drink, she decided it was not so scandalous enjoying oneself thus, especially on a particularly cold and gloomy evening when only the tangy cider could warm one's belly so divinely and chase the chill away. Besides, she was finding Phoebe's lighthearted spirit rather infectious.

She nibbled on a macaroon and sipped again of her cider while Phoebe perched on a chair behind her, wielding her brush and tending to her unbound hair. The fire sputtered, illuminating the darkened room with a yellow glow and capturing Elizabeth's unwavering attention. She basked in the warmth of the fire and the heat spreading like honey through her belly and into her limbs. My, but the cider was unusually potent....

"Will there be dancing at this event, Miss Burbridge?" Phoebe asked, her soft voice drawing Elizabeth from her reverie.

"Dancing?" Elizabeth swallowed a huge gulp of cider, emptying her mug, and shook her head. "I wouldn't know...perhaps. Dear God, I hope not."

"Why not? Oh, Miss Burbridge, dancing is such fun."

Feeling an unusual heat in her cheeks, Elizabeth replied, "Perhaps, though I wouldn't know."

The brush paused midstroke. "You mean you've never danced?"

"I've never learned."

"Oh, how awful!"

"It is not so awful, Phoebe. The idea that *you* have done so causes me some distress."

"Well, thank heavens I have or *you* would never have learned! Now, up you go!"

Elizabeth shook her head emphatically and waved a hand. "Oh, no. This is not the time for a lesson."

"Oh, poohey! What better time than the present?" Phoebe grasped Elizabeth's resisting hand and hauled her to her feet. The amber eyes widened slightly when Elizabeth swayed and clung to Phoebe's plump arm for several moments.

Pressing her fingers to her temple, Elizabeth smiled rather whimsically. "My, but it's unusually warm in here, don't you think?" She loosened her wrapper and shook her head. "And I must be a bit more tired than I'd thought." Quite suddenly her eyes flew wide and she erupted with an enormous hiccup that echoed through the room until it was obliterated by an uproarious howling. In another instant, both girls were bent over at the waist, clutching at their bellies as if in pain, though it was laughter, unbridled and silly, that rendered them thus. Yet another hiccup nearly proved their undoing and they all but fell to the floor, overcome by their hysteria.

Wiping a tear from her eye, Elizabeth sniffed and attempted to regain her breath, though controlling herself seemed beyond her realm. Doing her best to muffle another giggle, she glanced at Phoebe and sputtered, "I...I feel so strange...so... Why on earth is everything so blastedly funny?"

Both snorted and doubled over yet again until Elizabeth found her voice. "If I didn't know better, I would think it was that cider..." She paused as a thought occurred to her, and at that precise moment her gaze locked with Phoebe's guilt-ridden countenance. "Phoebe, what is it? What in God's name did you do? It *is* the cider, isn't it? For God's sake, tell me!"

"I...I..." Suppressing a smirk, Phoebe confessed, "I dipped into Father's rum. You see, he has often remarked that the brew adds just the right amount of kick."

Elizabeth stared at the girl. "Rum?" she croaked, pressing a hand to her temples. "Dear God, I'm intoxicated."

Phoebe nodded vigorously and stifled a giggle behind her hand. "As am I. Perhaps I added a bit too much."

"I'll say!"

And with that, both burst forth with another round of hysterical giggles, which culminated in Phoebe's grasping Elizabeth's hands and setting off about the room in a version of waltzing heretofore unknown to the civilized world. Around and around the room they danced, bellowing melody after melody for all the world to hear.

Upon passing by a low table, Elizabeth spied her book, the gift from Alec, and bent to retrieve the red velvet ribbon tucked between the pages. She looped it around her neck then tied it into an enormous bow atop her head, allowing two long streamers to dangle down either side. She twirled about the room, reveling in the feel of her unbound tresses, and on a whim left her wrapper and her slippers in a heap before the fire. She danced before the flames, head flung back, feeling the air upon her bare legs and the plushness of the rug between her toes. Lifting her arms above her head, she hummed aloud the lovely waltz playing so vibrantly within her mind and swayed in rhythm to the music.

As such, she was completely unaware that another had imposed his presence upon their merrymaking. Unaware, that is, until she ended her dance with a huge sigh and a whimsical smile, only to find her glazed eyes fixed upon the hulking figure standing just inside the room. The eyes fastened upon her were unreadable and harshly penetrating, but Alec Sinclair's all the same.

Chapter Nine

Elizabeth's next hiccup was met with a stony silence that sliced through the cheery ambience like a finely honed blade that served to sober both girls in the span of one hammering heartbeat. With a trembling hand, Elizabeth brushed aside a red velvet streamer that had managed to plop upon her nose and conjured up a faint voice, while her eyes did everything but meet his. "Lord...*hic!* Alec..."

Something flared in the depths of his eyes as they lowered momentarily from hers to sweep her from head to toe and back again as if it were his birthright to do so at such a leisurely pace. Had Elizabeth known that the fire burning softly behind her left very little to the imagination, she would have flung her wrapper about her with more than her usual amount of embarrassment. As it was, she turned to retrieve the robe and slippers and, in so doing, afforded a pair of smoky eyes the luxury of her silhouette in profile. Had she known the depth of passion her display aroused, she would have fled the house, nay, the country, without a backward glance. As it was, she donned the wrapper, knotting it at her waist, and pulled the ribbon from atop her head, wishing desperately not to hiccup again.

"Father..."

"Phoebe." The deep voice reverberated through Elizabeth and she knew even without looking at him that he had donned his thoroughly unreadable expression. "Elizabeth."

She glanced up hastily and clutched at the ribbon. Offering a weak smile, she gave an airy laugh. "We were...dancing."

His face remained passive. "Is that so?"

"Why, yes, Father." Phoebe materialized at Elizabeth's side and grasped her hand. "It seems Miss Burbridge is attending an event rather soon that will require her to dance, and we were simply . . . practicing."

His head inclined slightly, his eyes intently focused upon Elizabeth. "Is that so?"

"Oh, yes, Father, and she'll be on the arm of her new beau, Basil! Isn't that marvelous?"

His expression remained unreadable. "Marvelous."

Phoebe frowned and bit her lip with indecision. "I . . . I, uh, believe I shall be off to bed." She squeezed Elizabeth's hand and, with a conspiratorial wink and a smile, murmured in her most docile voice, "Good night, Miss Burbridge . . . Father."

"Oh yes, good night, Phoebe," Elizabeth managed to say, biting her lip against any giggles that threatened, then forcing a yawn behind her hand. "My, but it must be getting late. I shall retire, as well." Attempting to follow closely at Phoebe's heels, Elizabeth found her path suddenly blocked by an expanse of chest she found difficult to ignore.

"Elizabeth, a moment of your time."

With eyes cast downward and fixed upon nothing in particular, Elizabeth replied, "That would not be seemly."

She hastened to brush past him, then nearly cried out with frustration when his hand shot out to encase her wrist in his steely grip. Her eyes flew to his, then widened as he pulled her closer until her heaving chest all but touched his. Indeed, it seemed that with every breath she took Elizabeth felt the whisper of contact between them as if his chest were made not of corded muscle but molten steel capable of searing her to the core.

The firelight hollowed the rugged planes of his face, sharpening the chiseled features and lending him a harshness that set Elizabeth's blood coursing through her veins and her heart hammering within her breast. His eyes blazed with an emotion of their own and his mouth twisted into a wry smirk.

"You obviously gave little thought to the seemly and unseemly when you chose to discard your robe and frolic about my parlor like some woodland nymph. You had Holmes and

Lewis the coachman so agape I had to remind them of their manners. No doubt a score of passersby perched at the front window for a closer look."

Elizabeth gulped past the knot in her throat. For some blasted reason, the manner in which his eyes blazed and his beard-roughened cheek tensed suddenly proved rather humorous, given the circumstances, and she had to bite the insides of her cheeks to keep from erupting with an ill-timed giggle.

His eyes narrowed upon her, his grip tightening about her wrist. "What the hell's the matter with you?"

"Me?" Elizabeth erupted with a disbelieving laugh. "It was not I who stormed in here like some big wounded boar to forcibly restrain innocent maids." Twisting her hand from his grasp, she shook her tumbled tresses from her eyes. "Take your glowering and barking elsewhere, Alec. I'm in desperate need of my bed." With a haughty lift of her chin, she turned and, much to her horror, tripped over the red velvet ribbon dangling from her hand. Not that the rum in any way contributed to a graceful step.

In a flash, powerful hands swept about her waist, saving her from falling on her nose yet sparing her not one ounce of the embarrassment that poured over her like a bucket of ice-cold water. Or perhaps the undeniable heat of his hands spanning her waist, lingering far longer than was necessary to get her feet beneath her, flustered her beyond measure. Whatever it was, she found she could not meet his gaze when he turned her toward him and bent to peer closely into her eyes.

"If I didn't know you better, I would think that you were..." He paused to lean even closer to her, as if he were listening for her breathing, and she was assailed with his spicy, woodsy scent and her legs threatened to dissolve beneath her yet again. His gaze shifted to the empty mugs lying innocently enough upon the table. "You're drunk," he stated flatly.

Elizabeth managed a noisy swallow and her eyes finally met his. He paused for the briefest of moments, then threw his head back and roared with laughter. Elizabeth stared in mute horror, then abandoned her quest to remain impassive. Her laughter bubbled forth, mixing pleasantly with his hearty chuckles and filling the room with a cheery ambience once again.

For several moments, she was completely unaware that his hands remained about her waist, but when he suddenly ceased laughing and their eyes met above a looming silence, she grew supremely conscious of far more. His hands moved against her waist, the thumbs brushing feather-light over her ribs and sending waves of shock through her that brought a gasp to her lips. Retrieving her scattered wits, she pushed his hands aside and forced an airy laugh. "I really . . . I must see myself to bed. Good night."

Elizabeth remained blissfully ignorant of any attempts made to stop her this time, for she spun about and fled the room without a backward glance. She scurried into her room, slamming the door so forcibly in her wake that the sound echoed throughout the house before coming to rest upon the broad-shouldered figure staring thoughtfully into the dying fire.

Fairly early the next morning, though somewhat later than was her wont, Elizabeth emerged from her room and descended the stairs on legs so blastedly unreliable she had to grip the rail with both hands. Squinting against the brilliant sun flooding the breakfast nook, she carefully made her way to her chair, eased herself into the cushiony seat and pressed her palm against her pounding head, closing her eyes.

"Good morning, Elizabeth. I trust you slept well."

Her eyes flew wide to meet Alec's infernally raised brow and amused smirk just across the table from her. Bestowing a chilling glare upon that atrociously cheery visage, she lowered her head into her hands once more. "You're still here?"

"I live here, remember?"

"That does little to ease my plight."

His chuckle filled the room. "I'm afraid there's relatively little *anyone* could do for you, Elizabeth. Could it be, perhaps, that your generous consumption of rum and cider last eve left you with a monumental hangover?"

Elizabeth squeezed her eyes tight against that mocking tone he applied so liberally whenever he spoke to her. He was so jolly and dapper, impeccably garbed and grinning from ear to ear

like a well-fed lion. At the moment, she would gladly endure
this "hangover" if he would leave her to do so in peace. Silence, therefore, proved the best reply, and she soundly ignored him, peering about the table for the teapot. Spying it just
out of reach, she attempted to rise, when he all but bounded
from his chair with a cheery, "Allow me." He placed the tea
before her then reseated himself, much to Elizabeth's annoy-
ance, which she made little effort to hide. This only seemed to
feed his twisted sense of humor and he gave her a dazzling grin
that would have rendered her a breathless, quivering mass had
she not hated the cad so intensely.

"So, tell me, Elizabeth, what is this event that drove you to
frolicking last evening?" He paused as if lost in thought, then
offered in a voice positively dripping with gallantry, "I would
be more than happy to instruct you to dance in a manner more,
shall I say, *fitting* for public display."

Elizabeth scowled in his general direction and waved a hand,
indicating the door. "Go away. You make my head positively
ache."

She received a soft chuckle in reply and he shifted in his
chair, drawing her gaze to his fingers toying idly with the flat-
ware before him. Such powerful hands he possessed. She
scowled all the more at the thought.

"I trust you intend to abandon this unattractive mood in favor of your typical lighthearted manner before accompanying
this Basil to your event? You may risk losing him if you do
otherwise."

"One cannot lose what one does not have," Elizabeth replied irritably, attempting to nibble at a warm muffin.

"Ah then, I wish you luck in acquiring him as your beau."

Elizabeth abandoned the muffin and gritted her teeth. "I
harbor no such desires. Basil is simply a friend, and a friend he
shall remain."

"And woe unto he who wishes to be otherwise, eh?"

She scowled at his empty plate. "Are you finished?"

He toyed with his teacup. "So where did you meet this
friendly fellow? Surely so pure and chaste a miss did not stumble upon him by her own doing."

Elizabeth shot him a look of disgust. "You no doubt find it difficult to believe there exists one female whose sole purpose in life is *not* to acquire a beau."

"I would be less than truthful with you, sweet Elizabeth, if I did not admit that such a preoccupation of women's minds makes my life a hell of a lot more enjoyable."

Elizabeth grimaced. "Thank heavens Basil feels differently."

"You neglected to mention that the poor sot was simpleminded."

"Sot?" She hastened to her friend's defense in a strident voice. "Why, I would wager a hefty sum that he's not the type to habitually indulge in spirits, and as for his intellect, Alec, let me just say this. One does not achieve his lofty status of honored philanthropist without the benefit of a certain amount of brilliance. Why, he is so highly thought of here in London that he's being honored at that gala event I shall attend with him, benefiting education for the poor and underprivileged." Elizabeth donned her best smug look. "So there."

Alec suddenly frowned and leaned his forearms upon the table. "What did you . . . ?"

His words remained forever lost upon Elizabeth, for at that moment Phoebe padded into the room wearing a forced smile and a lopsided bow atop tumbled ringlets and a face devoid of color. She squinted as if in pain as the brilliant sunlight met her bleary eyes, then groped for a chair and sank into it with a heavy sigh.

The ever-so-helpful Alec hastened to place before her a cup of warm tea, which elicited a wince and shake of her head. With a smirk, he remarked, "I believe it would serve us well if I were to inform Cook that her cider was unusually potent last evening, Phoebe. Judging by your pallor, I would say you overindulged by just a few cups. Or perhaps you joined Elizabeth in her pillaging of the rum, though one has to wonder whose idea it was in the first place."

"Mine," the two young women said in perfect unison. They exchanged startled glances, which drew Alec's thoughtful regard, though Phoebe's blush proved far more revealing than any words at the moment.

His gaze swung to Elizabeth, and he was favored with her
first attempt at a smile all morning and a helpless lift of her
shoulders. "I . . . well, it's an old family custom to mix the two
brews. Perhaps I was a trifle heavy-handed. I shall reimburse
you for . . ."

He waved a dismissing hand. "That's entirely unnecessary.
Besides, despite the pains you feel today, I would venture to say
you made little dent in the rum supply." His eyes flickered over
her and she felt a sudden compulsion to remind the man of his
manners. "Put your excess coin toward the dress fund, Elizabeth. Surely your Basil expects you to be garbed in something
besides *that* awful excuse for a gown."

Elizabeth's gasp of outrage was obliterated by Phoebe's
quick response. "Oh, but, Father, Miss Burbridge has every
intention of acquiring a beautiful new dress! But the event is
just ten days hence! Oh my, but have you engaged a couturier?
And what of the color and fabric? Just imagine the possibili-
ties!"

Elizabeth raised her brows as if she, too, delighted in such
trivialities, and her eyes flickered to Alec. She was met with a
look of such sudden intensity she nearly fled the room. "Red
velvet," he murmured.

Phoebe's gasp of glee went unnoticed by the others. "Now
there's an idea!"

For some reason, beneath his unwavering regard, Elizabeth
felt entrapped, ensnared and exposed, as if with one searing
glance he could sweep aside every attempt at modesty, every
chaste thought. He looked as if he would say something, then,
apparently thinking the better of it, slid his chair from the table and rose to his towering height. Tossing his linen napkin
upon the table, he gave them both an encouraging grin. "I shall
leave you both to nurse your ailments. Have little fear, it will
be but a faint memory by midafternoon." He paused to deposit a kiss upon his daughter's head, then strode from the
room, leaving a shaken Elizabeth to confront, yet again, the
jumble of emotions he awakened within her.

In spite of her exhaustive efforts to the contrary, Elizabeth
stood before her full-length mirror ten days later, wearing what

her mother breathlessly referred to as "that ravishing red velvet confection." She had refused to abide by the choice of color not just once but scores of times, only to be hastily and rather carelessly dismissed by the effervescent Gigi. The woman, though brilliant with a needle and thread, possessed such a wicked tongue that Elizabeth nearly died of humiliation at least a dozen times. Leonora and the ever present Phoebe, however, found the couturier's lack of good taste engaging and responded with high-pitched squeals of delight and low, throaty giggles whenever the commentary grew exceptionally risqué. Both heartily agreed with the choice of color and fabric, reassuring a stricken Elizabeth that red was *her* color.

Elizabeth would consider it a feat to parade in the dress before the servants, much less a roomful of highbrow philanthropists, without collapsing in a scandalized heap. Surely the frock's color alone would raise a few brows. She wondered with growing anxiety at the response to the low neckline and the poufed three-quarter-length sleeves poised just off her shoulders. That alone left her feeling all but naked. But the scandalous manner in which her bosom threatened to spill from the gown filled her with such unabashed terror that she clutched at the fabric as if to keep herself contained.

With a disapproving *"Tsk! Tsk!"* her mother brushed her hands aside for the hundredth time and wagged a finger. "Elizabeth, for heaven' sake, you must forget about your bosom."

Elizabeth tugged again at the bodice. "I fear I cannot."

"And neither will your Basil," Gigi drawled in her throaty, wicked tone as she tended to Elizabeth's coiffure with expert hands. She had coiled the glossy locks loosely about Elizabeth's head and caught them at the back with an enormous red velvet bow. "This self-consciousness you feel because of the dress, your hair... because of your innocence, it will all vanish in an instant when *he* looks at you. Trust me, darling, the right look from the right man and you will be positively overflowing with confidence."

"Basil is not my beau ... merely a friend."

Gigi shrugged and added a final pat to the bow. "But a man nevertheless. Trust me, darling, no man will be able to take his eyes from you tonight. You are an absolute vision. Such a transformation I have never seen!''

"Oh, Miss Burbridge, you are so beautiful. I wish Charlotte Lambert were here to see you!'' Phoebe clasped her hands to her mouth. "And wouldn't Father be surprised that we took his suggestion for the color.''

Elizabeth felt herself wince, though she managed to bestow a heated glare upon her mother's arched brow.

"My, my,'' Leonora drawled, running her hands over Elizabeth's tiny waist then adding an extra pouf to the huge bustle, all the while keeping her eyes upon her daughter's averted face. "One can only imagine the man's reaction? So, tell us, Phoebe, where *is* your Father this evening? I would enjoy meeting the man.''

Elizabeth shot her mother a frigid look, which Leonora wisely chose to ignore in favor of the rapt attention she turned upon Phoebe.

The young girl shrugged. "Some business function, though one never knows with Father. If he is in London, chances are he will stay here for the night.''

"Mmm...'' Leonora mused in a tone that sorely tested Elizabeth's resolve not to pinch her mother's slender arm. Had Phoebe not been present, she would have erupted with a strident scolding and a heated denial of whatever it was her mother was implying. Leonora turned to face her daughter, though her attention remained on smoothing the invisible wrinkles in the gown. "He may see you yet, darling.''

Holmes's soft rapping upon the door announcing Basil's arrival served to send the room into an uproar. Before she could do more than embrace her mother and murmur her thanks, Elizabeth found her black velvet cloak about her shoulders and a fur muff pressed into her hands while the trio burst forth with their last words of advice, all of which were lost upon Elizabeth. Indeed, as she made her way from the room with the twittering voices in her wake, she could not deny the nagging sense of dismay that the man awaiting her was not Alec Sinclair.

Chapter Ten

Elizabeth paused at the top of the stairs to catch her breath, her nervous gaze focusing on the black-cloaked figure standing just inside the front portal. She could have sworn he lingered far too long before his reflection in the mirror, smoothing his sleek hair, then leaning closer to flash himself a toothy grin. Her tread upon the stairs apparently snatched him from his preoccupation, for he uttered a startled grunt, as if he'd been caught with his hand in the cookie jar. Spinning about, he drew a deep breath, puffing up his chest, and gallantly strode to meet her at the bottom of the stairs.

When her eyes met his, her heart fell to her toes and she had to avert her gaze lest he sense her distress. The look of shock swept across his ruddy features so quickly that had she not been so supremely self-conscious of her appearance, she would never have noticed. Much to her dismay, however, she saw it for what it was, along with his hasty attempt to paste on a smile while he held a hand to the door. Dear God, he hated her... hated the dress. It was all wrong.

She drew the cloak tight about her neck with one hand, clutching fiercely at her muff with the other. He was such a gentleman, in his elegant evening attire, while she looked no better than some shameless tart with nothing but mischief on her mind. Poor Basil! He was obviously too chivalrous to abandon her upon her doorstep with a hastily dreamed up apology, even if he would save face with his philanthropic peers.

She refused to meet his eyes as he assisted her aboard his black barouche. Perhaps she should afford him with her own excuse and save the poor man's hide. She opened her mouth, only to be struck with a horrid thought. If she did indeed plead a suddenly aching head, this would surely cast her in even worse a light than the blasted dress, leaving Basil with little choice but to choose another partner for his project, which she had little intention of relinquishing without some sort of fight. Thus, she bit her tongue, managing a smile in his direction as he seated himself beside her and motioned to the driver.

Silence hovered about them, serving as a reminder that neither had spoken, save for their murmured exchange of greetings. Elizabeth stared at her muff and tried to call to mind some appropriate comment, though none seemed to materialize upon her knotted tongue.

"You look lovely."

Basil's words tore through her like the slice of a jagged knife. Dear God! Could a man be more selfless, more sensitive to her needs? That he could still speak with such genuine feeling, despite the distress he so valiantly concealed, convinced Elizabeth he possessed the most sterling of characters.

"Thank you," she managed to reply, slanting her eyes at him, only to avert them quickly to her muff. He peered so intently at her she almost threw herself from the vehicle in shame.

His voice jarred her once again. "I was a trifle surprised by your note instructing me not to retrieve you at Dunlevy. How long will you be visiting your friends?"

With an attempt at a casual shrug and a light manner, she replied, "Oh, perhaps a few weeks longer. They're...old, very old family friends...and I see them so infrequently." She looked away, closing her eyes against the sick feeling that rose like acrid bile whenever she lied through her teeth. Even a man of Basil's fine character would be incapable of concealing his horror if she were to reveal under whose roof she slept, night after night. What in God's name had she been thinking to accept Alec's offer in the first place? And why, oh why had she allowed her mother, of all people, to oversee the creation of this blasted dress?

"Perhaps I know them," Basil ventured. "Their name?"

Elizabeth hesitated. "Uh... Al— I mean, Sinclair. I'm sure you've never heard of them."

Elizabeth detected a hesitation on Basil's part as if he were lost in thought a moment. "No...the name is unfamiliar. And is your mother visiting, as well?"

"Oh, no. You see, she lives here in London and...travels. When Father died—"

"Oh, I had no idea. I'm terribly sorry."

"Thank you, but you see, he died when I was very young. I never really knew him."

"Your mother must be dreadfully lonely."

Elizabeth forced an airy laugh. "Oh, she manages somehow. So, what of your family?"

"I'm afraid I, too, lost my father when I was very young. Mother passed on ten years ago, and Stepfather is a good man. I've remained with him, aiding with his business ventures and projects of this sort. Now that he's ailing..."

He paused, far longer than he had previously, and Elizabeth had to glance at him for fear she had erred once more by asking him so personal a question. She was, however, struck with a fleeting sense of disquiet when she was met with a penetrating, powerful look. For some reason she knew it was not grief he displayed and was taken aback when he asked, "May I call you Elizabeth?"

She blinked several times. "Of course."

He leaned closer to her, so close that she could smell his hair tonic. Her eyes flew to his and the thumping of her heart eased when she viewed the sincere appreciation in the depths of his dark eyes. For some blasted reason she was assailed with the vision of Alec's tousled hair, devoid of anything but its windswept scent, as he lowered his lips to hers....

"Elizabeth, I cannot tell you how grateful I am that you have agreed to assist me. My only hope is that you will not find yourself with little time for other pursuits, such as your work...or perhaps a beau who might feel a trifle ignored."

Elizabeth glanced away and Alec's arrogant smirk loomed into her consciousness. "I have no beau."

"A shame, if you ask me."

Elizabeth flushed beneath his regard. "I find that my work does not lend itself to such frivolities."

"Indeed. A passion for one's work makes life worth living, though, and I'm certain you'd agree, finding someone who shared that passion would truly test one's resolve to remain unwed."

She was given little chance to ponder Basil's remark, for the barouche pulled to a stop. Grasping his outstretched hand, she stepped from the buggy then allowed him to escort her toward the entrance of an enormous white marble building. As they proceeded up the few steps, her widening eyes surveyed the grand entrance, flanked by four enormous white marble columns and brilliantly lit by more than a score of flickering gas lamps. Twin doors of heavy polished wood swept open before them and they found themselves swallowed by a tremendous crowd. The ceiling overhead, three stories above them, was ornately carved marble with intricately painted domes that echoed with the din of the throng below.

Women drifted past by the score, glamorously outfitted from head to toe in every imaginable shade of taffeta and silk, sporting enormous bustles and the latest in hats and leaning on the arms of elegantly garbed escorts. The orchestra was strategically positioned before an imposing fountain whose gentle fall of water lent the lyrical strains an appropriate accompaniment. Impeccably attired gentlemen with thoroughly somber expressions hastened about balancing silver trays laden with sparkling glasses of what Elizabeth soon discovered was champagne, for Basil rather efficiently retrieved two glasses and pressed one into her hand with an encouraging smile.

"Champagne. Try it."

Raising her glass to his in a silent toast, she managed the smallest of sips, then watched with some surprise as Basil drained his glass in one gulp. Glancing away, she instinctively reached to test the fastener at the top of her cloak. Poor man! So nervous he was! Her eye scanned the crowd and, in particular, the myriad gowns on display. She supposed she should have drawn some measure of confidence from the styles the other women wore. Though try as she might to convince herself otherwise, she was quite certain that none of the colors was as bright a red as hers nor the fit quite as...dramatic. She clutched at the clasp of her cloak and nearly died when Basil's eye swept over the garment.

"Shall I?" he offered, extending his arm.

"No...no! Thank you just the same!" she replied a little too heartily, and snuggled within the velvet folds. "I fear I'm still a bit chilled."

Basil flashed a grin and stopped a servant in his tracks to obtain yet another glass of champagne. "Nothing like a little champagne to chase the chill away."

Elizabeth smiled gamely and sipped again, allowing her eyes to venture about the throng. "There must be over two hundred people here."

Basil nodded and the keen eyes darted about. "Indeed, and it is a shame I know so very few of them. You see, my work with Stepfather keeps me inordinately busy with relatively little time to enjoy the socializing that is so very much a part of a philanthropist's obligations. I feel, however, that generous donations and time spent on pursuing projects such as ours benefit the cause far more than making idle chitchat in order to meet the proper people. Don't you agree?"

"Oh, indeed," Elizabeth murmured, averting her gaze lest he detect that his every word struck some chord within her, as if he knew exactly what to say.

"You're not disappointed?"

"Oh, heavens no! I've never been very good in crowds. Besides, it is an honor simply to witness your receiving such a token of esteem." Elizabeth paused, feeling his eyes intent upon her, as if the mood between them had suddenly changed dramatically.

"No more an honor than escorting a beautiful and intelligent young woman to such an event," he said, and received in reply a gulp and a blush, accompanied by a murmur of thanks. He leaned closer to her, his hand grasping hers. "Elizabeth, I have such respect for you. Indeed, I would find myself drawn to you regardless of your physical beauty. Oh, dear Lord, I've spoken out of turn. Please...you needn't turn away." Much to her surprise, he drew her fingers to his mouth. "Lovely Elizabeth, perhaps I speak too soon."

Elizabeth felt the urge to tug gently upon her hand, still soundly clasped in his. "You've caught me somewhat by surprise."

He seemed to study her trembling fingers. "I fear I cannot help myself. I've never met another quite like you, a woman who so completely embodies that which I desire in a wi— Oh, there I go again. Forgive me. It is highly unprofessional, and if we are to work alongside one another, I promise I shall keep a tight rein upon my feelings, though it will be a test of will, to be sure, and . . ."

At that precise moment, Basil chose to reach for yet another glass of champagne from a fleet-footed servant. Perhaps due to his preoccupation with Elizabeth, he made his move a tad too late, or perhaps his two previously ingested glasses had rendered him a trifle clumsy. Whatever it was, his movements were less than nimble, and in the process of retrieving his glass he upset two others, which tumbled from the tray, spilling cool champagne down the entire length of Elizabeth's cloak.

Gasping in shock, she jumped several steps back and hastened to sweep the champagne from her sodden garment. Over the din of mounting panic in her ears, she heard Basil's effusive apology and the murmurs of several others who had witnessed the accident. One stepped forward to swipe a crisp white handkerchief over the cloak, which Elizabeth held away from her at an angle with one hand until someone removed her glass from her grasp.

The bystander wielding the handkerchief spoke brusquely to Basil. "On the table, there, over by the orchestra. More napkins, man, she'll need more napkins."

Basil's "Oh, of course," and the indignant brow he raised were both lost upon Elizabeth, for at the sound of the bystander's voice, her head snapped up and wide violet eyes met smoky gray.

"Alec!" Her hand brushed his handkerchief away as if it were suddenly aflame.

"Elizabeth." The mischief in his otherwise innocent grin was unmistakable. "You're looking well, my dear."

Her teeth gnashed. "What are you doing here?"

"What are *you* doing here?" His eyes strayed a moment to Basil's departing form and hers followed, focusing on Basil's sleek black head as the poor man wandered aimlessly about in search of napkins. Elizabeth's gaze swung to the rugged profile towering above her and her heart fluttered to life within her breast. Alec looked incredibly dashing in his formal attire, all crisply starched black and white, with his hair typically windblown and entirely too masculine for such an occasion. His topcoat and trousers were as well tailored as any of those in attendance, yet somehow the length of his muscular legs and the breadth of his chest made the ensemble almost risqué. Indeed, the man virtually screamed virility. The cynically raised brow he bestowed upon her did little to ease her plight. "Your friend Basil isn't wasting any time, is he?"

Elizabeth's brows swept together in a perplexed frown. "Excuse me?"

The gray eyes flickered over her. "Then again, perhaps you caused the man to forget his manners." His gaze locked with hers. "Red velvet. It suits you."

Elizabeth's mouth fell open then snapped shut with a decided click. "He has been nothing but a gentleman."

Alec stuffed his handkerchief into his trouser pocket. "A gentleman might refrain from wooing his lady until he'd found a more intimate location. A fragrant garden, soft music, dim lights... They would, no doubt, aid his cause." His hands freed the clasp of her cloak and settled about her shoulders before she even realized, unmindful as she was of anything but the sensuous purr of his voice.

"Stop it!" she hissed, attempting to twist from his grasp, only to realize he'd whisked the cloak from her shoulders. She pressed a trembling hand to her décolletage as the heat of her flush collided with the cool air sweeping her bare skin. Her voice failed her, though she was very much aware of Alec's eyes upon her and that he, too, did not speak for several achingly long moments. Some baser instinct told her it was not contempt or revulsion smoldering in his eyes, though this offered her little insight as to why she should suddenly feel as if he'd stripped her of *all* her clothing.

"I can understand why you wanted to keep the damned thing on," he muttered, drawing a pace nearer. Elizabeth would have turned and fled had Basil's gracious tone not crashed upon her befuddled senses.

"Elizabeth, I managed to locate several napkins and..." He skidded to a breathless halt before her, extending a handful of linen napkins, which were soundly ignored. Elizabeth almost groaned with shame when his eyes widened and traveled the length of her dress, then rose to fix upon the display of her bosom.

"My God... Elizabeth..." was all he managed through his slackened mouth.

Elizabeth reached for her cloak, only to choke with frustration when Alec chose that precise moment to drape the garment casually over his arm, just out of her reach.

"I couldn't have said it better myself," Alec drawled in a tone that implied many an impure thought.

Basil swung a stormy brow upon Alec. "Who the hell are *you?*"

Alec shifted the cloak in his arms and extended his hand, nearly brushing Elizabeth's bodice as he did so. Her eyes fixed upon the men's hands as they clasped and she was struck by the thought that Alec's looked as if it could crush the other man's with one beefy squeeze. "Sinclair. Alec Sinclair. A friend of Miss Burbridge."

Basil's dark brows drew lower in a thoughtful frown. "Sinclair... Sinclair..." His eyes widened and darted between Elizabeth and Alec several times. "You're the—she's staying with *you?*"

Alec gave a half smile that verged upon a smirk. "I don't believe I caught your name, old chap."

"Christy, Basil Christy." Giving Alec a suspicious look, Basil reached for Elizabeth's cloak, a gesture that Alec either did not notice or purposefully chose to ignore.

"Christy... Any relation to Nigel Cosgrove, by any chance?"

"My stepfather." Basil's voice, laced with unsuppressed irritation, made Elizabeth wonder why the two men seemed to have taken an instant dislike to each other. She glanced at

Alec's unreadable visage, noting that he seemed to be enjoying himself in some perverse way.

"I do some business with Nigel from time to time," Alec offered.

"Oh, of course," Basil quickly replied with a glance at Elizabeth. "Now I remember."

Alec's gaze narrowed upon the other man. "I don't seem to recall Nigel ever mentioning you."

"Basil is heavily involved with philanthropic work," Elizabeth piped up, much to both men's surprise. She found herself the object of two heated stares. With a game smile, she waved her hand lightly. "Perhaps that's the reason."

"Of course," Alec replied. His eyes lingered upon her longer than was appropriate, and she was left to wonder how long he would have stood there staring had an elegantly attired, white-haired gentleman not appeared at his side at that moment. After lending the man his ear, Alec turned to Elizabeth. "A matter requires my attention. Elizabeth, I shall tend to your cloak." His gaze flickered to Basil. "Christy. Enjoy your evening." And with that, he turned on his heel and disappeared into the crowd.

Without realizing it, Elizabeth released her breath with a tremendous *whoosh*, which drew Basil's eye from the departing figure. His scowl seemed to deepen when his eyes found hers, prompting a response. Elizabeth said the first thing that popped into her mind. "My, the champagne. I'm rather warm of a sudden."

Basil's eyes momentarily grazed her bare shoulders and she groaned inwardly, for no woman, despite the amount of champagne she'd gulped, would be even remotely warm in a gown so daringly cut. Though when Alec had looked at her a few moments before, she'd felt the heat of her blush clear to the toes of her red satin slippers.

If Basil harbored the slightest suspicion at her reply, he was gentleman enough to let it pass and he gestured to a flight of stairs leading to the balconied mezzanine overlooking the main floor. "So, does this Alec Sinclair have a wife somewhere?" he inquired as they mounted the stairs.

Elizabeth hesitated in her reply. "They divorced quite some time ago."

"I see. Any children?"

"One. A daughter, Phoebe. She attends Dunlevy." Elizabeth searched the ruddy face for any hint that his was not simply idle curiosity. After all, she should have explained all this to him before. Why hadn't she?

"How very convenient." His hand grasped her elbow and guided her to a spot along the carved railing directly above the fountain. The orchestra's melody drifted to them, and for a moment Elizabeth lost herself in the lyrical strains until Basil's terse tone snatched her attention. "Really, Elizabeth, at the risk of seeming too forward, I must say that your staying on at the Sinclair town house without a chaperon is somewhat out of the ordinary." He leaned closer to her and his brows rose. "People may talk."

What people? "I really don't think—"

"Elizabeth, you never know what kind of a man Alec Sinclair may be, what his reputation could be! I find him rather arrogant, to be perfectly honest." He looked at her sharply, as if suddenly struck by a thought. "And what does Miss Percy think of all this?"

Elizabeth was saved from fabricating a response when some commotion directly below them drew their attention to the white-haired gentleman standing before a huge podium. The crowd grew quiet and the gentleman's deep voice echoed through the place. From what Elizabeth could discern, the man had the honor of bestowing thanks upon two of the most generous benefactors to the cause. Her eyes lifted to Basil's profile and her smile faded when she glimpsed his rigid countenance, the tightly held mouth and narrowed eyes focused intently upon something below. Why, if she hadn't known any better, she would have thought the man was seething with anger.

"Basil, perhaps you should go below to accept..."

Elizabeth's words died on her tongue when the name Nigel Cosgrove rang clearly from below, followed by the brief explanation that, due to illness, Nigel was unable to attend and his solicitor, Charles Boyd, was present in his stead. Elizabeth's surprise at this escalated into full-blown shock when the second of the benefactors was announced.

There was no mistaking this man as he moved to the podium, towering head and shoulders above the rest of the crowd and moving with an athletic grace better suited to taming his wild stallion, Sebastian. Yet he seemed perfectly at ease before such a throng, his smile easy, almost boyish, as he accepted the token of appreciation. Dear God, the man almost looked humble, if it were possible! Elizabeth's focus narrowed on that handsome countenance, even more captivating, or so it seemed, as he stood before the crowd and spoke briefly on the urgency of the cause. Alec Sinclair, the eccentric heathen who wolfed down his food, kept a menagerie of equally eccentric friends and harbored not a care in the world for proper decorum, was a champion of *her* cause. Arrogant man! Why hadn't he told her?

"Well, well," Basil mused. "You didn't tell me your friend Alec possessed any altruistic tendencies besides those he reserves for beautiful young schoolteachers."

Elizabeth chose to ignore his insinuation in favor of defending herself. "I hadn't a notion. Why, I would think you'd have known of the man, as involved as you are."

"Ah, Elizabeth." Basil's tone grew wistful. "Therein lies the problem. You see, as oftentimes happens with causes such as this, typically the individual who commits the most time and effort is not the one to receive the praise." He inclined his head below. "Like Boyd over there." Elizabeth's eyes followed. "You see, Elizabeth, the man is an opportunist, capitalizing on any and every opportunity to further his own interests at Stepfather's expense."

"And yours, to my eye!"

Basil donned a sheepish smile. "Why, I never would have thought of it that way, my dear. My dedication leaves me far too busy to haggle with Boyd over such frivolities."

Elizabeth had to shake her head with wonder at this selfless man, though for some reason she found it difficult to believe that Basil would step aside for Mr. Charles Boyd, whose diminutive stature, small features and large protruding ears made him look very much like a mouse. She now understood the steely eyes Basil leveled upon the little man meandering about below, yet decided freshening up a bit might serve her better than pressing this matter. She excused herself, politely declining his offer to accompany her with a suggestion that he find them something to eat among the buffet tables.

Navigating her way through the crowd proved far easier than securing directions to the women's toilette, and she found herself in a wide hallway following a pair of chattering older ladies whose heavily powdered faces looked in need of retouching. Their pace was quite slow, which, in addition to testing Elizabeth's patience, allowed her opportunity to venture long glances into the huge rooms on either side. Most of the doors were open, offering any so desirous an opportunity to slip away from the crowd for a few private moments. Elizabeth was surprised to find the rooms empty, save for their scattering of elegant gilt furniture, though when she passed one particular room, the sound of deep voices drew more than a momentary glance. This she regretted immediately.

No sooner had she glimpsed Alec's dark head than his eyes lifted and locked with hers. With what had to be a hastily mumbled apology to the three gentlemen beside him, he appeared at her elbow before her scurrying feet could deliver her elsewhere.

"Looking for someone, Elizabeth? Me, perhaps?" His voice, close to her ear, caused her to stiffen, though her step did not falter. Unfortunately, the two older women had disappeared and she did not know where she was going. She barely noticed his light grip upon her elbow when he spoke in a gently teasing tone. "Your Basil needs his head examined for allowing you to venture about unescorted. There's little telling who you could bump into."

"Indeed!"

"Ah, a little surly, I see. Is your beau not showing you a good time?"

Elizabeth ground her teeth and shot him a vexed look. He returned a lazy smile, which only added to her frustration when she realized they'd come upon the end of the hallway.

Alec peered curiously at her and lifted a brow. "Now where, my lady?"

"Where are *you* going?"

"With you, of course."

Elizabeth twisted her arm from his grasp, only to find her hand encased in his. Suddenly, he was pulling her along behind him, striding quite determinedly into yet another deserted room. "Release me, this instant!" she huffed.

Alec turned abruptly and Elizabeth was graced with a sweep of his eyes that instantly parched her throat and snatched her words away. "Relax, Elizabeth. I only wish a word with you."

"And I you!" she returned with force.

He smirked and held a hand before him. "Ladies first."

Drawing a breath, she attempted to cross her arms over her chest in a manner that would lend her a sterner demeanor. Much to her dismay, however, the gesture only served to push her bosom nearly out of her gown, a veritable feast for the smoldering eyes that fastened upon the high curves. She swung about, clasping a hand to her flushed décolletage and wincing at his softly murmured words.

"You're far too beautiful to be embarrassed by a look of appreciation. Surely your Basil has given you his share."

Drawing herself up with a deep breath, she cast him a stormy look. "Basil is a gentleman, and one who manages to keep such ... such ..." She shook her head, at a sudden loss. "Such *notions* to himself."

His chuckle filled the room. "Then the man deserves a medal, for that is an endeavor that escapes me."

"As does speaking the truth." Elizabeth turned an unflinching glare upon him. "Why didn't you tell me you were going to be here, and that you are so involved with a cause you *must* know I feel strongly about?"

His eyes narrowed upon her. "Is that why you're so angry? I'll admit it was indeed a blunder on my part, for I suppose you would have come with me then, instead of your Basil."

"Stop mocking me!" She gasped with outrage then nearly clawed his eyes from his head when his gaze dipped to her bosom for several excruciatingly long moments. "Have you no decency?"

"Have a care, sweet Elizabeth," he murmured. "It's not every day that I am privileged with such magnificent displays. I fear I cannot help myself."

Something in his tone and the undeniable look in his eyes sapped the anger from Elizabeth in one fleeting moment and filled her limbs with molten lead. She swallowed, attempting to call to mind some reason why she felt such hostility toward him all of a sudden. Intuition told her it was not simply his secrecy regarding this function. No, she knew all too well the reason for her ire, this feeling that she was out of control. Hadn't Gigi said it best? *The right look from the right man...*

"Oh, for goodness' sake. Can it be? Alec? Alec Sinclair?"

At the sound of the sultry feminine voice, Elizabeth peered around Alec's broad-shouldered frame at the beautiful woman lingering with some uncertainty in the doorway. She was slightly shorter than Elizabeth, slim yet undeniably curvy in her off-the-shoulder dress of rich emerald green taffeta. Her honey blond locks were swept from her face, and when a slow smile teased her full lips, Elizabeth was struck by a gnawing familiarity. There was no denying that this woman and Alec knew each other, for when the woman spoke again, Elizabeth felt something akin to fear grip her.

"Why, of course it's you. I should have known." The amber eyes sparkled like twin stars. "No man can fill a doorway quite like you, Alec."

"Celestine."

From her vantage, Elizabeth watched the back of Alec's head nod briefly as he replied, then he turned to Elizabeth, all but ignoring the other woman. Her gaze flickered over Elizabeth in a manner that left Elizabeth with no doubt that if this Celestine did not know Alec *very* well, she certainly wished she did. A fair brow lifted ever so sightly and the amber eyes slid to Alec's profile. "Ah, I see. Perhaps we shall speak later, hmm?" And with that, she turned and disappeared in a rustle of crisp taffeta.

"Who was that?" Elizabeth blurted without thinking.

"Who?" Alec replied distractedly, and she felt his eyes playing upon her hair, sliding unhurriedly over her face.

She gave him a befuddled look. "Who? That woman. Who is she?"

"Oh... her." He scowled in the general direction of the doorway and his hesitation only made Elizabeth's heart hammer all the more urgently. "Nothing to concern yourself with, Elizabeth. She's merely the woman I was once unfortunate enough to call my wife."

Chapter Eleven

Basil eyed his heaping plate of canapés with suspicion and no small measure of disdain. God only knew *why* people took the time to create such concoctions when they looked fit for neither man nor beast. He nursed his drink and cast a keen eye over the crowd in search of one particularly ravishing, ebony-haired wench in red velvet. Perhaps *she* would be more appreciative of the effort some poor soul had expended on creating the food. To his eye, Elizabeth Burbridge was not only the most naive and gullible of maidens but also the most thoroughly tenderhearted, as easy a prey as he could have hoped for. If only she weren't so beautiful, so desirable, enough to make a man lose his mind.

Basil gulped from his glass. This he had not expected. The transformation she had undergone from plain schoolmarm had left him nearly agape. And to make matters worse, she seemed completely oblivious to the effect she had upon him, blinking her enormous violet eyes and parting those full lips, shivering delicately within a dress that clung to her curves like a second skin and all but begged to be ripped from her supple body. He swallowed past a suddenly dry throat and cursed his empty glass.

If he didn't watch out, he might abandon his original intent and find himself being led about by that which sprang to attention between his legs. His grip tightened upon his glass and he clenched his jaw with determination. *No* woman was beautiful enough to make him sacrifice a bloody fortune. A distraction, yes, and one whose charms he fully intended to sample at great length. He simply had to proceed with caution lest she even suspect his intent. The only problem with caution, however, was that damned Sinclair. How in God's name was he to woo the lady when she was living beneath that arrogant bastard's roof? Judging by the manner in which Sinclair looked at Elizabeth, her virtue was already in jeopardy.

Basil sucked in his belly and thrust out his chest as his eyes scanned the room. Where was the rutting bastard? He'd have no trouble spotting the man, he was so blastedly tall. How he detested men taller than he, and obviously stronger. Where the man had acquired his muscles, Basil would never know, but he was certain he'd never known a firmer grip on a man. He snorted. Sinclair was all brawn and no brains; he knew the type. Lacking in finesse and a tender, knowing touch. Elizabeth would realize this all too soon, if she hadn't already. Though if he didn't know any better, he would have sworn she'd bloomed into a blushing red rose when Sinclair had happened by.

Heaving an agitated sigh, he shifted his weight and pondered setting out after Elizabeth when a high-pitched female voice from behind the pillar at his back caught his attention.

"Prudence! Prudence Proudfit! How are you, darling?"

Basil's heart leapt. *Prudence Proudfit?* The same Prudence Proudfit, possessing of the wagging tongue, who corresponded regularly with Nigel? Best to see himself from this place before the woman spotted him and Elizabeth and requested an introduction. His eyes darted about for an appropriate spot to abandon his canapés, when he found his attention drawn to their conversation once more.

"Did you see who's here? Celestine Sinclair . . . DuBois."

"Celestine DuBois? Alec Sinclair's wife?"

"Can you believe it?"

"How does she look?"

"See for yourself, darling. She's over there. By the fountain, in that god-awful green dress."

Basil's eyes sought out the honey blonde poised enticingly before the fountain. The dress looked fine to him. So did she. Now he knew Sinclair was a fool.

"Oh, she looks awful."

"My, but she's aged terribly."

Basil couldn't suppress a smirk. Women. Jealous and snippety even at their advanced ages. Celestine Sinclair DuBois looked no more than a score and ten, if that.

"What's she doing here?"

"Why, haven't you heard? It's the talk of London. Her husband, Theo, died rather suddenly."

"Oh, yes. Theo DuBois. The rich one."

The woman snorted in so unladylike a manner even Basil had to raise a brow. "Rich? Pah! At one time, yes, fabulously wealthy. But from what I hear, he died penniless. One can only imagine how *that* came about. Why, just look at her. It takes no practiced eye to see that those jewels are mere paste!"

"Poor Celestine." The sarcasm dripped from the woman's tongue. "I seem to recall she left Alec due to his lack of fortune."

"Of course, darling! Theo was everything Alec was not at that time. Rich, powerful and extremely well connected socially. We all know that's what the dear girl was after, despite the fact that she'd had Alec's child."

"True, but to leave a man like Alec Sinclair. Why, the woman must have been insane!"

"Oh, she was never in love with him, though I cannot imagine how one *couldn't* fall in love with the man."

"Hardly the grieving widow, is she. Presumably here to acquire yet another socially prominent, fabulously wealthy husband?"

"Well, you must promise not to tell . . ."

"Darling, do I ever?"

"She's staying with Lord and Lady Castlethorpe, Theo's very old friends, and Lady Castlethorpe confided in me that Celestine is after Alec!"

"Indeed!"

"Why, it makes perfect sense! He's still handsome, God only knows, but he's also rich and socially prominent."

"Ah yes, but he'll never take her back. Mark my words. He'll never forgive her."

"Well, of course, if there's another woman . . ."

"I'm not aware that there is. The man is quite private, you know, but I don't believe another woman would matter, darling. Men like Alec Sinclair can be deceived and humiliated but once. He'll never take her back."

"She's bound and determined to try, nonetheless."

"Ah, there's Lord and Lady Castlethorpe. Perhaps we should just happen by and see what we can squeeze out of them."

Basil peered around the pillar as the women scurried off, then his eyes settled upon Celestine. The luck! Lord and Lady Castlethorpe had spent the Christmas holidays with Nigel. It would not be out of the ordinary were he to pay them a brief social call and, in the process, just happen to meet the lovely Celestine. Indeed, it would serve him well to enlist her help in achieving his goal, which in turn would aid her cause to ensnare Sinclair. Of course, he had little intention of confiding everything to her. He'd already taken enough of a chance with Felicity. God only knew there was no trusting a woman.

A twisted version of a smile parted his lips for several moments until he realized Elizabeth had been gone far too long. A quick glance about assured him that Alec Sinclair was also nowhere to be seen. A claw of anxiety gripped his insides and he unceremoniously thrust his glass and plate at a passing servant before shoving his way through the crowd.

Elizabeth stared at Alec for a moment and felt her mouth open and close with a silent "oh." His *wife?* Little wonder Celestine had looked familiar. Phoebe was the image of her mother. For some reason she could not fathom at the moment, her dearest wish was to flee from him, from what it all meant, from the undeniable attraction she felt between them.

"I really must get back," she said, lifting her skirt and attempting to brush past him.

"Where the hell are you going?" His hand shot out to encase her wrist, stilling her feet momentarily.

Elizabeth flashed him an angry glare and attempted to free her hand. "Basil is waiting for me. Really, Alec! Resorting to force to detain me is uncalled-for and—"

"Celestine means nothing to me."

Elizabeth stared at him, dumbstruck. "What on earth are you talking about? I simply want to return to my escort. Now, my hand, if you please."

His eyes narrowed upon her so that Elizabeth wondered if he could see into her thoughts. "As you wish," he said, and followed directly at her heels as she hurried from the room.

Though she was unable to meet his gaze, Elizabeth was very much aware of his towering presence keeping pace with her. The tripping of her heart proved adequate hindrance to speaking and they proceeded down the hall in silence until they spied a dark form hastening toward them, wearing what could only be described as a murderous expression.

"Your Basil looks to be in some sort of foul mood, as well," Alec remarked. "Could it be you two do not enjoy one another's company?" His hand lightly touched her in the small of her back, sending a shiver through her limbs. "Then again, perhaps he's jealous. You may want to ask him."

"*Jeal—*"

Alec offered her little opportunity for rebuttal. Giving her a sly wink, he pasted on a huge smile that screamed self-confidence and bellowed, "Basil! So good to see you again! Enjoying yourself, old chap?"

Basil stopped, his eyes traveling back and forth between the two of them. Scowling in Alec's direction, he snorted. "Don't 'old chap' me, Sinclair. Elizabeth, I'm afraid I've received a message of some urgency and we must leave. Your cloak, my dear?"

"I'll fetch it," Alec offered before Elizabeth could reply, though when he moved as if to brush past Basil, the other man's hand shot out to press against one brawny shoulder.

"No, Sinclair. *I'll* fetch the lady's cloak."

Elizabeth watched with mounting anxiety as Alec's brow grew stormy and his eyes flickered over Basil's hand, still upon him. Her heart thumped an erratic beat in anticipation of a sparring that never came.

"As you wish," Alec replied with a brief but ever-so-sarcastic nod at Basil. "I deposited it with an attendant, just around the corner." His eyes slid to Elizabeth. "Enjoy the remainder of your evening."

"Bastard," Basil muttered beneath his breath as he glowered after Alec's departing form. As if he suddenly realized Elizabeth stood beside him, he spun about and gave her a wide apologetic smile. "I'm sorry, my dear. There's something supremely annoying about that man, though I won't waste your time with such nonsense." He held a hand before him. "Shall we?"

Closing the door softly behind her, Elizabeth pressed her palm to the wood and strained her ears for some clue that Basil had departed. For some reason, she was quite certain he stood outside that door for several moments, waiting, before the crunch of his boots upon the snow and then the crack of reins assured her that he was gone. Heaving a tired sigh, she turned and started for the stairs, when a deep voice stilled her feet and brought her head about.

"So, did he get what he wanted?"

She skidded to a halt inside the front parlor and found herself staring at Alec, who was settled quite comfortably upon the sofa. A fire burned low in the hearth, its amber glow casting his hair in a flaming copper hue and shadowing the planes of his face so that his eyes were unreadable. He sat low in his seat, his legs stretched forever before him, contemplating the drink he held in one hand. He'd doffed his topcoat and waistcoat and had loosened the buttons of his shirt to reveal a dark furred chest that held Elizabeth fascinated for several long moments. A trembling bubbled forth within her as she stood, openly staring upon the one man who had no business arousing such thoughts.

He inclined his head. "Did Basil get what he was after?"

Elizabeth stared uncomprehendingly at him. "Whatever are you talking about? And why were you spying on me?"

He erupted with a hoarse laugh. "Elizabeth, need I remind you once again that I live here? I was but innocently enjoying a brandy in my parlor. No harm in that. It's certainly not anything akin to squeezing myself between the stair railings and spying upon those below enjoying a Christmas day."

Elizabeth's cheeks flamed with embarrassment at the notion that she'd been caught. Arrogant man! She spun about as if to flee the room and his blasted conceit, when his words stopped her.

"So, little inquisitive mouse, did you learn anything from your spying, or should I perhaps ask Basil?"

He had risen as silently as a cat and stood quite close to her. Close enough that she could detect the brandy on his breath and the clean scent that was his alone. Much to her chagrin, she realized her eyes were focused on the expanse of his bare chest.

"You speak in riddles, Alec," she murmured, feeling the need to draw her cloak close about her.

"You stood out there long enough. There was only one thing on the man's mind, Elizabeth, and I can assure you, it was not hot cocoa."

She swung her gaze to the fire, though the heat of the flames paled in comparison to that emanating from the man before her. "Pray, tell this innocent what the man wanted, Alec."

"Oh, perhaps a few not-so-chaste kisses to keep him all warm and snug for at least a fortnight or two."

Elizabeth had to shake her head. "Men. You're all alike."

"Oh, so he *did*..."

"Indeed!" Elizabeth swung blazing eyes upon him. "Perhaps it's this blasted dress that causes such mistaken notions!"

Alec's eyes met hers above the glass poised at his lips. "I can assure you, a woman never looked so fetching."

Elizabeth snapped her mouth shut, then turned and paused before the fire, feeling the delicious anticipation seeping into her limbs and dissolving any anger that dared remain. "Basil and I are merely friends."

"Don't fool yourself. He's after far more."

Elizabeth mulled over his words and listened to him refill his drink. No doubt his strange mood had prompted such an indulgence. Celestine's return must have proven more of a surprise than he was willing to admit.

"Would you care for a brandy?"

Elizabeth raised a brow. "I presume this, too, shall warm my blood?"

"One can only hope," came the response, and before she could say otherwise, he'd pressed a glass into her hand. "Sip slowly, Elizabeth. This is a mite stronger than Phoebe's hot toddies."

She did as he'd instructed, allowing herself several tiny sips of the brew, then several more, for she found the brandy quite soothing. "You don't seem overly fond of Basil."

"Something about the man."

"He said the same of you."

"Is that so?"

"Perhaps he thinks you're as arrogant as I do."

"One could say the same of him, though that's hardly adequate reason to thoroughly dislike the man. Indeed, you seem to like him well enough, arrogance and all. No, I find myself wondering how the man could have forgone dancing with you this evening. Business obligations be damned."

"It's just as well." She felt his eyes upon her, and the flush mounting in her cheeks had little to do with the fire. Something in his manner compelled her to respond. "I...I fear I've never danced."

"Indulge me, just this once, Elizabeth." His hands were upon her before she could respond. "You will, of course, have to remove this." The cloak landed in a heap upon a nearby chair.

She found herself rubbing her arms as if she had caught a sudden chill despite the warmth of the room. Unable to meet his gaze, she turned toward the fire once again. "Really, it's not necessary." She nearly jumped from her skin when he loomed close at her side. Dear God, the man didn't even have to touch her. With every fiber of her being she *felt* him. "I...I've never found myself in need of the skill."

"You can't remain a prude your entire life, Elizabeth." Her sharp glance met his hooded expression, then his lips parted in a dazzling smile. "You know, it wouldn't kill you to loosen up a bit." He glanced about in a rather covert manner, then whispered, "The venerable Miss Percy isn't secreted behind some door somewhere, is she? And your ever-so-impressionable pupils are all tucked away in their beds. Just an innocent dance. You've nothing to fear."

"We have no music," she offered lamely, and managed a weak, trembling smile when he moved to the column of shelves beside the hearth and produced a music box.

"Strauss's *Tales of the Vienna Woods.*" He cocked a brow as he wound up the box then set it upon the table before the fire.

The sweet tinkling seemed to fill the small room and plucked at Elizabeth's resolve. *Prude?* God only knew she'd never given the matter much thought, but suddenly the idea that she might never know what it felt like to dance in the arms of a man like Alec Sinclair brought a hollow ache to her soul. Her eyes flickered over him, standing so tall and magnificently handsome. Any woman would be a complete fool to squander such an opportunity. And though she might, on her worst days, be considered by some to be a prude, she was certainly no fool.

Swallowing the last of her brandy, she set the glass aside and moved before him, mindful of the surprised brow he raised. He offered her little insight to his thoughts, however, as he drew nearer and slipped one arm about her waist, then grasped her hand in his.

"Your fingers are ice-cold," he murmured. "And you're trembling."

"Just nervous, I suppose," she replied shakily, all too aware that the proximity of his bare chest to her exposed bosom would normally have sent her into a swoon. "Or perhaps it's the brandy."

"Relax, Elizabeth. You might try looking at me. It's not chic these days to feign disinterest in your dance partner. Perhaps you could attempt to look upon me as if you harbored some fondness for me. The more the better, of course, which makes it all the more fun for those watching."

"No one is watching," Elizabeth said, still unable to meet his gaze. God only knew how close they were.

"All right." He gave a soft chuckle. "We'll try that later. Now, just relax in my arms—that's it—and move your feet. Oh, and you may want to put your other hand—yes, the one that's dangling there—put it upon my shoulder. That's it."

"I . . . I've no idea how to do this." How on earth was she to concentrate on moving her feet when his skin seemed to pulse beneath her fingertips and his shoulder felt as solid as granite?

"You're doing fine." His breath fanned the tendrils curling against her face.

"I don't recall seeing partners dance this close."

"Oh, this version is nothing compared to the newer," he replied with a slow smile. "Would you care to try it? I find I prefer it above all others."

"I suppose I could try."

"Now, this requires you to loop both your arms about my neck. You may have to step a little closer or your derriere will look rather funny, especially with that damned bustle."

"You don't like it?" Elizabeth did as she was told, shocked to find her fingers upon his hair, which curled over the back of his collar.

He gave her a wicked smile. "I like everything about your dress, trust me. Now step just a bit closer."

She hesitated, then complied and nearly swooned dead away when his hands swept about her waist and pressed her full against him. "Alec! I don't think . . ."

"Now close your eyes and tip your head back, just so."

His finger beneath her chin left her little choice, and the twinkling in his eyes spurred her on to close hers. "I think you're teasing me," she murmured, feeling a soft smile part her lips.

"Would I ever do such an awful thing to you?" His hands moved about her waist, spanning the supple velvet and sending shivers through her. "Why, that could be fun."

"Now I know you're teasing me."

His voice was suddenly very deep, husky, and should have served as some sort of warning, had Elizabeth not been such an innocent. "No, darling Elizabeth, you're the tease, though how you can be so damnably unaware of it . . . of what you do to mere men . . ."

Elizabeth's eyes flew open. Dimly, she was aware that the music had stopped, perhaps some time ago. Her ears were filled with the hammering of her pulse and her frantic silent pleas. Even as his mouth descended to hers and he drew her closer still, she knew that this was wrong, so thoroughly improper, yet perfectly wonderful and far too powerful to deny.

His mouth moved over hers so softly at first she almost collapsed in a trembling heap from the sweet pleasure. Instead, she clung to his shoulders as if the roaring in her ears were some tempestuous wind that threatened to sweep her out of his powerful embrace. Her lips parted with a soft moan and she turned her face to draw a breath. His mouth pressed against her cheek then lowered to her neck, and she had to gulp for air when he crushed her to him.

"So beautiful . . ." he whispered against her throat, then his mouth captured hers once again, only with far greater urgency.

Elizabeth knew a sudden overwhelming panic that she could control neither him nor herself, that she was bound for disaster, yet she could do naught but cling to him.

"Sweet, open your mouth," he rasped against her lips.

She pushed vainly against his shoulders. "I . . . I cannot . . ."

"You'll love it, I promise." His hands wandered up her back, caressing the slender curve, then swept about her narrow rib cage. His voice trembled with suppressed emotion. "God, but you feel good . . ." He lowered his lips to press against the hollow of her throat. "And you smell like a warm spring meadow . . . so damned sweet . . ." His deep murmur sent tremors through her limbs. "Open your lovely mouth and let me kiss you the way you were meant to be kissed."

With a moan of despair, she dissolved in his arms, parting her lips to the sweet taste of him mixed with warm brandy. His kiss was so passionate his beard-roughened face branded her skin. She felt as if he would inhale her very being, draw life's breath from her. The bubbling heat rose like a kindled flame, low in her belly, spreading like molten fire through her limbs and bringing with it a mounting urgency all its own. She felt his hand in her hair, the silken tresses tumbled to her waist, the pins scattering to the floor.

His hands caught in her hair for a moment, then cupped her face, tenderly stroking her cheekbones. Fathomless gray eyes captured hers and she was afforded but a momentary glimpse of the unbridled passion in those smoky depths before he swept her hard against him. Again, his hands spanned her waist then rose unheeded over her ribs to boldly cup her breasts. The contact, and his obvious intent, proved enough to bring Elizabeth crashing to her senses.

"Oh, God..." she groaned, twisting from his embrace. She spun about, drawing a trembling hand to her swollen lips, feeling her skin burning from his touch. Gulping for a breath, she pressed a hand to her quaking belly, then nearly collapsed when she felt him close behind her. The heat of his chest against her back branded her as did the palm traveling across her belly. His lips pressed against the side of her neck, sliding over her shoulder.

"Don't run from me," he whispered.

Elizabeth closed her eyes. "I must...."

Her words lodged in her throat and panic seized her when she detected a muffled sound from the doorway behind them. Alec, apparently, heard it, as well, and they spun about as one to confront a wide-eyed Phoebe clutching at her flannel nightgown and staring at her father's arm wrapped about Elizabeth's waist.

Chapter Twelve

Phoebe stared with some confusion at Elizabeth. "Miss Burbridge! Whatever is the matter? Are you ill?"

"Oh my, yes!" Elizabeth burst forth, pressing a hand against her forehead and all but collapsing into Alec's ever ready arms. This took very little effort to accomplish, for the mere thought that Phoebe had witnessed their indiscretion buckled Elizabeth's knees and set the room spinning about her.

"Oh my goodness, how awful for you! Little wonder you're home so early. Poor Basil."

This last drew a sharp look from Alec.

Phoebe rushed forward to lay a comforting hand upon Elizabeth's arm. "My goodness, your throat is so flushed and your skin so warm. Heaven only knows what ailment you've got! Father, we must get her to bed! Carry her, will you?" Wringing her hands with worry, Phoebe turned and started for the stairs. "Hurry! Follow me!"

"Of course," Alec murmured, giving Elizabeth a wicked look.

"That's quite all right," Elizabeth muttered, attempting to right herself, though she realized this was impossible, for Alec appeared bent upon carrying her to her room. He was apparently having little trouble going along with this ploy. His arms slipped beneath her legs and she found herself with little choice but to loop her arms once again about his neck.

"Oh, this is awful!" Phoebe's voice echoed throughout the foyer. "I shall have Cook prepare you some soup."

Elizabeth could only manage a tiny smile in Phoebe's direction as the child preceded them up the stairs, then almost groaned aloud when Alec paused for the briefest of moments to press his lips to her throat.

She squirmed in his arms. "What on earth are you doing?"

"What do you think?" His voice was so casual, she wondered if the man had lost his senses, then realized he had indeed when his eyes slid from hers to her bosom and he lowered his mouth to the high curves.

"Alec, please. You've lost your mind."

"Indeed I have," he murmured against her skin. "Have you?"

Before she could reply, Phoebe's hurried footsteps and urgent tone set Alec's feet moving again, though they did little to temper the passion looming like a wild beast in his eyes. Elizabeth shuddered with a sudden fear of his unleashed desires, knowing full well she would be powerless to stop him. What had she become?

He proceeded in his most gallant manner to her chamber and deposited her, per Phoebe's instructions, in the middle of her bed. If Elizabeth had been aware of the picture she presented him, all tousled and flushed, looking perfectly ravishing, she would not have dared to lift her eyes to him before he departed. God only knew why she did. Perhaps she wished yet another glimpse of hollowed cheekbones or bared chest as he lingered beside the bed. In her wildest dreams, she had never imagined such power in a man's gaze. In that fleeting moment when their eyes met, she knew beyond a doubt that, had Phoebe not been present, he would have taken her upon that very bed. For as fleeting a moment, she wished that he would.

She knew he left the room when the door banged forcefully behind him, startling her, though her eyes remained lowered. Phoebe drew forth her nightgown and assisted her in removing her dress. She lent the child's idle chatter half an ear and hoped that Phoebe would assume her mood was in keeping with one so ill. Thus, when Phoebe doused the candle and slipped from the room, Elizabeth drew the sheet to her chin and prayed for sleep. For some time, however, she found herself staring into the darkness, feeling the pulse beating vibrantly in her limbs with naught but the memory of Alec's kiss playing in her mind.

Quite early the following morning, Alec stood scowling from the parlor window, watching the coach bearing his daughter back to Dunlevy. Shoving an impatient hand through his hair, he glanced at the mantel clock then swung his gaze to the stairs.

With a growl of frustration, he strode to the foot of the stairs and paused, listening. Only Cook's muted humming reached his ears. Giving an agitated grunt, he mounted one step, then another, and paused, peering curiously upward. Where in the hell was she? And better yet, why was he so damned concerned?

He had to give a wry laugh at the thought. Indeed, sometime during the night, despite his restless sleep, his newly awakened, brandy-enhanced passion of the prior evening had given way to unadulterated chastisement in the stark light of day. What in God's name had come over him? At one point in that parlor last evening, when she'd looked at him with those come-hither eyes, all aglow in her red velvet, he'd found himself wondering how easy it would be to fall in love with the girl.

He shook his head and mounted another step. It was the damned dress, though God only knew he'd never seen a more beautiful woman. Beautiful and intelligent, but beyond that, far from his type. In love with her? What a notion. True, her innocence intrigued him and her blasted prudish manner seemed to make her all the more engaging. And when she'd appeared at that gala, as desirable as any woman could ever hope to be, he'd been possessed by one thought alone, and that had been to ravish her beyond her wildest dreams and the consequences be damned.

A sound from below drew his attention and he all but snarled at Holmes when the servant cast him a questioning glance. Thrusting a hand into his trouser pocket, he scowled again and proceeded up the stairs, two at a time.

At the top of the stairs he paused to listen once more. He wasn't quite certain, but the soft singing he detected was far too melodious to belong to Cook. Very slowly and rather cautiously for a man moving about his own house, he started toward her room, cursing the sudden leap of his pulse. For one so ingenuous, she'd surely made a mockery of his past experiences with women. Perhaps her innocence reminded him of his own, lost so long ago, and swept aside the sour memories of another woman he'd once been foolish enough to think he loved.

Celestine. His mouth twisted into a disgusted smirk. What *that* woman wanted from him now, he could only venture a guess. Widowed, lonely and, by the looks of it, hungry for far more than food. He'd seen that look about her before and he wasn't going to make that mistake again. Marriage was a bad idea, something he had taken great pains to avoid, though something a virtuous and upstanding girl like Elizabeth would expect, especially after handing him her virtue on a red velvet platter.

He clenched his jaw resolutely. He had to apologize to her and manage to keep himself from her and this damned town house.

As he drew nearer to her room, he realized Elizabeth's sweet voice filtered into the hallway through her partially opened door. His feet stilled and he listened for several moments to the melody, recognizing Strauss's *Tales of the Vienna Woods*. He swallowed, as if realizing for the first time how difficult a proposition it was, keeping himself from a woman in love with him. He'd done it before, rather effortlessly, with a score of women. Elizabeth would prove just as easy. Raising a hand to the doorknob, he leaned forward to peer around the door and froze.

She stood before her dressing table, clad only in sheer white pantaloons and a shift, though the latter was as yet unlaced. Her back faced the doorway, though the mirror before her afforded Alec with an unimpeded view as she slowly proceeded about her toilette. The pink rays of the sun slanted through the windows and fell upon her unbound tresses tumbling about her slender shoulders then cascading in an ebony torrent to her waist. The silken mane swung hypnotically as she drew a damp sponge over a slender arm then across her shoulders. When the sponge dipped between her breasts, Alec's breath caught in his throat and his eyes fastened upon the full mounds. From her narrow rib cage they swelled, as exquisite as he could ever have imagined, as luminescent as the finest of white porcelain, with thrusting nipples the color of the palest of pink roses.

His mouth parted and his eyes narrowed as she passed the sponge across her breasts then lower to her softly rounded belly. Without even touching her, Alec was certain her skin felt like silk, downy soft, fragrant . . .

His eyes wandered over her back appreciatively, over the slim hips and softly rounded derriere, then down long slender legs whose curves beckoned for his touch. *She* beckoned for him, and for the briefest of moments he was consumed with a desire that threatened his sanity. He moved forward as if in a trance, his eyes fastened upon her, aware only of the urgent need filling him. He pushed the door open, intent upon taking her on the floor, if need be, when her humming stopped and she bent to retrieve the sponge she'd dropped. As she did so, still oblivious of his presence, she afforded Alec a clear view of her profile.

In the pale morning light she looked like an angel, so unaware of herself as a woman. Thus, when Alec's eye fell to her innocently parted lips, he had to retreat, so overcome was he by the enormity of what he'd contemplated doing. He paused not a moment outside her room but strode quickly down the hall and descended the stairs in search of something to ease his plight. A brandy would do quite nicely, though beneath Cook's all-knowing eye, very strong tea would have to suffice.

When Elizabeth entered the breakfast nook not a quarter of an hour later in search of a quick bite and some tea, she encountered Alec's stormy brow and their eyes locked before she could spin about and beat a hasty retreat.

"Elizabeth!" he barked. Her heart leapt like a startled frog. "Where the hell are you going?"

"School," she replied, feeling the heat of her blush. "I'm late."

"They're not expecting you," he grumbled, giving her a sweep of his eyes before wincing into the teacup he held. "Phoebe intends to inform Miss Percy that you are abed . . . with some strange ailment."

"Oh." Elizabeth pondered this for a moment. "Well then, I'll inform Miss Percy otherwise."

"I'm afraid that may be a little difficult."

"Why is that?"

"Lewis and the coach just left with Phoebe. Unless you plan to make your way to Dunlevy aboard Sebastian, you'll have to remain here until they return."

His darkening scowl swept over her again. Obviously, a night of grim contemplation had wrought a dramatic change of heart, for his entire demeanor bore little resemblance to that of the dashing and sensuous man of last evening. His brusque manner and barely concealed anger served only to confirm the suspicion crouching deep in her mind, a suspicion honed and fostered by years of her own mother's heartache: he'd determined to make a go of it with Celestine. What else could it possibly be? After all, it made perfect sense! Hadn't her mother warned her time and again *never* to become involved with a man claiming to have no feelings for his long-departed wife?

Perhaps his change of heart would have pleased her had she not spent the majority of *her* night reliving those glorious moments when he'd embraced her, when his lips had claimed hers, when his powerful length branded her his. Contemplation of her actions in that parlor, though fleeting, had proven unforgiving, leaving her filled with self-disgust, loathing this weakness she had no idea she possessed, and knowing full well that she had best avoid Alec altogether. Little wonder she was but a jumble of conflicting emotion, a lost soul yearning for the unattainable. . . .

"Well?" His voice echoed through the tiny room, and Elizabeth could not help but remember how that same voice had sounded murmuring softly in her ear. "What do you wish to do?"

She drew an unsteady breath and clasped her hands primly before her. "I suppose I shall wait, then . . . uh, in my room. Good day." She turned, but his impatient bark stilled her movements.

"Perhaps I could take you."

She couldn't help but lift a brow. "On Sebastian?"

"Why the hell not?"

Why, indeed! "I think not."

"Fine!"

"Fine."

"I presume you're still afraid."

"That's not the reason."

"Then I'm left with only one other possible conclusion. It's my company that you wish to avoid."

She flushed and averted her face, wincing at his wry laugh.

"I suppose it's an honor to be the sole reason for keeping one so devoted from tending to her duties," he snarled.

Her ire sprang to life at his implication and she swung blazing eyes to him, waving one hand in the direction of the door and placing the other upon a slim hip. "Go then, untether Sebastian, lest your ego grow too cumbersome for even that mangy beast to bear!" She lifted a haughty brow. "I'll fetch my cloak." And with that, she swept from the room and up the stairs, nursing her wounded pride and unaware of the scowl that dissolved into an appreciative smile with one shake of Alec's dark head.

Her indignation did not ease one whit in the short time it took Alec to saddle his mount. Nor did the crisp morning air prompt even the tiniest of shivers within her woolen cloak, so intent was she on her thoughts. She barely flinched when Alec led the animal to a stop before her and held out a hand to assist her. She returned his stoic expression with a curt nod and ignored his proffered hand. Blast his gallantry! She could mount just as well by herself.

She paused not a moment to contemplate her actions and, knowing no better, inserted her right foot in the stirrup. Sebastian swung his head about to eye her curiously as she grasped a handful of black mane and attempted to pull herself up. As her luck would have it, the horse chose that moment to shy away from this blundering amateur. His quick movement sideways threw Elizabeth off balance so that her left foot slipped on the snow just as her right foot fell from the stirrup.

Had it not been for Alec's quick response, she would have fallen in a flustered heap at his feet. As it was, she could do naught but erupt with a breathless, "Oh, my goodness!" when one hand slipped about her waist and another imposed itself upon her derriere, lifting her into the air then depositing her soundly upon her rump in the saddle. Without a moment's hesitation, and before Elizabeth could catch her breath, he swung up in front of her and grasped the reins.

She had but a moment to silently curse his broad back before he clicked the reins and Sebastian leapt forward. Deciding it better to avoid falling off the blasted animal, she wrapped her arms fiercely about Alec's waist, where they remained for the duration of the ride.

Alec's grin faded into a scowl and he pulled his hat low over his eyes, attempting to concentrate on something besides the soft and supple woman pressed against his back. He shifted uncomfortably in the saddle. With every jostle and bounce, he felt as if her breasts seared the layers of clothing between them to burn like twin flames into his back.

What the hell was the matter with him? Why was he behaving as if he were a love-smitten lad and she Aphrodite incarnate?

His eyes narrowed in thought. He had only himself to blame for his quandary. If he hadn't been so foolish as to peek into the woman's boudoir so early in the morning, he wouldn't be plagued by the vivid image of her exquisite half-naked body bathed in morning sunlight. Though his spying upon her did not sit well with him, God only knew, a team of six horses couldn't have driven him from that room had he been assured she was willing. He needed to keep away from the girl. So why had he offered to take her to school?

He clenched his jaw and closed his eyes as if in pain when Elizabeth shifted in her seat, unknowingly caressing his tightened abdomen and rubbing her breasts against him in a most provocative manner. If the girl didn't watch it, she'd find herself on her back, melting a good bit of snow beneath her while he quenched his need for her. The undeniable tightening in his trousers deepened his scowl and brought a tic to his bronzed cheek. Best to get her to Dunlevy, prim, proper and completely unsullied. Then he could return to the town house and remove anything he could possibly need for several weeks, surely enough time to find a woman, a beautiful, seasoned and worldly-wise woman upon whom he could ease this lust that filled his every thought and who would sweep aside every image of Elizabeth.

The thought merely deepened his scowl.

Elizabeth's arms wrapped tighter about Alec's waist as Sebastian broke into a smooth, undulating lope. The wind brought tears to her eyes, which blurred her vision, though by the muffled thud of the horse's hooves, she was certain that they had left the city limits.

She sniffed and buried her face against Alec's back. His coat was made of the finest wool, warm and smooth to the touch and smelling distinctly of him. Her palms moved unconsciously over his belly until the feel of ridged, corded muscle through layers of clothing sent a tremor through her. She stilled her hands immediately and found herself wondering if his stomach sported the same smooth dark hair that covered his chest. She gulped for a breath, convinced that he could detect the thumping of her heart just as she could all but feel his pulse beneath her fingertips. Biting her lips, she raised her eyes and found herself contemplating the back of his head.

Dear God, but she hated him! If it hadn't been for him, she would still be blissfully unaware of her immoral soul. She scowled at the russet head. She didn't even like the man! Let him go back to his ever adoring wife! She could have him *and* all his eccentric, immoral ideas. Elizabeth had every intention of immersing herself in her work, her lifeblood. If that couldn't sweep the vivid images of last evening from her mind, nothing could.

After a time, they came upon Dunlevy's entrance, an enormous wrought-iron gate at the juncture of a tall stone fence that encircled the school's grounds. Alec pulled Sebastian to a halt outside the gates, and for a moment Elizabeth wondered if he were going to deposit her there. The school was still a good distance from the entrance.

"Are you all right?" he asked curtly.

Elizabeth frowned, both at his concern and his tone of voice. "Fine." She couldn't help adding, "If it was such a bother to bring me, Alec, you never should have offered."

He twisted around to give her a wary look. "What the hell are you talking about?"

Her eyes flickered over his windburned cheeks, knowing that they would be cold and damp to the touch. His stormy brows drew together and prompted her response. "You're in such a foul mood, grumbling and roaring like a wounded boar, it is an easy conclusion to draw."

"Indeed. I've a lot on my mind." He cocked a brow. "And what of you, Miss Burbridge? You seem positively brimming with more than your usual stoicism this morning. Are you troubled, as well, perhaps?"

Elizabeth managed a shrug. "Perhaps."

"Then I shall save you the trouble and speak for both of us. I'm afraid I must apologize for my behavior last evening. It was uncalled-for and entirely out of line."

"Yes . . . I mean, I see."

"The brandy, you know."

"Of course."

"Yes, well . . . I'm certain you'll agree we should keep our distance from one another."

"Of course. I shall look for other lodgings as soon as—"

"No!"

"No?"

"No, for God's sake, don't do that!"

"Alec, it is *your* house, not mine, as you have been wont to remind me."

"No matter. I have another in which I intend to keep myself. There's no reason for you to look for other lodgings. I insist."

"If you insist . . ."

"I do."

"Fine."

"Fine."

Her eyes met his and she swallowed. "Do you wish me to dismount here? I . . ."

"Woman! Don't be a damned fool!" He swung about and clicked the reins, sending Sebastian through the gates and up the winding snow-covered drive.

They rode in silence, though the wind roaring unheeded through the trees would have made conversation impossible. Not that Elizabeth had much to say. She was far too busy wondering why she didn't feel something akin to elation. The man was going to stay away from her. Wasn't that what she wanted? So why on earth did she have this gnawing sense of loss?

Her musings were short-lived, for when they stopped before the imposing structure, she was struck by the familiarity of the coach parked directly beside them. She had but a moment to ponder this, when the front portal burst open with more than its usual bang and Basil marched onto the porch.

"Elizabeth! What in God's name happened to you?" Basil skidded to a halt at Sebastian's side and cast a suspicious look upon the pair.

"Christy." Alec dismounted and presented Basil with his back while he swept Elizabeth from the saddle. "It's a trifle early in the day, isn't it, for all your good-deed doing?"

Basil's eyes narrowed upon the hands that lingered about Elizabeth's waist longer than was necessary, and his heavy black brows swept downward. Choosing to ignore Alec's barb, he growled. "Sinclair, what the hell are *you* doing here?"

Alec cocked his head, peering beneath the rim of his hat, and flashed Basil a dazzling grin that snatched Elizabeth's breath. "Why, assisting the lady, of course. She found herself in need of transportation."

Basil looked apoplectic and waved a hand toward Sebastian. "On *that?*"

The sarcasm in Alec's voice was not difficult to detect. "Why, yes, Christy. This four-legged beast has more than sufficed for centuries as man's most common form of transportation. The lady was more than willing."

Elizabeth noted the furious tic in Basil's jaw as he stared at her, nearly dumbstruck. "Elizabeth, the notion! Whatever were you thinking, parading about London with *him* on horseback, for God's sake?"

Elizabeth stared blankly at Basil for several moments, realizing she hadn't given propriety much thought this morning. Her tone was even, though his strident words and insistent attitude did not settle easily upon her. "Rest assured, my every thought was to reach Dunlevy as soon as possible. But I must say I resent your implication that—"

"Forgive me, my dear Elizabeth, of course. I never meant, well . . . From now on, consider my coach at your disposal."

"Thank you, Basil, but that is not necessary."

Basil glared at Alec. "Indeed it is! Elizabeth, listen to me, only heathens and lawless ruffians meander about without a coach."

Alec clasped his hands behind his back and looked amused. "Heathens and lawless ruffians? In these parts? Surely you jest, Christy. Why, the trip was rather enjoyable—surprisingly warm and cozy, of course, being that we were in the same saddle."

The deep scarlet suffusing Basil's face was the only testament to any anger he suppressed. He stepped forward between the two and slipped his arm about Elizabeth to guide her forward. "You're shivering, my dear. Let us get you inside where I *know* it's warm and cozy."

Elizabeth ventured a smile and started forward, then glanced over her shoulder at Alec. He stood very tall and still, staring after her with nothing akin to a smile upon his face. His manner was drawn and tense, his jaw sharp and hollowed, and his eyes bored into hers beneath the rim of his hat. She proceeded inside with Basil, bent upon accomplishing enormous amounts of work. This was achieved with more than her usual amount of tenacity, for she found that the image of Alec standing thus plagued her throughout most of her day and well into the coming weeks.

Chapter Thirteen

"My mother has returned."

Elizabeth glanced up to find Phoebe perched at her desk, awash in a jumble of grief and indignation. Returning her quill to its well, Elizabeth pushed her work aside into one neat pile and leaned her elbows upon the desk. "I know."

Phoebe's eyes flew wide. "You do? Miss Burbridge, why on earth didn't you tell me?"

"It was not my place, Phoebe, but your father's."

"Indeed!" Phoebe huffed. She flopped into a chair directly before Elizabeth's desk. The late afternoon sun slanting through the windows settled upon the child's pout and set her tumbling ringlets aflame. "I had to find out from Mrs. Pettibone, of all people! Do you believe it? The servants know more than I!"

"Perhaps your father had a reason for—"

"Of course he did! He's been away nearly every night, perhaps he hasn't found the time. But for goodness' sake, Miss Burbridge, she's been in London for over two weeks now!"

"You mean to say you haven't seen her yet?"

Phoebe pursed her lips. "Oh, I've seen her. She's come here, once or twice, after Mrs. Pettibone refused her entry to the house. Mrs. Pettibone never forgave Mother for leaving us. She all but tossed her from the doorstep!"

Elizabeth couldn't resist. "And your father?"

Phoebe shrugged. "He doesn't say much about Mother. He never has. Do you know that I still don't know the real reason she left?"

"I thought there was another man."

Phoebe waved a hand and grimaced. "Miss Burbridge, don't be so simpleminded! Charlotte Lambert says parents never tell you the whole truth about anything."

Elizabeth raised a brow. "Is that so?"

"Indeed! Charlotte says she knows of a young girl whose *father* ran off with another man! Can you believe it?"

Elizabeth stared at the girl.

Phoebe raised self-important brows. "Well, the mother thought she should tell her daughter every last detail and the poor child has stuttered something awful ever since."

Elizabeth blinked several times. "That is indeed a story worth remembering."

"Anyway, Mother's grieving, though God only knows she doesn't behave as if she is." Phoebe raised eyes brimming with distress. "Oh, Miss Burbridge, she's full of remorse over leaving us, says a day has not passed that she doesn't regret her actions. Now she wants to reunite with Father, move back into the house and . . . and become my mother again!"

"Oh, Phoebe!" Elizabeth rushed to the stricken girl and cradled the golden head against her. "She was your mother even when she wasn't living with you. And she always will be."

Phoebe raised a tearstained face. "That's the very reason for my distress! Oh, how I wish she were not my mother!"

"Phoebe, you can't mean that."

"I do! I swear it, I do!"

"Now stop. You're angry and justifiably so. In time you will feel differently."

Phoebe's eyes widened with indignation. "Oh, no I won't! I shall never forgive her!"

Elizabeth could not resist wiping a stray tear from the child's cheek and smoothing the hair from her damp brow. "You will, Phoebe, trust me, but it will take time. Perhaps her eagerness has upset you."

"Eagerness! I'll say! Why, she's so entirely convinced that she can get Father back, she's nearly gushing about it!" Phoebe buried her head in her hands. "Oh, I know not what to think! It occupies my every waking moment!"

Elizabeth sank to her knees beside Phoebe's chair and lightly stroked the child's hair. "Now, we can't have that! My goodness, you've been doing awfully well with your studies, so much so that I remarked on it to Miss Percy just the other day."

Phoebe lifted her head. "You did?"

"Why, of course. She was extremely pleased."

"She was?"

"Oh my, yes. I even broached a subject with her that I've been meaning to discuss with you for some time now."

"You did?"

"Of course. You see, you've quite a knack with young children, Phoebe. I saw you with Willie and Constance's little brood. They adore you! You would make a wonderful teacher."

"I would?"

"Miss Percy will need someone with your skills in a few years."

The amber eyes sparkled with unrestrained joy. "She will?"

"Of course! You must, however, be sure to keep up with your studies. I'm afraid you cannot afford to be distracted."

"Oh, I won't allow it, Miss Burbridge! Thank you so!"

Elizabeth smiled. "It was none of my doing, Phoebe. You should be proud of your accomplishments."

"Oh, I am! Inordinately so!" Phoebe leapt to her feet and threw her arms about Elizabeth. "Thank you just the same. I shall look to you as my sole inspiration."

Elizabeth flushed. "Oh, for heaven' sake, don't do that!"

"And why shouldn't I? You're intelligent, beautiful, and by the way, Charlotte and I simply adore the way you've been wearing your hair. It's quite chic, Miss Burbridge."

Elizabeth raised a hand self-consciously to her loosely knotted hair then plucked at the tendrils curling about her face. "Do you think so?"

Phoebe erupted with a sly wink and a grin. "It's Basil, isn't it."

"Who?"

"Basil! Your beau! You can tell me, Miss Burbridge!"

"Tell you what?"

"Why, he's here every day, working alongside you into the wee hours of the evening, then escorting you home. Why, it's obvious from the way he looks at you that he's in love with you!''

"Phoebe! For heaven' sake, how would you know?"

"Oh, Charlotte says there's no mistaking *that* look!"

"Charlotte seems rather advanced for her age," Elizabeth muttered with a raised brow. "Just brimming with wisdom, isn't she?"

"Now don't try denying it. Ooooh! I hope you marry him!"

"What?"

"Oh, you silly goose, you heard me! I hope you marry him and have lots of beautiful babies!"

"Phoebe! Cease this nonsense!" Feeling the blush flaming in her cheeks, Elizabeth waved a hand before her to shoo Phoebe from the room.

Giving Elizabeth a saucy wink over her shoulder, Phoebe started for the door. "Call it what you will! You're doing a shameful job of keeping this from me."

"It is but a figment of your overactive imagination. And you can tell Charlotte that, as well. Now good day."

"I suppose Basil's coming by this evening?"

Elizabeth sighed impatiently. "Quit lingering, Phoebe. For your information, he has already come and gone."

"A pity. What on earth shall you do all evening?"

Clasping her hands before her, Elizabeth pursed her lips with determination. "I've another, rather pressing engagement." And though Phoebe was well out of earshot, scurrying toward her room, Elizabeth muttered aloud, "And one that cannot wait."

With a resolute set of her head, she gathered her things and set out in search of her coat and Lewis, the coachman. He knew well the way to the Sinclair country home. Her step was purposeful and her intent unwavering. This time, nothing would deter her from her purpose. Nothing.

Alec looked up from his work and rubbed weary eyes. Laying his quill aside, he rested his elbows upon the desk and pressed his fingers to his throbbing temples. His bleary gaze settled upon the fire, though he achieved little solace staring upon those gentle flames. The lengthening shadows prompted him to light a lamp but he chose to linger in the gathering dusk, hoping that a few moments' respite might ease his tension. God only knew a brandy would help. His gaze wandered to the decanter upon the sideboard.

"What the hell," he grumbled, rising from his deep leather chair and pouring himself a liberal draft. He sipped slowly and paused to stare into the fire. Funny how a simple taste could conjure an image, a memory and all the feelings that accompanied it. Indeed, as the liquor worked its way through him, his mind filled with the image of long slender limbs swathed in a sheath of red velvet, luminescent skin as smooth as the finest of silks, and full pouty lips parted with a whimsical smile as her head tilted to his.

He scowled into his glass and pondered refilling it, though he knew if he did he would accomplish nothing in the way of constructive work for what remained of the night, a chance he could ill afford. Indeed, his duties had occupied him late into the evening, every evening for the past several weeks. God only knew, if offered the briefest chance, he'd have found himself at the town house seeking Elizabeth on more than one occasion.

He studied his empty glass with brooding eyes. So much for setting her from his mind. The thought that he would prefer an evening spent in her chaste company to that of any number of women, eager and willing to warm his bed, settled heavily upon him.

"For God's sake, I'm no damned eunuch," he growled, setting his glass aside with a pronounced thud. He'd be damned if he didn't get her out of his system, tonight! He knew of just the place, very exclusive, catering only to the most elite clientele. He'd patronized the establishment but once, very long ago, just after Celestine had left, and the memory, though vague, was more than vivid enough to suit him. His pulse quickened and he spun about with a determined set to his jaw, when quite suddenly a crimson-clad female form filled the doorway.

He stopped short, his eyes assessing her from head to toe, missing not the slightest detail. The unmistakable look in her eye and the cut of her dress brought the familiar scowl to his features and a foreboding tone to his voice. "Celestine, if you value your life, you will see yourself from my house post-haste."

As if she hadn't heard, Celestine ventured several paces into the room. "Oh, come now, Alec, can't we let bygones be bygones?" She shrugged delicately within her velvet cape, enough to allow it to fall off her shoulders, laying bare her generous bosom all but offered up for the taking by the low scoop neckline. Her hair was caught loosely at the top of her head so that several blond curls tumbled artlessly to her shoulders and one nestled coyly between her breasts.

Alec's eyes dropped to the unabashed display, then rose to find her glittering amber gaze sweeping heatedly over his torso, lingering upon his hips, then literally flaming over his legs. The woman left little doubt as to what she was after.

Her eyes met his and she arched a delicate brow. "You're looking awfully good, Alec."

He stared at her, unmoved, knowing full well she wished desperately for him to return the compliment. Not that he wouldn't have found her irresistible at one time, very long ago, and, no doubt, many men would still be hard-pressed to find a woman to rival her beauty. But he knew that beneath the honey blond veneer lay a heart of ice and a twisted, scheming little mind that could never be trusted.

"Well!" With a saucy smile that curved her heavily rouged lips, she moved to the fire, quite close to him, and allowed her cape to slide to her elbows.

Alec observed her through hooded eyes and found himself very aware of the cloying, musky scent of her perfume, so much so that he was left to wonder if she'd bathed in it. How in God's name had he ever thought himself in love with such a creature?

"So, aren't you going to offer me a drink?" She turned and smiled. "I fear I'm in great need of one."

"Get the hell out, Celestine," he muttered, moving past her to shuffle distractedly through the papers piled upon his desk.

"Alec, please . . ."

"You heard me."

"You're not being fair."

He spun about so quickly Celestine jumped. "Fair?" His hand shot out toward her and he gave a caustic laugh. "Don't jest with me. Get out."

She moved toward him, a desperate, pleading look in her amber eyes, and he gave her his back before she could get any closer. "Alec, please, we must talk."

"Nothing you could possibly say holds any interest for me."

"You don't mean that. What about Phoebe?"

He raised his head and gave the darkened windows a disbelieving look. "Yes, what about Phoebe, your only child, the one you abandoned ten years ago?"

"Oh, Alec, don't be so cruel . . . oh!"

Alec closed his eyes and shook his head with wonder at the woman's wiles. Her muffled sobs echoed through the small room, followed closely by delicate sniffling and her murmured, "I . . . I seem to have misplaced my hankie, Alec."

Heaving an agitated sigh, he turned and offered her his linen handkerchief. She accepted it, raising shining eyes and a meek little smile. He studied her bent head, surprised at the pity he felt for her. Then, when she seemed to pause and draw the handkerchief almost lovingly against her cheek before making good use of it, Alec had to wonder if this was yet another ploy.

"I . . . I've been to see her, you know, at that school she attends." She shrugged. "I certainly hope it is adequate for her."

"More than adequate."

"And her teachers?"

"The very best England has to offer, I can assure you."

Celestine seemed satisfied, though Alec wondered if the woman had given the matter even a moment's thought over the past ten years. "She looks good, a trifle plump, but then again, I was just like her at that age. And look at me now."

Alec kept his bearing impassive though his patience was wearing thin. "What's your point, Celestine?"

She waved a perfectly manicured hand. "We talked."

"I'm surprised she even spoke to you."

"I fear she was a trifle worried about making a scene in front of her friends. Though God only knows, that awful Mrs. Pettibone left me with little choice but to seek her out at the school! The woman won't allow me to step foot in this blasted castle!"

"She's always been the most obedient of the servants, though tonight I believe Casper's flu required her attention. Had it not, I doubt you would have stepped foot in the place."

Celestine pursed her lips in exasperation. "Alec, Phoebe seems fine on the surface, but for heaven' sake, the girl needs a mother."

"No mother is preferable to one who cares more for herself than her child."

"Oh, Alec, you judge me too harshly."

"And you try my patience, Celestine." He turned to his desk, waving a hand to the door. "Need I show you the way out?"

"Oh, Alec!" Before he could react, she moved in a rustle of taffeta, slipping her hands about his waist, clutching at his tightened belly beneath the linen of his shirt. Burying her face in his back, she sobbed brokenly, "Oh, Alec, forgive me...you must!"

Grasping her hands, Alec spun about and attempted to set her from him, which proved far greater an undertaking than he'd imagined. Perhaps her desperation had manifested itself in an uncommon strength. Whatever the reason, he found that the moment he'd grasped her hands, she threw herself against him, driving him back a few paces against his desk.

"Oh, Alec..." she moaned, rubbing herself wantonly against his entire length. "How I've missed you, darling! You remember, don't you, the passion we once shared, the love..."

"Love?" His jaw tensed with his mounting anger. He grasped her firmly about the waist in an attempt to ease her from him. "You're making a fool of yourself, Celestine."

She flung her arms about his neck in a stranglehold, burying her face against his chest. "Kiss me, darling, just once... dear God, how I've missed you."

"Celestine, don't make me embarrass you." His words were gruff and he turned aside his face with revulsion as she began to feverishly kiss his chest, his neck, his cheek.

"Oh, Alec, I don't care," she moaned huskily, grasping his face in her trembling hands. "All I know is that I want you ... desperately...." And with that, she pressed her lips to his so forcefully that Alec was momentarily caught off guard. Ah, but he should have known. He felt her hands in his hair, her hips grinding against his, and for the first time in his life he considered employing brute force with a woman simply to get away from her. Then another voice, ringing clear and true through the room, crashed upon him like a bucket of ice-cold water.

"Oh my goodness!"

Chapter Fourteen

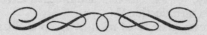

Elizabeth's throat went bone dry. "I—I'm awfully sorry. I—" Just as she spun on her heel to flee the room, Alec's bark filled the air.

"Elizabeth!"

Somehow, he had managed to pry himself from Celestine's embrace in time to grasp her arm. His hold upon her seemed made of finely tempered steel. Elizabeth's gaze found the floor and she cursed the tears that threatened.

"Let me go . . ." she whispered for his ears alone.

"Look at me," came the muttered response in a tone so thick with emotion Elizabeth had to dare a glance at him.

Their eyes met for the briefest of moments, colliding like the fiercest of storms, until hers fell to his cheek, his neck, his shirt, before fixing upon his mouth. The stain of Celestine's rouged lips left little doubt in Elizabeth's mind that she had indeed intruded upon a most intimate moment. Her eyes swept about, noting the purposefully soft lighting, the empty glass, the crimson cape still lying upon the floor where it had been hastily discarded in the heat of passion. An ache welled in her throat.

His grip upon her arm tightened and his eyes bored into hers. "Listen . . . it's not what you think."

"Don't flatter yourself, Alec," she ground out. "Phoebe is my sole concern."

"Phoebe!" In a rustle of crimson taffeta, Celestine rushed forward, laying a hand possessively upon Alec's arm. The woman looked so flushed and breathless that Elizabeth felt an overwhelming urge to slap her silly. "My darling daughter! What's happening to her?"

Drawing her cloak close, Elizabeth attempted to ignore Celestine's hand clutching at Alec's sleeve or the fact that the woman's breasts were all but out of her gown. "Perhaps you should ask your husband."

For some reason, "husband" seemed to please Celestine tremendously, for she crooned and plucked at Alec's sleeve. "Darling, an introduction."

Alec's stormy glare fixed relentlessly upon Elizabeth. "Celestine DuBois, Elizabeth Burbridge, Phoebe's teacher."

Celestine arched a delicate brow. "Is that so, Miss Burbridge? It *is* Miss, is it not?" Her eyes narrowed. "You look a trifle familiar. Could we have met before?"

Elizabeth lifted her chin a notch. "I attended a benefit for better education several weeks ago. Perhaps it was there."

For several moments, Celestine seemed to search her memory, then she leaned forward with a wave of her hand. "Oh, of course! Now I remember! You were talking to Alec and you were in that red...velvet...dress." Her smile faded as if she'd been struck by a sudden awful thought, and her eyes flickered to Alec then to Elizabeth and back again. With a smile that never quite reached her eyes, she positively purred, "Well, if you've anything to say regarding Phoebe, I'd like to hear it. After all, I am her mother, you know."

Oh, how Elizabeth knew! Her blurring gaze slid over the feline form curled against Alec, past the stain marring what had been a spotless sweep of white linen shirt to the eyes boring almost savagely into hers. He stood stoic, immobile, unreadable. Though he seemed almost oblivious to the woman rubbing herself all over him, he made no moves to discourage her, which Elizabeth deemed ample encouragement for a woman of Celestine's obvious appetites.

Attempting to control the trembling in her voice, she said, "No...no, I can see this is not the time. It can wait. Good evening." With a curt nod, she swept toward the door and would have flung herself through that massive portal and into her coach without a backward glance had Alec not followed closely at her heels. He caught her arm as she hurled the door wide, allowing a blast of angry January wind to sweep into the foyer, accompanied by a tumble of fresh snowflakes.

She spun about and attempted to wrench her arm free. "Your crude methods of detaining me are wasted, Alec!" she warned, aware that Celestine lingered just ten paces away in the study door, shivering delicately within her flimsy taffeta.

"Elizabeth, you're too damned stubborn for your own good. Listen to me." His hold intensified upon her, spurring her frustration. The wind ruffled his hair, yet he seemed oblivious to the harsh elements.

Elizabeth tugged urgently to free her arm. "If Phoebe is your concern, you shall receive a full report on her progress by post." Her eyes strayed to Celestine for the briefest of moments before focusing upon him once again. "Perhaps you and your lovely wife could discuss it together then."

"She's not my wife!" Alec roared into the howling wind. "And you damned well know it!"

"That's of little concern to me, Lord Sinclair. Phoebe is my priority and the sole reason I have anything to do with you!" Of their own accord, her eyes slid to the stain upon his lips, his cheeks, his chest.... "How I loathe you at this moment," she ground out, yanking her arm from his grasp. Without a moment's hesitation, she spun about, clutching at her skirts, and lurched toward the waiting coach just as her tears spilled to her cheeks.

The door slammed with a ferocious bang and Alec spun about to fix a deadly look upon Celestine. "Get the hell out!"

"Alec..."

"Now!"

She shrank from him as he strode determinedly past her, directly to his discarded glass, and poured himself a hefty portion of the brandy.

"Darling, whatever is the matter?"

He drained the glass in one gulp and shot a deprecating glance at her. "Before I do you bodily harm, get the hell out of my house, Celestine. And don't come back."

She eased forward, spreading her hands wide in supplication until his glower stilled her progress. She gave him a suspicious look. "Why, Alec, you're awfully angry of a sudden. Perhaps this mousy Miss Burbridge holds some fascination for you."

"Hold your tongue, woman!" he barked, refilling his glass.

"Ah, I see. For heaven' sake, you must be awfully desperate to find such an old maid appealing!"

He glared at her over the rim of his glass. "Celestine, even on your best of days, your beauty pales in comparison to hers."

She gaped at him and clutched a hand to her bosom. "My God, Alec, you're in love with the girl!"

He stared at her then drained his glass. "If I am, it has little bearing on my decided lack of feeling for you. Now, get out."

"I can't believe it! It's almost laughable!" Her throaty laughter sent a chill of murderous rage through Alec.

"Get out!" he roared, slamming down his glass and taking several steps toward her. Apparently the fists clenched at his sides caused Celestine to consider doing just that, and she backed slowly toward the door.

"Now!" The ferocity of his roar proved the final straw, as did the cape he hurled at her, which sent a wide-eyed Celestine through the front door as if she ran for her life.

The slam of the door echoing throughout the house nearly obliterated Alec's bellow of unmitigated frustration. For a moment he pondered his fists, still clenched at his sides, fists he could well use upon himself, damned idiot that he was to have allowed that . . . *that* . . . into his house. He spun to the brandy again and stopped just short of another glassful. He had never been one to seek solace in spirits before. Now was certainly not the time to start. His life was enough of a shambles as it was.

Elizabeth. Damned stubborn, foolish woman! Why the hell was he so besotted with the girl? Why the hell did it matter so damned much that she understood he would never feel even the slightest warmth or desire for Celestine? God . . . all he wanted was to sweep the pain from those enormous violet eyes, to penetrate yet again that chilly reserve, that carefully tended veneer. . . .

His eyes strayed to the curved set of windows and the snow falling in huge flakes beyond. A sudden gust of wind rattled the panes and served as a grim reminder of the harshness of this winter night. Running a hand swiftly through his hair as if to brush aside the effects of the brandy, he snatched his coat from a nearby chair and set out determinedly for the stable.

Basil stood at his dark bedroom window, staring at the snow swirling upon the cobblestones below. The soft sounds of stirring from his bed beckoned him to rejoin Felicity upon the tumbled sheets yet again. He'd hesitated not a moment in bedding the eager maid the instant she'd entered his room this evening, little suspecting that his ardor had been stoked to the limits of his endurance not by her but by the woman he'd come to desire more than any other in his life.

Elizabeth . . . immune to his charms, even startled by his bumbled attempts to seduce her, and for those very reasons all the more alluring. A virgin witch-goddess, she was, and the woman he intended to marry before the month was out, by God, or he'd die trying.

Felicity's tiny hands slipped beneath his robe to encircle his waist and she pressed her naked warmth against his back. The tiny hands stilled their soft stroking of his belly and Felicity's voice took on a plaintive tone that drew him unpleasantly from his thoughts. "Basil, what is it? You've said she believes your ploy. What could be troubling you?"

Basil turned, his hands rising to fondle Felicity's derriere in a distracted manner. "Oh, she's responding quite well. If it weren't for that damned Sinclair . . ."

"Who?"

Basil released her and stalked about the room, his hands thrust into the pockets of his robe. "Alec Sinclair, that's who! The damned bastard's got her beneath his roof!"

"So?"

Basil stopped short and stared at Felicity as if the girl hadn't a brain in her flaxen head. He barely noticed that she was stark naked. "So? How can I get anywhere with the girl if she's living with that man?"

Felicity moved to the bed and drew the sheet around her shoulders. "Our Elizabeth? Living with a man?"

Basil resumed his pacing. "Well, she is, damn it all! I know not why. The mere mention of the man's name and she blushes clear to her toes. Can't even look me in the eye for quite some time thereafter.'' His eyes narrowed. ''If I didn't know any better, I'd think she was in love with him.''

''Sinclair...Alec Sinclair...'' Felicity raised a wide smile. ''Oh, yes! I know him! He's been to the house to visit Lord Cosgrove from time to time. Oh, he's very dashing, handsome, and so nice.''

Basil stared at the girl. ''For God's sake, Felicity, I don't need to hear that!''

For several long moments, the young maid peered closely at him, until a pout formed upon her lips. ''Why, darling, you're acting as if *you're* in love with *her!*''

Rolling his eyes heavenward, Basil sighed heavily. ''Now, you know very well it's part of the plan that I seduce the girl.''

Felicity's narrow shoulders shook with first one soft sob, then another. ''But you needn't enjoy it.''

Unmoved by the girl's display, Basil turned again to the windows, where Elizabeth's face loomed vividly. ''It's not my fault that she's beautiful...and intelligent. All a man could ever hope for in a wife.''

''Oh, Basil!''

''It will only make it that much less bothersome to marry her.'' Ignoring Felicity's blubbering and sniffling, he muttered half to himself, ''What would the old man do if I introduced her as my bride? The thought is almost too tantalizing to dismiss.''

''You seem rather certain that she will marry you, Basil, despite Alec Sinclair.''

''I can always threaten the girl, Felicity, expose her for what she is, who her mother is, though I've enlisted some help in distracting Sinclair.''

Felicity rose from the bed and moved to stand in a tear-stained heap before him. ''Help? From who?''

Basil cocked a supremely self-assured brow. ''Sinclair had a wife at one time. I've been to visit the woman. After exchanging a few simple pleasantries, I had little trouble convincing her that we could help one another's causes immeasurably.''

Felicity stared at him. ''You didn't tell her why?''

Basil heaved an agitated sigh. "What, do you think me daft? Of course I didn't tell her! She simply believes me to be desperately in love with Elizabeth, seeking only to ensure that Sinclair does not pose any great threat." He reached for her, sweeping the sheet to the floor and drawing her against him. "We alone share this secret, Felicity. It's imperative that it remain thus. You will benefit immeasurably by it."

"But if you marry her, what becomes of me?"

Basil smiled wickedly and his hands roved over her back then cupped her full breasts. "It will only be until Nigel dies, darling Felicity, and the fortune becomes mine."

With a soft sigh, Felicity swayed against him. "But once you marry her, Lord Cosgrove will surely discover your plot."

"So? She's his sole heir. He will not disinherit her. His love for her far outweighs his contempt for me."

"You seem so sure of this."

Drawing her hard against him, Basil stared into her innocent eyes. He wasn't about to tell her that he had every intention of killing Nigel should the old man ever consider altering his will in any way after Elizabeth became his wife. Basil pressed his lips to her neck and nipped at the soft skin. "Trust me."

"But what of Elizabeth, then, once you inherit the fortune? If I am to be your wife..."

Basil almost laughed aloud at the girl's naiveté. To think that he would forsake Elizabeth Burbridge to take a simple maid as his wife! True, Felicity's body fit well into his hands, her limbs supple, her passion genuine. Yet even with her in his arms, he couldn't help but envision Elizabeth thus.

"Time, darling, give it time..." was all he could murmur in response as his hands wandered. Had Felicity but known of his wayward thoughts... His mind filled with the image of Elizabeth before him, her red velvet dress sagging from her shoulders to reveal her bosom in all its ivory-skinned splendor. He felt her hands threading through his hair, her soft voice murmuring *his* name, not Alec Sinclair's. In his mind's eye, her hair fell in a heavy ebony curtain about them, and he inhaled deeply of her fragrance, nearly insane with his desire for her.

"Ah, Elizabeth, my love..."

Felicity jerked so violently he was sent sprawling upon his backside. "What the hell is the matter with you?" he bellowed.

Felicity drew a trembling hand to her bosom. "Me?" she shrieked. "You called me Elizabeth!"

Basil rose shakily to his feet, searching frantically for a response. "You imagined it. Come here."

"No!" she shrieked again, and he winced. "I did not imagine it! You think me a fool!"

He took several steps toward her. "I would never think such a thing, darling Felicity." Grasping her trembling hand, he murmured, "Get a hold of yourself, darling. If I did call you by another name, it is only that I am consumed by this. I must succeed. For both of us."

For several moments, Felicity stared at him as if she experienced some difficulty believing him. When her eyes flickered to his chest, Basil knew a relief so great he nearly whooped with joy. When her eyes moved lower still and widened appropriately at his unabashed display of passion held in check, Basil needed no further invitation. With a sweep of his arms, he lifted her from the floor and bore her to the bed. He'd be damned if he'd allow her another moment to reconsider. Even a woman as gullible as Felicity could not be deceived forever.

Chapter Fifteen

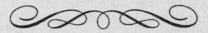

Before Elizabeth could slip her cloak from her back and dust the snowflakes from her hair, she was met with Winifred's startled expression as the maid skidded to a halt before her.

"Miss Burbridge, ye look as if the devil were on yer tail!" The plump woman eased the cloak from Elizabeth's shoulders and folded it neatly over one arm. "A storm's a-brewin' out there, to be sure."

"Yes, it is." Elizabeth caught a glimpse of her reflection in the foyer mirror and nearly winced. Her eyes were puffy, her cheeks blotchy, and the tip of her nose glowed a bright red, all from a very good cry.

"Lass, ye look awful, if'n ye don' mind me sayin'. 'Tis a frightful cold ye've got, eh?"

Elizabeth ventured a weak smile.

"We'll tend te that in a jiffy!" Winifred slipped a plump arm about Elizabeth's shoulders and guided her into the parlor. "Now sit yourself down, right here, before this nice cozy fire. Here's a blanket fer yer legs." The maid smoothed the damp tendrils from Elizabeth's forehead. "I'll stoke a fire in yer room and bring ye up a nice warm bath. Like me own mother used te say, there's nothin' like a hot bath an' a warm snug bed to cure what ails ye."

A sharp pang sliced through Elizabeth's heart as Winifred bustled off toward the kitchen. Bidding the woman farewell would be heart-wrenching indeed, but scant reason to delay her departure. If it weren't for the blasted storm, she could be gone this very eve. Why, she had no more right to remain here . . .

A broken sob escaped her lips. Tears welled and slipped
down her cheeks, splashing heedlessly upon the woolen blanket covering her lap. *His* blanket, in *his* house, his and Celestine's. She was no better than an intruder, a homeless waif,
foolish enough to believe that she could live in Alec's house and
remain immune to the man. Trembling fingers rose to her lips
as the memory of the kisses they'd shared in this very room
tumbled over her, then suddenly an unbridled anger sent the
blood coursing through her limbs.

"Dear God, how I hate him! If he would but walk through
that door, I would claw his bloody eyes from his—"

At that moment, the front portal burst open with a ferocious bang and a swirl of snow. Before Elizabeth could leap to
her feet, the door slammed shut with equal ferocity and three
heavy and determined footfalls brought a snow-covered Alec
skidding to a halt just inside the front parlor.

Winifred's concerned voice filled the foyer. "Lord Sinclair,
sir, yer soaked to the bone!"

Alec glowered at the maid. "Not now, Winifred."

"But, sir . . ."

The snow-covered brows gathered in a deep scowl. "Go
home, Winifred. You won't be needed until morning. Inform
the rest of the staff of the same. Oh . . . and thank you."

The maid's eyes widened and her face grew extraordinarily
pale. She glanced between Alec and Elizabeth, bobbed her head
and opened and closed her mouth. "I . . . er, sir, 'twouldn't be
seemly . . ."

"Woman, I don't give a damn!" he bellowed, turning so ferocious a scowl upon the poor maid that she fled the foyer,
clutching at her cap to keep it upon her head.

Elizabeth rose on unsteady legs, clutching the blanket, her
eyes sweeping over his bulk. His face looked frozen, whipped
by a frigid wind, yet he made no move to discard his coat to
warm himself before the fire. Indeed, he seemed unaware of his
physical state, so intent was his focus upon her. Her anger
sputtered yet refused to die. His abrupt manner in dismissing
the staff and what that implied brought the color high in her
cheeks and the words tumbling from her lips.

"You weathered a tempest in vain, Alec, if it is I you seek. I've nothing to say to you."

"Fine," he muttered, impatiently shrugging out of his coat and tossing it carelessly aside. With two long strides he stood before her. "Then I trust you won't interrupt me, because I've got a hell of a lot to say to you."

Elizabeth lifted a haughty chin. "I've no use for your mindless prattle. Step aside and let me pass."

"Not on your life." His hands upon her arms forced her to resume her position upon the settee.

"Nothing you could possibly say would interest me, Alec. Now, let me pass!" She clawed at his hands, then shoved at him in an attempt to flee. With a curse, Alec swung one long muscled leg over hers and pushed her flat on her back, pinning her arms with his.

His face loomed close above hers, his chest pressing against her heaving bosom. When he spoke, his breath, smelling of warm sweet brandy, fanned her cheeks. "Stop fighting me, you little she-cat. I'm a touch stronger than you."

Elizabeth's heart thumped wildly within her breast, and when his eyes narrowed upon hers then lowered to her mouth, she knew a sudden dread. "Surely even *you* would hesitate in taking an innocent maid against her will?"

His eyes burned intently into hers. "Trust me, Elizabeth, when I take you, you will be more than willing."

"When?" she shrieked. "You conceited cad! Go back to your Celestine! Perhaps she wishes to feed that ego I so abhor!"

"I don't want Celestine."

Elizabeth couldn't resist a wry incredulous laugh. "Forgive me if I don't believe you, Alec. I don't think she would, either. Typically, kissing a woman does not imply abhorrence. Even I know that!"

"And that's about all you know," he gritted through clenched teeth. "Did it ever occur to you that things might not be as they seem? Not everything in this world, my innocent Elizabeth, is as black-and-white as you would like it to be."

"What the devil do you mean?"

"For God's sake, Elizabeth, the deceitful, scheming Celestine arouses in me nothing but disgust."

"Disgust? You have an unusual way of showing it! Don't take me for a fool, Alec. It was not disgust that I saw in that study."

A dark brow lifted wickedly. "My, my, Elizabeth, how your claws bare—"

"You conceited ass! It's Phoebe's welfare that concerns me, nothing more!"

"Ah, yes. My daughter. The one destined for doom." He released one of her hands. "Truce?"

She nodded, brusquely, and he eased himself from her, pulling her to a sitting position. He remained close beside her, holding her hand far longer than was necessary. She yanked it rather obviously from his grasp.

"You really don't like me, do you?" he asked, as if he truly could not comprehend such a thing.

"The enormity of your ego never ceases to astonish me, Alec. No, I don't like you in the least. I never have and I never will."

"Who are you trying to fool, Elizabeth? Me or you?"

Beneath his regard, her purpose wavered. Never had the man looked so good. His hair shimmered with melted snow, beckoning for a hand to sweep the droplets aside. A day's worth of stubble only seemed to enhance the chiseled jawline and lent him a ferocity in keeping with his mood. His shirt clung to his muscled chest like a second skin, plucking incessantly at Elizabeth's resolve to remain physically unaffected by the man. If only her entire torso weren't burning from the feel of him pressed against her. If only he weren't sitting so close, his thigh resting against hers, his hands capable of reaching for hers without warning.

She lifted a hand to brush a stray curl from her shoulder, only to clasp it hastily in her lap when she realized that a trembling had seized her. Clearing her throat, she raised a level gaze to him. "It's a heinous injustice, what you have done to the poor child."

"What now, Elizabeth? Don't tell me, did you find a spider in your bed or a snake in your desk?"

Her anger sprang to life in the face of the man's thickheadedness, his mocking smirk, his casual dismissal of her concerns. "You bloody arrogant lout! It is a disgrace and the very reason I ventured to see you this eve, fool that I am! You have allowed her to agonize over this situation with your blasted wife for far too long! She deserves much more than a passing moment of your precious time! Why, the girl is aching over this! She needs guidance, though God only knows why I'm telling *you* this, a man of no morals, a complete roué—"

He slanted her a wicked glance. "Why do I get the distinct feeling that it's not Phoebe who agonizes so over this."

"Ugh!" Elizabeth cried with a frustration that suddenly knew no bounds. "The conceit! Be gone! I've nothing more to say to you!" With that, she scooted from the settee and ran for the stairs.

"Oh, no you don't!"

She nearly shrieked when Alec's footsteps echoed in her wake. As if the devil were indeed after her, she dashed up the stairs, down the hall, clutching at her skirts, knowing, even without looking, that he followed closely at her heels. This was all too evident when she raced into her chamber and attempted to slam the door closed behind her. With a fierce bang, Alec shoved the door wide and without preamble strode into her room.

She spun about before the fire, pointing to the door. "If it is your desire to shake every door from its hinges in one evening, you are doing an excellent job!"

"Shut up, Elizabeth."

"What?"

"Listen to me—"

With an impatient toss of her head, Elizabeth shrieked, "Listen? To what, pray? More of your inane ramblings, full of conceit? Thank you, but no, I've had my fill!"

"Is that so?" He reached her in two huge strides, grasping her shoulders and shaking her firmly, his eyes blazing into hers. "You'll listen because you want to. Because you need to."

Elizabeth froze, pinioned by the force of his gaze, the untested strength of his arms. "I don't need anything from you." The words tumbled from trembling lips. "I hate you . . . hate your flimsy excuse for paternal guidance . . . your damned arrogance . . ."

The firelight shadowed the hollows of his jaw and flamed in his fathomless eyes. "Don't speak too hastily, innocent one, for there is so much more between us, isn't there? Listen to me." He drew her roughly against him, his voice a hoarse murmur. "God only knows why, but I want only one woman, desire only one." His hand slid around to cup her chin and his thumb rubbed as soft as thistledown along her jaw. "You, Elizabeth. Only you."

Elizabeth's knees buckled and she twisted and slumped in his arms. "No . . . God, no! How foolish do you think me?"

He caught her against him. "You seek the truth, Elizabeth. Don't run from it now."

Tears welled, tears of frustration, of longing, of confusion and pain. Her eyes lifted to his. "The truth?" she whispered. "You stand before me, smelling of another woman, wearing the stain of her lips across your chest, and you wish me to believe you?"

"She wanted it, Elizabeth, not I," he said, wiping her tears aside. "To what end would I stand before you thus and not speak truth?"

To what end, indeed! Yet he allowed her but a moment's thought. With one sweep of his hand, he ripped the shirt from his back so violently that Elizabeth spun about, the blood pounding ominously in her ears. A tremulous anticipation bubbled to life within her, and a mind-numbing fear threatened her sanity when she heard the soft splashing behind her.

"Look at me." His voice was so sensuous she could not deny him or herself, despite her every wish to do otherwise.

She turned and her breath caught in her throat at the sight of him standing bare-chested beside the bathtub Winifred had so graciously provided. He passed a sponge over his jaw, then lower, across the bronzed expanse of chest, wetting the smooth dark hair and sending tiny rivulets down the ridged muscles of his belly to disappear inside his trousers. Elizabeth's eye was drawn to his arm as it flexed, again wiping the sponge over his shoulders and across the powerful ribs. His torso was lean and heavily muscled, as beautiful as she could ever have imagined.

And twice as imposing. Her fear compelled her to turn away and clutch a hand to her breast.

"Please..." A groan escaped her lips. "Take yourself from my chamber, Alec. You must."

"I can't." And then he was behind her, his hands spanning her waist, turning her, drawing her close. His damp chest pressed solidly against her, sending a delicious tingling through her breasts, plucking at her crumbling will. His hands cupped her face, his thumbs rubbing gently over her cheekbones. "You've nothing to fear from me."

Hopelessly, she shook her head and the tears spilled from her eyes. "Oh, but I do..." Her words were lost in the shudder that coursed through her when he pressed his mouth to her cheeks, kissing away each of her tears. "You're everything I despise...I struggle against."

"You can't hide from yourself forever." He removed the last of the pins from her hair, catching his hands in the silken tresses. "Lord, but you're beautiful...." His mouth found her neck, just below her ear, and his nuzzling made Elizabeth's breath catch in her throat.

"Touch me," he said, drawing one of her trembling hands around his neck. "Feel me. I won't hurt you."

Elizabeth's world swam crazily, all coherent thought melting like snow in her hands. "But, Alec, I..."

"Touch me." He gathered her close, pressing her full against him, his mouth playing upon her throat. "Use both hands, Elizabeth."

She tried, her palms sliding over bare shoulders, warm and undeniably strong, yet she detected a faint trembling in him. That she affected him thus sent a wave of giddiness through her and her hands ventured slowly down the sinewy length of arm, across his flexing back, then lower to his waist. How vibrant he felt, how natural it seemed to explore him thus, yet her fears could not be denied.

"I...you mustn't...we mustn't... It's so very wrong and I..." With a helpless groan, she allowed her head to fall back beneath the onslaught of impassioned kisses possessing her throat.

"You want it as much as I," he rasped against her neck. "Don't deny me, yourself. I won't hurt you. I promise..."

Before Elizabeth could catch her breath, his mouth swooped upon hers, parting her lips like the brand of a white-hot flame. Her fears scattered like startled birds and she melted into his arms, clinging to him as wave after wave of mounting desire surged forth, seeping into her limbs, coiling deep within her belly, never to be denied again. His passion awakened the sleeping lioness within her, drawing forth raw, primitive sensations that banished her fears and granted him every privilege. Thus, when the warmth of the fire caressed the bare skin of her back, then her shoulders, as he eased her dress from her, she could only cling helplessly to him. He knelt before her, tossing the dress into a forgotten heap at her feet, then slipping the straps of her chemise from her shoulders.

"Ah, Elizabeth..." he murmured hoarsely, his hands making quick work of the pink laces and allowing the flimsy garment to sag from her breasts. His eyes flamed over her exposed skin and he cupped her breasts, his thumbs brushing over the sensitive peaks.

Elizabeth sagged against him. His lips seared her skin and she could do naught but caress his head, pressed close against her, feeling the heat of his ragged breath upon her bosom, his hands urgently stroking every ounce of will from her. Her lips found his hair, and she inhaled his scent, wrapping her arms about his shoulders as if she couldn't draw him close enough. She luxuriated in his mouth moving heatedly over her breasts, but when he gently captured one nipple, she gasped. "Alec...don't. I..."

"Ah, Elizabeth..." His hands circled her waist then ventured lower to cup her derriere. "I couldn't stop if my life depended on it."

Elizabeth's breathy reply was lost in his deep groan as he rose and pulled her fiercely against him. Her chemise dissolved into a soft pile at her feet, drawing a gasp from her that he silenced in an instant with his kiss. Murmuring unintelligibly, he caught her up in his arms and bore her to the bed, looming in the darkness as it had in her subconscious for so long.

His eyes captured hers for a fleeting moment and so many words, still left unsaid, passed between them. "Do not deny me," he rasped hoarsely, placing her gently upon the sheets.

Her hands caught in his hair, eliciting from him a deep groan of pleasure as an undeniable urgency filled her, a yearning for him, for what she instinctively knew he alone could bring her. She gazed upon him as he shed his trousers and stood naked, proud and glorious before her. What should have sent her fleeing from the room only brought a hint of color to her cheeks, as did the passionate sweep of his eyes over her trembling body. Then, in one sensuous movement, he was upon her, his mouth tasting hungrily of hers, his hips pressing her into the soft bed. His passion engulfed her, obliterating the last vestiges of her resistance. Her desire flowed like molten fire, and she clasped him to her. Beneath his insistent touch, she parted her thighs, welcoming the searing pain of his thrust with an anguished cry that dissolved into soft whimpers beneath tender then impassioned kisses. These whimpers soon become soft gasps of unbridled desire, pure sensual delight as his hips moving sensuously against hers banished reality and lifted her to the heights of passion. He left her suspended at the pinnacle for but a fleeting, agonizing moment, until the flames bursting within her set her atumble amidst the brilliance of her womanhood finally discovered.

Emotions welled from depths heretofore uncharted, bringing tears from her eyes and a choked gasp from lips that found Alec's and clung. He gathered her close, burying his face in her neck. His pace intensified and he plunged deep within her, drawing a cry from her lips. She pressed her face to his shoulder, clasping him closer. His final thrust was accompanied by a throaty growl and a shudder that tremored through Elizabeth, as well, and she returned his languid kisses and soft sweet whispers with her own.

When he rolled from her and drew her close against him, she could do naught but burrow into his warmth, curving her arm over his chest, her hand into his hair, and nestle cozily within his arms, content, for the moment, simply to find sleep.

*   *   *

Alec closed his eyes. The skin beneath his hands felt like the finest of silks, her hair, tumbling over him, a fragrant cascade of shimmering satin. She was woman, soft, warm, yielding, and capable of a passion, an innocent sensuality, that rendered him her captive.

She stirred, burrowing closer to him, and the softest of sighs parted her lips. In an instant, his desire sprang to life, banishing any disquieting thoughts, and he shifted, cradling her in his arms and lowering his head to nuzzle at her breasts. At first his pace was leisurely as he suckled her, slowly caressing the swelling mounds. And then she moaned in her sleep and drew him closer.

He required no further encouragement. He eased her beneath him and rose above her, allowing his gaze to venture unheeded over her slumbering form. Her ivory skin shimmered in the soft firelight, playing gloriously over the swelling curves and shadowed hollows that captured his fascination. She was long of limb, sleek, slender, delicately boned, yet with an undeniable lushness that drew him irresistibly. As if entranced, he lowered his mouth to caress her narrow ribs, then swept lower, over the downy softness of her belly, slightly curved, warm, rising and falling with each breath she drew.

The blood pounded in his ears when her hands caught in his hair, caressing, urging, and he ventured lower still, into the dark curls beckoning him. He nuzzled her there, delighting in her soft moan of pleasure and struggling to keep his passion at bay. His hands grazed her hips then cupped her derriere, lifting her closer to him, when he grew dimly aware of a pounding, as if from very far away.

At first he thought it only the drumming of his pulse in his ears, but then it grew more insistent. He resisted, yet the urgent pounding continued, bringing a twinge of concern. With a scowl, he lunged from the bed, scooping up his trousers from the floor and impatiently tugging them on before stalking angrily from the room. Whoever it was would have hell to pay if his mission were not of the utmost importance.

Through the darkened halls he strode, acutely aware that the pounding on the front door had grown fierce, accompanied by an urgent calling of his name. He navigated the steps two at a time and swung the front portal wide. A blast of frigid air assailed him, deepening the furrowed brow he directed upon this unfortunate soul.

"Oh, yer lordship, sir!" Hiram whisked his cap from his head and held it tightly against his chest. His wide eyes noted Alec's bare torso then rose to meet Alec's gaze as if he suddenly realized the harm that could befall him were he not to spit out whatever it was that brought him to his lordship's door so late in the night. "I'm so very sorry, sir, te awaken ye..."

"I was awake." Alec gestured the coachman inside. "Come in, man. Warm yourself from the storm."

"Aye, sir. Thank ye, sir." Hiram gave Alec a sheepish smile and ambled into the foyer.

"Well?" Alec demanded, closing the door behind him. His yearning for Elizabeth was indeed very strong and he found himself growing agitated with Hiram's gaping about as if he'd never stepped foot in the place before. "Out with it, man!"

Hiram jumped as if caught unawares. "Oh, of course, yer lordship. A messenger came te the house, sir. He said a ship ran amuck in the harbor, bein' as there's a storm an' all. Sideswiped one of yer ships, sir. She's burnin' out o' control." He cringed beneath Alec's furious gaze. "I—I came as soon as I could, sir, not knowin' where te find ye. Mrs. Pettibone was nowhere te be found, an'—"

Alec clasped the man firmly upon the shoulder. "You did right, Hiram. I will be but a moment." He strode quickly to the stairs. "Saddle Sebastian for me," he barked over his shoulder, mounting the steps three at a time. "Posthaste! And a mount for you, as well. We'll travel quicker and easier on horseback."

Hiram's reply was lost upon Alec as he made his way back to Elizabeth's room. The sight that met him nearly proved enough to keep him there—to hell with his entire fleet of ships. Indeed, far more than the warmth of the fire beckoned. He knelt upon the bed, careful not to disturb her slumber, and bent to kiss her mouth. He tasted of her breath upon his lips then nuzzled her neck, breathing deeply of her fragrance. Of their own accord, his hands swept the sheet aside and found the softness of her breasts, and his desire raged.

"How you've captured me," he whispered against the warmth of her neck, almost shedding his trousers yet again. With a groan of the purest frustration, he rose and pulled the sheet over her then turned and hastened from the room, knowing full well that he would find neither warmth nor sleep for what remained of the night. Then again, he mused with a sly grin, had he remained in her bed, sleep would have proven just as elusive, if not more so.

Chapter Sixteen

Upon awakening the following morning, Elizabeth stretched as languorously as any woman ever had after a night of love-making. The ache in her muscles and the soreness between her thighs drew her from her dreamy state, yet her lips still curved with a soft smile. A flush warmed her cheeks and she snuggled beneath the sheets, eyes closed, instinctively reaching a hand in search of a fur-covered chest. Cold empty sheet was all that awaited her. She sat up, pushing her tangled mass of hair from her eyes and clutching the bed linens to her bosom.

"Alec?" Blinking the sleep from her eyes, she peered about the deserted room. One glance at the fog-enshrouded windows assured her the storm still raged, proving scant temptation to those of sound mind to venture out-of-doors. So where was he?

Her eyes flickered to the closed door and her ears strained for some sound. Perhaps he had ventured below for something to warm his belly before stoking the fire. She frowned, attempting to ignore the ominous gnawing in the pit of her stomach. Slipping from the bed, she shivered against the cold air and the icy chill of the barren floor beneath her toes and searched for her robe. As she turned, her eye fell upon the stain of her virtue marring the otherwise immaculate expanse of white sheet and she froze.

The enormity of what had occurred last eve descended like a pall over her, sweeping aside any vestiges of whimsy in favor of cold, cruel reality. Suddenly she grew shamefully aware of her naked state, of her lips, bruised and swollen from passionate kisses, and of the rawness between her thighs, as if she felt it for the first time. The silence in the house swelled around her, broken only by the rattling of the shutters beneath the onslaught of the storm's fierce winds. Instinctively she knew she was very much alone. Surely he hadn't left her?

Clutching the sheet about her shoulders, she sank to the bed and attempted to stave off the dread looming in the back of her mind. Yet, amidst her jumble of emotion, one thought rang clear. She had given herself to a man freely, without reservation or the benefit of marriage. With a groan of despair, she gave vent to her distress. The tears slipped heedlessly down her cheeks and she hung her head woefully in her hands. Dear God, she was a shameless tart, a wanton ruled only by her primitive carnal needs! She had become that which she despised most and she had only *him* to blame! Oh, to be so doomed! The tears spilled to the sheet she clutched and she buried her face in the cotton until she realized with a start that it smelled distinctly of him. She thrust the sheet aside, when suddenly the vision of Alec standing naked beside the bed formed in her consciousness.

"It is indeed my penance to bear the burden of this memory for the rest of my life," she choked hoarsely. She bit her lip, attempting to stave off another sob, but failed miserably, and the cry burst forth, accompanied by another moan of despair. "I gave myself to him believing myself in love with the man!" Passing a trembling hand over her cheeks, she pulled at the sheet and sighed heavily. "He, however, harbors no such delusions. No doubt that is the very reason he fled this room, braving the tempest lest I awaken to mewl and cling to him, harboring naught but the preposterous notion that I will soon become his bride! And I did, indeed, awaken thus! Dear God, I have become my mother!"

She allowed herself the leisure of a good cry until a grossly disturbing thought wriggled into her mind. Her eyes stared unseeing and her heart pumped angrily in her ears. It had been the cad's intent all along that this should happen! He had meant to keep her here as his mistress, safely ensconced within his house, forever eager and willing to indulge his every fancy! And how easy she had made it for him!

With a hissing breath, she threw the sheet aside as if the mere sight of it sickened her and strode to the armoire, flinging the doors wide. Four identical brown muslin dresses hung neatly in a row and she removed the first from its hanger. After a very quick, very cold washing of the night's activities from her, she donned the dress and carelessly swept her hair from her face to tumble freely to her waist. Such was her haste to get herself from that room.

Not that she was in any hurry to come face-to-face with Alec. God only knew she'd have killed the man were she to have found him loitering about below stairs. As it was, she found the house deserted save for Cook, and had just stoked a fire in the parlor when the front door burst open.

"Oh, Miss Burbridge! Thank heavens you're safe!" A snow-covered Phoebe, looking as if the wind had gotten the better of her, rushed into the room. "I simply had to see how you were faring with this storm!"

Elizabeth raised a knowing brow. "It was adventure you sought, Phoebe. No doubt the day loomed positively unbearable with no classes and the storm threatening to keep you indoors."

Phoebe shrugged a saucy shoulder and gave a sheepish smile. "You may be a tad on the mark, Miss Burbridge, but honestly, it was your company that I sought above all else. Besides, what better place to be found snowbound, with nothing but hot cider."

Elizabeth felt a smile curve her lips at the memory. "Oh, no you don't. Not for me. How on earth did you make your way? Did you summon Hiram?"

Phoebe's cheeks flushed a telltale pink and she lifted her shoulders in a helpless gesture. "Not exactly. You see, Father would not have approved of my venturing about in this weather. So I was left to secure help from Dunlevy's stable hand. You know, the rather handsome one with the curly blond hair and the trousers that fit him like a second skin."

"Phoebe!"

"Well, it's awfully difficult not to notice!"

"You could try!"

"I fear I cannot. Besides, it seems he favors me, as well. Actually, it was a relatively simple task getting him to bring me here in the coach." Phoebe's innocently raised brows proved more than enough to pique Elizabeth's curiosity.

"Phoebe, surely you didn't bribe the poor young man!"

"Of course I did!"

"Phoebe! You *are* destined for doom."

"Oh, Miss Burbridge!" Phoebe turned to exit the room and gave Elizabeth a saucy smile. "I'm counting on *you* to see to it that I'm not! Now, I must see what Cook's been up to all morning in that kitchen. I'm positively starving!"

How infectious the child was, brimming with vitality and a hunger for adventure. How dear she had become in so short a time. Far too dear, indeed, to abandon in the face of some heinous misunderstanding with Alec. Dear God, had she taken leave of her senses? Had she indeed risked her reputation, all that she had strived for, as well as Phoebe's trust, for the sake of some sordid tryst that meant nothing to Alec? A few intimate caresses and she was eager to forsake everything of worth in her life. How on earth was she to go on?

An insistent pounding upon the front door drew her unceremoniously from her thoughts. "Basil!" she exclaimed upon swinging the door wide. "What are you . . . ?"

He swept past her, along with a gust of frigid air, impatiently brushing the snow from his hair. He glanced about, scowled, then slipped his cloak from his back.

"Basil, for heaven' sake, why are you out and about in weather like this?"

He rubbed his hands together and indicated the parlor. "Your fire looks awfully inviting, Elizabeth. Shall we?" With his hand upon the small of her back, he guided her into the room. "The storm seems to be easing somewhat, though I would have come regardless. There's a matter that could not wait a moment longer. You needn't look so startled, my dear. It is not a subject that will cause you distress."

He settled close beside her upon the settee and she grew very aware of his eyes lingering on her hair, then dropping to her mouth. It seemed his wont, of late, to stare at her in this way, which made her extremely uncomfortable. Instinct dictated his preoccupation was not related to their work, which seemed to occupy less and less of his energy lately. Indeed, he appeared far more intent upon wooing her, a pursuit that did not settle too favorably upon her this particular morning.

Gathering her hand in his, he lowered his eyes as if he didn't quite know how to begin. "Elizabeth, your living here causes me great distress. You see, I know very well why you're here, thanks to young Miss Sinclair. You needn't explain why you found it necessary to keep the truth from me."

"Basil, it is really none of your concern."

"Oh, but it is. You see, Elizabeth, in the few short weeks I've known you, I rather suddenly realized that, well . . ." His eyes bore deeply into hers. "I'm in love with you, Elizabeth. Deeply so, I'm afraid."

Her jaw sagged. "You're what?"

A flicker of confusion scudded across his heavy brow. "I'm in love with you."

Elizabeth could only stare at him dumbly for several moments. "This is quite a surprise, Basil."

He scooted closer until the length of his leg brushed intimately against hers, and he gazed upon her with such unabashed hope that Elizabeth felt a pang of guilt slice through her. Perhaps she had enticed him in some way, though she'd never intended to. Dear Lord, her life was a shambles!

The light stroking of his hand upon hers captured her attention and she attempted to ease herself from his grasp. "B-Basil, please, it's awfully early."

He erupted with a deep chuckle yet made no move to release her hand. "Oh, my little innocent, my love for you knows not the passage of time, nor can I restrain my emotions until after the sun has properly reached its zenith."

"Perhaps you should try," Elizabeth replied with a bit more impatience than she would have liked to display.

Lurching from the settee, she fought to contain the shudder that threatened at the feel of him pressed urgently against her, of his hands upon her. Yet she did not wish to hurt this dear man. After all, her life's current state of upheaval wasn't Basil's fault. He had weathered the storm so terribly early in the day, driven by his need to unburden his soul to her. She should feel elation or, at the very least, gratitude and some lightening of heart.

Thus, she did not flee from his touch, as instinct dictated. Instead, she turned toward him and found herself in his arms, with his mouth descending to hers.

"Basil!" She shoved against his chest. "Basil, please!"

His hold loosened upon her, though his gaze grew decidedly stormy. "What is it now? Certainly not the blasted time of day. It's Alec Sinclair, isn't it?"

"What?"

"You needn't don your innocent, wide-eyed look for my benefit, Elizabeth. Are you in love with the man?"

"No!" Elizabeth cried so quickly and in such a strident voice that she was certain Basil harbored serious doubts as to her sincerity. She drew a shaky breath and managed a weak smile. "I mean, for goodness' sake, don't be silly."

"Are you aware that his wife, Celestine, is here in London?"

Elizabeth forced a lifting of innocent brows. "Is that so?"

Basil studied her so closely she was convinced those black orbs penetrated her every traitorous thought. "And rumor has it that a reconciliation is in the making."

"How nice."

"Indeed, it was only a matter of time, or so I've heard. Celestine simply had to return. Apparently, Sinclair has been eagerly awaiting her reappearance for quite some time now. I guess time has healed those wounds, though a child is a strong bond between two people, despite their differences, and could prove a formidable reason for reconciliation."

"Of course."

"And there's little denying their passion still burns true."

Elizabeth started visibly. "Excuse me?"

Basil gave her a slow understanding smile. "Of course, you're atrociously naive with regard to this and may find it a tad incomprehensible. But they had to marry due to the child they'd conceived out of wedlock, this daughter." He leaned close to her and uttered distastefully, "Their love child."

Elizabeth gulped and suddenly yearned for a cool glass of water. Basil, however, did not miss a beat.

"Being young and foolish, this Celestine gave up her passion for Sinclair for Theo DuBois, a man somewhat older, very well connected with society and fabulously wealthy. It seems our young Sinclair at that time was a relatively penniless young lord, titled but lacking the social stature and, perhaps most of all, the desire to acquire social position. As much of a recluse as he is now."

Resisting the overwhelming urge to leap to Alec's defense, Elizabeth bit her lip and murmured, "Indeed."

"Well, according to what I've heard, Celestine regretted her decision to leave after a relatively short time, though her husband's ailing health kept her at his side for years. Upon his death, though she grieved, of course, she hastened back to London and the ever eager Sinclair. One can only imagine how much they yearn for one another. That kind of passion, innocent Elizabeth, *never* dies."

Elizabeth's heart hammered in her chest. Summoning a strength of will she did not feel, she remarked, "It is a mystery, Basil, why this should be of any importance to me."

Basil gave her a knowing look. "Let me just say this. Imagine the talk, Elizabeth, which might be a subject of much discussion already, even as we speak. A young, innocent schoolteacher...living beneath the man's roof, unchaperoned. Not only are you jeopardizing your reputation, you are risking your position at Dunlevy."

"I would never intentionally do such a thing!"

"Intentional or not, it's what it looks like that matters. And this situation literally screams of immorality."

"Basil! How could you think such a thing?"

"Believe me, Elizabeth, it's not difficult, especially seeing the way Sinclair looks at you! Surely you've a notion!"

Elizabeth gulped and opened her mouth, yet the words of rebuttal, of blatant denial, would not materialize on her tongue. Basil required no further encouragement.

"Ah, I see. It's as I expected." He swept her into his arms and cradled her head against his chest. "Darling, you must leave this place, get yourself from beneath the man's roof before he forces himself upon you. He will, you know. I know the type well. That Celestine is back in his life is of little consequence. The man will keep his mistresses whether he's married or not. Dear God, the talk I've heard ... the man's a cad, an utter roué." Tilting her head up to his, he searched her eyes and said, "You've only one course of action, my love. Marry me."

Elizabeth blinked several times and squeaked, "What?"

A loving smile curved his thin lips and his hands ventured along her back. "You heard me, lovely one. Marry me, come live with me in my grand manor, far from Sinclair and his depraved notions. I shall protect you, love you, honor you with my name, something *that* man will never do. Say you will, darling."

Awash in a hopeless sea of confusion, Elizabeth slid from his arms and pressed a trembling hand to her aching brow. "Basil, I ... I can't give you an answer just yet."

"Of course, love. Think on it, leisurely if you must. Take your time. But I await your response eagerly and ever so hopefully." He grasped her hand and pressed his lips against it. "Do not keep me waiting for too long, my darling."

She gazed after him for some time after the front door closed behind him. With a sudden thought, she glanced at the windows and experienced a flood of relief. The storm was indeed subsiding, at least enough that even she might dare to venture about. Without further thought, she hastened in search of her cloak and Lewis the coachman. She had a call to make. One that had been a long time in coming.

So intent was she on her thoughts that Elizabeth failed to notice the plump form secreted just inside the drawing room, not ten paces from the parlor. A grin dimpled the rosy cheeks and the child all but clapped her hands together with glee. Her brief repast of Cook's delicious concoction had prevented her from eavesdropping on the entire conversation, but she had heard more than enough.

"Ooh, Miss Burbridge is betrothed! And to that wonderful Basil!" she gushed in a breathless voice as her eyes followed Elizabeth's speedy dash up the stairs. Best not to let Miss Burbridge know that she'd overheard. The woman had far more important things on her mind. Like a wedding! "Oh, I must tell Cook, and Holmes, and of course Father. He'll be so surprised!"

And with a last giggle of delight, she retreated as quietly as her soaring spirits would allow.

Chapter Seventeen

"Mother?" Elizabeth ventured but one step into the darkened room. A lone candle burning very low upon a small table cast the faintest of shadows through the tiny parlor. The heavy drapes had been drawn, the hearth left cold, leaving little doubt that the tiny form huddled upon the settee for warmth, at the very least. "Mother? Is that you?"

The figure started and swung a countenance both pale and drawn and frighteningly unfamiliar to Elizabeth. Violet eyes locked with violet until the woman quickly turned away as if she were terribly ashamed. "Oh yes, Elizabeth." The voice was undoubtedly that of her mother, as was the manicured hand she waved toward the door. "'Tis a dreadful day to come calling. Perhaps another time."

Elizabeth moved farther into the room and perched upon the settee. Her eyes swept over her mother, swathed in a shimmering gold silk robe, and she found herself startled by the unkempt tangle of auburn hair, which was typically so elegantly coiffed. Some sixth sense told her that her appearance and the trembling of her mother's shoulders were not due to any slight ailment.

Hesitantly, she reached a hand to Leonora's shoulder and gasped with surprise when that slight movement elicited a moan and a broken sob. "Oh, Elizabeth!" Leonora wailed, flinging herself into her daughter's arms.

Elizabeth found herself tempering her growing concern as she cradled the auburn head to her chest. The sobs finally gave way to choked hiccups and long, drawn-out sniffles, which Leonora chose to bury in the coarse muslin of Elizabeth's dress.

"I'm . . . I'm so dreadfully sorry you had to see me thus," Leonora choked. "Had I known you intended to call I would have . . . But, darling, I . . . I know not what to do! Oh, Elizabeth!"

"Mother!" Elizabeth lifted her eyes heavenward in a silent plea when her mother dissolved in a heap of sobs. "Mother, you must tell me what dreadful thing has happened."

Leonora dabbed gently at her swollen eyes and idly fingered her robe, her gaze lowered to her hands. "P-promise me you won't scold . . . or laugh."

Relief washed over Elizabeth like a cool spring rain. This "ailment" was nothing more than some blasted falling-out with a beau! Elizabeth willed herself to remain unruffled. "I promise."

Leonora sniffed. "'Tis that awful Reggie. It seems he has decided to return to his wife!"

"I thought he wasn't married."

"So did I!" Leonora seemed to draw herself up with renewed spirit. "It seems our titled lord has a wife all tucked away in the country somewhere. They've been estranged for some time, though little good that does me now! And to think he paraded me before his entire family at Christmas! No doubt they thought me some woman of easy virtue!" Leonora lifted a hardened gaze and held up a finger for emphasis. "*Never* trust a man, Elizabeth, especially a married man. They want but one thing, and if you accommodate them, if you make it easy for them in any way, they will use you heartlessly. And God help you if you fall in love with them. You will be a lost soul, mark my words."

Elizabeth's blood ran cold, her deepest fears realized. Naive though she was, Leonora had the benefit of experience, and for once Elizabeth chose to listen. "Mother, I'm terribly sorry."

Leonora waved a hand and grimaced. "Oh, don't be. It was my mistake, after all, and one from which I will learn, yet again. Let me tell you, though, never again will I carry on with a man unless he is as eligible as they come and all but upon bended knee before me, ring in hand. And even that holds no guarantees." She patted Elizabeth's hand encouragingly. "Thank heavens you have a profession, darling, which won't necessitate a man to keep you. You will never have to be bothered by such nonsense. Now, what brings you here, darling, on such a day? Not that I don't enjoy seeing you but, well, you know..." Leonora leaned a bit closer and whispered, "Did anyone see you, darling?"

"Mother! The coachman Lewis delivered me and awaits outside. He knew not whom I came to visit and I informed no one else of my plans. Rest assured, your secret remains safe."

"And yours, darling. So?" Leonora urged with a smile. "What is it that brings you here with your hair all atumble and your cheeks flushed so rosy." A slender hand rose to her half-opened mouth and the look in her eye was enough to bring the color flooding to Elizabeth's cheeks. "Oh, darling, don't tell me! You...and Alec...and...Oh, Elizabeth!"

Elizabeth put a quick end to her mother's hearty embrace. "Mother, it's not Alec. I mean..." She paused, awash in confusion and a jumble of emotion, then blurted, "Basil proposed."

"He what? Oh, how lovely! My daughter is going to be a bride before me! Darling, I'm so happy for you!"

"Mother! Please, listen to me! I have not accepted...yet."

"Why not, you silly goose? Proposals from eligible men do not hang on trees!" Leonora's brows lifted and a wicked smile curved her lips. "Ah, I see. It *is* Alec that has you in such a state. You're in love with him, aren't you. Oh, and by the looks of it, dreadfully so! Ooh, how delicious!"

"Mother, my life is not some sordid novel!"

"It could be, darling! You have all the necessary ingredients!"

Elizabeth studied her hands clasped primly in her lap. "It seems that Alec's wife has returned...rather...she used to be his wife."

Leonora bit her lip. "Oh, I see. Hmm, well, that does make things a trifle sticky."

"Sticky!" Elizabeth exclaimed, throwing her hands into the air and all caution to the wind. "He is determined not to marry again, insists she holds little interest for him and..."

"Ah, so you've discussed this with him, hmm? This is getting better and better. Do go on, Elizabeth."

"But I'm not certain that I believe him. You see, they have a daughter... a very strong bond."

Leonora nodded. "There's no denying that. A child between two people binds them forever. But, darling, he won't remarry her for that reason alone."

Elizabeth chewed at her lip. "Perhaps. It's just that I have the distinct feeling that his intentions with me are not... honorable... in the least."

Leonora stared blankly at her daughter then her mouth fell open. "Surely he hadn't taken you to his bed?"

Elizabeth closed her eyes. Hearing it was twice as bad as thinking it, if that were possible.

"Oh, Elizabeth, what have you done, darling?" Leonora shook her head woefully. "This is worse than I'd ever imagined! What are we going to do?"

"That's why I'm here," Elizabeth said, and found her trembling hand reaching for her mother's.

"You seek advice from a veteran, darling, though I hope my mood doesn't impose itself too heavily upon you." Leonora bent her head in thought then patted Elizabeth's hand. Raising eyes filled with a certain sadness, she offered an encouraging smile. "Marry Basil, darling, posthaste. It will save you from inevitable doom. Oh, don't look at me in that manner! You don't have to stop loving Alec! Indeed, you won't be able to help yourself! If that you could! *But*— and this is very important—if you marry Basil, live beneath his roof, sleep with him if you can bear it, have his children and make a life with him, the temptation to run to Alec's bed will grow less and less over time. However, if you don't marry Basil, try as you might to avoid him, Alec will impose himself upon you, charm you, woo you until you will be naught but putty in the man's hands. And then you will be truly lost. Not only will your reputation be sullied to the point that no man worth his salt will have you for his wife, but you will jeopardize your teaching, your very livelihood. And if you lose that, my dear, you will end up no better than I."

"Mother..." Elizabeth felt the tears spring into her eyes and she clasped her mother's hand to her breast. "If that I could one day be as wise as you, I would be grateful."

Leonora blinked several times then averted her face, though her trembling lower lip betrayed her. "Oh, stop it. You're embarrassing me. Now, go on, do as I say. Marry Basil, and for heaven' sake, invite me to the wedding!" Leonora's sparkling eyes darted about as if she were already lost in the planning of the event. "Why, you'll need a lovely trousseau for your wedding holiday, especially for your wedding night. Something truly delicious and..." Her eyes found Elizabeth's troubled countenance. "Darling, whatever is the matter? Now you mustn't pine away for Alec if you intend to make this a success."

Elizabeth closed her eyes and shook her head. "It's not that, but the mere thought of lying with Basil, especially after I...well, you know...with Alec and... Mother, I am but used goods already!"

Leonora gave a low, throaty laugh and waved a dismissing hand. "Oh, for goodness' sake, is that all that's bothering you? Just listen to me, darling, for I am a master at...well, let's just say that your Basil will never know the difference. He will think you as innocent and untouched as the day you were born."

"So, I am to begin my marriage with an act of deceit."

"Now, now, Elizabeth, let's not split hairs, hmm? Surely you didn't think yourself the first bride to feign innocence in the arms of her groom? Have you been living under a rock, darling?" Leonora grimaced and shook her head. "I presume Miss Percy has not seen fit to educate you thus. Now, where shall I begin with our little lesson? I know, let's start by practicing a few breathy moans, as if his mere touch were enough to send you into a swoon. Try it." Clearing her throat, she half closed her eyes and flung her head back, murmuring breathlessly, "Ooh, Basil...darling..."

Elizabeth stared at her mother. "This is ludicrous."

"Try it! Ooooh, Basil..." Leonora's voice was as deep and sensuous as the sumptuous blue velvet hanging at the windows and called to mind all sorts of intimate thoughts.

"Oh, Basil."

"For heaven' sake, Elizabeth! You want him to think you're about to swoon, not retch!"

"It's the latter that will no doubt occur!"

Leonora shook her head wistfully and her gaze grew dreamy. "I was once in love with a man, helplessly so, just as you are with Alec. Darling, I will not lie to you. You will never forget him, your first love, but you will go on. If you feel you must, when you're with Basil, pretend that you're in Alec's arms. That should elicit the proper response. But for heaven' sake, *don't* call him Alec. Dear God, there's no telling what that could do to your marriage. Now, when Basil takes you to his bed . . ."

When Elizabeth emerged from the parlor not more than an hour later, her cheeks still flamed from the candid words she'd exchanged with her mother. The lingering embrace they'd shared spoke volumes of the new bond she sensed between them, albeit a bond forged by her foolishness. Indeed, as she gazed upon her mother's careworn features, she realized that in the span of that one morning she'd achieved an understanding of her mother that heretofore she'd had little inkling of. She left her mother with tears shining in her eyes and boarded the coach, intent upon righting the disaster she had made of her life. But first she had to speak with Phoebe.

Before Sebastian skidded to a complete halt upon the snow-covered cobblestones, Alec eagerly dismounted, handing the wheezing stallion over to a dumbstruck Holmes with a distracted nod and an unintelligible murmur of instructions. The servant stared after his lordship then eyed the frothing stallion before him with a certain hesitation. Never in all his years under Lord Sinclair's employ had he seen him treat his animal thus. Indeed, the beast looked as if he had been ridden into the ground. The servant raised a curious brow. There was no denying that his lordship had been in a great hurry to return.

"Good morning!" Alec bellowed cheerily through the kitchen, halting his purposeful stride beside a startled Cook to bestow a resounding kiss upon the woman's softly lined cheek. Her girlish giggle and the sudden stain in her cheeks elicited a huge grin from Alec and he peered innocently into the enormous pot before her then scooped up a handful of apple muffins. "Mmm, and warm, too. Don't ogle me so, woman! I've been up all night battling a damned fire! We almost lost the ship!" He popped an entire muffin into his mouth and gestured to the ceiling. "Have Holmes bring a hot tub up for me, will you?"

The muffin did little to appease the gnawing hunger in Alec's belly, but of that he was only vaguely aware. Nor did the searing ache in his shoulders or the pain in his back temper his lighthearted mood or deter his thoughts. Indeed, a night's worth of backbreaking labor to save his ship had left him but all the more eager to return to the woman awaiting him above. Perhaps she hadn't yet stirred and still slumbered peacefully upon her bed, warm, soft, yielding . . .

His heart hammered within his breast and his determined stride lengthened, taking him swiftly through the house and up the stairs three at a time. His grin returned and he ran a hand briskly through his hair, though he knew this would do little to improve his appearance. Unkempt, unshaven, covered with grime and smelling from head to toe of smoke, he was not at all fit for greeting his love. Perhaps she would be willing to join him in his bath. God help him if she wasn't willing, though what he intended to say to her should appease even the slightest remorse she might harbor.

I love you, darling Elizabeth. Marry me.

The words sprang immediately into his mind and tumbled effortlessly from his lips in the softest of murmurs. His heart swelled with emotion, emotion he had kept at bay, tried to deny but was powerless to combat any longer. How could she refuse him?

His step was jaunty, his eyes brimming with anticipation when he pushed her bedroom door wide. Taking several strides, he paused, his eyes scanning the deserted room, the cold empty hearth, then lingering upon the stain marring the sheet. His lips curved into a smile and his heart raced. He *hadn't* imagined last eve, though God only knew, in the wee hours of the morning, when he had been on the verge of collapse, his muscles resisting the slightest movement, the memory of their union had seemed but a wondrous dream.

With an urgency that could be denied not a moment longer, he exited the room and retraced his steps, bounding down the stairs then skidding to a halt when his eye fell upon Phoebe, cozily ensconced within the parlor.

"Phoebe. What are you...? Never mind. Where's Elizabeth?"

Phoebe's wide-eyed stare traveled over her father's soot-covered form from head to toe and back again. "Father! What on earth happened to you?"

Alec waved an impatient hand. "A fire, aboard one of the ships. Where's Elizabeth?"

"Oh my goodness! How awful! Thank heavens you weren't hurt! I was wondering where you were, though the servants had little notion. I thought that rather strange. Do you know they all took the evening off, Father?" Phoebe shook her head as if she were truly stricken at the thought of such carelessness.

"I dismissed them early last eve," Alec muttered distractedly, feeling an undeniable urge to shake his precocious daughter as an apprehension began to build deep within him. "The storm and... Never mind. Where's Elizabeth?"

Phoebe blinked several times. "Why, Father, you seem rather upset and..."

"Where the hell is Elizabeth!"

"Father!"

"Phoebe, damn it all, find your tongue!"

"You needn't raise your voice," Phoebe scolded him, which nearly proved Alec's undoing. The child's amber gaze suddenly lit up and she clapped her hands together with glee. "Oh, Father, I've the most wonderful news!"

Alec couldn't resist a shake of his head and a hoarse laugh. "I can only imagine. Save it, will you, until later, for I've got some news of my own. Where is Elizabeth?"

"*You* have some news, as well? How wonderful! Go ahead, Father, tell yours first."

"Damn it, Phoebe, this isn't some game! Open your ears, child! Where is Elizabeth, your Miss Burbridge? You do remember her, don't you?"

For several excruciatingly long moments, Phoebe chewed her lip. "Oh, she left."

"She what?"

"She left. Just a short while ago."

"With whom?"

"Oh, all by herself, though I believe Lewis took her."

"Where did she go?"

Phoebe shrugged and raised her hands in a helpless gesture. "She didn't say." Her Cupid's bow mouth suddenly lifted into a mischievous grin as if she harbored some deep, dark, thoroughly delicious secret. "But I've an idea." She clasped her hands behind her back, and to Alec's jaded eye she looked as if she truly enjoyed the torture she inflicted upon him. "I would venture to say she dashed off for some clandestine meeting with her betrothed."

Alec frowned. "But I didn't summon..." Something in Phoebe's self-satisfied manner gnawed at him until a horrible thought blazed across his mind. "Her what?"

Phoebe grinned from ear to ear. "Her betrothed. Basil!"

Alec's world reeled. "Christy?"

"Oh, Father, do you know him? He's tall, dark, very dashing. Isn't it just too wonderful?" Phoebe drew her hands to her breast. "I just knew it! He's been in love with her for *so* long. It was only a matter of time! Oh but, Father, don't let Miss Burbridge know that *you* know. Let's just keep it our little secret for the time being. You see, I overheard them..."

"When?"

"Oh, quite early this morning. He ventured by for a visit, though he had but one thing on his mind, no doubt about it! Ooh, you should have seen them, in a torrid embrace and..."

"Where did she go?"

Phoebe raised her brows then gave her father a suspicious look. "I don't know. The school perhaps. That's where they always meet."

Alec stared at his daughter, hoping desperately that this was all some confounded game, some joke...aye, that's what it was. A ruse to muddle his weary mind. Yet his pulse thundered ominously in his ears. "Surely you misunderstood, Phoebe. Elizabeth would never marry Christy."

Phoebe shook her head with conviction. "Oh no, Father, I heard perfectly. Miss Burbridge positively adores Basil. Ooh!

They'll have such darling children and... Father? Father! Where are you going?'' Phoebe scurried after Alec as he strode swiftly toward the kitchen.

He barely heard her, such was the din of the blood roaring in his ears, of the rage and confusion rattling his brain, of the mind-numbing fear that he had lost her. He pushed the kitchen door open with a bang that elicited a frightened yelp from Cook, then threw the back door wide with equal force.

"Holmes!" he barked into the chill morning air. "Saddle Sebastian, man!"

"Father! Surely you've not going after her!" Phoebe skidded into the kitchen and lunged after him. "Father, please! What on earth is wrong with you? I thought you'd be pleased!"

"Ha!" Alec snarled. "Holmes! Show your face!"

Phoebe plucked insistently at his sleeve and her tone was beseeching. "Father, you *mustn't* tell her that I overheard them! She will be awfully stern with me! Father, are you listening? You haven't told me your secret!"

"What secret?" Alec muttered, then bellowed with frustration when Holmes peeked out of the stable and uttered a confused, "Sir?"

"Blast!" Alec snapped, setting out for the stable as if to do something physical harm. One look at his still wheezing mount convinced him that if he was going to chase Elizabeth about the English countryside, it was not to be upon Sebastian's back.

"Another mount!" he raged to a dumbstruck Holmes.

With a noisy gulp, Holmes eyed his lordship with something akin to fear. He indicated the stall directly beside Sebastian's. "Perhaps old Ichabod will suffice, sir."

Alec glared at the swaybacked gray gelding dozing peacefully in the next stall. Swinging a thoroughly disbelieving look upon Holmes, he waved an impatient hand toward Ichabod. "You've got to be joking. That's it?"

Holmes nodded. "I'm afraid so, sir. The coach is in use at the moment, sir."

"Damn it, man, I know that!" Alec ran a hand briskly through his hair and scowled again at the old gelding. "I don't suppose the blasted animal is shod? It would be my only stroke of luck thus far."

"I believe he is, sir. You see, Cook enjoys a nice quiet ride from time to time and old Ichabod is just her speed."

"How very nice for Cook," Alec grumbled, then set out for the back of the stable. "So be it. Help me saddle him up, Holmes, if you can rouse the damned animal. I've a maiden to retrieve, and I'll be damned if I let a sorry old nag keep me from my purpose." He strode about grumbling and muttering, completely oblivious to the others present. "Damned foolish woman . . . some mistake . . . some . . ."

Mistake indeed. His mind flew, searching, delving for some explanation, for some logical reason why his Elizabeth would flee him for another. For Christy? He paused, scowling at nothing in particular. Then again, perhaps he shouldn't assume logic had anything at all to do with it. After all, the woman he'd so boldly taken to his bed the night before was no ordinary virgin. He'd known that well, so why the hell had he been so damned cavalier, so bloody certain that she awaited him, snug and cozy, harboring not the slightest remorse, needing nothing more upon awakening than what a cold lonely house could provide?

He closed his eyes as a dreadful thought blazed through his mind. He'd left her to confront the enormity of their passionate night together . . . alone. No comforting words. Nothing. Lord . . . what a woman like Elizabeth could do with that. Surely he hadn't bungled it so entirely? Surely she had more faith in him than . . .

His mind echoed with her words of the previous night. She didn't even like him.

He gritted his teeth. Like him? No doubt at this very moment she hated him.

Chapter Eighteen

Upon returning to the town house, Elizabeth hastily swept her cloak from her back and set out in search of Phoebe. Upon entering the parlor, she was instantly met with Celestine's cool gaze. The woman stood before the fire, unflinching in emerald green velvet, wearing a fake smile that oozed sweetness. Phoebe's, however, seemed forced from the depths of some overwhelming panic.

"Oh, Miss Burbridge!" Phoebe gushed, racing from her seat to throw her arms tightly about Elizabeth's waist, her eyes shining with unspoken pleas. Elizabeth brushed the tendrils from the child's face and offered an encouraging smile.

"Well, well, Miss Burbridge, we meet again," Celestine purred. "How nice that you and Phoebe are so...chummy. Phoebe darling, I'd like a word alone with Miss Burbridge. Run along and find some milk and cookies, hmm? Sit, won't you, Miss Burbridge?" Celestine indicated the settee in a manner befitting the lady of the house, which did far more than pique Elizabeth's ire and kept her feet planted firmly. Celestine raised a brow. "No? Well, shall we not mince words? You see, Miss Burbridge, I know your game, my dear, and though I positively hate to be the one to tell you, I'm afraid it won't work."

"Excuse me?"

"Oh, you can cease the wide-eyed innocent guise you've no doubt honed upon the likes of my husband."

"He's not your husband."

"Oh, but he was, my dear, and if anyone knows Alec, it is I. Now then, it takes no genius to see that you are hopelessly in love with the man."

Elizabeth had to avert her gaze, for hearing those words spoken from this viper's vile tongue sliced through her with deadly intent.

"Ah, the telltale blush gives a virgin away every time."

Elizabeth waved a hand to the door and did everything she could to suppress the trembling in her voice. "Take yourself from this house, Celestine. We've nothing more to say to one another."

"The truth hurts that much, eh? My dear Miss Burbridge, you're not the mistress of this house, nor should you harbor any delusions. Love him though you might, I'm afraid you are doomed, at best, to the role of kept woman, though God only knows what Alec could possibly see in you." Elizabeth felt those glittering eyes sweep her from head to toe. "You're passable, I suppose, in a puritan sort of way, though what kind of body you feel you've got to hide beneath that horrid dress one can only begin to imagine."

"Sheathe your claws and be gone!" Elizabeth railed.

Celestine lifted her shoulders in a delicate shrug and took several steps toward the door. "I'll leave of my own accord, you needn't toss me out. I came to see Alec, though it seems we've both just missed him. You see, I came to deliver my goodbyes, Miss Burbridge. Ah, you look positively stricken."

Stricken, indeed! What the devil did this mean? "You're leaving London?"

"I'm off to Italy, my dear. The Adriatic coast is incomparable and I've met a . . . well, let's just say I've a friend who maintains a villa there. Besides—" Celestine waved an airy hand "—I find that I'm not particularly . . . shall I say, *needed* here. My dear Miss Burbridge, make haste and flee, for Alec has no intention of ever marrying again. Take yourself from beneath this roof, posthaste, before your heart is irreparably broken and your life full of naught but despair."

Elizabeth's silence prompted a low throaty laugh from Celestine. "Ah, and I can see that my words hold some credence with you." A wicked smirk curved her lips. "One can only imagine what Alec has done already to inspire such, shall I say, *faith* in him?''

Elizabeth slanted the woman a fierce look. "If you believe the man to be so horrid, why on earth did *you* want him?''

A blond brow rose haughtily. "My dear Miss Burbridge, if that we could pick and choose the ones we fall in love with, but, alas, we cannot. Heed me well, for I'm speaking to you as a woman, not a foe, my dear. Your choosing to remain here bodes nothing but trouble for you.'' With a rather smug look, Celestine swept her cape about her shoulders, tossed Elizabeth a breezy *"Arrivederci!"* then beat a quick and airy leave.

Elizabeth stood motionless for several moments, attempting to make sense of her jumbled thoughts. She achieved some comfort knowing that Alec had indeed spoken the truth regarding his lack of regard for the woman, for this had obviously served to hasten Celestine's departure. Yet that mattered so very little at the moment. Alec could have one wife, ten wives, twenty mistresses. The fact remained, he never wished to marry.

She nibbled thoughtfully at a finger. To what end would Celestine offer such advice if not for the very reason she indicated? By week's end, the woman would be basking in the Adriatic sun, comfortably ensconced within some posh and elegant villa. Why on earth would she even care what Elizabeth chose to do unless she truly wished to spare her the inevitable grief, the heartache... Dear God, the woman had no other motives! And she *had* been married to the man at one time....

A muffled groan escaped Elizabeth's lips and she pressed a palm to the dull ache that spread painfully through her belly. What further provocation did she require? Her opportunity to escape her fate had presented itself in the form of a gracious and rather timely proposal this very morn, an opportunity that, in her lifetime, might never again present itself. She stared blankly from the windows. She might be in love with Alec, fool that she was, but she was smart enough to know her weaknesses. Alec was certainly that, and more.

Not thirty minutes later, Elizabeth alighted from her coach and paused to draw a steadying breath, assuring herself that her legs were well beneath her. At her knock the front door opened wide and she found herself in an enormous white marble foyer. Her mood did not lend itself to glancing about, and as a result she stood stiffly just inside the front door, nervously tapping a toe and studying the floor while a very somber-looking servant ventured off to announce her.

Not thirty seconds later, Basil, looking as if his tail were on fire, bounded down the sweeping stairs and skidded to a breathless halt before her. Grasping her elbow, he steered her to a shadowed corner of the foyer.

"Elizabeth. Is something amiss?" he muttered in so soft a voice she wondered if he wished not to be overheard.

Elizabeth lowered her eyes and found herself contemplating Basil's shoes, which weren't shoes at all but soft silk slippers in the deepest shade of scarlet. Never had she imagined that her sensible brown shoes would one day find a home beside scarlet silk slippers belonging to her husband. "I've given your proposal a considerable amount of thought."

"In two hours, Elizabeth?" Basil frowned in a thoroughly disbelieving manner until his ruddy complexion grew atrociously pale. "Perhaps you've made your decision in haste."

Elizabeth shook her head and smiled gamely. "No, Basil. It is a decision I intend to abide by for the rest of my life."

Basil gave her a weak smile and she detected a trembling in his limbs, causing her to raise a reassuring hand to his arm. "I wish to become your wife, Basil, and . . ."

Her next words were lost amidst Basil's gasp of the purest joy, and he bent his head, clasping her hand to his mouth and mumbling incoherently against it for several moments. "Oh, my darling . . . my darling Elizabeth . . ." was all she could detect, though for some blasted reason, any delight proved atrociously evasive for her. Indeed, his next words struck naught but a melancholy chord within her.

"Oh, my darling, let us hasten to retrieve your belongings. I'll be damned if my betrothed will be living under another man's roof, by God! You shall move in here, my dear, today! No, now don't look so stricken. It will all be very proper, of course, until the wedding, which we shall have to schedule for very soon." Basil smiled in so wicked a manner, Elizabeth felt her insides flip-flop. "You see, my darling, I must have you as my wife, very, very soon, or I shall die of wanting you."

"Basil!"

He gave a chuckle, deep and throaty, and ushered her to the door. "Now, be a good girl and wait for me in your coach. I shall be but a moment."

"Damned mule!" Alec grumbled, pulling the lumbering animal to a stop and slipping from the saddle. Nonetheless, he scratched the gelding fondly between the ears and rubbed the nose that inevitably swung about in search of some treat. Alec had to laugh despite his frustration, and he dug into his pocket for a carrot, which he extended to that seeking muzzle. He glanced toward the stable and his heart leapt, suddenly filled with an undeniable joy. "Lewis. Lewis, my good man!" he bellowed, hastening to the coachman, who was bent upon some task beside his vehicle. "You're back!"

Lewis glanced up and eyed his lordship as if he were rather taken aback by the enthusiastic greeting. "Sir?"

Alec's smile felt as if it stretched from ear to ear. "Where is she?"

"Sir?"

"Elizabeth, man! Is she inside?"

Lewis blinked several times as if to gather his thoughts, then shook his head. "Oh, nay, sir. She's gone."

Alec stared at the coachman. "Gone? Where the hell is she now?"

"Sir, I believe she has taken up residence at the Cosgrove estate."

"She what!" Alec nearly roared with unmitigated frustration, throwing his head back as if he were speaking heavenward. "What the hell is going on?"

"She left not an hour past, sir, with all her belongings. It seems the lady and Basil Christy are betrothed and . . ."

Alec flung a look of such murderous intent at Lewis, the poor man nearly fled the stable. "Damn it, man, tell me something I don't know!" With a disgusted snort, he flung Ichabod's reins aside and set about pacing the stable as if he knew not where he was going. "What the hell is a man supposed to do?"

"Sir?"

Alec bent his ferocious gaze upon Lewis. "To hell and back to the damned school I went, and she wasn't even there! All that way, through the storm on that…that…" He snorted and flung an arm toward Ichabod, who, in spite of the commotion, dozed peacefully beside his stall. "Oh, for God's sake." Alec ran a hand through his hair to knead the knotted muscles at the base of his neck. If only his frustration could be so easily assuaged. He knew he had only himself to blame for all this, that he'd best be about winning her back. He'd be damned if he'd give up that easily. The woman had, after all, awakened this morning in his damned bed!

"Don't ever love a woman, Lewis," he muttered.

"Sir?"

"They'll make a fool of you every time." Drawing a deep breath, he rubbed his eyes then clasped Lewis heartily upon the shoulder. "I suppose I'd best see myself into a hot bath. What do you think? She'll never have me looking like this."

Lewis nodded dumbly and stared at Alec. "Sir."

"Don't look at me in that tone of voice, man. I know damned well what you're thinking! And you know what? You're absolutely right." Alec cocked a brow. "There's nothing half as rewarding as making a fool of yourself over the woman you love."

And with that, he strode purposefully from the stable.

"Darling, you're trembling," Basil murmured, leaning forward upon the coach seat to clasp Elizabeth's gloved hands in his own. His heavy brow furrowed with concern. "You've spoken not a word since we left Sinclair's. Have you experienced a change of heart, God forbid?"

Elizabeth shook her head and managed a weak smile. Of course she couldn't tell Basil she felt sick, hideously ill to the pit of her stomach. "It was not the manner in which I would have liked to leave Phoebe."

"Phoebe? Who is...oh, yes. Sinclair's daughter. I saw nothing out of the ordinary there. You explained yourself succinctly, and she seemed satisfied."

Elizabeth shrugged and swung her watering gaze to the passing city streets. Indeed, the news of her betrothal had found a ready and eager ear in Phoebe, not that Elizabeth had expected anything less than a euphoric response from the girl. However, when Elizabeth had appeared with her belongings in tow, there was little mistaking Phoebe's bafflement or her immediate distress. Heedless of Basil's presence, she'd thrown her arms about Elizabeth, sobbing brokenly into her brown cloak and pleading for her to stay. Elizabeth heaved a wistful sigh as the melancholy bubbled forth within her. Dear, sweet Phoebe, so innocent despite her mischievous streak. How she would be missed.

"Now, darling, allow me to put all your worries to bed—" Basil flashed a wicked smile "—so to speak. You've nothing to fear of the staff. And Stepfather is a relatively harmless old bird. However..."

His pause and the tone of his voice aroused some sixth sense in Elizabeth and she peered curiously at him.

Basil patted her hand in a distracted manner and bit his lip, as if unsure of what to say. "Well, you see, though he possesses a sound business mind, I'm afraid he recently has acquired this nasty and rather alarming senility with regard to his family life. He seems to think he has some long lost children that have been kept from him for years."

"Oh my goodness, the poor man!"

"Aye, it's a dreadful shame, and naught but a figment of his imagination. Not an ounce of truth to any of it, I can assure you. He once even suggested that one of the maids was his daughter, if you can believe it! Imagine that! Well, I thought it best to inform you, lest the man take some wild notion about *you* into his head, God forbid. We all humor him. There's little else we can do, you see, for he is dreadfully ill, on top of it all, with one foot all but in the grave."

"How awful."

"Indeed. It is a tragedy and one for which I grieve daily. With him, my dear, tread lightly. Oh, and one more thing. Keep the matter of his feeblemindedness to yourself. We all do, lest the poor man overhear some loose talk and find himself bed-ridden for days. Now, enough said, eh?'' He patted her hand then glanced from the window. ''Ah! We've arrived!''

Basil assisted her from the coach and inside, where he deposited their cloaks upon a waiting servant with curt instructions to take Elizabeth's things upstairs to one of the guest chambers. Graciously, he ushered her into the front parlor to find warmth before the blazing fire. Their entrance startled two maids, busy at their work, such that they spun about in confusion. The older of the pair, a very plump, gray-haired woman, attempted to hasten from the room, mumbling an apology, while the young blond maid seemed all but rooted to her spot with mouth agape.

''Ah, Brunhilde!'' Basil called after the older maid. ''A moment of your time, if you will.'' Slipping an arm about Elizabeth's waist, he drew her forward and, to Elizabeth's eye, flashed a huge, triumphant smile. ''Brunhilde, Felicity, it is with great pleasure that I introduce my fiancée, Elizabeth Bur-bridge.''

Elizabeth could not help her surprise at their reactions to this announcement. Brunhilde glanced over her from head to toe then directed what could be described as a furious look at Basil, which for some unknown reason only deepened his grin. Felicity, on the other hand, never managed to snap her mouth closed but stared at Elizabeth, the color draining from her face until she was as white as a sheet.

''Why, you . . . I should have known!'' Brunhilde uttered in so threatening a tone that Elizabeth expected the woman to take her broom to Basil at any moment. She nodded tersely at Elizabeth, then spun on her heel.

''Oh, Brunhilde,'' Basil called after the stomping form. ''Would you be so kind as to inform Stepfather that I wish a word with him?''

In reply, he received naught but a resounding ''Humph!'' before Brunhilde slammed the parlor door closed behind her.

Basil chuckled and bent close to Elizabeth's ear. ''Don't mind her, darling,'' he whispered, squeezing her waist in a manner that made Elizabeth want to squirm from her skin.

"She can be a testy old thing, believe me. Indeed, I suspect she liked you." Before Elizabeth could even nod her head in reply, Basil lifted a brow at Felicity. "That will be all, Felicity."

With a wide-eyed nod, the poor maid scurried from the room, one hand clutching frantically at her apron and the other pressed to her mouth. As Elizabeth's eyes followed the flustered girl, she could not suppress the feeling that the two maids seemed none too pleased with her. However, Basil's arm about her waist, drawing her close against his side, served to knit her brow with far more immediate concerns.

She stiffened when he took the liberty of pressing his lips to her throat. "Ah, my darling, alone at last."

"Basil!" She shoved with all her might against his chest.

"Elizabeth, I'm your betrothed, soon to be your husband." He scowled when she held her arms close about her and evaded his grasp. "Darling, I only want to touch you, hold you close the way I have longed to do these many days and nights. Surely you will not deny me that?"

Elizabeth swallowed with great difficulty, attempting to tamp down the shudder of distaste that threatened. She mentally shook herself; as distressing as it was, she could not for the life of her imagine wedding a man who aroused such feelings. She supposed this sort of thing was to be expected, since she'd left Alec's bed just that morning. Her eyes widened and flew to Basil's furrowed brow. Dear God, he must never suspect such a thing!

Reaching a tentative hand to his, she forced a wavering smile. "Basil, it's only nerves."

He drew her hand to his lips. "Forgive an impatient bridegroom, my dear. I hope my desires do not prove the better of me before we wed. We must make it soon, very soon."

Elizabeth's heart gave a frightened leap. "How soon?"

Slipping an arm about her waist, he drew her closer and his eyes darted desperately over her face. "As soon as possible. I have no great need for a large affair that will require weeks, even months of preparation. Just an intimate gathering of a few friends that we could plan for, oh, perhaps in a week's time."

"A week?" Elizabeth squeaked.

Basil flashed a wicked grin. "Or sooner, if I have my way."

Elizabeth pressed her palms against his chest once more, lest his ardor indeed prove the better of him. She was coming to know that certain glint in his eye all too well.

At that moment, the parlor door burst open to admit a grumbling Brunhilde, who paused to growl through her clenched teeth, "Lord Nigel awaits ye in his study."

Basil clasped his hands and rubbed them together with great energy. "Very good!" Holding a hand toward the door, he gave Elizabeth a smile brimming with unrestrained glee. "Shall we?"

Elizabeth, left with little choice, preceded both Basil and Brunhilde from the room, though she remained very much aware that the maid's unwavering glare fixed heatedly upon them. Through several long halls they proceeded until Basil's hand upon her elbow steered her to a stop before an imposing set of mahogany doors.

"Now relax, my darling," he whispered in a voice laced with suppressed excitement. Elizabeth could only assume he was as nervous as she, though he had a look about him not unlike the cat who'd swallowed the canary. She hadn't a moment to ponder this, for he pushed the doors open and urged her to step into the room.

The fire blazing in the hearth illuminated the tiny room, rendering the quarters stuffy and uncomfortably warm. The figure huddled within a huge chair directly before the fire, however, seemed oblivious to this. One gnarled hand clutched at an enormous wool blanket that covered his slight form, and the other, dangling at an odd angle over the arm of the chair, moved absently over the head of a rather mangy-looking dog lying at his feet. Were it not for that one movement and the narrowed glare he'd fixed upon the flames, Elizabeth would have thought Lord Cosgrove slept. As it was, she found that fierce hawklike profile and the cloud of unkempt white hair stirring more than an idle curiosity within her.

When, after several excruciatingly long moments, he abruptly turned toward her, she started at the raw intensity of manner he displayed. He spoke not a word, though none was necessary to reveal the depth of the emotion that seemed capable of consuming the frail man. Beneath his fearsome regard, Elizabeth felt her heart plummet to her toes. There was little mistaking it. Nigel Cosgrove was not happy in the least.

"Stepfather," Basil ventured in a booming voice that startled Elizabeth. Indeed, she nearly stumbled when his hand at the small of her back pressed her forward a pace. "It gives me great pleasure to introduce my fiancée, Elizabeth Burbridge."

Lord Cosgrove's unflinching glare remained upon Elizabeth as if Basil were not present. Though she thought it her imagination, Elizabeth could have sworn she detected a softening of his manner as he stared upon her, an easing of what seemed the permanent scowl that deepened the crease between his bushy white brows. The clench of his jaw, as well, seemed to dissipate, and for a moment Elizabeth found herself musing that Lord Nigel Cosgrove must have been a very handsome man at one time, long ago, before the passage of time and the ravages of some unspeakable grief had taken their toll upon him. Indeed, gazing upon his emotion-racked countenance, Elizabeth knew without a doubt that this man battled demons, none of which were her doing. This elicited an unexpected sigh of relief from her, serving to remind her that she hadn't drawn one breath since entering the room. Her lips quivered then lifted with a trace of a smile. Lord Nigel's reply did far more than startle her.

"My dear Elizabeth, your beauty knows no equal, your intelligence no bounds." His eyes narrowed upon her with a fierce intensity. "So tell me, my dear, why on earth would you condemn yourself to hell with the likes of him?"

His words were spoken so casually, as if he discussed the weather, with nary an inflection of the undeniable contempt he harbored. Elizabeth gaped at him for a moment as he flashed her a cockeyed grin. "You have your mother's eyes, you know. Do you know who your father is, my dear?"

Dear God, Basil had been right! The man was surely off his rocker!

Basil, apparently as stunned as she, managed to gather his thoughts with startling dispatch. "Ahem...er, Stepfather, I can see this is a bad time..."

"A bad time?" Nigel barked, suddenly full of ire, and he turned blazing eyes on Basil as if seeing him for the first time.

"And when has it ever been a good time to lay ruin to a man's life, eh, Basil?" A gnarled hand waved toward the door. "Get the hell out, man . . . Oh! No, no, my dear Elizabeth, you may stay. Indeed, please stay and comfort an old man." The piercing eyes beheld Basil and a crooked finger wagged at the younger man. "We've so little time, you know. I have a strange feeling my end is growing frightfully near." Nigel motioned to the settee and his smile settled upon Elizabeth. "Sit, please sit. Warm my heart, my dear, for just a moment."

"No!" Basil waved a hand as if the idea were unthinkable. "No, I'm afraid my darling Elizabeth really should see to her unpacking, shouldn't you, my darling? Perhaps later, Stepfather, when the mood is more fitting."

Elizabeth heard but a grumble and a grunt from Lord Cosgrove as Basil guided her to the door. However, just before they left the room, Nigel's booming voice called after them. "Oh, do make sure your 'darling' sleeps with a knife beneath her pillow, eh, Basil, you bloody . . ." What remained of his words was lost in a sudden fit of guttural coughing the likes of which Elizabeth had never before heard. The spasms seemed to go on indefinitely and with such fervor that they could be heard even after Basil closed the door behind them.

"Shouldn't you see to him?" Elizabeth asked.

Basil shook his head. "No, it will pass in a moment. Besides, I've a matter I must speak with him about. I'll tend to him in a few moments."

His airy disregard and the hint of a smile she'd glimpsed settled uncomfortably upon her but he offered her little time to muse on this. Grasping her hands in his, he focused on her slender fingers and shook his head regretfully. "I'm so dreadfully sorry, my darling. He's in one of those moods of his. Of late, he's been striking out at nearly everyone close to him. Me most of all! God only knows why! The doctors tell us nothing." He raised a pain-racked expression, which plucked at Elizabeth's heart.

"Of course, it's a dreadful shame," she murmured, though amidst all her empathy, she could not bring herself to hold him close. Instead, she eased her hands from his grasp. Before she could draw a breath, Basil's arms slipped about her waist and pulled her unyielding form against him. For some blasted reason, Elizabeth could not help thinking that his length pressing against her felt nothing like Alec's steely frame. Fortunately for her, Basil mistook her blush for one befitting an innocent bride and he reveled in it.

"Ah, but you fire my blood, vixen," he murmured wickedly, lowering his mouth to her neck.

Elizabeth shuddered and fought against a mounting panic. "Basil, please . . . the servants . . ."

Her wince at her banal response was lost amidst Basil's guttural laugh. "Darling, they expect it of us. Now, we mustn't disappoint them, hmm?"

Elizabeth squirmed with all her might against him. "I'm afraid we're going to have to disappoint them, just this once, Basil. I really must lie down. I'm afraid I've developed a raging headache."

And with that, she hurried down the hall in search of a pillow upon which to ease her fears, all too aware of the black scowl lingering in her wake. She had little intention of appeasing the servants or Basil anytime soon. Let Basil's scowl deepen and his blasted ardor mount. For all he knew, she was an innocent, untouched, chaste and pure as the driven snow.

Time. She needed time, something Basil seemed dreadfully intent upon keeping from her. A week, one sole, lonely week in which she must forget Alec Sinclair enough to achieve some measure of affection for the man she would call husband for the rest of her life. The man with whom she would soon share a bed.

Chapter Nineteen

Basil stared after Elizabeth's swinging skirts as if momentarily hypnotized by the movement. Then, drawing a deep breath, he turned and entered the study once again.

Nigel sat clutching at his throat, reaching a shaking hand for the glass left just out of reach on a nearby table. Basil paused before the old man and slanted a glance at the water.

"You need a drink, old man? In a moment. First, I wish a word with you." He ignored the gurgled sound his stepfather emitted, which bore scant resemblance to his typical roar. "You, of course, realize my true intent with Elizabeth Burbridge, your long lost daughter by that whore Philippa Valentine."

Nigel's eyes widened and his face grew scarlet, but Basil paused for only one breath.

"Really, Stepfather, it was a shock to discover that you had been unfaithful to my mother so very early in your marriage, and with a trollop, no less. Why, if for that one reason I should despise you." Basil clasped his hands behind his back and gave a self-satisfied smirk. "Ah, but there is more, is there not? You see, the comely Miss Burbridge will soon inherit a sizable fortune, one which, as fate would have it, I have long thought would be mine. Tsk, tsk! Such luck, don't you agree, to find myself betrothed to the girl?" He erupted with a wry laugh. "It was so dreadfully simple, you know. She has little notion that you're her father, of course. She thinks you some senile old bird. Won't believe a word you say. A naive wench, but then again, I like them that way. Makes bedding them all the more fun."

A ghastly growl filled the air as Nigel glared at Basil, eyes blazing, and clutched at the arms of his chair as if to pull himself to his feet.

Unmoved, Basil shook his head and sighed with melodrama. "It would be a pity if she were to meet with some untimely demise. But then again, if circumstances alter in any way..." He fingered his chin as if lost in thought, then lifted a wicked black brow. "I would wager that if your will were altered *in any way,* I would be forced to kill the wench, for I fear I would be overcome with my anger. You can understand that, old man."

Nigel's face had grown a deep, mottled purple, his eyes wide, angry pools that suddenly opened even more. Frantically, he clawed at his neck with one hand and with the other clutched the air before him in a violent effort to elicit Basil's help. The younger man looked on, impassively watching his stepfather's agony, before strolling to the glass of water and lifting it in a mocking toast.

"To you, Stepfather," he drawled, raising the glass to his lips. "And to your will. May I live long and prosper, eh?"

Nigel's hands gripped his throat and his eyes rolled back into his head. For some reason, the thought that the old man might be dying right before his eyes did not instill the usual terror in Basil. Perhaps because he was so certain that his plan would work. Indeed, a smile curved his lips despite the hoarse wheezing from Nigel. With a sigh, he refilled the glass and attempted to thrust it into Nigel's clawlike hand.

When this proved hopeless, he shrugged and strode to the door, flung it wide and bellowed down the hall, "Brunhilde! Dear God, woman, hurry. It's Stepfather! Fetch the doctor! I fear it's apoplexy!"

Elizabeth stood before the parlor fire, staring into the flames and feeling atrociously silly. How quickly a tragedy could render one's worries but a fleeting memory. Nigel lay struggling for his life, for every breath. How could she pace before this fire and selfishly ruminate upon what she had not two hours before considered the great calamity of her life?

The jostling of fine china behind her drew her attention to Felicity, who had padded silently into the room bearing a delicate tea service. If the maid's intent had been to disappear as stealthily as she had appeared, she failed miserably, for the porcelain perched at a precarious angle upon the silver tray she carried, just seconds from crashing to the table.

Elizabeth rushed to assist the maid, placing one hand firmly upon the tray to right it. Together, they lowered the service safely to the table. She glanced up, a smile curving her lips. "My, but that was close!"

Felicity's face remained averted. "My lady."

Elizabeth's eyes flickered over the young girl, noticing the slight trembling in her fragile limbs. "Oh, for heaven' sake, please address me as simply Elizabeth. I fear 'my lady' conjures up all sorts of disagreeable visions."

Hesitantly, the maid's enormous pale blue eyes lifted and Elizabeth was struck by the young girl's delicate beauty. She mused on this but a moment, for the girl still trembled, causing Elizabeth to draw the most likely conclusion. Reaching a hand to the maid's arm, she offered, "It is indeed a dreadful shame what has happened to Lord Cosgrove, but the doctor is tending to him now. We must think positively, you know. Why, if Basil hadn't acted so quickly, Lord Cosgrove could be much worse off."

Felicity bit her lip and lowered her gaze. "My lady, Lord Cosgrove is the finest of men, deserving of the very best care, our love and devotion . . ." Her eyes rose and locked with Elizabeth's. "As if he were our own father, my lady."

Though the maid's comment struck an odd chord in Elizabeth, she nodded as if she understood. "Of course."

"Ah! Well now, thank you, Felicity!" Basil's abrupt entrance brought Elizabeth's head about and served to snap Felicity to attention and prompt yet another trembling spell, as if the young maid were afraid of Basil.

Basil cocked a brow and indicated the door. "Felicity, I believe Brunhilde requires some assistance in the dining room. We must still eat, you know, despite this awful tragedy." He swung his gaze from the departing maid to Elizabeth and shook his head. "Such a nervous twit, and clumsy, as well. One can only wonder why Stepfather keeps her on staff. I'd have sent the wench packing long ago."

"Basil!" Elizabeth could not suppress her shock. "She's a lovely young girl. A bit unsettled, true, but one can easily overlook that. She seems extremely fond of Nigel, and this day no doubt has caused her great distress."

"Ha!" Basil guffawed, moving to the sideboard to partake of the brandy. "Indeed, she should be fond of the man. He took her on, inexperienced as she was, when no one else would give her the time of day." He turned to Elizabeth and waved his full glass for emphasis. "My darling, you mustn't go attaching yourself to every young maid we employ. They're a fickle lot, faithful only until a better opportunity presents itself."

That undeniable gnawing of uncertainty and dread began again in the pit of Elizabeth's stomach as Basil gulped his drink. Something in the confident set of his head, the tone of his voice, the jauntiness of his step, almost as if the man had just triumphed over some foe...

"How is Nigel?" she asked, watching closely for some glimpse of sorrow, some emotion, as he refilled his glass.

"Well, you know doctors and all, my dear, they can't really say with these things, but it appears he..." He paused, holding the now empty decanter upside down over his half-filled glass and spilling several drops on his hand. "Damn! We're out of brandy." He frowned agitatedly at Elizabeth and indicated the empty decanter, as if it provided indubitable evidence. "You see there. Precisely my point. It's Felicity's duty to keep the liquor well stocked."

Elizabeth stared at him. Surely he was joking....

An urgent pounding upon the front portal followed closely by a flurry of activity in the foyer drew Elizabeth's attention. Basil's, as well, for he abandoned his brandy to search for a towel. Finding none, he grimaced, wiped his hands on his trousers and strode toward the parlor door.

At that precise moment, Brunhilde's plump form appeared as she bustled breathlessly into the room, extending a hand before her. "'Tis so nice te see ye again, Lord Sinclair!'' she gushed.

Elizabeth's heart plummeted to her toes and she had to grip the back of the settee for support. It was good that she did, for when Alec swept through that doorway, looking every inch the dashing roué, her knees buckled beneath her and the room swayed before her eyes.

Both Felicity and Brunhilde took it upon themselves to ease Alec's cloak from his back. Elizabeth nearly expected a tiff to result over who should bear the tremendous burden of carrying the thing from the room. Brunhilde easily won that battle, blushing beneath Alec's smiling regard and fiddling rather self-consciously with her hair. A flushed and flustered Felicity clasped and unclasped her hands, then indicated the tea sitting directly before Elizabeth.

Before Elizabeth realized, Alec's gaze followed the maid's trembling hand and locked upon her. Her breath was snatched from her and she foundered, lowering herself upon the settee and casting an unsteady gaze at Basil, who stood rooted to his spot, black eyes blazing upon Alec.

"That will be all, Brunhilde...Felicity.'' Basil's gaze fixed upon the young maid, who seemed suddenly incapable of anything beyond blushing becomingly. Only when Alec nodded and smiled at her did she appear to find her feet beneath her and scurry from the room.

"Sinclair,'' Basil choked. "What the hell are you doing here?''

"Christy,'' Alec drawled, mocking a bow then raising a dark brow. "So you do indeed reside here. One would never have guessed, since you always seem to be out.''

"How the hell would you know?'' Basil demanded with a furious scowl.

Alec inclined his head and gave Basil a wide, confident grin, waving the attaché case he carried as if for emphasis. "Nigel and I are business partners. I come here quite often.''

Basil eyed Alec warily then hastened to the settee to clasp Elizabeth's hand and draw her to her feet directly beside him. Slipping one arm about her waist, he pulled her very close against him and his hands moved in a most irritating manner from her waist to pause just at the underside of her breast.

Elizabeth had little notion she possessed the strength of will to allow Basil such liberties, but she would have died before doing otherwise beneath Alec's all-seeing gaze. Her eyes skidded over Alec's expanse of chest then rose to fix upon Basil's profile. Funny, she'd never noticed the cruel hook to his nose.

"I have every reason to linger these days, Sinclair." Basil cocked his own brow then turned glowing eyes to Elizabeth. "My Elizabeth has finally come to her senses and vacated that hovel you dare to call a town house. We plan to wed in a week's time."

The few moments of silence proved too much for Elizabeth to bear. Risking a glance at Alec, she experienced what could only be described as furious dismay at his reaction. His dark brows shot up and he gave her a look of such wide-eyed surprise, followed quickly by a huge smile, that she nearly slapped him.

"Indeed!" he replied with gusto. "My congratulations to the happy couple! What a surprise!" He extended a hand to Basil and the two exchanged a hearty handshake. Glancing at his palm for a moment, Alec frowned then rubbed his apparently sticky hand upon his trouser before gracing Elizabeth with the same wide smile. "Miss Burbridge. May I say that no one is as surprised by this as I." Before she could say or do otherwise, Alec grasped her hand and brought it to his lips.

His breath lingered upon her hand, his lips moving warm and slow over her trembling fingers, his eyes boring relentlessly into hers. It was such a simple gesture, appropriate under the circumstances, yet performed thus by Alec it seemed as sensuous as any deed he could enact behind a closed bedroom door. As for Elizabeth's reaction, it was as if in that one moment she relived their entire night of passion.

"Th-thank you, Al—Lord Sinclair," she managed, snatching her fingers from his grasp to tremble hesitantly at her throat before plucking at her hair. Blast the man!

"Your pending vows seem to sit well with you, Miss Burbridge," Alec remarked, inclining his head at her. "May I say that you've never looked quite so...*fulfilled*. Yes, that's the word. Fulfilled, and sporting such a becoming blush."

Elizabeth gritted her teeth with mute frustration. "It is indeed a happy state I occupy, and one that is entirely Basil's doing."

"Ah, Christy," Alec boomed, clasping Basil upon the shoulder with such force he let out a noisy rush of air. "One would never have thought you had it in you."

Basil frowned, as if he missed Alec's meaning.

"Now, Miss Burbridge," Alec drawled smoothly. "As happy as she will be over this news, my daughter, Phoebe, will surely miss you at the town house. Indeed, she seems to have grown exceedingly fond of you."

Try as she might, Elizabeth could not ignore the innuendo looming in Alec's words. And in those blasted hooded eyes. "I am just as fond of her. However..."

"Now, now, Elizabeth," Basil piped up, squeezing her waist yet again. "The girl has a mother, you know. By the way, Sinclair, word has it you and Celestine DuBois stand to reconcile forthwith."

"That depends on whom you talk to."

Elizabeth had but opened her mouth to speak her news regarding Celestine when Basil's hand began a slow, agonizing journey up and down her side. "Well, there you have it, Elizabeth," Basil proclaimed. "No sense in developing these little friendships with other people's children when you will soon bear your own little brood, isn't that right?"

Elizabeth stared at Basil. "My what!"

"Now, darling," Basil crooned. "There's no need to keep it all a delicious secret. I intend to have as many children as you can bear. We've the means and certainly the, shall I say, gumption."

Elizabeth ignored the wicked gleam in his eyes yet found the sly wink he cast Alec nearly enough reason to end their betrothal right then and there. Pursing her lips, she glared at Alec and all but screamed in frustration when he cocked a brow at her over a thoroughly mocking half smile.

"And what of Miss Burbridge's teaching career?" Alec asked in that infernally innocent tone of his. "Bearing a brood will require more than a little time and energy on her part, no?"

Basil erupted with a chuckle and waved a dismissing hand. "Oh, that. I believe this little lady will find herself far too busy breeding to be concerned with other trifles."

This was too much! The fury mounted uncontrollably within her, threatening to burst forth in a ferocious tirade, when a resounding rap upon the door echoed through the room.

"I beg your pardon." A short, bespectacled, white-haired man ducked his head into the parlor before venturing several paces forward. Over one arm he carried his cloak and in the other clutched a small black bag. A worried frown plagued his brow and he directed his comments to Basil. "Son, your stepfather is not well."

"What?" Before Basil could reply, Alec spun about and loomed before the older gentleman. Extending his hand, he hastily introduced himself then swung a stormy brow upon Basil. "What the hell is going on?"

"Don't look at me like that, Sinclair?" Basil barked, drawing shocked expressions from both Elizabeth and the doctor. "This is none of *my* doing. Stepfather suffered severe apoplexy earlier today."

"What?" Alec confronted the doctor once again. "So, how is he, man?"

The doctor shook his head. "Not well. The stroke was rather severe. I'm afraid he's confined to bed and, at this point, seems incapable of communicating."

"What the hell happened?" Alec growled, pushing a hand impatiently through his hair.

The doctor blinked several times at Alec, as if he wondered if the man would do him bodily harm. "One can never predict these things. I've advised him time and again to remain calm, relaxed, stable. He was doing so well. I can only venture to say that some unanticipated trauma most likely brought this on."

A cold dread seeped into Elizabeth's limbs. Surely the news of her betrothal to Basil had not proven distressing enough to bring about a stroke!

"He can't communicate?" Basil asked. "You mean he can't speak?"

The doctor shook his head.

"And he can't write."

"That's correct. A tragedy, I tell you."

Basil moved a step forward. "And what of his chances for making some sort of recovery?"

The doctor adjusted the spectacles perched upon the end of his nose. "In situations such as this, one can't say. He could recover fully, given time and the proper care. Then again, he may never progress from this state."

Alec's scowl found the doctor once again. "Is he lucid?"

"It's difficult to tell. My advice would be to let him rest for several days. No visitors, lest that tire him unnecessarily."

"Damn..." Alec muttered, striding to the windows as if the mere sight of the doctor sickened him.

"Basil, my deepest condolences to you," the doctor said. "And if there's anything I can do for you, please don't hesitate to summon me."

"Indeed I shall," Basil replied, stepping forward and holding a hand to the door. "Shall I see you out?"

Elizabeth stared after the doctor, an overwhelming sadness welling within her. Alec's low voice rumbling through the room snatched her attention. He stood at the windows, staring out.

"He's a brilliant man, Elizabeth. Believe me, I know. You see, he and my father were partners long ago, long before I was of an age to be of any help in the business and well before they made their fortunes." He gave a wry, brittle laugh. "I was but a lad of ten and seven, newly married, with a wee babe and a young wife to care for, struggling alongside my father when he died suddenly, and Mother not long after. And without hesitation, Nigel made me his partner. Taught me everything I know of the shipping business. I owe my success to that man."

"He alone did not make you the man you are today," Elizabeth murmured in so soft a voice that she wondered if Alec even heard her. Several moments passed, then he turned and their eyes locked. It was as if a knife had been plunged into Elizabeth's soul. Dear God, how did one stop loving a man?

Perhaps, as was her wont, she revealed her thoughts. Or perhaps Basil's conspicuous absence played upon Alec's restraint. He moved toward her, his eyes full of some potent emotion she could not fathom. There was pain, and grief, and something more...anger, and a burning intensity. She couldn't have moved if her life had depended on it. He loomed before her, larger than life, and reached for her hand.

His thumb brushed softly over her fingers. "Your hands are like ice...."

"Well now, Sinclair, weren't you just about to leave?"

Elizabeth spun about, clasping her hands before her and giving Basil a forced smile.

"Indeed. There's little to be accomplished here today," Alec muttered. "I do intend, however, to call...frequently."

"I'm afraid that won't be necessary," Basil said.

Elizabeth slanted a glance at Alec's raised brow, awaiting his response with far more anticipation than she deemed appropriate. "Oh, but, Christy, I'm afraid it's very necessary. You see, I always keep a sharp eye on my investments, and Nigel's health is of the utmost importance to me."

Elizabeth found herself overcome with dismay at Alec's reply. Business! That was it? Better yet, why the devil was Alec doing business with a senile old man? For some reason, she couldn't believe that Alec would do such a thing, no matter the ties binding them.

And then his eyes locked with hers. "I presume this has put a damper on your wedding plans."

Basil frowned. "How so?" He gave a forced laugh and drew Elizabeth close against him. "Ah, but, darling, even this tragedy cannot keep me at bay." He cocked a brow at a very surly-looking Alec. "Can you blame me, Sinclair? I fear I cannot wait to bed the girl."

"Basil!" Elizabeth cried, pushing his hands from her with unrestrained anger and humiliation.

"Well, well, this seems as good a time as any to take my leave," Alec interjected, though his words belied the savage look he directed at Basil. With a curt bow, he turned and strode in his own magnificent manner from the room.

"Darling! Darling, where on earth are you going?" Basil's urgent voice followed in Elizabeth's wake, though this caused her not a moment's pause as she left the room without a backward glance. "Darling, what is it? Are you upset by my little slip of the tongue?"

In silence, Elizabeth marched on, through the foyer, directly past a lingering Alec and up the stairs. Behind her, she heard Basil skid to a halt at the foot of the stairs and clear his throat, but her step did not falter.

"Er... darling," Basil ventured in a beseeching tone. "Of course, I understand your need to rest after such a trying day... Sinclair, what the hell are you looking at? Get the hell out!"

In reply, Basil received a hearty chuckle followed by a slam of the front portal that echoed through Elizabeth's soul far longer than it lingered through the halls.

Alec scowled at the door as it banged closed behind him, wondering if the force of his fist would mar the smoothly polished wood. Were it Christy's twisted smirk looming before him, he wouldn't have paused long enough to consider anything but the satisfaction gained from beating the man to a pulp. He clenched his fists at the thought of the man's hands all over Elizabeth and he closed his eyes as the memory of her slumbering peacefully in his bed loomed painfully in his subconscious. He'd be damned if he was going to give her up without one hell of a fight, whether she wanted him or not. Though to choose a man like Christy... Could she be that desperate?

Taking several steps toward his coach, he paused and glanced at the second-floor windows, wondering behind which curtain she stalked angrily about. Actually, he should have thanked Christy for aiding his cause. Either the man was bent upon losing Elizabeth or he harbored little knowledge of the workings of that particular woman's mind. Not that Alec had one up on him regarding that.

His eyes narrowed in thought. Nay, to his eye, Basil seemed to be parading his betrothal to Elizabeth a trifle too jauntily for his own good. Alec could well understand the man's urgency to wed her, but at the risk of losing her? Surely he wasn't *that* sure of himself. Then again, hadn't he himself been guilty of the very same? Perhaps Elizabeth had given Christy ample reason to believe this wedding would indeed take place in a scant week. Alec could scarcely believe the woman he'd held in his arms last eve would readily agree to marry such a man. Or would she? Damn . . .

White-hot anger surged through him. To hell with the damned woman and her games! He'd had enough! He'd—

Like hell he'd had enough. It would take more than a flimsy betrothal to a fraud like Christy to dissuade him. Far more. With a frown troubling his brow, he turned on his heel and strode to the coach, intent upon making more than a simple nuisance of himself in the Cosgrove household for many days to come.

Chapter Twenty

Long after Elizabeth watched Alec's coach roll slowly down the curved drive she paced about her room, mulling and grumbling and clutching angrily at her skirt. The echo of her heels upon the polished mahogany floors matched her fevered pulse and she paused long and often to peer from the window at the spot below where Alec had stood. With an indignant pursing of her lips, she observed Basil depart soon thereafter. She found herself hoping that he would keep himself occupied away from the house for what remained of the day. She harbored scant desire to exchange words with the man lest he spew forth more of his insufferable ideas regarding their union.

She paused and gave a wry laugh. Union, ha! If he were the last man on earth . . .

Her belly twisted painfully into a knot. Blast it, but he might as well have been the last man on earth, for he alone offered salvation from Alec Sinclair. Naive though she was, she knew beyond a doubt that her incessant trembling and fluttering when Alec was about were not the result of her blinding hatred for the man.

She shook her head and scowled at the sun-dappled winter landscape. "Fool," she grumbled, folding her arms over her chest. "The man does not love you. Your marrying another caused him but the briefest moment's pause. So you won't be available to warm his bed at his choosing. He'll find another, and another after that, and you will be all but forgotten amidst some perfumed embrace. . . ." Her scowl grew more fierce as the tears stung her eyes. "Ooh! How I hate him!"

At that moment, the bedroom door burst open with Felicity's breathy, "Oh, m'lady!" followed closely by a shuffling of many feet upon the floor. Elizabeth spun from the windows and found herself staring with mouth open as Felicity and Brunhilde, along with the older gentleman servant, Cecil, marched into the room, their arms laden with boxes and packages. These they deposited upon the bed, then the chaise, until only the floor provided ample space. Without a word, they disappeared then returned bearing even more packages, until finally Basil appeared in the doorway wearing a huge grin. He took several paces into the room then deposited upon the floor the large trunk he carried. Dismissing the servants from the room with a wave of his glove, he looked smugly at Elizabeth.

"Well?" he asked, waving a hand about.

"Well what, Basil?"

He erupted with a disbelieving laugh. "Elizabeth, don't be daft, my dear."

Elizabeth arched an angry brow. "*Daft,* Basil, I—"

He held up a hand and shook his head. "Forgive me, my darling. Poor choice of words."

"An annoying habit you have acquired of late."

"And well I know it, my darling. I have come asking your forgiveness, hoping that you will find it within your heart."

Elizabeth's cool eye swept about the room, over the trunk, which was no doubt filled to the brim with gowns, the boxes with hats, the packages with stockings and shoes and gloves. "A heartfelt apology would have sufficed, Basil. I shan't require an entire new wardrobe every time we argue."

"Oh, but, darling, you were in need of a few things and, as your betrothed, I took it upon myself to procure several items. I've a discerning eye and guessed at the size. You can't tell me you're not just itching to get your little hands upon all this finery?"

Elizabeth stared at his sly grin, the patronizing tone of his voice grating upon the very fiber of her being. What did this man know of her? Her discomfiture must have shown for in an instant he was before her, upon bended knee no less, clasping her hands in his in so desperate a manner, pleading for her to accept his gifts as a token of his apology.

Accept them she did, finally, though this caused her tremendous disquiet. She mulled over this after Basil had ambled off and Felicity returned to assist her in dressing for dinner. Her disturbing thoughts were banished for a time as she found her attention drawn once again to the melancholy young maid.

Felicity moved about silently, her gaze averted, her head lowered, responding to Elizabeth's attempts at conversation with quick nods and shakes of her head. When Elizabeth drew forth one particularly lovely gown made of the crispest of pale blue cottons, however, Felicity paused for several moments to stare at the thing as if it were spun of gold.

Elizabeth smiled at the girl. "Take it. It's yours."

"B-but, m'lady, I cannot."

"Of course you can. Here, take the matching slippers, as well. We're about the same size. You may have to hem it an inch or two. Oh, don't look at me like that! Besides, I look positively dreadful in that color and it's perfect for you."

Felicity hugged the dress to her bosom and her eyes shone with unshed tears. "Oh, m'lady, 'tis so generous! How can I ever thank y—"

"Just help me finish tending to this mess. Oh, and do you perhaps know a thing or two about arranging hair?"

A ferocious bang from directly below caused Elizabeth's eyes to meet Felicity's in the mirror. Pausing long enough to allow the maid to tuck one final pin into her coiffure, she swept from the room to stand at the curve of the stair railing. The sounds of voices raised in anger echoed through the foyer, accompanied by an insistent stomping of feet.

"'Tis Lord Sinclair," Felicity said. "He's back."

"He's back!" Elizabeth cried, clutching one hand to her thumping heart and the other to her hair. Her wide eyes noted Felicity's curious look and she cleared her throat and assumed a dreadfully sedate tone. "He's back. Well, perhaps I should see what the commotion is about, hmm?" She hesitated a moment, then turned to the maid and tugged at the low neckline of her new gown.

Felicity gave her a smile, obviously sensing Elizabeth's distress. "Oh, m'lady, Lord Basil shall be pleased."

Elizabeth's smile faded ever so slightly. "Lord Basil... of course. You don't think the neckline is too low? And all these bows and ribbons and this enormous bustle..."

Felicity laid a hand upon her arm and gave Elizabeth a gentle nudge. "You'd best hurry. They seem to be in some sort of tiff."

Tiff indeed. When Elizabeth finally found them in a small study at the rear of the house, Basil looked as if he were on the verge of apoplexy himself. As for Alec, he seemed unruffled, moving purposefully about the room unpacking his attaché and stacking papers neatly upon a huge desk while Basil stormed to and fro, bellowing and blustering.

"I said get out, Sinclair! Your bloody arrogant ass is not needed—"

"Basil!"

Both men turned to stare at Elizabeth poised in the doorway. That her eyes immediately met Alec's should have told her something. However, it was his low appreciative whistle that captured her, prying from her that telltale blush she could not control. She refrained from fanning her heated décolletage lest she succumb entirely to the role of love-smitten ninny.

"Elizabeth, my darling!" Basil surged toward her, his eyes flaming over her. "You're a vision, my dear."

"Basil, what on earth is the matter?" Elizabeth asked, ignoring, for the moment, Basil's preoccupation with her bosom.

His head snapped about and he jabbed a finger at Alec, who had seated himself in the deep chair behind the desk as if he meant to occupy that position for some time.

Basil gnashed his teeth so fiercely Elizabeth could hear him. "Damn it, Sinclair! I wouldn't get too comfortable if I were you. You're in another man's house."

Alec cocked a brow. "Indeed. Nigel has welcomed me many a time. In these circumstances, I harbor little doubt that he would wish my presence whenever I see fit to impose myself upon you." His eyes flickered to Elizabeth and he gestured toward the door. "Go on about your evening. I've already had my dinner, so you needn't fret over me."

Basil's face turned a deep crimson. "Fretting was not what I had in mind, Sinclair. You have no purpose here!"

"Purpose?" Alec flashed a grin that shot white-hot flames through Elizabeth. "Nigel and I are business partners, Christy, and he retains a large portion of the paperwork here. Due to his recent illness, it's only fitting that I assume complete responsibility for these matters. I wouldn't want our company ledgers to fall into the wrong hands, now would I?"

"What the hell are you insinuating, Sinclair?"

Alec shrugged. "I'm practicing sound business judgment, that's all. Nothing more. That is, unless I have reason to doubt, say, you, Christy."

Basil clenched his fists ominously at his sides. "Take what you need and get out."

With a hearty chuckle, Alec shook his head. "You've got to be joking, man! It would require two coaches to empty this room. No, I'm afraid you'll be seeing a lot of me for some time, until Nigel's recovery, of course." Alec leaned back in his chair, his smoky eyes intent upon Basil. "This causes you some distress, Christy, any fool could see that. One has to wonder at your lack of involvement in all this. Then again, perhaps your time is better occupied with other pursuits."

"Indeed it is!" Basil huffed indignantly. "Why, my own dear Elizabeth can vouch for the endless hours we've spent on improving the education of the poor."

"A worthy cause indeed," Alec mused softly. "Ah, that reminds me." He turned his attention to sorting through the pile of papers before him until he found what he sought. He waved a copy of the London *Times*. "Here it is. I presume you shall be leaving on the morrow, then."

Basil stared at Alec. "What?"

"Why, I only assumed, being as dedicated to the cause as you seem to be, that you would be attending in Nigel's stead the opening of the new school in Stratfordshire. It's the talk of the philanthropic world, you know."

For several moments, Basil stared at Alec, then directed a smile at Elizabeth. "Oh, yes! How frightfully silly of me! The new school in Stratfordshire. You know the one, darling?"

Elizabeth bit her lip. "I'm afraid I've been a bit preoccupied at Dunlevy to even read *The Times*. It's wonderful, just the same."

"Indeed it is!" Basil piped up, rubbing his hands together. "Just a momentary slip of the mind, you know. Far be it for me to know positively *everything* that is of some significance to our cause, but this—" he nodded his head vigorously "—*this* has been on my itinerary for some time, yes, quite some time now." He paused as if in thought, then looked horror-stricken. "Stratfordshire! Why, that's a full day's ride!"

"So it is," Alec observed, then advised graciously, "You'd best leave this very evening."

"Of course," Basil muttered, his philanthropic fervor apparently dwindling. "I assume you shall be going, Sinclair?"

"Regretfully, no, I shan't."

"Of course you shan't," Basil mocked scornfully. "Indeed, it's such a distance, perhaps I, too, shall forgo—"

"Oh, Basil, you mustn't!" Elizabeth cried rather enthusiastically. "I would attend if I could. It would be shameful if we purposefully ignored such an event."

"Of course," Basil grumbled. "I do hate to leave you so soon, my darling, though it will be but for one day." He slipped his arm about her waist and drew her close against him. "Shall we see to dinner and afterward perhaps a little sherry?"

"Sherry..." Elizabeth repeated with a resounding lack of heart, wondering if the memory of sherry exchanged on Christmas Eve loomed as clearly for Alec as it did for her. A glance at his lowered head offered her little solace. "How lovely."

Lovely it wasn't. For what remained of the evening until his departure, Elizabeth fought off Basil's endless attempts to brazenly fondle her. The man seemed positively bent upon pawing her, regardless of who looked on. A servant's presence only seemed to heighten his ardor, if that were possible, as did the sherry, which he consumed with gusto. In response to all his advances, Elizabeth simply pushed against him, doing her very best to avoid his heated gazes. God only knew what awaited her once she wed him.

That thought settled ominously upon her as the front portal closed behind him. With her arms wrapped protectively about her, she wandered aimlessly into the parlor. Silence welled, broken only by the ticking of the mantel clock. The hour was late, well past nine, and the servants had long since ceased their muffled padding about, clearing dishes and dousing lamps. Her ears strained for some sound, some evidence that Alec was still about. Surely he had taken his leave long ago? Just in case, she'd best seek her bed . . .

"What the devil are you doing here?" she demanded at the sight of Alec looming like a stoic fortress in the doorway.

"You know damned well why I'm here," he muttered, pulling the doors closed behind him. "Sit down, Elizabeth."

"I will do no such thing!" she huffed. He turned and took several steps toward her. Her eyes widened. "And don't you dare try to force yourself upon me!"

"Force myself upon you?" He gave a wry laugh. "That would be a first."

Elizabeth sputtered and hissed, failing miserably at retaining her composure. "You arrogant lout! Let me pass!"

Alec remained blocking her path to the door with hands on his lean hips and a wicked glint in his eye. "You know what I think?"

Elizabeth gritted her teeth and tapped a toe impatiently. "I don't suppose it would matter if I did or not, would it?"

"I think you're afraid of me."

"You? For heaven' sake, why? You've but an arrogant, ill-mannered lout with nothing but heathenish thoughts plaguing your mind."

"And for those very reasons you find me irresistible."

"You conceited cad! Be gone, before I summon Cecil to drag you out."

"Don't fool yourself, Elizabeth. You awoke this morning in *my* bed, remember?"

"I'm trying desperately to forget." She waved a hand as if to conjure some reason from thin air. "It was not I in that bed with you. It was but a momentary lapse."

"It was you all right, and it lasted far longer than a moment."

Despite the heat of her blush, Elizabeth raised her chin haughtily. "It meant nothing to me, Alec. If it had, would I have accepted Basil's proposal of marriage? Indeed, would I be here, wearing this gown of his choosing?"

Much to her chagrin, his eyes lowered for several painful moments. "I should have known. You'd never have chosen such a frock. It's a bit too...you know, all those bows and frills..." His eyes, now a deep smoky gray, lifted to hers. "Your beauty needs no such enhancement. Just a simple...low-cut gown of the richest material, a gown just begging to be taken off."

Suddenly breathless, she spun about to fan her flaming décolletage.

"Look at me, Elizabeth. Confront the damned truth, woman! You're beautiful, sensuous, a woman who knows well the pleasures to be found in my bed."

"Stop it!" she shrieked. "I won't listen to another word!"

In an instant he grasped her by the shoulders, spun her about, shaking her gently, but the restraint in his touch spoke volumes of his frustration, as did the ferocious clenching of his jaw. "Why won't you listen? Because I speak truth, you little fool, and you damned well know it. Why do you insist upon denying who you are, what you were meant for?"

"Release me!"

"Not until I'm finished with you."

"Is that so? Well, I'm finished with you, you arrogant bloody bastard!"

"And you, you're but an innocent little victim, eh? All those damned self-righteous, puritan attitudes have done nothing but enslave you to upholding something you truly don't believe in. Stop squirming and listen to me. This cloak of chastity, this shroud of moral doom and gloom you huddle within...how you've quaked with fear that someone would sweep that veil aside, revealing the sleeping seductress within you, the woman I held in my arms and made love to so passionately."

"No!" she cried, the tears stinging her eyes. "It was all a mistake, a dreadful mistake I shall regret as long as I live!"

His grip grew painful on her arms, his voice a harsh rasping, as if he struggled for control as much as she. "Regret? Oh, you'll feel regret all right, after you marry Christy. But we both know why you'd do something so foolish, don't we?"

Her shining eyes found his and her heart skipped a beat.

For several long moments, his eyes dipped to her mouth and she grew very aware of his muscled length pressed heatedly against her. "He's safe, isn't he?" he growled. "All full of pomp and circumstance, an overblown fop who could never stir your blood. And all well and good, because that's what you think you want."

Frantically, she shook her head, attempting to control the trembling that had seized her. "No . . . no. I . . . I . . . love him."

"Love him, you say? God, Elizabeth. How far do you want to push me?" His expression hardened into a sheet of etched glass. "Do you think he knows the first thing about love? Oh, he desires you all right, as any red-blooded man would, God help him. But love you? I fear that the pompous Basil Christy is capable of loving no one but himself."

"And well you know the type!" Elizabeth snapped, resuming her struggle with refreshed vigor. "You're not half the man Basil is! How you deign to compare yourself to one so honorable, so . . . so—"

"And how you leap to the man's defense," he snarled. His hand caught in her tumbling hair, yanking her head back until her shining eyes met steel-cold orbs. "Obviously talk will do me little good. Not that it ever has with you. Maybe this will convince you."

With a groan of utter helplessness and despair, Elizabeth found herself lost beneath the firebrand of his mouth, as unable to stop this as she was the tides. A slave, she was, not of her blasted virtue but of her wanton soul, the soul that craved him with every fiber of her being, the soul that was his, would forever belong to him no matter in whose bed she slept the rest of her life.

Tears slipped from her eyes, slid along his beard-roughened cheek. She tasted them as their tongues entwined and danced in an age-old rhythm. The flames of his passion lapped at her will, at every last ounce of her resolve, threatening her sanity as his mouth found her throat . . . When suddenly he released her, she nearly collapsed in a heap.

"That should give you something to think about while you plan your wedding," he growled. With a clipped, "Until tomorrow," he turned and stalked from the room.

Elizabeth released her breath with a strangled groan when she heard the front portal bang and the sounds of horses' hooves and coach wheels upon the snow. She stared at the empty doorway, tears blurring her vision, the cold empty silence of the house descending upon her, and knew without a doubt that she feared most not the man she loved, but the woman who loved him.

Chapter Twenty-One

When Elizabeth emerged from her room early the following morning, it was with some trepidation that she tiptoed down the stairs and peeked into the deserted study. Wondering at her nagging dismay, she turned to seek her morning tea when her eye caught the issue of *The Times* Alec had pulled forth the night before. She scanned the page for some mention of Stratfordshire. Ah, there it was, at the very bottom; not a large article, which surprised her.

Her mouth fell open and she gave a gasp of unmitigated horror. It was not the new school that was of interest in the small town of Stratfordshire. No, indeed! Alec had sent Basil off to witness the annual livestock exhibition featuring, of all things, Tuddlemire's famous seventy-stone pig. *Seventy stone.*

Wide disbelieving eyes swept the newsprint yet again, and her heart thundered within her breast. There was no denying it. The only event of interest occurring in Stratfordshire this day was that involving some bloody pig! Why, that arrogant...

"But Basil fell into the trap so handily," she pondered half-aloud. "He was so convincing in admitting it had simply slipped his mind when, in all truth, there never was such an event!" Cold dread seeped through her limbs and she had to lower herself to the chair as the ramifications settled ominously upon her. He'd deceived her. Suddenly there loomed those doubts that had plagued her...his lack of knowledge with regard to certain educational advances, for instance, which he had brushed off as momentary slips of the mind and she had accepted without question. Or his claiming at one time to have been involved with Nigel's business ventures, which Alec had also handily proved false. And what of his feelings for her?

A shadow filled the doorway and she glanced up, her anger flaring, half-expecting Basil's twisted leer and... Her heart leapt to her throat. "Alec?"

He strode toward her, his penetrating eyes pinioning her to her seat. "Why do I get the feeling that you never expect me to be here? Don't you know by now that I'm a persistent man?"

"And a bloody vicious one, at that." She thrust the paper at him. "What you did to Basil— It was unforgivable."

He cocked an arrogant brow. "Snooping, Elizabeth?"

"I was not snooping!"

"How do you women do it?"

Elizabeth stared at him, thoroughly bewildered. "What the devil are you talking about?"

Alec folded his arms over his chest. "Is it instinctive or a perfected art?"

"What?"

"Your uncanny ability to rationalize your every action. I've never met a woman that couldn't talk herself into believing absolutely anything, and believe me, some of it boggles the mind. Men, ha! We muddle along, pondering and deliberating, attempting to make reason out of something that defies rationale." He paused and glared at her. "Like your marrying Christy, for instance."

Elizabeth couldn't resist a lofty raising of a brow. "You needn't tax yourself, Alec. That is something that requires little in the way of muddling over."

"Indeed. The man made it awfully easy for me, did he not? I suppose you'd have me feeling guilt-ridden...."

"Guilt-ridden? *You?* Ha! *This* from a man who purposefully sent Basil off to some godforsaken livestock exhibition!"

"What you see is a man with a purpose. Cease this charade, Elizabeth, and thank me properly for exposing your devious Basil for what he is, though I honestly believe he has very little to do with all this."

Elizabeth flung a scowl over her shoulder, turning her back upon him and strolling before the windows. "You've made a fool of him. No doubt he was confused. He's awfully busy, you know.''

Alec gave a wry laugh. ''Doing what? Keeping his chair warm at some faro table, or occupying some strumpet's bed?''

Elizabeth whirled about heatedly. At first she thought her fury born of some deep-rooted need to defend her betrothed. But Alec's arched brow made a hasty mockery of that and served to illuminate the true reason. She was defending herself and all her naive and virtuous notions that Basil had so cleverly preyed upon. Just as Alec had. ''Do not slander the man with your inane accusations when he's not about to defend himself.''

''Don't tell me you require more?'' A brawny arm swept before him, his voice bouncing off the rafters. ''What the hell does the man have to do to prove he's a fraud? And don't tell me you haven't had your suspicions.''

Elizabeth turned from him, from the truth looming in his words, dangling before her, just within her grasp. Her gaze focused on the sun-dappled winter landscape and she thought of Basil speeding home, his anger building with every passing mile. ''Would you mind telling me why he did it, Alec?''

''One would readily assume the obvious, of course. He fell in love with you and chose deceit as his method. I can hardly blame him.'' His eyes flamed over her so brazenly, so full of impudence, yet with such devastating consequences Elizabeth had to press a hand to her quaking stomach. ''It is his misfortune that you were already in love with another long before he came along.''

A violent shudder rippled through her, though she managed to erupt with a disbelieving laugh. ''Are you mad?''

''Mad? Perhaps, a little.'' Suddenly, he was very close behind her, his hands encircling her waist to lie possessively over her belly. ''A certain amount of madness is to be expected when one is in love.''

''Alec, take your hands off—'' Elizabeth spun about with mouth sagging open. ''What did you say?''

His hands cupped her face, his thumbs tracing over her cheekbones and his lips lowered to brush with an infinite tenderness over hers. ''I'm in love with you, God help me,'' he murmured against her mouth. "I would never have taken you to my bed if I weren't, don't you know that?"

Elizabeth's world reeled, her head swam, her heart thundered and the tears slid from her eyes. He loved her! Yet for a man such as he, a wily, crafty man, a man used to his women wherever, whenever, love did not necessarily mean...

His lips burned against her throat, his hands caressing her ribs then the tender sides of her breasts, sending waves of delicious sensation coursing through her. "Stop pushing at my hands, Elizabeth, and get your damned cloak." His mouth captured hers in a hungry kiss. "You're coming with me. Now."

Breathless, numb with desire, she stepped back from him a pace, one hand at her trembling lips and the other outstretched as if to keep him at bay. As if that one slender arm could accomplish such a feat! "No, Alec."

He grasped her hand and pulled her to him so tightly the breath was driven from her in a rush. "What is it? You want an apology? You want me to say I regret taking you to my bed? Well, I don't. My only regret is that I left you to awaken alone, to fight a damned fire, to save one bloody ship. I'd have forsaken the whole damned fleet had I thought I might lose you. Foolish woman," he muttered, drawing her close. "Forgive a foolish man, will you? Get your things. *Now.* I'm not an overly patient man."

She eased herself from his arms and found her eyes upon his throat and the dark hair visible above the open neck of his shirt. He loved her! But did that mean...? "Alec, you know I simply can't go with you...stay at the town house as your... your..." Her lower lip trembled, the tears poised upon her lashes then falling to her cheeks.

"Elizabeth, for God's sake, I can't spend the rest of my life with you if you insist upon all this crying and—"

"What did you say?"

He shoved an impatient hand through his hair. "Not this again. Listen, we should see ourselves from this place before Christy returns, intent upon dismembering me. Trust me, I'd face an army to have you, but if we can at all avoid a confrontation today I'd rather—"

"I can't."

"Why the hell not?"

Elizabeth closed her eyes, dreading his response, yet she could not, would not, allow herself to acquiesce to him so easily. "For so successful a man, you really are obtuse."

"Obtuse? *And* arrogant? A man could do worse. Woman, do I have to hoist you over my shoulder?"

Elizabeth lifted her chin and peered haughtily down her nose. "What I had in mind was not quite so barbaric." She drew a shaking breath and plunged on. "Upon bended knee would do."

He stared at her. "Bended knee? Hmm, bended knee." He fingered his chin thoughtfully for several moments. "Bended knee," he murmured, appraising her with a sweep of his hooded eyes as if the idea plagued him.

Elizabeth's heart ceased its frantic thumping for an agonizing moment. The glint in his eye would have provided sufficient clue that he merely toyed with her if she were not still immersed in that wonderful and dreadful state of doubt. Just as the color drained from her face and she envisioned before her endless years as Alec's mistress, he dropped to one knee before her and grasped her hand.

"My darling Miss Burbridge," he said with the greatest of sincerity and a dazzling smile, "marry me. Be my wife. Bear my children."

Her smile felt as if it stretched from ear to ear. She raised a hand to caress his tousled head as she'd longed to do so many times. The blush staining her cheeks felt glorious and the renewed thumping of her heart was music to her ears, as was his voice and the words he spoke. She laughed softly. "Alec, you can get up now. I—"

At that moment, Felicity and Brunhilde skidded to a very quick and noisy halt inside the door and stared with matching dumbstruck expressions at Alec, still bent upon one knee. To Elizabeth's astonishment, he grinned like a devil and nodded at the two maids. "Good morning, ladies."

Elizabeth did everything she could to suppress a giggle. "Alec, do get up."

"I can't." The innocent look. "You haven't given me an answer. Will you marry me?"

Her heart soared. "Yes, Alec, I will marry you, be your wife and bear your children, as many as you'd like."

Alec cocked a brow at the two maids, still frozen to their spots, and made no move to rise to his feet. "Did you hear that? She loves me. Do you think I ought to kiss her?"

At this, Brunhilde scurried from the room, followed closely by Felicity, who appeared to be grinning from ear to ear. In one swift movement, he rose and crushed Elizabeth to him, his mouth swooping over hers in a kiss so passionate and full of such wicked promise she had to gasp for air.

"Get your things," he muttered hoarsely, pressing his lips to her forehead. "And be speedy about it or I *will* hoist you over my shoulder."

She pressed her palm against his shirt, feeling the steady beat of his heart. "Listen to me, Alec. Just one moment." His hands roved over her back, spanned her waist and drew her hips tight against his. He didn't appear to be listening. "Alec, please. I will come, but not now. I must speak to Basil first, alone. It's only proper."

"Proper? You can talk about propriety after what the man has done?"

"He is my betrothed."

"Ah, that one step below knighthood."

"I'll come tonight. Not one minute after I tell him."

"I'll come for you."

"No, Alec. I wish no bloody confrontations, no dueling of egos for my benefit. I shall leave by my own means. He employs a coach, which I'm sure will suffice."

Alec's eyes narrowed. "And what if he refuses to let you leave? Locks you up somewhere."

Elizabeth smiled. "Then you'll simply have to rescue me, won't you? Alec, he may be a master at deception but I don't think he harbors any ill will toward me. After all, he's a reasonable man. He won't stop me."

* * *

The resonant bang of the front portal reverberated through Elizabeth's chamber and stilled her hands, busy at the task of packing her meager belongings.

"Elizabeth?" Basil's voice rang through the foyer. "Darling! Where are you?"

Elizabeth frowned. Certainly not the voice of a man bent upon dismembering another. With a sense of foreboding, she hastened from her room and down the hall to wait at the top of the stairs. "Basil? Basil, I'm here."

He skidded into view at the foot of the stairs and gave her a huge grin. "Ah, my darling! How I've missed you!"

With gusto, he bounded up the stairs to loom before her, one step below her. Elizabeth felt the blood draining from her face, very slowly, as she stared upon his smiling countenance. Ice-cold dread filled her limbs. "How was it?" she managed.

He waved a hand and shrugged with all the nonchalance of one who'd grown frightfully bored with such functions. "Oh, you know, the usual. Lots of hullabaloo and notables."

Elizabeth stared at the cool black eyes, at the pleasant lift of his mouth, as if he were indeed happy to be home. "And Stratfordshire... Is it as quaint as I've heard?"

"Oh yes, quite so."

"A lot of farmers?"

"Oh, a remarkable number. Why, the streets literally bulge with livestock in that town. And the pigs! My word, the pigs are of a size... why, my darling, you couldn't imagine."

Elizabeth was dumbstruck. Indeed, she couldn't imagine how the man could stand before her, looking deep into her eyes, wearing a self-assured smirk as if he'd just accomplished a hard day's work, and lie to her! Brazenly, and with such aplomb! It galled her and sent a chill racing up her spine.

"You're lying," she stated flatly.

It was Basil's turn to stare. "I'm what?"

Elizabeth folded her arms across her chest and tightened her jaw. "You heard me. You're lying."

Basil erupted with a short laugh, though the blood had drained from his ruddy face. "Lying? Me? Ha!" He cleared his throat, attempting to bring his shrill voice down an octave or two. "Whatever are you talking about?"

Elizabeth felt the anger flare in her cheeks. "For bloody hell's sake, stop it, Basil! With every word you speak, the deeper your hole becomes. And the more you demonstrate your atrocious disrespect for me." She turned and stalked angrily toward her room with him but a half stride behind her.

"Elizabeth, please! What has come over you?" His voice oozed with plaintive appeal. "If that bastard Sinclair..."

Elizabeth stopped before her opened chamber door and spun about. "Alec has nothing to do with this flagrant deceit you've practiced upon me!"

His eyes suddenly gleamed with murderous intent, plaintive appeal all but forgotten. "Alec, is it?" he sneered. "Why that... I'm gone but one damned night and the man lays claim to my woman!"

"*Your* woman!" Elizabeth cried. "I am not chattel, Basil, nor am I some simpleminded wench harboring nothing but the desire to breed for the rest of my days! How frightfully little you know of me. I suppose it's what prompted you to ply me with deception." Her eyes narrowed upon him. "To what end, Basil, pray tell? Why the guise?"

In response, Basil shook with his rage, or perhaps with disbelief at being found out. His eyes, for some reason, darted inside her chamber to her opened trunk. Aghast, he grasped her harshly about the shoulders. "You're not leaving, I can promise you that. What were you planning? To run off to Sinclair?"

Elizabeth tempered the gnawing apprehension in her belly and twisted in his grasp. "It's of little consequence where I flee. I'm leaving because of your lying, your deception and, yes, because I realized I cannot marry a man I do not love."

Something very evil flared in the depths of those black orbs, something that shot like quicksilver through Elizabeth. "Get in there," he commanded, shoving her into her room and slamming the door behind them. With a rough jerk upon her arm, he drew her full against him. "Tell me that again, Elizabeth. You don't love me, eh? And well I know why. It's Sinclair, that..." He yanked so violently upon her arm she cried out. "He set me up. He knew all along, didn't he. That bastard! Made a fool of me. A fool!" He spat the word out as if it left some awful taste in his mouth.

Elizabeth stared at him, overwhelmed by his abrupt and astonishing change in manner. Drawing upon some measure of calm, she lifted a brow. "At least you admit your deceit, though that offers little solace."

His grip did not lessen one whit, his wrath one measure. "You think I'm going to let you walk out of my life like that?"

Elizabeth tugged upon her arm, horrifyingly aware of the maniacal grin sliding across his face, twisting his mouth and glittering in the depths of his eyes. Her voice began to tremble. "Basil, there's little need to prolong this. I don't wish to cause you any embarrassment, but the wedding is off."

"You're not leaving."

"Basil, stop this! Release me!"

"You're going to marry me." He spoke as if he hadn't heard a word, as if he were lost in his own mad delusions.

"Basil, I'm dreadfully sorry, but I'm afraid that's not likely. You certainly don't want a wife who doesn't love you?" Her smile, as faint as it was, quivered upon her lips then dissolved beneath his fathomless gaze. Was he beyond reason? "Basil, I am in earnest. Release me."

He stared at her as if seeing through her for several long moments, then his eyes dropped to her bosom crushed against him. Elizabeth's hair stood on end. She sensed the urgency in his grip upon her, though that strength, held momentarily in check, could force her to do just about anything. And suddenly she knew it all too well.

"Oh, you'll be my wife, all right," he ground out, his eyes boldly raking her length before his arms pinioned her against him. His rank breath, stale with day-old rum, fell heavily upon her face. "And you'll warm my bed at my command." The black eyes glittered evilly into hers and he laughed coarsely when she shrank from him, clawing at his hands roving about her waist. "You'd best get used to my touch, lovely one. I'm a man of ferocious appetites, as you will soon fully realize." Those black slits lowered to her mouth and he smirked. "You needn't fret. My prowess is unparalleled, Elizabeth. You will be begging for it one day, I can assure you."

"You're mad," she whispered hoarsely, her purpose growing frantic. "You cannot force me to marry you... to sleep in your bed. I won't, I tell you!"

"You will have little choice."

"You make it sound as if I will be some sort of slave!" Elizabeth shook her head feverishly. "The day will never come!"

"Ah, but the day is upon us." His fingers grasped her jaw harshly and twisted her face to his. Licking his lips as if he savored some morsel, he lifted a malicious brow. "My darling Elizabeth, I believe you know a woman named Philippa Valentine...."

Chapter Twenty-Two

The repast had long since lost its aroma and lay cold and tasteless in chafing dishes along the sideboard. The low flames flickering in the flat sea of wax in the dozen or more crystal candlesticks bore little resemblance to the tall and elegant white tapers of several hours before, when Alec had commenced his pacing to and fro; when he had first experienced the twangs of apprehension deep in his belly, which had, in three hours' time, burgeoned into an overwhelming suspicion that all was not to go as planned.

He scowled at the mantel clock, which seemed to be keeping astonishingly fast time this eve. The hour of ten had come and gone on silent feet, whispering through the deserted household, yet drumming mercilessly upon his mind, each tick of the clock a grim reminder that Elizabeth had yet to arrive.

His feet, which had tested at great length every carpet in the household over the past few hours, stilled at the bay window overlooking the dark deserted street. He glanced derisively at the full yellow moon mocking him from high in the cloudless winter sky, and found himself wishing that some blasted storm had prevented her coming. Where the hell was she?

He presented the windows with his back and for the briefest of moments contemplated the brandy decanter, then shoved a hand through his hair and lowered himself to the settee. He flipped through a book, replaced it upon the table, then made a quick inspection of his boots. With a grunt, he rose to his feet, paced about, then stopped before the windows once again. The moon and the deserted street. Unchanged.

Of course she was coming. Something unforeseen had delayed her. She loved him, didn't she? She knew his intentions. So... she would come.

He clenched his fists at his sides. She should have been here by now. Something had happened...something unforeseen and beyond her control. That bloody Christy! So what the hell was he doing mooning from the windows like some love-smitten fool? He wanted her, tonight...now...in his arms, upon his bed...

In three huge strides he swept into the foyer and flung his cloak about his shoulders. Without pause, he threw the door wide, took two steps, then all but mowed down a tiny lad scurrying up the steps.

"Sir! Pardon me, sir!" The young boy skidded to a halt, bobbed his head and extended a tiny hand. "A message fer ye, sir."

With a growing sense of foreboding, Alec snatched the white envelope from the lad's grasp, pressed a few coins into his hand, thanked him, then spun about, slamming the door behind him. His fingers made quick work of the envelope, though the slight shaking of his hands startled him. His eyes scanned the feminine scroll, fixing for several minutes upon Elizabeth's signature. He read the brief letter several times in the foyer, then again three more times in the parlor. And again as he stood staring into the night from the parlor window, though this time his brow was knit not with an impatient scowl but with a grim finality. He'd been wrong, grossly wrong. To her, it had all been a game, and this her final play. Final indeed, for he stood thus, the letter crushed in his hand, until the moon saw its zenith and hung low in the sky once again.

Elizabeth rapped softly upon the door, feeling the anxiety welling painfully within her, then brushed a trembling hand over her cheeks. Her face was hot to the touch, a sorry testament to the tears that had slipped heedlessly from her eyes all evening long. Perhaps it was this tearstained visage that tugged at Brunhilde's heart when the maid opened the door.

"May I see him?" Elizabeth asked. She sucked in her breath when the maid hesitated a moment before drawing the door wide. Offering Brunhilde a weak smile of thanks, she swallowed and stepped into the shadowed interior.

Nigel lay in an enormous mahogany bed, its dark velvet drapes ominously black and heavy. A lone candle burned upon a table beside the bed. Beside that sat a chair and a blanket and Brunhilde's sampler. The air was oppressively hot, thanks to the fire blazing in the hearth in the corner of the room, though Elizabeth would have found breathing difficult regardless.

Her father lay frail, feeble and, worst of all, motionless upon the bed, an insignificant dip in the feather ticking, so withered were his limbs. Thankfully, his eyes were closed, though his breathing was heavy and labored.

"How is he?" she whispered to the maid.

"He sleeps, lass."

Elizabeth felt Brunhilde's eyes upon her, though she could not drag hers from the bed. She licked her parched lips. "If that I could have known him before all this. I . . . I would have liked to very much."

"And he too, lass, more than ye'll ever know."

The tears slipped from Elizabeth's eyes, that endless tide of remorse she had scant ability to deny at the moment, and one she knew would plague her for many days to come.

"I've some tea brewin', lass," Brunhilde murmured, laying a comforting hand upon Elizabeth's arm. "I'd best see to it."

When Elizabeth's eyes met Brunhilde's sympathetic gaze, she nearly doubled over with grief. So many souls harboring such secrets, and to what end? This? Would she ever know the man who suffered upon that bed? Why was she to be denied her father, the man she had believed dead these many years, now that she had found him?

She moved to the bed, her focus upon the pale form. As if he were cognizant of such things, she willed the tears from her eyes and lowered herself beside the bed. Her gaze flickered to the wizened hand clenched upon the sheet covering his chest. Hesitantly, she reached for that hand, gasping at the coolness of his skin, the fragility of those fingers she imagined had once possessed great strength. Indeed, he must have been something that score and five years before when he'd met her mother; a man of power, strength, good looks and, no doubt, mountains of charm. Enough, at least, to thrust Leonora into the talons of unrequited love for the remainder of her life.

Elizabeth's eyes lingered upon his hands then rose again to the drawn face and the cloud of hair, which she imagined was once as ebony as her own and just as untamed. What else had this withered old man bequeathed to her? The sweep of his brows implied a truly stubborn nature, as did the determined set to his bony jaw, even in his sleep, which brought a faint and fleeting smile to Elizabeth's lips. The independent, boorish type no doubt, full of his own convictions and hell-bent upon achieving them.

Her mind wandered, drawing forth the memory of him huddled in his chair just minutes from a brush with death. What had he said with that cockeyed smile? *You have your mother's eyes.... Do you know who your father is...? We've so little time.... I have a strange feeling my end is growing frightfully near.* And she had thought him daft! He had been speaking the truth, all but throwing it in her face for her to so casually deny. The poor man! No doubt the shock of her being presented to him as Basil's betrothed had proven too much for him. He'd guessed Basil's plot, of that she was certain, so why on earth hadn't he told her outright? The clammy grip of dread descended upon her heart.

Was Basil that powerful, that unstoppable...that cruel, to parade her flagrantly before her own father, knowing full well what that could do to the man? How malicious his arrogance! How supremely self-assured he was! Enough to make one's blood run cold. And she was his prisoner.

Nigel stirred, moaning in his sleep and gripping her hand with a strength that jolted her. She leaned closer, gulping for air, and spoke softly. "Father, it is I, Elizabeth." A noisy swallow followed, then a hasty sweep of her hands over her eyes. "Father, I may never understand the reasons, but I forgive you...and Mother. I more than anyone know the folly of love, the inevitable heartbreak. You see, I too love in vain, as Mother did, and I shall be forced to keep myself from Alec, as Basil's wife, for fear that I shall lose all that I have devoted my life to attaining. This secret, if divulged, would cast me from

Dunlevy in a heap of shame. I would never find teaching work again."

As she gazed at his face, an abundance of grief poured over her. "It is all that I have known! The one truth in all this, my pillar of strength . . . my heart's desire until . . ." A sob escaped her lips and she hung her head. "Oh, but the uncertainty of love! If that I could see my way clearly through this! If only I were one to take my commitments and my aspirations lightly, I would flee to Alec buoyed by the knowledge of the contentment I would find in his arms, regardless of the shambles Basil would make of my reputation. But what of Alec and his reputation? Would he, too, cast me aside for not speaking the truth with him? Indeed, I have lied to him . . . to Miss Percy . . . to dear Phoebe . . ." The tears fell to her lap, tiny dark spots upon the coarse muslin.

A few moments of silence passed. "So you see my plight. How I am torn, yet I know that I face greater risk if I do not comply with Basil's wishes. Perhaps you would find disapproval with that. I know Mother would. If that I were light of heart, an adventuresome soul. Instead, I am as bound by this as I am by my beliefs, and I fear I can do little else." She offered a faint smile. "I also wish to remain with you, here in this house, and despite Brunhilde's unwavering good care, I too wish to see to your recovery. It is all that is left us, you know."

Drawing a deep breath, she wiped the last of her tears aside and attempted to draw her hand from his. She paused, her heart leaping when his grip tightened upon her, and she stared at those brittle fingers squeezing hers.

"Oh, Father, you hear me . . . ." She choked on a soft sob. After a time, she sensed he had drifted into sleep once more and she was able to ease her hand from his. Rising to her feet, she turned and padded to the door, only to find it partly ajar. The reason for this presented itself forthwith when she drew the door wide and encountered Basil's eerie smile.

"Well said, my dear Elizabeth," he sneered, his black eyes glittering into hers. He folded hairy arms over his chest, drawing Elizabeth's eye to the flaming scarlet silk dressing gown flowing about him.

"Your manner is as revolting as your gown," she ground out through clenched teeth. "The least you can do is allow me the courtesy of speaking to my father in private."

He leered at her. "I was but passing by."

"Do not make me loathe you any more than I already do," Elizabeth stated coldly. "You may find me more than a trifle intractable."

The black orbs glittered like cold marbles. "A mite frisky this evening, aren't we?" He leaned closer and his vile breath assailed her. "Need I remind you that I hold your life in my grasp? If I were you, lovely one, I would try my very best to remain as tractable as I possibly could."

Elizabeth matched his glare with her own. "Blackmail does not sit well with me for some reason. Give me a few days, will you. Perhaps then the mere thought of you shan't cause me to retch." She couldn't resist a deprecating sweep of her eyes over him. "Don't trip on your sash, Basil."

With grim determination, she presented him her back and stalked to her chamber, head held high despite the apprehension seeping through her limbs. With infinite care, she locked the door behind her, hoping beyond hope that the bolt would keep that monster and his vile purpose at bay for one more night, at least. If only she could resign herself to her fate, perhaps the emptiness and grief that overwhelmed her would somehow ease.

Very early the following morning found Elizabeth at her desk. The classroom was cold and empty, lit only by the sun rising in all its rosy winter glory, though she remained oblivious to this. And though she blinked several times to clear her vision, she was still as incognizant of what lay before her as she'd been when she'd first laid unseeing eyes upon it. Perhaps it was for lack of sleep, that elusive commodity she had so valiantly sought into the wee hours of the morning, until at last she had given up and summoned the coachman to deliver her to Dunlevy in the hopes of accomplishing some work. As her luck would have it, however, the moment she'd settled herself behind her desk and the mountain of paper piled high upon it, sleep seemed all that she was capable of.

She closed her eyes, very slowly, then opened them once more, forcing every ounce of her concentration to fix upon the parchment. It was simply not to be. Her thoughts were as jumbled as her emotions and within seconds the words blurred. A loud rapping upon the opened door brought her to her feet with a hollow scrape of her chair.

"Elizabeth?" Miss Percy peeked around the doorjamb. "Ah, here you are." The dark eyes peered keenly at her over thick bifocals. "It's rather early in the day to be so fervently embroiled in one's work. However, lest you think that I question such dedication, which I don't, it seems you're not alone in seeking accomplishment at this hour." Miss Percy turned. "Lord Sinclair, sir."

Looking as dashing as any man could ever hope, Alec appeared in the doorway, filling that space with his broad-shouldered, black-clad frame. His unreadable stare fixed so heatedly upon Elizabeth that she completely forgot about her spectacles, still balanced upon her nose.

Miss Percy attempted to peek over his shoulder, no doubt straining on tiptoe to accomplish the impossible. "Lord Sinclair wishes a word with you about Phoebe," came her deep voice from behind one brawny shoulder. "He has some grave concerns I think you should address, posthaste."

Elizabeth nodded, not that Miss Percy could have seen her, for Alec took several steps forward then shoved the door closed with a *thwack* of finality. Edwina Percy was not the type of woman one slammed doors upon. Alec, however, seemed unconcerned with that bang of heavy wood and the ghastly expression that no doubt fixed upon the headmistress's face.

Elizabeth's heart pounded as he drew nearer, his black cloak billowing about slim hips and long legs. His attire was immaculate, his hair ruffled and in desperate need of a good shearing, though this only enhanced the undeniable masculine bravado that was so much a part of him. He stopped directly before her and Elizabeth's heart thundered in her breast. She drew a deep breath, gripping the sides of the desk for balance.

Chapter Twenty-Three

"What the hell is going on?" Alec's voice rumbled ominously through the hollow room, echoing off the stately rafters and resounding through Elizabeth's rigid frame. Her fingers gripped the edge of the desk in a manner that belied the forced levity of her voice.

"Good morning, Alec. I believe I explained all that in my letter."

"*Letter?* You call this a letter?" A crumpled piece of parchment, which indeed bore little resemblance to a letter, waved before Elizabeth's eyes until Alec thrust it into his pocket with a disgusted snort. He took a step closer to her and his brows met in his most ferocious of scowls. "It is but a hastily penned missive. I'm not some simple country bumpkin thinking myself in love with you, someone you can play for a fool. I require far more in the way of an explanation than some—" He yanked the letter from his pocket yet again and shook it before him for good measure, a frown of disdain creasing his chiseled features. He took yet one more step closer, poised not a handbreadth from her. His tone was flat, his expression unreadable. "Why didn't you come? And don't give me any of that duty rubbish."

Elizabeth stared silently at him for several moments, drawing upon the strength these four walls provided, the staunch reminder of all that was good and worthy, all that she had committed herself to these many years. Alec and all his muscled virility suddenly seemed out of place here, in a room so used to housing innocent young women seeking to enrich themselves, in a place she called home. This was her security, her future, something she could not risk even for a man such as he. She lifted her chin a notch and matched his unwavering gaze with her own. "I fear I've misled you. I apologize."

His mouth twisted cynically. "Lest I grow even more confused, was it your agreeing to marry me that threw me, or perhaps the bestowing of your virtue upon me? There isn't a man in all of England who would have been misled by that."

"Lower your voice, Alec, Miss Percy might—"

"I don't give a damn what Miss Percy might!" he roared, towering mightily above her. His eyes narrowed. "Perhaps I was wrong in thinking you the type of woman who would never play games, for I believe this is indeed just that. You play with fire, woman. Have you considered the price you may pay for such folly?"

Elizabeth willed a steadiness to her voice. "It is never folly to stand by one's word. As I explained to you, Alec, after considerable thought, I have determined to abide by my word and marry Basil."

An ominous tic began in his fierce jaw. "Even *you* can't be that pious and self-sacrificing."

Elizabeth's mind frantically sought some believable train of thought. "Why does it come as no surprise to me that you cannot understand such logic?"

"Because I happen to be a man of sound mind!" he bellowed, looming like a fearsome lion before her, his stormy eyes turbulent. "You push me too far, Elizabeth. Lord, woman, what do you want from me!"

Elizabeth gulped. "I . . . I wish to be left alone, Alec."

"Alone?" He glowered at her as if he practiced great restraint. "Not twelve hours ago you wished to be my damned wife!"

"I spoke too soon, you see. I was confused . . ."

"Confused?" So feral was his scowl, his fists clenched at his sides. "Look upon confused, my dear Elizabeth, for here it stands before you. Aye, you've muddled my mind, played upon me like the most seasoned of wenches. Is it all a guise? Indeed, a game, the likes of which even Celestine would envy! And how I've exercised patience, thinking I knew you!" He shook his head and glared at her. "How I played into your hands, wooing and waiting upon bended knee, then waiting again. And for what? Some damned high-flown gibberish about keeping one's word to marry some fop. Some…" He released his breath with a slow hiss. "I've had enough game playing for one lifetime, Elizabeth, and I'm through waiting. Turn about. Gaze out the window if you must, but damn it, woman, speak the truth."

Indeed, she sought that bleak winter landscape over the ferocity of his manner, the harshness of his tone, the finality in his words. "I speak the truth. I shall marry Basil, Alec. I must—"

In an instant she was facing him, her breasts crushed against solid brawn, her wide eyes staring into his. The strain upon him was undeniable, the tension etching lines in his bronzed face and flowing like molten steel from his grip upon her arms. His eyes blazed, his jaw tightened and his voice was hoarse. "I don't know what the hell has gotten into you since yesterday, but I damned well intend to find out." He ground the words out, tightening his hold upon her.

"Alec, please . . . not here . . ."

A flame leapt in his eyes. "What? Are you worried that these hallowed halls may crumble in shame, or that your Miss Percy lurks behind the door, ever at the ready to save you from any pursuit that is less than chaste? Perhaps that is why you seek this haven. Where but within this fortress of puritan consciousness could you seek that strength of moral fiber you feel you cannot live another day without? Are you perhaps seeking absolution for your misdeeds?"

"How your mocking falls trippingly from your tongue, Alec," she retorted. "Far be it for me to deny you your solace seeking aboard your mighty beast, Sebastian! So what if I draw some peace from these hallowed halls? It's all I have known to comfort me these many years. How dare you even deign to deny me that, or worse yet, to belittle such an endeavor?"

His eyes narrowed, his jaw clenched. "Seek what you must here, but for God's sake, don't marry Basil as some sort of penance."

Elizabeth squeezed her eyes tightly upon the tears yearning to be shed. Penance? It was a life sentence. Her heart swelled with the agony of it all. With a strength of will she had never before imagined she possessed, she pushed against him with a shake of her head. "I'm sorry, Alec. I fear I shall never be able to make you understand."

"Understand!" He gripped her arms, bending his head as if he sought to capture her evasive gaze. "Look at me," he growled. "For God's sake, woman, I love you."

"Stop...please..." She twisted futilely in his grasp.

"I'm never going to stop," he muttered harshly, pulling her closer and clasping a hand beneath her chin. "I want you as my wife."

"Alec..."

His hands upon her shook with his rage, and he growled, "As the mother of my children."

"Please...no..."

He swept her roughly against his entire length, his eyes glittering dangerously into hers. "I want you in my bed."

She groaned.

His hands spanned her waist, his rasping words almost incoherent, such was his restraint. "I want you at my side...now and as I grow old. I want you as no man has ever wanted a woman. And I shall not be denied."

Her mouth opened in meek protest, but her voice caught in her throat as his lips swooped upon hers with a ferocity that buckled her legs beneath her. Tears of frustration and pain slipped from her eyes, yet she clung to him as the tempest swept over them. Every protest, every minute thread of logic, her very will split asunder in that aching moment when she surrendered completely to him. He knew it. She knew he knew it, yet she did not care. If this was indeed to be the last time she would be in his arms, she intended to savor it.

Their passion was irrefutable, but there was something more, a desperation and an urgency that brought them together like storms colliding. Gone was the gentle coaxing in his manner, the sweet and leisurely awakening of her response. His kiss was fierce, all-consuming, allowing but the slightest gasp of breath before resuming with even more intensity.

Elizabeth's world reeled and she clutched at his shoulders as if she could never draw him close enough. She gasped for a breath when his mouth released hers to claim the slender column of her throat, and she sagged weakly against him.

His hands caressed her ribs and boldly moved over her breasts, his thumbs brushing with leisurely impudence over her nipples, which drew a breathless gasp in response. His laugh was low, confident, full of an arrogance that set her aflame with need. "You are mine, now and always," he murmured against her parted lips. He clasped her chin and his eyes bored into hers. "Seek the truth in your heart. Only there will you find the solace you so desperately seek elsewhere."

Without warning, he released her, turning on his heel and leaving her to clutch at the desk and stare after him. When the door slammed in his wake, she was aware not of the thundering of her heart, the rawness of her lips or the tingling in her limbs, but of a bleak emptiness that ensnared her as completely as it seemed to fill the room.

Basil closed the door softly behind him. Despite the barrage of less than kind words Brunhilde had chosen to fling at him, he wore his self-satisfied smirk as comfortably as his dressing gown. Bloody old cow! How she wished to deny him any opportunity to check up on the old man, permanently perched, as she was, beside Nigel's bed. So be it. He'd required but a hasty glance to assure himself that Nigel's condition had not improved. Indeed, the old man looked about as close to death as one could be.

A movement farther down the hall drew his attention and his pulse quickened at the sight of Felicity. And from what he could see, she looked as delectable as a puff pastry. He hesitated not one moment. After all, things were going exceedingly well. Chastity and all that be damned. He deserved a good romp.

As stealthily as a cat, and wearing a feral grin, he padded down the hallway, stopping behind the young maid, whose arms were laden with freshly laundered linens. He watched with silent amusement as she struggled with the doorknob to a linen closet. Then, just as she managed to pry the door open, he cupped her derriere and ground his turgid manhood into her backside.

"Basil!" she cried breathlessly, spinning about so hastily the linens tumbled to the floor around them.

"Who else?" He grinned wickedly, roughly pulling her to him and carelessly fondling a breast.

With wide eyes darting frantically about, Felicity pushed meekly against him. "Look what you've done to my linens!"

"So? Launder them again. You've nothing better to do, have you? Then again . . ." He raised a wicked brow and glanced at the huge closet. Grasping her hand, he pulled her behind him and into the closet, silencing her breathy retort with a savage kiss.

Ignoring her protests, he impatiently brushed her hands aside to tear at the buttons of her dress. Spreading the starched cotton wide with a growl, he bent his head to suckle the high curves of her bosom. He chuckled at her acquiescence as she melted into his arms like the softest of butter. When his hand groped beneath her dress and slid along her thigh, however, she tensed and pushed against him once again. Surely he wasn't losing his touch? His fingers hooked in the elastic of her pantaloons and he yanked them down. "Don't resist me now. You don't want to be the reason for disrupting such a successful week thus far, now do you?"

Felicity's feeble attempts to dissuade him with her tiny hands failed miserably, and soon her pantaloons lay in a heap around her ankles. "B-be gentle, Basil," she sighed, sagging against the wall as he tugged upon his sash to allow his robe to hang loosely about him. He made quick work of his trousers and soon grasped her roughly beneath her derriere, lifting her from her feet as he pressed against her.

"I must say. . ." she breathed, clutching at his shoulders and drawing quick gasps of air, "you seem very jaunty for a man whose betrothed agreed to marry another."

"*What?*"

As if a bucket of ice-cold water had descended upon him, Basil jerked upright, releasing Felicity so suddenly she nearly crumpled to the floor. His passion fled so speedily he tugged his trousers up lest Felicity glimpse his lagging desire. "What did you say?"

Drawing a trembling hand to her lips, Felicity stared blankly at him. "Elizabeth. She agreed to marry Lord Sinclair. Oh, you should have seen him! On bended knee, he was, even when Brunhilde and I came in. And she . . . Basil!"

With brutal force, Basil's hand closed about Felicity's throat and he pinioned her against the wall with a dull thud. Ignoring her horror-stricken look of terror, he growled ferociously, "I don't care to hear of the man's prowess. What in God's name is the matter with you? Why didn't you tell me sooner?"

A tear slid from the corner of Felicity's eye and she trembled in his grasp. "I thought she would tell you. She's in love with him, you know. 'Tis plain as day, and he with her."

"Listen to me!" he hissed. "She loves *me,* do you hear me? I am the man she agreed to marry! And if Sinclair thinks he can foil that, he cannot. If she thinks she can bear my name and dally in that bastard's bed, I'll simply have to kill her." At Felicity's gasp, he sneered, "I will not be cuckolded, do you hear me? And I will not have the servants in this house thinking otherwise! Do you hear me? Do you?"

He was only dimly aware of Felicity's vigorous nods, for he flung his robe about him and stalked angrily from the closet.

Alec labored mightily over Sebastian in the stable. Despite the frosty, late afternoon air, he had shed any outer garments and rolled the billowing sleeves of his shirt to his elbows as he worked. The compatible scents of liniment and fresh hay filled the small quarters as he rubbed the salve into Sebastian's glistening coat with an ardor that brought sweat to his brow and a satisfying ache to his muscles. To this he remained unaware, his mind as consumed by his thoughts as his body was with the task at hand.

It was the least he could do for the animal, having ridden Sebastian hither and yon about the damned English countryside for a large portion of the day. From Dunlevy, he'd stormed off to the country estate to see to his mail and any other items requiring his attention. Then, at a ferocious clip well suited to his mood, he'd ridden into London and to the harbor for a rather superfluous inspection of his fleet of ships. As usual, all were in fine shape, operating smoothly and requiring little in the way of attention from him. Feeling superfluous himself, he'd swung Sebastian's nose in the direction of the town house, knowing damned well that he wished to avoid the place until evening. Too many images sprang to his mind whenever he but passed through the place.

A fire in the hearth drew forth a startlingly clear vision of Elizabeth in a transparent gown frolicking before the flames. The slightest glimpse of the parlor conjured up the memory of a sensuous dance and lithe curves swathed in sumptuous red velvet. Even the sunlight taunted him with the image of an angel at her toilette, her luminous skin aglow in the rosy rays, the lushness of her body rendering him momentarily insane....

Sebastian's snort of disapproval and a wary sideways glance served to snatch Alec from his troubled musings.

"Sorry, boy," he murmured, patting the stallion's neck. "I'm a little heavy-handed today." A movement at the stable door drew his eye to the somber-faced Holmes, lingering in the doorway as if he were out of his element in such a place.

"Ah, Holmes," Alec greeted the servant, wiping his hands upon a rag dangling from his pocket. "What brings you out into the cold, man? Surely it's not some heretofore unknown desire to labor over a sweaty animal?"

Holmes remained impassive. "Hardly that, sir," he intoned, clasping his hands behind his back and sending Sebastian a bored look. "You've a visitor, sir. A young lady."

Alec stared at the servant for several moments then tossed the rag aside and reached for his coat, lying upon a nearby stool. He could barely temper his grin. "Ha! Do I know her, or what? Never once did I harbor the slightest doubt. Not the slightest." He could hardly suppress his excitement, carelessly running a hand through his hair before flinging the coat over one arm and moving past Holmes at a determined pace. The servant's words stilled his booted feet.

"'Tis not Miss Burbridge, sir."

Alec swung about and found himself tempering a scowl instead. "Of course. Thank you, Holmes. I'll see to the young lady."

"She's in the parlor, sir."

His guest did indeed await in the parlor, though upon entering, Alec couldn't locate her for several moments. A slight movement in the corner of the room finally caught his attention, and with some surprise he noticed that she perched upon the very edge of a small chair as if she were afraid of marring the fabric. He realized with far greater surprise that he hadn't recognized her at first due to the blotchiness of her skin, the puffiness of her eyes.

"Felicity!" He hastened to the girl, trembling fearfully upon her perch. A chill of dread raced through his veins. "Felicity, for God's sake, what is it? Elizabeth . . . Something's happened to Elizabeth."

Chapter Twenty-Four

When Elizabeth stepped through the massive front portal of the Cosgrove mansion, it was with a purposeful tread. As if in keeping with her mood, the foyer was deserted and dimly lit, the servants no doubt having taken to their quarters at this late hour. And justly so. The hour was well past nine, an ungodly time for a schoolteacher to be returning from her day of toil and trouble.

She harbored little doubt that Basil lurked somewhere, his keen ears pricked, his beady black eyes peeled for her appearance. Little did he know that the reason for her tardiness had scant to do with Dunlevy affairs and absolutely everything to do with Alec's unforeseen and thoroughly enlightening visit early that morning.

No sooner had the door slammed behind Alec when the sudden realization of what she must do crashed upon her with all the force of a legion of cannons. True, the tears had spilled and the reservations had reared their ugly heads, but amidst all this, one thought rang clear and true. The greatest sacrifice she could make would be a lifetime with Alec, and she had no intention of denying herself that, no matter what she lost in the process.

A sound from the parlor drew her attention and she proceeded toward the partially opened door, her tread muted by the thick rugs. The sound of muffled voices reached her ears, assuring her that Basil was indeed one of those ensconced within the room. The other voice was higher in pitch, softer, with a decided breathiness. Felicity?

Some primitive instinct took hold as Elizabeth grasped the doorknob. Instead of flinging the door wide, thereby announcing her arrival, she merely ventured a hesitant and very quiet peek around the heavy wood.

Basil and Felicity stood in such a way that Elizabeth's presence went undetected. Felicity apparently tended to something at the sideboard, though Basil seemed intent upon thwarting her efforts, standing close behind her, obscenely close, both hands fumbling feverishly at her disheveled bodice. Then, with one swift movement, Basil spun her about and bent his head to her exposed bosom while his hands roved freely over her hips and thighs. Elizabeth, the eavesdropper, could do naught but stare.

"Basil, please..." Felicity moaned, though to Elizabeth's eye, the manner in which the maid sagged in his arms belied her plea. "Haven't you had enough for one day?"

"Enough?" Basil replied in a growling voice. "You have warmed my bed for the past few months so well, wench, I fear I cannot get enough of you, even after this afternoon."

This afternoon!

"But, Basil, once you are wed, it would not be fitting for us to continue our..."

Basil gave a thoroughly wicked laugh from somewhere deep in Felicity's cleavage. "I have every intention of continuing to bed you at my leisure even after I'm wed. Desirable though she may be, and believe me, her charms would tempt a saint, Elizabeth will find it beyond her means to entirely satisfy me. Besides—" Basil's fingers delved into Felicity's bodice, eliciting a moan from the young maid "—I intend to keep her on her back and breeding as much as possible. I have no intention of remaining faithful to her during that time. What man would, after all?"

His words seemed to strike some chord of dismay in Felicity, for she jerked upright and made a feeble attempt at fending him off. "Are you saying that you do not find a woman with child desirable?"

Not to be denied, Basil grasped her hands in one of his and continued his ravishment of her bosom. "Perhaps I may, one never knows. When the woman is one's wife, one has little choice, but—"

"And if she were not your wife?"

"Felicity, my luscious girl, stop this gibberish and let me..."

Perhaps something in the young maid's voice penetrated that fog of lust into which Basil had descended, for he sprang from her as if she were suddenly aflame. "What did you say?"

Felicity shrank from him. "I...I...oh, Basil, I love you so and I...I believe I am carrying your child."

"You're what?"

"I...I thought you'd be pleased."

"Pleased!" he shrieked. "It's not mine, I tell you!"

The tears spilled to Felicity's cheeks and she shook her head so fiercely the pins tumbled from her hair. "Basil, I was a virgin when you took me and I have sought no one but you ever since. I love you. I..."

Elizabeth could endure no more. With a hand pressed to her mouth, she turned and fled, racing up the stairs and to her room. With trembling hands, she bolted the door and sank to the floor against that heavy wood. Her own tears spilled unheeded, tears of anger, yes, at the true extent of Basil's deception, at his effortless manipulation of her, at the glimpse she'd achieved of his vile and thoroughly debauched character. But these tears were also shed for Felicity, that innocent child who had committed the most heinous blunder of all: she had fallen in love with that demon.

Quickly, she rose to her feet and hastened to the armoire to fling the doors wide. Her eye passed unseeing over the array of silk, satin and taffeta gowns, Basil's feeble attempt at coercion, until she found her few identical brown muslin frocks. These she swept from the armoire along with her shoes and underclothes, tossing them upon the bed. From beneath the bed, she pulled forth her trunk and, without preamble, stuffed her belongings inside. Snapping the latches closed, she heaved the trunk into her arms and turned toward the door, only to stop dead in her tracks.

How on earth was she to escape unnoticed with Basil below and no means of transportation conveniently awaiting her? Her hesitation lingered but a brief moment as her thoughts flew.

Then into her mind emerged a plan, a delightful and daredev-ilish plan, the likes of which she had never before even consid-ered herself capable of attempting, much less accomplishing. With a determined set of her shoulders and a decided twinkle in the depths of her eyes, she placed the trunk in a corner and turned once again to the armoire.

Those silk, satin and taffeta gowns, as it turned out, proved excellent bed-stuffing material. She surveyed her work with a confident eye. In the darkness, if one so happened to venture into her room to peek at her or, in Basil's case, to accost her, the bed would appear to be inhabited. Elizabeth could not help a smirk at the image of a rutting Basil achieving naught but a handful of taffeta. She gave the bed one last look then opened the door.

A quick glance in either direction assured her that no one lurked about. Closing the door behind her, she turned, not in the direction of the front stairs but toward the back of the house and the dark, narrow staircase reserved solely for the servants' use.

Not more than a few moments later, the curtains in Eliza-beth's room billowed with the cold breeze sweeping through the room. A window closed without a whisper of sound and a dark form emerged from behind the curtain and moved stealthily to the bed. Without pause, the figure bent, extending one brawny arm to sweep a hand boldly over the sheet, whose curves and hollows were so visible in the moonlight. In an instant, the form jerked upright then tossed the sheet aside and thrust one hand into the pile upon the bed. A lopsided smile slid across the prowler's face when he held up a pale satin gown. With care, he replaced the gown and drew the sheet over the pile once again, poking and tucking until it once again resembled a lithe female form deep in slumber.

With a light heart and purposeful tread, he left the room as he came, making his way to the ground below as agilely as a cat. He paused but once, his attention drawn by the scene in the parlor. He did not linger long before turning and disappearing into the night.

* * *

In horror, Basil again and again stared at Felicity then at her belly before he spun about and headed straight for the brandy. His skin crawled when her hand plucked at his sleeve and she mewled softly behind him, though this did not impede the urgent filling and draining of his glass three consecutive times. Only then, after the liquor had adequately numbed him, did he lend her breathy but ever-so-plaintive voice his ear.

"Basil, please, listen," she said, tugging again at his sleeve. "I think I have a solution."

Basil closed his eyes and shook his head in wonderment at the girl's naïveté. Could a wench be more dim-witted? He poured himself another draft and drained it as quickly as he'd done the others. Wiping a hand across his mouth, he turned to face her and cocked a brow. "What is this solution of yours? I'm simply dying of curiosity."

Momentarily flustered, Felicity blushed, then clasped and unclasped her hands several times before finding her tongue. "I fear that I have grown rather fond of Elizabeth these past few days. Very fond, actually, and feeling as I do about her, and about Lord Sinclair, I thought it in her best interests and those of everyone involved that I...oh, Basil!" Desperately, she flung herself into his arms, clutching at him and sobbing into his silk gown. "I have been so foolish, but it is only because I love you and wish to be your wife more than anything! We can marry now!"

"Is that so?" Basil could not help raising an amused brow, though this dissolved into an angry scowl when he realized what her tears must be doing to his gown. She, however, paid little heed to his attempts to pry her hands free and resumed her sobbing with dramatic fervor.

"Yes! We can marry and raise our child."

"Is that so? And what of the fortune, my dear? Are you suggesting that I do away with your chum Elizabeth soon after I wed her?"

Felicity stared at him, horror-stricken. "Oh my goodness, no! Never that! We don't need the fortune, Basil. You could find work. We could even live with my family. They are poor, of course, and live in a small village. But there are ten children to help with the farm and—''

Basil's guffaws echoed through the room. "Me? On a god-forsaken farm? With *ten* children? Ha!" With a disbelieving shake of his head, he removed himself from her grasp and bent over the decanter once more. "That's no plan you harbor, my dear, it's a joke. Now leave me to my musings, will you."

"But, Basil . . ."

"Oh, and by the way . . ." He tossed the words nonchalantly over one shoulder. "If I were you, I would seek employment elsewhere, posthaste. I don't need some swollen, clumsy servant ambling about, causing havoc in this household."

"Basil!"

He donned a cool look and turned to face her once again. "Don't tell me you're surprised? Are you indeed that naive? Felicity, this is a lesson I would have thought you'd learned. Men of my station would never, *ever* marry a woman such as yourself. True, I desire you in my bed, as many men will, and due to your position you should comply with those desires. But as for love . . ." His laughter drew a shudder from Felicity, who could only stare at him with mute horror. "I do not love you, nor would I ever be capable of such an emotion with you. As for that child you shall whelp . . ." He waved a hand at her belly. "Why, I'm rather certain that, with the help of a few gold coins, I could convince the stable boy to claim it as his. So you see, dear sweet Felicity, it is *I* who have all the solutions. Now, if you please, leave me."

Felicity's mouth sagged and she appeared to gasp for breath. "I . . . I cannot."

"You can, my dear," Basil muttered, indicating the door. "Simply place one foot in front of the other and off you'll go to your little bed."

Felicity didn't move. "I'm sorry, Basil, but I simply cannot allow this. Indeed, I fear I have given you little alternative but to marry me. I believe that Lord Sinclair knows of your plot and intends to foil it."

Basil's eyes narrowed upon her as the blood ran cold in his veins. "He what?"

"He intends to thwart your scheme to marry Elizabeth. He loves her so . . ."

"You're lying."

Felicity's gaze was suddenly unflinching. "I speak truth."

He weighed her words, the grim finality of it all descending upon him. "How the hell does he know?" he roared. "How?" Then, amidst his blinding rage, he detected the undeniable guilt plaguing Felicity's brow, the plaintive appeal in her eyes, the unabashed hope. His heart seemed to stop for several moments. "You?" he managed in a strangled voice. "You told that bastard Sinclair?"

"I did it for us, Basil!"

Basil clasped a hand to his brow and shook his head with disbelief. "Do you realize what you've done?" He turned and stared at the brandy, then rubbed his eyes as if to clear his mind and began a fervent pacing. "Of all the people in London, you had to tell *him?*"

"Why, of course. He loves Elizabeth."

"Listen to me," Basil hissed, grasping Felicity by the shoulders and shaking her so hard he heard her teeth rattle. "Nothing is going to stop me, *nothing!* Not you and your harebrained ideas of love, and certainly not Sinclair. That bastard will have to turn this country inside out and kill me to find Elizabeth, and by the time he does, she will be my wife. Do you think he'll want her after I've had her? I think not."

Despite the wild-eyed look of terror in her eyes, Felicity managed a weak shake of her head. "I truly believe he would want her under any circumstances."

"Ha!" Basil sneered. "That shows how much you know of this world, wench."

"Or perhaps how little you know of true love, Basil," came the murmured response, though he barely heard her. "Basil, where are you going? Basil, please don't leave me!"

Without pause he strode from the room and up the stairs, barely mindful of Felicity scurrying frantically in his wake, so consumed was he. Only when he reached the top of the stairs and Felicity lunged after him did he pause.

"Get the hell away from me!" he barked, twisting about and shoving hard against her. "Go, wench." He waved a hand to he stairs at her back. "Go warm some poor lout's bed. I've no further need for you."

A grief-stricken Felicity would not be denied. "You cannot kidnap Elizabeth! He shall hunt you down. Oh, Basil . . ."

Grasping her hands in a brutal grip, he vowed, "No one will ever find me, I can promise you that. Now get . . . *away* . . ."

His final shove against her coincided with poor Felicity's recoil from him. For one catastrophic moment, she teetered precariously on the edge of the top step, one hand reaching desperately for him and a silent cry upon her lips. Then she tumbled, landing soundly upon her back before somersaulting heels over head like a flimsy rag doll to land in a crumpled, lifeless heap at the foot of the stairs.

Like a man possessed, Basil raced down the stairs and dropped to his knees beside her. As if in a trancelike state, he drew her into his lap, cradling the blond head that hung at an odd angle from her neck and feeling the bile rising in his throat along with something dreadfully foreign to him. Sorrow . . . ? He knew without a doubt that she was dead, the color already vanishing from her skin, the life from her blood.

Any remorse he might have come close to feeling, however, was surpassed by his unrivaled instinct for survival. Glancing about, he sprang to his feet then paused, staring at Felicity and rubbing shaking fingers into his temples. He turned and raced back up the stairs, pausing only when he reached Elizabeth's room. A hasty peek inside assured him that she slept and he silently thanked the fates. An ear pressed against the wood of Nigel's chamber door satisfied him that Brunhilde still read aloud to the old man, her deep voice droning on and on incessantly. Back down the stairs he sped, stopping yet again to stare at the lifeless form, half-anticipating her to get up.

With a noisy gulp, he scurried into the parlor and retrieved a full bottle of brandy. Cradling this in his arm as if it were precious cargo, he flung his cloak about his shoulders and, with one last look at Felicity, thrust the front portal wide.

Just as he stepped into the frosty night air, a horse and rider, moving at a rather speedy but erratic clip, thundered from around the side of the mansion, directly past him to disappear into the night. Startled, Basil stared after the pair as the horse's hooves upon the cobblestones faded into the muffled sounds of evening. He shook his head. No doubt some randy stable hand bent upon acquiring a lady of the evening to satisfy whatever plagued him. The lad's pace was adequate testament to an urgent plight, though Basil could have sworn from what little he had seen that the horse bore no saddle. He frowned momentarily then shrugged. An urgent plight, indeed.

He mused on this but a moment, his own atrocious situation hovering about him like a shroud. With a grunt, he withdrew the brandy and lifted it to his lips, drawing upon that bottle like a starving babe. Glancing about the shadowed terrace, he pondered for a moment then drew again upon the bottle. The brandy would serve him well this night. Indeed, what better companion to chase away the chill and while away the hours here, upon this terrace, in full view of the front portal, lest that bastard Sinclair happen to descend upon them, intent upon whisking Elizabeth away from him. Ha! The idea!

He settled himself upon the cold bricks, well into the shadows, and huddled within his cloak. A slight turn of his head afforded him an unimpeded view of the staircase and Felicity's body still lying upon the floor. Cold fear pricked through him. He banished it with a gulp of liquor.

When she was discovered, and it was only a matter of time before Brunhilde ventured past, he would have a front row seat. Only then, when the entire household had been roused to hysterical confusion, would he amble through that portal, his gait leisurely, his manner relaxed and affable, fresh from an evening spent with his cronies. His inebriation would only lend his story credence, as would his utter shock and dismay over Felicity's demise. He had deceived many a soul before with remarkable ease. That his life could be at stake now caused him only a moment's pause. He drew again on the bottle, belched, then gave a hoarse laugh. They would never suspect him. After all, as far as he was concerned, he'd neither seen nor spoken to Felicity all evening. Who knew better?

Elizabeth pulled on the reins with all her might, erupting with a frantic "Whoa!" as she'd heard Alec command when he'd wished to halt Sebastian. To her intense relief, the animal finally complied, skidding to a stop upon the cobblestones so suddenly she was nearly thrown from his back. With a decided hesitation, she released the handful of black mane she clung to so frantically and pressed a shaking hand to her heart, drawing enormous gulps of air into lungs that threatened to burst. Her mount swung a curious look upon her, and she patted his neck with as much confidence as she could muster.

"Good boy," she muttered, drawing strength from the ears that pricked at her voice and willing her pulse to a normal speed. Perhaps he was one of the more feebleminded of his breed and, as such, unaware that his rider was thoroughly petrified, almost to the point of losing her mind. Indeed, she already *had* lost her mind, for here she sat, astride this mangy beast, clad in a tattered version of her typical gown, her pantaloons glowing like beacons in the moonlight as they peeked from beneath her cloak. And in her wake she'd left a poor young stable hand harboring the vow that he wouldn't tell a soul of her flight.

He'd simply stared and nodded dumbly as she'd first demanded a mount, one of the more docile in the stable, then insisted that the beast need not be saddled. Time did not allow such a convenience. Besides, she'd reasoned, if one did not know how to ride, a saddle, especially one of those designed exclusively for women, would be of little help.

With nary a thought as to what she might be doing to the young stable hand, she'd hastily done away with the bottom third of her dress, enabling her to straddle the horse's back. At the lad's instruction, she'd dug her heels into the horse's flanks, only to have the very life drawn out of her as he'd dashed from the stable and around the manse as if his tail were on fire. Docile mount, indeed!

She drew a deep breath and glanced behind her. They were out of sight of the manse, yet something told her she would not be safe until she'd reached Alec's town house. Her eyes darted warily about and she pulled her hood close about her face. At this hour, alone on the streets of London, she had far more to fear than Basil.

Her pulse leapt and a shiver of apprehension raced through her, sweeping aside, for a time, her fear of the horse beneath her. Grasping the reins tightly, she pressed her heels gently into the animal's sides and guided him down the dark street.

Chapter Twenty-Five

Elizabeth had but lifted a hand to rap upon the door when it was flung wide and she found herself swooped into a pair of steely arms. Dimly, she was aware that her feet had left the ground and that the door had banged closed behind her. She struggled to catch her breath, which proved close to impossible, for Alec's mouth descended upon hers with such intensity she nearly swooned. She clung to him, luxuriating in his warmth, his strength seeping through the folds of her cloak and branding the entire length of her chilled and trembling body. Her fingers delved into his hair, cradling his head as her lips parted again and again beneath his. He mumbled incoherently against her mouth, his words of love but a hoarse murmur full of passion and restraint that gave flight to Elizabeth's heart.

With one swift movement, he lifted her into his arms, his eyes capturing hers before roving heatedly over her. When he glimpsed what remained of the hem of her gown, her pantaloons and her exposed legs, he did not pause in his swift mounting of the stairs, though he managed to raise a wicked brow.

With a groan of pure helplessness, she clung to him as he strode down the hall and into his chamber. He lowered her to the burgundy velvet covering the massive bed with little ceremony. Leaning upon his hands on either side of her, he gazed deep into her eyes. Elizabeth's hands moved over the contours of his face, caressing the bearded jaw, tracing the hollowed planes, before pressing against the firmness of his chest. "Alec, please, you must heed me but one moment."

He moved as if he hadn't heard her, rising beside the bed and tearing the shirt from his back in one swift movement. It fell in a careless heap of white cotton at his feet, an unnecessary testament to a growing impatience of which Elizabeth was more than aware. As aware as she was of his eyes, pinioning her to the bed, and of him, looming magnificently, muscled and bronzed, vibrant and full of an undeniable need. As if with a will of their own, her eyes roamed freely over his furred chest, past the washboard stomach to his hand, that powerful hand poised at the top button of his trousers.

Her heart leapt and she scurried from the bed, feeling the heat of her blush and a trembling to rival that of the most chaste of maidens. How her passion mounted to match his, despite all the words she had yet to speak! Words that simply must be spoken before she lay with him upon that bed.

He moved toward her slowly, as purposeful as any man could hope to be. She backed away from him, from the bed, until a low dresser pressing against the backs of her legs impeded her progress. Gripping the dresser, she held one hand before her in a meek attempt at fending him off. This drew the slightest lift of one corner of his mouth and then he was before her, his hands encircling her waist then roving over her hips in his bold manner, claiming her body as easily as he had her soul.

"Alec, please," she groaned, grasping his hands and attempting to still their quest by holding them tight against her chest. This proved a grievous mistake. With a throaty chuckle, he spread his hands over her bosom, then cupped her breasts as his mouth found hers. His thumbs brushed over the peaks of her breasts, eliciting a breathless gasp and nearly sending her into a swoon.

"Alec . . . you would be proud of me," she managed to say, struggling for some semblance of sanity. "Indeed, even I was rather proud."

"Is that so?" Such nonchalance, as if he would have responded thus no matter what she had said, as if he indeed had one very pressing purpose. His hands cupped her derriere and clasped her hard against him. "Yield to me, love . . . now."

Elizabeth's world reeled. "Alec, you must listen. I fear I shall be condemned to Newgate prison for my deeds earlier this night."

"Is that so?" She glimpsed the slight lift of his lips before he gathered her close and nuzzled her neck. "Tell me, sweet angel, what heinous act did you commit, other than losing half of your dress? To my eye, keeping legs like those concealed beneath some damned skirt is criminal enough."

"I stole a horse."

This proved sufficient for a momentary digression and a huge grin. "You what?"

She couldn't help the smile playing upon her lips as her eyes met his. "I didn't actually steal it. I sort of borrowed it. To ride." Her smile faded. "Such was my haste to flee."

That telltale flame leapt in his eye and he drew her tightly against him. "It warms my heart that your need was as undeniable as mine, love. Be it borrowing or stealing, I don't give a damn how you got here. Indeed, I would have stolen you myself had you not come on your own." His mouth lowered to brush unhurriedly over hers. "They're bound to realize at some point that your mound of taffeta and satin is simply that, and not some comely maid in slumber. Then again, by the time they do realize, you shall be my wife."

Elizabeth gasped and stared up at him, wide-eyed. "How on earth did you know?"

Alec swept a stray ebony tendril from her cheek. "My dearest love, I was certainly not going to leave our future in your hands a moment longer, even if I had to steal you, screaming and kicking, from that house." His lips slid across her cheek, over her temple. "Enough talk."

Elizabeth's eyes fluttered, yet her purpose would not be denied. "Alec, please, I must speak with you of certain circumstances that may alter your feelings for me."

"Nothing could change the way I feel about you," he murmured, lowering his head to her bosom. "You know, even through this damned muslin, you have the most beautiful breasts." He pressed the mounds to his face. "Soft and full and in desperate need of unbridling."

"Alec, please! There is something about me that you do not know."

"I know that I love you more than I could have ever hoped to love a woman. I desire you like no other. You could no more put an end to that than you could the rising of the sun." He gathered her close and his eyes blazed with passion. "Elizabeth, sweet innocent, my love for you does not ebb and flow with the tides. It's not subject to whim, nor is it something I can control. God only knows, I tried."

"You what?" Elizabeth cried.

Alec shook his head with mock disbelief. "Never mind. Suffice it to say, I was hopelessly smitten from the moment I met you."

"Oh, Alec," Elizabeth sighed, drawing his mouth to hers for a leisurely kiss and forgetting all that she had wished to say. "And I, too, loved you from the very start. I...Alec!"

His chuckle belied the urgency of his hands freeing the pins from her hair.

"Alec, please...I...I've lied to you."

His hands did not falter until her hair fell unheeded to her waist. "You're so beautiful...."

"Alec, you didn't hear me. I said I..."

"I heard you," he said in so casual a tone Elizabeth found herself startled. "Sometimes circumstances force one into playing a part, a game— God help me, even assuming a guise or lying." His eyes locked with hers. "I know all about your mother, Philippa Valentine, your father, Nigel, and Basil's scheme of blackmail."

Elizabeth's shock knew no bounds. "B-but how did you...?"

"It seems Felicity was in on Basil's plot from the very beginning. Upon finding herself suddenly overcome by guilt and a genuine concern for you, she sought me out this afternoon. Not that what she had to say made a damn bit of difference. Do you really think any of it matters in the least to me?"

"Oh, Alec!" Elizabeth threw her arms about him.

"Now that's more like it." He laughed, holding her close. "Elizabeth, there's only one thing you could do that may, just may, enrage me beyond measure."

Elizabeth lifted wary eyes. "And what is that?"

A smirk teased his lips. "If I have to wait this long each and every time I wish to take you to my bed, I will be far from a happy man."

Elizabeth raised a coy brow. "It's not proper, you know. After all, we aren't yet wed."

"So you keep reminding me," he muttered, indicating the windows. "Would you like me to venture forth into yonder cold night and rouse some poor cleric from his toasty bed to see to the nuptials? If you simply cannot wait another night, I will fetch him, you know. God knows *I* cannot wait another night."

She felt his fingers upon the hooks at the back of her dress yet again and realized, as the flames leapt in his eyes, that he indeed practiced great restraint. That this filled her with confidence surprised her far less than the sudden impishness it also elicited.

With eyes lowered, she pushed softly against his muscled chest, aware that he was lowering his mouth to hers. She turned her head at the last moment such that his lips found her cheek. "I'm sorry, Alec, I still don't think..."

She gasped as cool air and warm seeking hands caressed her skin, drawing forth shivers of delight as they moved over her back. With a soft groan, she turned from him and found herself staring at her reflection in the dresser mirror. When her eyes found his in the mirror, every last ounce of resistance fled in the span of a heartbeat. She was but an instrument beneath his hands, and she felt herself melting as her dress fell into a heap at her feet. Her shift and pantaloons followed and her eyes fluttered closed at Alec's sharp intake of breath.

"Open your eyes," he rasped hoarsely. His hands slid slowly over her hips, caressed the soft curve of her belly then cupped her breasts. "Look how beautiful you are."

"I can't...I..." Yet she did open her eyes in spite of herself, and nearly dissolved in a heap at the sight. She shook her head and dropped her gaze. "How can I stare upon myself this way with you, when I have never done so alone? It's shameful."

He lifted the curtain of her hair and pressed his mouth against the back of her neck. "Trust me, there is no shame in this. If you have spent the last twenty-five years shunning your lovely body, then I intend to spend the rest of my life making it all up to you."

With a low growl, he turned her in his arms, crushing her to him, then suddenly lifted her, allowing her but a brief gasp for air before soft velvet pressed against her back and warm man against her breasts, her belly, the length of her legs. With soft whimpers that fell unheeded from parted lips, she clasped him to her, rejoicing in the branding flame of his mouth against hers, along her throat, over her breasts. She inhaled him, she tasted of him, her fingers caressed him as if she wished to commit him to memory in the span of one solitary night. Like the possessed soul she was, she arched, she stretched, she moaned, as if all at his bidding. And when he rose naked and glorious above her, she welcomed him eagerly.

Before the fire's last ember sputtered and died, Alec took her three times. The last, in the wee hours of the morning, was a languorous journey of caresses that lingered, lips that savored and bodies that mingled with slow, sweeping strokes. Their soft murmurs drifted through the darkened chamber, soon dissolving into the deep sighs and even breathing of contented sleep.

Basil awoke with so violent a start that his head snapped against the bricks at his back. With a curse, he blinked several times and shook his head, then allowed his bleary eye a hasty look about to find his bearings. One hand fished inside his cloak to retrieve his pocket watch. His movements were stiff, his joints rebelling against the chill that had permeated to the bone. He held the gold fob up to the meager light of the window and squinted at the watch for several moments, then cursed again before stuffing it back into his pocket and struggling to his feet.

He swayed, much like a man aboard a ship tossed carelessly about the sea, his eyes focused intently before him as if that alone would level the earth beneath his feet. Perhaps, just perhaps, he had imbibed a tad too much.

A movement from the window accompanied by a high-pitched wail drew his attention. He stared, transfixed for several moments at the sight of a frantic Brunhilde crouched over Felicity's prostrate form. For one blessed moment, he'd forgotten about Felicity. The enormity of it all weighed on him and he shivered within his cloak before shrugging and rubbing a shaking hand across his damp brow. Sweating? In this chill? Indeed, he was sweating. The cold, clammy sweat of guilt. Guilt? Ha! He'd make certain they'd never suspect.

He shoved himself off the wall, staggered across the terrace and through the front portal. Brunhilde barely glanced up at the sound of the door banging behind him and her mournful wails echoed off the high ceilings. Two female servants stood beside Brunhilde, wringing their hands and chewing at their lips, attempting rather unsuccessfully not to stare at Felicity. The manservant Cecil brushed past Basil as if he were not even there and stooped beside Brunhilde to lay a hand upon Felicity's throat.

Basil retrieved his voice, albeit a slurred croak. "Wh-whath happened?"

Brunhilde's head snapped up and Basil was afforded her mottled, teary-eyed visage contorted with anger. "Can't ye see, ye bloody bastard? She's dead, I tell ye! Dead! And I'm of a mind that ye had somethin' te do with it!"

Basil stared at the woman, then, in an overdramatic gesture, clasped a hand to his heart. "Me?" He swayed then stumbled, managing a caustic laugh. "I have been at the gaming table with several of my chums for the better part of the evening and—"

"Oh, shut up!" Brunhilde roared, looking upon him as if he stank from far more than an overindulgence in spirits. "Don' jest stand there, do somethin'!"

Basil had to force his gaze from Felicity, from the pale skin he had found so enchanting, skin that was now sickly gray and no doubt eerily cold to the touch. He glanced about. Where was Elizabeth? Surely the commotion would have disturbed her sleep. Indeed, he knew very well that she was an extremely light sleeper, for he had listened at her door these several nights past as she'd tossed and turned upon her bed. She should have been streaking down those stairs at this very moment.

With a shaking hand, he delved into his pocket and withdrew a linen handkerchief. This he pressed to his nose in a rather delicate manner, as if the mere sight of Felicity proved too much for him to manage. "Excuse me," he croaked, making his unsteady way to the stairs and choosing to ignore Brunhilde's snort of disgust.

He navigated the stairs with amazing agility, considering his state, though the mounting sense that something was awry brought the blood pounding in his limbs. He flung Elizabeth's chamber door wide without preamble. The dim hallway light illuminated the still form upon the bed. Basil's breath caught in his throat. She was too still.

He staggered to the bed and snatched the sheet aside with one vicious tug of his hand. With a violent curse, he buried his hands in the mass of gowns, flinging them aside as if he expected to find Elizabeth beneath the mound. His anger exploded in his mind, obliterating the last vestiges of any inebriation, and he lurched from the room and down the stairs.

"And where are ye off to now?" Brunhilde cried in his wake.

Basil's step did not falter. "I'll fetch the doctor," he muttered through clenched teeth.

He staggered to the darkened stable, to the small tack room at the rear, where he lit a lantern with shaking hands then dropped to his knees. Frantically, he cleared the hay from one spot on the floor then clawed at the cold earth with his bare hands. He did not have to dig for long until the top of a smooth black box appeared in the dim light. At the sight, he grew so frenzied his limbs shook uncontrollably and it took him several attempts to pry the box open. When he finally raised the lid, it was with a maniacal reverence that he lifted the heavy black pistol from its berth.

He handled it with infinite care, a loving gentleness ill-suited for such a weapon and its intended purpose. This pistol was his salvation. Indeed, he intended to use it, and use it well, for he knew beyond a doubt in whose bed Elizabeth slept. A menacing grin slid across his face as his fingers traced the tarnished brass plating before he tucked the pistol into the top of his trousers. Alec Sinclair would not see the next sunrise.

Chapter Twenty-Six

At first, Elizabeth thought it some horrid nightmare she could banish by sweeping her hand through the tumbling fall of her hair and snuggling closer to Alec's naked warmth. But the vision proved relentless in its pursuit, drawing Alec suddenly upright in the enormous bed, his body all taut, coiled muscle and his arm snatching her close to his side.

Basil stood at the foot of the bed, wielding a satanic grin, a dim lantern and an enormous pistol leveled directly at Alec. His gaze, however, was all over Elizabeth. So marked was his unbridled lust that Alec uttered a low growl and jerked the bed sheet over Elizabeth's legs. With shaking hands she clutched the sheet close to her bosom, well aware that Basil had already gotten an eyeful.

His evil black stare remained unflinchingly upon her as she struggled with the sheet. "You sheathe yourself in vain, wench," he uttered in a strangled voice that belied the peculiar grin twisting his mouth. He waved the pistol menacingly and leaned forward until all that was visible in the shadow of the lantern was the feral gleam of his teeth. "You shall be mine."

"I wouldn't put any money on it." Alec's deep voice rumbled low and equally as menacing through the chamber.

"Ah, he speaks!" Basil gave a caustic snort and his eyes flickered over Alec. "Quite the brawny one, aren't we, Sinclair? Tell me, why is it you big powerful types always manage to get the girl? Surely it is some atrocious misconception. My dear Elizabeth, you are aware that a man's sexual prowess is not determined by..." He waved the pistol almost disdainfully toward an area just below Alec's waist. "How shall I put this...? Why, my dear, the man is a veritable fortress! The size of his—"

"That's enough," Alec snapped. "State your business, Christy, then take your leave, posthaste, before I make you wish you'd never stepped one foot inside my house."

"Strange words from a man found in flagrante delicto with another man's betrothed," Basil sneered, wiping a sleeve over his mouth and gulping for a breath. "She was mine!"

"She was never yours." Alec was so still, his voice so deep, so ominous, Elizabeth felt a chill course through her.

"You bastard!" Basil pointed the pistol squarely at Alec's chest, his thumb upon the hammer cocking the gun with an undeniable *click.* "I should kill you now!"

"No!" Elizabeth wailed, flinging her arms about Alec.

"Don't fret, love, he has but one bullet," Alec drawled, as if that provided any reassurance. "Tell me, Christy, where did you dig up such a relic of a firearm? One would think a man bent upon killing another would at least be sporting a revolver capable of firing six rounds."

Basil glowered at Alec. "It was my father's most coveted weapon, and his father's, as well. It suits my purpose, for these bullets never miss their mark, I can assure you." His mouth fixed into a thin line when his gaze flickered over a stricken Elizabeth clinging with all her might to the man at her side. "You love him."

Elizabeth nodded frantically, as if that would matter in the least to Basil. "Yes, I love him with all my heart."

"A pity." The coldness of Basil's tone settled with grim finality around Elizabeth's heart. "Then he must certainly die, but not before I have inflicted some of my own torture upon him. Just as he has done to me...here..." His eyes flickered to the sheet sagging from Elizabeth's bosom.

"Nothing is worth another man's life!" Elizabeth cried.

"Ah, but, my dear, you are worth that and more," Basil replied. "You see, Elizabeth, I intend to risk everything, even a bloody fortune."

"But what of Felicity?" Elizabeth implored. "And the baby she's carrying? Your baby?"

"Indeed," Alec drawled in a lazy tone that seemed extraordinarily cavalier under the circumstances. "I understand congratulations are in order."

"Shut the bloody hell up, Sinclair!" Basil barked, scowling at Alec. "So she told you that, as well, eh? Blast, but I should have known! Never again shall I trust a woman with a secret. Never! First that wife of yours, Celestine. Ah yes, we were co-conspirators—" Basil waved a disparaging hand at the bed "—against you two. She was as game as they come, at first. All eager and willing and full of teasing smiles and lingering pats upon the arm when she thought she might possibly ensnare *you* once again. Stupid woman, and fickle to boot. She all but abandoned our plot once you made it abundantly clear you wanted no part of her."

He shook his head and a snide curl twisted his lip. "Then there was Felicity, the most naive of them all." He shook his head and gave a cruel laugh. "Stupid girl thought if she divulged the whole scheme I'd marry her. Ha! I took care of that."

Alec's eyes narrowed. "Some convenient accident, Christy?"

Basil paled visibly. "What did you say?"

Alec lifted a curious brow. "Just a lucky guess."

"Damn you to hell, Sinclair!" Basil roared. "How you enjoy making a mockery of us all!"

"You make it painfully easy, Christy."

"Is that so? So smug, you are, for a man without his pants and a pistol in his face! How I shall relish killing you, not only for sending me off to some godforsaken swine-infested hovel, but for this!"

In one quick movement, he yanked the bed sheet out of Elizabeth's grasp and flung it to the floor. Without a moment's hesitation, Alec sprang from the bed and lunged for Basil. Uttering a desperate cry, Elizabeth surged after him. With a moan of despair, she sank back upon the bed when the pistol pressed squarely into Alec's chest.

Though the hand wielding that gun shook, Basil's tone was even and deadly. "Don't make me kill you yet, Sinclair. You wouldn't want to take all the fun out of it for me." He inclined his head with one sharp movement. "Over there, Sinclair, just beside the bed, if you please. And would you mind making good use of your trousers? I wouldn't want the fair Elizabeth unduly distracted."

Alec hesitated a moment then complied, looming beside the bed with the look of the devil himself. Elizabeth attempted to scurry to him but Basil's harsh command stilled her movements.

"Stay where you are, wench!"

Elizabeth huddled upon the bed, drawing her knees to her chest and attempting to shield herself from Basil's glowing eyes with naught but her trembling arms. She lifted her eyes to Alec in a silent plea.

"Allow her to cover herself, man," Alec growled menacingly, his fists clenching at his sides as if he itched to use them.

"Not on your life, Sinclair," Basil replied with a pompous smirk. "I've waited a long time for this." His eyes, glittering shamelessly with his lust, settled upon Elizabeth, though the gun pointed squarely at Alec. "Lovely Elizabeth, indulge me just a wee bit, will you, before I tie your bastard lover to the bedpost. It will be his front row seat while I take you upon his bed. I find myself, however, growing impatient for another glimpse of your charms."

"You monster!" Elizabeth hissed. "You shall have to use that pistol upon me, for I would gladly choose death over lying upon this bed with you, or allowing you the merest glimpse of naked flesh."

"Now, now, sweet Elizabeth," Basil purred in a voice that raised the hackles along Elizabeth's spine. "I wish but one good look at you. Surely you're not suggesting that I tie you to this bed, flat upon your back..."

"Do it, Elizabeth."

Elizabeth stared horror-stricken at Alec.

Those smoky gray eyes stared right through her. "I said do it. Indulge the man."

The tears fell unheeded and she had to turn away from him as Basil's harsh laugh sliced coldly through her.

"You're not such a fool after all, Sinclair. Listen to the man, Elizabeth. Let me look at you...."

An acrid bile rose in Elizabeth's throat and she closed her eyes for a moment as if to gather her sanity. Where had reason flown? Why was Alec subjecting her to this monster's whim? Had he a plan? Surely he did. Her eyes sought him. There was little denying the anguish burning in those eyes, the yearning and the frustration. Yet she sensed something else, as well. Perhaps it was the slightest lift to the corner of his mouth. Or the self-assured manner in which he held himself. A man with a purpose. Had she ever known him to be otherwise? Yet, would he stand idly by while she allowed Basil the liberty...

"Let's have it, shall we, Elizabeth?"

She cringed from Basil's voice, a voice as bloated with arrogance as he was. Drawing a deep breath, she closed her eyes with grim resignation and lowered her hands on either side of her hips, sliding her legs flat upon the bed. The heat of her embarrassment pounded in her temples, coursed through her veins and rushed in her ears.

Basil's strangled voice reached her through the din. "Mother of God, but you're a vision...."

Elizabeth swallowed the bile in her throat as the tears streamed down her cheeks. She could bear it not another moment. Lifting her eyes to Alec yet again, she felt a tremendous surge of anguish deep in her belly. And then she saw it, the flicker of his eyes toward Basil, accompanied by an almost indiscernible lift of his brow, before his eyes found her once more. Then again, the same quick glance at Basil, only this time, the merest hint of a smile teased his lips when his gaze slid to hers. Why, the absurdity! Surely Alec was not enjoying this?

Elizabeth almost gasped with horror, yet when her eyes swung to Basil she immediately understood. As if entranced, Basil stared with slackened jaw upon her, his eyes, wide and blank, traveling over her then fixing heatedly upon her breasts. Suffused with shame, Elizabeth shuddered, then dared a glance at Alec. Much to her consternation and for the briefest of moments, he, too, ogled her bosom with unabashed appreciation. Men! Before she could turn away, he bestowed such a tortured look upon her that she knew in the span of that one moment he simply had to have some sort of plan. Yet he remained unmoving, shooting yet another quick glance at Basil and, in particular, the pistol lolling rather loosely of a sudden in his grasp.

Mustering all her feminine wiles, Elizabeth licked her lips and posed rather coyly upon the bed, drawing one slender leg along the other and shrugging a saucy shoulder. Her eyes dipped pointedly to her breasts, then she slanted Basil an innocent yet undeniably saucy look from beneath lowered lashes and summoned a breathiness to her voice. "Do you like them?"

Basil stared at her, his Adam's apple bobbing as frantically as his head. "Oh, indeed I do, very much. If I could but touch you I . . ."

"Well..." Elizabeth cast Alec her best shy and demure look, only to find herself momentarily captured by the flame leaping in the depths of his eyes. The brow he lifted left little doubt that he, too, was somewhat captivated by her performance. She gave Basil a sloe-eyed glance. "I suppose one little touch wouldn't hurt, if you promise to be gentle."

"Oh, I . . . I shall be more than gentle . . . I promise." Feverishly licking the spittle from his lips, Basil moved toward her, his eyes fastened upon her bosom, the pistol, all but forgotten, lowering slowly to his side. He knelt one leg upon the bed and reached a trembling hand for her, his shaking fingers poised just above her leg.

For one long, thoroughly agonizing moment, Elizabeth thought he would indeed touch her. And then Alec moved, lunging at Basil with such force that both men toppled to the floor.

With a frightened yelp, Elizabeth sprang from the bed and huddled in the shadows, clutching the sheet and staring horror-stricken at the two men wrestling upon the floor. Over and over they rolled, their arms thrashing, their legs skidding over the polished mahogany then catching upon the thick carpets. They pitched into a small table, sending it and the chair beside it crashing to the floor. Elizabeth's screams evaporated beneath the violence of their struggle, the groans, the growls and, most heinous of all, the sounds of fists meeting flesh. And then came the sound, the one sound that shot a chill of the purest terror through her.

From somewhere between the struggling men, pinioned by their straining chests, the pistol discharged. Elizabeth froze, rooted to the spot for one agonizing moment as her blood ran cold.

With a mournful wail, she flew to Alec, lying motionless atop Basil. The bitter smell of gunpowder filled the air, stinging her eyes despite the tears falling shamelessly to her cheeks. Trembling hands clasped about him without hesitation, and she gasped at the heat of his flesh, living flesh. . . .

And then, through the blur of her tears, he turned and his arms swept fiercely about her, crushing her to a chest devoid of wounds. He cradled her in his lap and she clung to him, sobbing brokenly against the strong beating of his heart.

Chapter Twenty-Seven

"And, therefore, I regretfully submit my resignation."

The echo of Elizabeth's words had long ceased resounding through Miss Percy's office. Indeed, nothing could be heard but the incessant ticking of a small clock upon the headmistress's ever-so-tidy desk. And, of course, Elizabeth's frantic pulse. She was certain Miss Percy detected it, as well, though the woman's unwavering stare offered little clue. In all truth, had Elizabeth expected anything more from the woman? The headmistress had just been told the entire awful truth. Why shouldn't she simply stare in that unreadable manner at the young woman she'd once proclaimed her most prized teacher, the same young woman who had lied to her countless times, whose everyday existence was but one horrid lie atop another?

"Elizabeth, I am dreadfully ashamed of myself."

Elizabeth stared at the headmistress. "Miss Percy?"

"Oh, my dear, I have done you an atrocious disservice."

"Me?" Elizabeth's eyes widened as the headmistress knelt beside her and grasped her hands.

"My dear girl, I have known of this secret of yours even before you first stepped foot through Dunlevy's gates. Indeed, your father was rather insistent that you be accepted into the school. Oh, don't look so stricken, for goodness' sakes. He has always wished only the very best for you and kept himself very much aware of both you and your mother's every doing. From the very start, he took me into his confidence regarding his relationship with you, requiring naught from me but a tightly held tongue and timely reports as to your progress.''

Elizabeth flushed. ''I had no idea that I was granted special privileges.''

''My dear, what you have achieved is all your own doing. No one else's.'' A heavy brow rose curiously. ''Elizabeth, surely you know me well enough to gather that I deem only superior performance deserving of the rewards you have attained.''

''Oh, of course. I never meant to imply—''

''And furthermore, how gullible a woman do you think I am?''

''Miss Percy?''

''Your mother—and her powdered face and lame excuses.''

Elizabeth's shame knew no bounds. ''Oh, Miss Percy, I...'' Her next words were lost forever, for Edwina Percy suddenly did something grossly out of character. She laughed. Indeed, she did much more than that. She guffawed, hooting and howling until her bifocals fell from their perch and twin spots of pink splashed her cheek. Elizabeth stared at her dumbstruck.

Miss Percy shook her head frantically. ''Elizabeth, do forgive me. It's positively wicked of me to find humor in all this, but really! Why, your mother was no more the grieving, reclusive widow than I!''

Elizabeth had to look away, so intense was her chagrin. Even Miss Percy's comforting pat upon her hand could not retrieve her composure for several moments.

''My dear Elizabeth, you have little reason to feel ashamed. Indeed, prudence dictates that I alone bear that burden for perpetuating the scheme, though God only knows I simply wished to spare you any humiliation.''

Elizabeth could not help the wistful shake of her head. ''How wrongly I judged you, Miss Percy, for I believed if you knew the truth, you would toss me from Dunlevy without hesitation.''

''Elizabeth! What sort of heartless creature do you think me?''

"Miss Percy, it was the school's reputation that I was thinking of."

"And what sort of reputation would Dunlevy bear, were it not for exceptional young women such as yourself, my dear? Elizabeth, you are a treasure to me, to Dunlevy. Not because of your impressive lineage or the size of your father's purse, but because of who you are!" Miss Percy waved a hand at the door. "Surely your Lord Sinclair cares naught from whence you came?"

Elizabeth flushed immediately and lowered her eyes to her fingers, which toyed with her reticule. "No, he doesn't, but he's atrociously unconcerned with propriety and—"

"Propriety has little to do with it, my dear. You alone harbor the highest of expectations of yourself and erroneously assume others do, as well. How on earth did you think to live up to all that? You couldn't possibly, you silly goose. Thank heavens you had the sense to fall in love."

"I . . . I must confess, I resisted as best I could."

"There you go again. I suppose he wasn't quite right for you, eh?"

"Actually, he wasn't. But, of course, I'd never intended to fall in love with him and—"

"My dear girl, we never do." Elizabeth was struck by the fleeting look of melancholy flickering across Miss Percy's brow and for the briefest of moments she detected the glimmer of tears in those dark eyes. "Just look at you, my dear. Now don't blush again, for heaven' sake. So beautiful you are in this lovely dress. And how your eyes sparkle at the mere mention of his name. I assume Lord Sinclair intends to do right by you?"

"We plan to marry this very day."

"He's a good man, Elizabeth. I've thought so from the very start." A twinkle of mischief appeared in Miss Percy's eye. "I must admit, I've always found him awfully pleasing to look upon." Her brow knit. "And your father. How is he?"

Elizabeth drew a deep sigh. "Not well. He suffered a stroke recently, though with the proper care, his recovery is hopeful. In fact, my mother intends to lend a hand. It's rather strange seeing them together."

"I can well imagine." Miss Percy rose and turned to contemplate the letter of resignation lying upon her desk. Very carefully, she tore the letter in half. "Very well, then, I shall simply pretend that I never saw this letter, Elizabeth, and—"

"Oh, but, Miss Percy, I simply cannot continue with my duties at Dunlevy. I shall be a married woman, and as such I shall...well...Alec seems rather bent upon us having a...I mean...I, too, wish to have a...very soon and..."

"Elizabeth, why is it you can never seem to spit out exactly what you wish to say? It's an atrocious habit you have acquired of late." Miss Percy shook her head with mock reprobation then leveled a knowing gaze upon Elizabeth. "I once knew of a young teacher as disciplined and as dedicated as you, my dear. Perhaps just as hard on herself, as well. She, too, fell in love with a truly wonderful young man and wished to marry. But her dedication proved too formidable a foe and she sacrificed love for her work, erroneously assuming she could never have both."

"An honorable woman. Her dedication knew no bounds."

"Oh, for heaven' sake, Elizabeth!" A glower fixed itself upon Miss Percy's stern features. "No doubt somewhere beneath all that lovely cream velvet you're wearing, guilt is rearing its ugly head. You fear that somehow you have failed for choosing to marry, am I right?" Miss Percy gave a scarlet-cheeked Elizabeth scant time for a response and shook her head vehemently. "My dear, banish every last vestige of that guilt. To this day, that young woman regrets her decision and she's not about to allow you to bear any unnecessary burdens of guilt." The headmistress raised a somewhat lofty brow at Elizabeth. "You needn't look so shocked, my dear, though even I find the thought of me being in love at one time rather startling."

"Actually, I was thinking how beautiful a bride you would have been."

This time, Elizabeth was certain that tears shone in those dark eyes, tears that momentarily dissolved that impenetrable wall, that fortress of morality Miss Percy had erected about herself. Without hesitation, Elizabeth's fingers sought her teacher's and clasped the plump hand.

"You will forever be that to which I aspire," Elizabeth murmured. "And you are treasured far more in my heart than you could ever be here at Dunlevy."

Edwina Percy offered a wavering smile then spun to the desk and rather awkwardly snatched her bifocals from her nose. "Go...go on. Your betrothed awaits, and as anxious as a prospective bridegroom could be, I'd imagine."

Elizabeth hesitated a moment then gathered her reticule close and rose to her feet. She stared at Miss Percy's determined profile then turned to the door.

"Elizabeth?"

Elizabeth paused, one hand poised upon the doorknob.

"Your position here is one that only you can fill, my dear. shall be content to await your return, should you see fit, once you have all those babies."

Elizabeth swallowed. "Thank you, Miss Percy. You are a dear friend." Before she dissolved beneath her tears, she swept the door open and exited the room.

For several long moments she stared thoughtfully at the closed door, musing upon the woman within, the woman she'd learned so much about in this one morning. Or perhaps she herself had proven the greatest lesson. With a thoughtful smile teasing her lips, she turned to make her way below and caught sight of the tall, broad-shouldered figure poised not ten paces down the hall. He stood, hat in hand, gazing expectantly upon her with an encouraging smile playing on his lips, as if he knew not whether he should indeed smile.

Their eyes met and her heart soared and swelled with an unabashed joy. She rushed forward, flinging her arms about him as if she hadn't seen him in months. "Oh, Alec, promise me we shall have many, many babies. Sweet pink little babies..."

"I promise," came his hearty response. "An unburdened soul is a happy one indeed."

"Oh, Alec, she's a marvelous woman. Truly marvelous. can't say enough about the woman. She—"

He gave her a smirk. "I take it the venerable Miss Percy has seen fit to retain your services? Why, my love, that is indeed a surprise, is it not?"

Elizabeth pursed her lips and shot him a mildly vexed look. "Cease your mockery this instant or I shan't wed you, you brute."

"Is that so?" A decidedly wicked and mischievous twinkle glittered in Alec's eye. He held a hand before him and bowed with dramatic fervor. "Your coach awaits, my lady, as does your impatient bridegroom. Make haste." When she passed before him, however, he caught her hand in his and drew it to his lips. His eyes, dusky gray and potent, captured hers and set her heart fluttering. "Beautiful, bewitching Elizabeth, I would surely be a man lost without you. Come, stand beside me at yonder altar as my bride, my cherished wife, forever to be mine."

"Oh, Alec," Elizabeth whispered, the tears slipping from her eyes, unheeded as she caressed his hollowed cheek. "I love you so..."

"Father? Father, it *is* you and... Why, Miss Burbridge! Just look at you!" As if conjured from thin air, Phoebe materialized before them. Her amber eyes widened and darted between them, very quickly at first, then focused upon Elizabeth's hand on her father's arm. "Why, my goodness, if I didn't know any better... Where are you off to?"

"We're going to get married," Alec announced with a huge grin. Phoebe gaped at him.

Elizabeth's eyes flew to Alec, then Phoebe, and back again.

"Well! It's about time!" Phoebe declared. With a giggle, she rushed forward and flung her arms about them. "Oh, Miss Burbridge! I couldn't be happier! Surely you know how fond I have always been of you! Why, ever since you promised never to tell Father that I... oops!" Phoebe's cheeks flooded with color and she pressed a hand to her mouth, then smiled wanly at Alec's curiously raised brow. "Well... how positively wonderful! You know, I just *knew* something was wrong with Father, as did all the servants. For the past several weeks he just stormed about, barking orders one minute then whistling cheerily the next.''

"Enough, Phoebe," Alec warned, gazing down the hall-way.

Unmoved, Phoebe gushed on. "He frightened poor Cook on more than one occasion, and Holmes! Why, they all thought Father had lost his senses or was frightfully ill and—"

"That's enough, Phoebe," Alec interrupted again, urging Elizabeth along with a firm hand upon her back.

Elizabeth's feet resisted as best they could and she couldn't help but send him a teasing smile, noting, as she did, the heightened color in his cheeks. "No, Alec, I would like to hear this."

"I'll bet you would," he muttered, giving Phoebe a hooded glare.

"And to think it was all because he was smitten with *you!*" Phoebe grinned deliciously. "Ooh, how jealous you must have been, Father, when she agreed to marry Basil! No wonder you were so awful! He wouldn't sleep! He wouldn't eat! I have never seen him so distraught...Father! Father...Miss Burbridge...wait!"

"Goodbye, Phoebe!" Alec's voice boomed throughout the stairwell.

"No! Wait!" Frantically, Phoebe scurried after them, breathlessly skidding to a halt as she caught them at the front door. "I'm going with you," she announced with a self-satisfied grin. "Surely you didn't think to deny me the wedding of my two favorite people, did you?"

"Me?" Elizabeth grinned mischievously at the young girl. "Deny you anything, my dear Phoebe? Never!"

Linking her arm through each of theirs, Elizabeth hurried toward the coach with a blissful smile upon her lips. Before her lay a future bright with hope, brimming with contentment, and full of a love she once believed possible only in a dream.

* * * * *

JAYNE ANN KRENTZ

A two-part epic tale from one of today's most popular romance novelists!

Dreams
Parts One & Two

The warrior died at her feet, his blood running out of the cave entrance and mingling with the waterfall. With his last breath he cursed the woman— told her that her spirit would remain chained in the cave forever until a child was created and born there....

So goes the ancient legend of the Chained Lady and the curse that bound her throughout the ages—until destiny brought Diana Prentice and Colby Savager together under the influence of forces beyond their understanding. Suddenly they were both haunted by dreams that linked past and present, while their waking hours were filled with danger. Only when Colby, Diana's modern-day warrior, learned to love, could those dark forces be vanquished. Only then could Diana set the Chained Lady free....

Available in September wherever Harlequin books are sold.

JK92

Rebels & Rogues

Dash vowed to protect gorgeous
Claren—at any cost!

The Knight in Shining Armor
by JoAnn Ross
Temptation #409, September

All men are not created equal. Some are rough
around the edges. Tough-minded but
tenderhearted. Incredibly sexy. The tempting
fulfillment of every woman's fantasy.

When it's time to fight for what they believe in, to
win that special woman, our Rebels and Rogues are
heroes at heart. Twelve Rebels and Rogues, one
each month in 1992, only from Harlequin
Temptation. Don't miss the upcoming books by
our fabulous authors, including Ruth Jean Dale,
Janice Kaiser and Kelly Street.

HARLEQUIN®

I N T R I G U E®

It looks like a charming old building near the Baltimore waterfront, but inside 43 Light Street lurks danger . . . and romance.

Labeled a "true master of intrigue" by *Rave Reviews*, bestselling author Rebecca York continues her exciting series with #193 TRIAL BY FIRE, coming to you next month.

Sabrina Barkley, owner of an herbal shop at 43 Light Street, finds that the past has a bizarre way of affecting the present when she's called in by ADA Dan Cassidy to consult on a murder case—only to be herself accused of murder *and* witchcraft. Sabrina's only defense is four hundred years old and an ocean away. . . .

> "Rebecca York's 43 Light Street series just keeps getting better and better. (In TRIAL BY FIRE) the devilishly clever Ms. York brews up a mind-blowing concoction of black magic and timeless romance that will fire your imagination and sear your soul."
>
> —*Romantic Times*

Don't miss #193 TRIAL BY FIRE next month. And watch for all the upcoming 43 Light Street titles for the best in romantic suspense.

LS92-1R

WELCOME TO

The quintessential small town, where everyone knows everybody else!

Finally, books that capture the pleasure of tuning in to your favorite TV show!

GREAT READING...GREAT SAVINGS...AND A FABULOUS FREE GIFT!

Each book set in Tyler is a self-contained love story; together, the twelve novels stitch the fabric of the community. The covers honor the old American tradition of quilting; each cover depicts a patch of the large Tyler quilt.

With Tyler you can receive a fabulous gift, ABSOLUTELY FREE, by collecting proofs-of-purchase found in each Tyler book. And use our special Tyler coupons to save on your next TYLER book purchase.

Join your friends at Tyler for the seventh book, ARROWPOINT by Suzanne Ellison, available in September.

Rumors fly about the death at the old lodge! What happens when Renata Meyer finds an ancient Indian sitting cross-legged on her lawn?

COMING NEXT MONTH

#139 BOSTON RENEGADE—June Lund Shiplett
After inheriting a ranch from her nefarious brother, spinster
Hanna Winters was threatened by outlaws searching for a missing
cache of stolen money. Yet the biggest threat of all came from
drifter Blake Morgan, who threw her well-ordered life into chaos.

#140 BODIE BRIDE—Isabel Whitfield
Spinster Margaret Warren believed she had everything she needed.
But when her father brought good-natured John Banning into their
home, Margaret was forced to recognize her loneliness—and her
undeniable attraction to the one man who infuriated her the most.

#141 KNIGHT DREAMS—Suzanne Barclay
Lord Ruarke Sommerville was drunk when he rescued French
noblewoman Gabrielle de Lauren from marauding soldiers and
impulsively wed her. Although the morning after brought
surprises, haste doesn't always mean waste—especially when the
courtship begins *after* the wedding.

#142 GYPSY BARON—Mary Daheim
Lady Katherine de Vere had always been loyal to king and country.
Nevertheless, when mysterious half-Gypsy Stefan Dvorak drew her
into a web of political intrigue, she began to doubt not only her
politics, but her heart, as well.

AVAILABLE NOW:

#135 THE RELUCTANT BRIDE
Barbara Bretton

#136 ROSE AMONG THORNS
Catherine Archer

#137 THE NAKED HUNTRESS
Shirley Parenteau

#138 THE DREAM
Kit Gardner